PRAISE FOR RUTH GLICK, WRITING AS REBECCA YORK

"Rebecca York's writing is fast-paced, suspenseful, and loaded with tension." —Jayne Ann Krentz

"Glick's prose is smooth, literate and fast-moving; her love scenes are tender yet erotic; and there's always a happy ending." —*The Washington Post Book World*

"A true master of intrigue." —*Rave Reviews*

"No one sends more chills down your spine than the very creative and imaginative Ms. York!" —*Romantic Times*

"She writes a fast-paced, satisfying thriller." —*UPI*

KILLING
MOON

REBECCA YORK

BERKLEY SENSATION, NEW YORK

This is a work of fiction. Names, characters, places, and incidents either are the product of the author's imagination or are used fictitiously, and any resemblance to actual persons, living or dead, business establishments, events, or locales is entirely coincidental.

KILLING MOON

A Berkley Sensation Book / published by arrangement with the author

PRINTING HISTORY
Berkley Sensation edition / June 2003

For information address: The Berkley Publishing Group, a division of Penguin Group (USA) Inc., 375 Hudson Street, New York, New York 10014.

ISBN: 0-425-19071-4

A BERKLEY SENSATION™ BOOK
Berkley Sensation Books arc published by
The Berkley Publishing Group,
a division of Penguin Group (USA) Inc.,
375 Hudson Street, New York, New York 10014.
BERKLEY SENSATION and the "B" design
are trademarks belonging to Penguin Group (USA) Inc.

PRINTED IN THE UNITED STATES OF AMERICA

10 9 8 7 6 5 4 3 2 1

CHAPTER
ONE

ROSS MARSHALL WAS dressed for stealth. Black knit shirt, comfortable black pants, black running shoes.

Just before sunset he pulled under the sheltering foliage of a low-growing maple and cut the truck's engine. After rolling down the window, he sat motionless behind the wheel of the Jeep Grand Cherokee, his dark eyes scanning his surroundings, his ears pricked for telltale warning sounds in the depths of the forest.

His senses were only those of a man. Still, he had trained himself to watch and listen with as much skill as a human could acquire. In the branches above him a few birds still chirped and rustled. And he saw a doe and a fawn come through the woods on the far side of the road. She stopped, sniffed the air, and tensed, then turned and bounded back the way she'd come, taking her offspring with her. He was sorry he had frightened her. Yet her instincts had been right.

As the gray of twilight edged into the darkness of night, he grabbed the knapsack from the seat beside him and exited the truck, uncoiling his six-foot-plus frame and brushing back the mahogany hair that fell across his forehead. For a moment he stood breathing in the scents floating on the spring air. Tipping his head up, he looked toward the heavens, toward the pinpoints of light winking to life in the black velvet of the sky.

As he focused upward, a vision stirred in his brain, and he imagined his long-ago ancestor standing in a sacred grove and asking the gods for powers beyond those of mortal men. His request had been granted. By the gods, or fate, or some cosmic jester. It had been granted for his sons, as well, and their sons after them, down through the generations.

Fingers of wind shaking the branches above his head brought Ross's mind back to the present. The world was different than it had been for his ancestors, yet some things never changed. Men still reached for the forbidden—and suffered the consequences.

His face set in hard lines, he hoisted his knapsack over a muscular shoulder and set off, blending into the shadows of the forest.

With an eagerness for the hunt, he quickened his steps, his running shoes crunching the brown leaves that still lay on the ground. The chain-link fence topped with razor wire was a hundred yards ahead. When he reached it, he squatted, opened his pack, and pulled out the wire cutters he'd brought. The pack contained other tools, as well. It would be too damn bad if he needed them later.

After laying his pack on a pile of leaves, he cut the links, and pulled the edges of the fence apart, making a hole wide enough to accommodate a low, lithe body. Then he quickly stood to pull the knit shirt over his head and toss it on top of the pack.

Pants and shoes followed. He hadn't bothered with underwear. The air was cold on his bare skin, but he stripped to the buff.

Closing his dark eyes, he called on ancient knowledge, ancient ritual, ancient deities as he gathered his inner strength, steeling himself for the feeling of disorientation, even as he said the words that he had learned on his sixteenth birthday.

"Taranis, Epona, Cerridwen," he intoned, then repeated the same phrase and went on to another.

"*Gá. Feart. Cleas. Duais. Aithriocht. Go gcumhdaí is dtreoraí na déithe thú.*"

The words and the blinding pain that came immediately after them had been the death of his older brother. Ross had had more luck. At least that was what he thought at the time, when he'd still been giddy with relief at his own survival. It was only later that he'd understood that he'd given up as much as he'd gained.

On that night so long ago, the words had helped him through the agony of transformation, opened his mind, freed him from the bonds of the human shape. He had tried more than once to watch in a mirror, but his vision had blurred as if his own consciousness rejected that which was beyond a man's comprehension.

But comprehension was apparently unnecessary for reality. Even as the human part of his mind screamed in protest, he felt his jaw elongate, his teeth sharpen, his body contort as muscles and limbs changed into a different shape.

The first few times he'd done it had been a nightmare of torture and terror. But once he'd understood what to expect, he'd learned to ride above the physical sensations of bones crunching, muscles jerking, cells transforming from one shape to another.

Thick gray hair formed along his flanks, covering his body in a silver-tipped pelt. The color—the very structure—of his eyes changed as he dropped to all fours, no longer a man but an animal far more suited to the forest around him.

A wolf.

A surge of freedom rippled through him, and he pawed the ground with the joy of a creature totally at one with nature. Raising his head, he sucked in a draft of air, his lungs expanding as his nose drank in the rich scents that were suddenly part of the landscape.

His body quivered. The blood sang in his veins. He wanted to throw back his head and howl for the sheer joy of it. But he checked the impulse, because the mind inside his skull still held his human intelligence. And the man understood the need for stealth tonight.

An owl screeched above him, flapped away into the night, and he saw the wings beat the dark air—saw the grace and power of the bird as it went in search of prey.

His own prey was on the other side of the fence. He pressed low to the ground, slithered through the hole he'd cut, then shook the dead leaves from his thick fur. Sniffing the wind again to get his bearings, he trotted into the woods. He knew that a house lay to his right, hidden by a dense stand of trees. Instinctively the wolf gave the place a wide berth—avoiding the evil that lurked there.

Eyes and ears tuned to his surroundings, he noted the rustling sounds of small animals scurrying to get out of his way. But he wasn't here to hunt the creatures of the forest tonight.

He had come to this tract of land for evidence that would satisfy human laws.

Scent was his most important sense, but his eyes were sharp, too, helping to guide him through the inky darkness under the trees. A quarter mile from his point of entry, he was stopped short by the thick, sickening odor of decaying flesh—too faint for a man to catch. Cautiously he approached a mound of newly turned earth where someone had dug in the forest floor, then piled the dirt back into place. The grave hadn't been there long. Only a thin layer of leaves and other debris had fallen to cover the fresh scar on the land.

He circled the mound, fighting the cloying scent, then pawed at the loose dirt, carefully removing the top layer of soil, and more. Less than a foot below the surface he discovered what he had been certain he would find—the partially decomposed remains of a woman's body, the flesh marred by stab wounds. Back-

ing away, he scratched in the leaves to clean the tainted
dirt from his claws.

Penny Delano, he thought. Or maybe Charlotte
Lawrence. Both of them had been missing for months.
Both of them, he was certain, had ended their young
lives on this piece of property. Alone, except for their
torturer. A son of a bitch named Donald Arnott.

It was Penny's parents who had hired him to find
their daughter—and his investigation had led him to
this grave in the woods. He had hoped that perhaps he
was wrong, but now there was little doubt where their
daughter was buried.

He was too focused on the grim pictures in his mind,
too sickened by his discovery, to hear the crackle of
dry leaves, the stealthy crunch of human footsteps.

The sound of a rifle shot and a bullet plowing into
a tree trunk inches from his head brought his mind
zinging back to his own present danger.

He was already sprinting into the cover of the forest
before the next slug splatted into the ground behind
him.

But he wasn't fast enough. The third shot caught him
in the right hind quarter, sending a shaft of fire through
the leg.

He didn't let it slow him down. Mind clenched
against the pain, he put on a burst of speed, zigzagging
through the woods, even as the sound of more bullets
echoed behind him. Despite the fire in his leg, he was
faster than any man as he circled into the forest, then
headed back toward the opening he'd made in the
fence, his ears tuned to sounds of pursuit.

Breathing hard, he reached the fence and flattened
his body to the ground, his right hind leg in agony as
he clawed his way toward freedom. Relief surged
through him once he was on the other side.

Panting, he stood on wobbly legs, staring at the
knapsack and pile of clothing he'd left on the ground.

If he changed back to human form, he could pick up
his belongings, carry them away. But transforming

now, when Arnott was closing in on him, was too dangerous. The shock of changing with a bullet in his body might knock him out cold.

When his wolf ears picked up the crunch of leaves in the distance, he was forced to make a decision. Snatching up his trousers in his teeth, he left everything else where it lay and headed toward the truck.

Arnott's own fence would stop him for the time being. He wouldn't be able to wiggle through the wolf-size opening—not without enlarging the hole. And the tools for doing that were on the other side.

Dragging the trousers along the ground, the wolf made it back to the truck and stood with his sides heaving.

As a wolf he was unable to utter the words of transformation aloud. But the silent chant echoed in his mind as muscle and ligament, skin and bone transmuted themselves once again—this time from wolf shape to human.

A cold sheen of sweat filmed his skin, but there was nothing he could do about the bullet torturing his flesh except grit his teeth and push past the agony. In the end, the effort was too much.

He realized he'd lost consciousness when he woke up on the ground beside the vehicle. He was still naked and now shivering with cold. His head was cradled in a pile of leaves and his leg was lying in a pool of blood.

Muzzy-headed, vision wavering, he longed to simply lie there on the cool ground and close his eyes again, but giving in to that impulse was a death sentence.

Summoning all his remaining strength, he pushed himself to a sitting position and grabbed his trousers, fumbling in the pocket for his keys. Thank God they hadn't fallen out during his wild dash to the truck.

Crawling toward the driver's door, he pulled himself up and managed to get the key in the lock. There was no point in wasting energy getting dressed. He simply tossed the pants onto the floor of the passenger side, wincing as his leg hit the console.

For a moment he sat gripping the steering wheel to keep from passing out again. Then he reached for the bottle of water he'd left on the passenger seat. Fumbling off the cap, he took a long swig, spilling some down his chest and belly.

With clumsy fingers he reached into the glove compartment and pulled out a first-aid kit. Unwrapping a bandage, he wound it around his thigh, stanching the flow of blood.

He held back a groan as he turned the ignition key, then pressed on the accelerator, wondering if he could stay conscious long enough to make it home. He'd made a mistake tonight by underestimating the man who'd dug the grave. Or maybe it had only been bad luck that he'd been discovered.

But it didn't matter what had gone wrong. Either way, he was in a hell of a mess.

DONALD Arnott stood with the rifle pointed toward the ground as he stared at the hole someone had cut in his fence.

Playing the flashlight beam over the forest floor on the other side of the chain links, he could see a trail of blood leading toward the road. The dog was hurt, all right. Maybe it was bleeding too bad to get much farther.

He swept the beam in an arc. When the yellow light struck a knapsack and a pile of clothing, he went rigid, then charged toward the fence, his fingers gripping the cold metal links as he stared in disbelief.

Holy shit!

He'd expected to come upon the big dog dazed and wounded—cowering against the barrier—waiting helplessly for the kill shot.

Instead he'd found someone had cut a damn hole in his fence. A hole large enough for the dog to squeeze through.

Turning, he trotted back to the house, where he

quickly exchanged the rifle for a Beretta and grabbed
a plastic trash bag. Then he jumped in his Land Rover
and sped toward the gate.

Jesus. What if he hadn't come outside tonight?

He'd been walking through the woods—the need for
another woman building in his gut like gas expanding
through a rotting body. It had been weeks since he'd
finished with Charlotte. And the memories of the things
he'd done to her no longer had the power to bring him
to hard, aching arousal.

After the first little blond bitch he'd taken, he'd
waited almost a year before daring to repeat the delicious adventure. Last time, he'd been able to hold off
for only a few months.

He made a guttural sound in his throat. Charlotte had
been too weak, given up too easily. And he hadn't
gotten the full measure of gratification he craved.
That's why he'd been so restless tonight. But he was
thankful now that he'd been out of the house because
he'd heard the animal digging, taken aim, and scored
a shot.

He screeched to a halt at the gate, jumped out of the
SUV, and worked the combination on the padlock. After driving to the other side, he carefully relocked the
barrier before barreling down the driveway and turning
right, heading for the spot on the road parallel to where
the knapsack was lying.

Was the man coming back for his stuff? Unlikely.
Probably he'd gotten the hell out of the area while the
getting was good, with or without the dog.

He found the knapsack and the clothing easily
enough. Squatting, he stared at the abandoned possessions, wondering if this were some kind of trap. Like
what? A bomb stuffed into a shoe?

With a snort, he pawed through the knapsack, finding a collection of tools. Then he picked up a shirt and
shoes. Only the trousers and underwear were missing.

Touching the discarded clothing sent a shiver of
dread slithering down his spine. Thrusting the feeling

aside, he stuffed everything into the plastic bag he'd brought, hoping the guy had been stupid enough to have put an ID tag on the knapsack.

That would make things easier, although it wasn't essential. Someone had sent a dog to his private grave-yard tonight—and he had to assume that it wasn't a random act of bad luck. Some bastard had discovered what he was doing and had come after him with a bloodhound. No, not a hound. Something with thicker, shaggier fur. Maybe a shepherd mix.

His hand clamped around the butt of the gun, the cold metal digging into his flesh.

He was going to find out who it was—because failure was not an option, not when failure meant the end of everything. Life. Freedom. And the sexual satisfaction he needed to exist.

CHAPTER
TWO

MEGAN SHERIDAN FOLDED her arms across her chest, rubbing briskly at the sleeves of her lab coat.

She'd already tried to turn up the heat, but a newly installed plastic box covering the thermostat made it impossible to change the setting without a key. One more Monday morning surprise at Bio Gen Labs.

"Is Walter trying to freeze off our fingers, then collect on the insurance?" she muttered under her breath.

Her coworker Hank Lancaster gave a sharp laugh and handed her a hot mug of coffee. The mug was a freebie from a drug company pushing a new diuretic, and the picture emblazoned on the side of the bright yellow ceramic showed a pair of kidneys.

"Here, maybe this will help. And don't let him hear you. He may think it's a good idea."

Megan rolled her blue eyes as she cupped her hands around the mug's warmth. Two years ago, after her medical internship at Johns Hopkins and a year of postdoc work, she'd had her pick of job offers from the biogenetic laboratories clustered around the Washington-Baltimore area.

She'd gone with Bio Gen because the CEO, Walter Galveston, had sold her on the potential of his up-and-coming company. Now in his early forties, Walter had learned the ropes at several area labs, then gone out on his own. After telling her he was looking for projects that would bring in money as well as scientific prestige, he'd listened attentively to her proposal for using gene therapy to treat Myer's disease, an inherited form of macular degeneration that struck in young adulthood. Walter had given the project priority at Bio Gen until some of the well-publicized deaths caused by gene therapy had hit the news.

Now he was holding up her clinical trials until she dotted every "i" and crossed every "t" in her proposal. Not only that, but in the past four months, she'd watched Walter shift her hours away from her project to routine paternity testing, chromosome studies, and genetic profiles—jobs that paid nice fees in the short run but contributed nothing to the basic genetic research that fired her enthusiasm.

From where she stood, it looked like Bio Gen had a cash flow problem. Only Walter hadn't bothered to share the information with his employees. And he hadn't bothered to come in on time this morning, either, Megan thought with a snort—then suffered a pang of guilt for her mutinous attitude. Bitching behind her boss's back made her feel uncomfortable. Yet sharing her frustration with her coworker was turning into a ritual, probably because their research goals were so similar.

She and Hank were both in their early thirties, both highly educated, both dedicated to their research projects. She'd gotten her MD, then realized it was impossible to keep her distance from her patients. She cared too much, was affected too much by their suffering and their deaths. And so she'd withdrawn to a safer venue—where she could impose the veil of lab procedures between herself and flesh-and-blood patients.

Hank had gone a different route—earning a Ph.D. in biology before coming to Bio Gen. He was different, too, in his feelings about people. While she appreciated the unique human qualities of each individual, he was the kind of man who classified everyone he met according to IQ. The smarter they were, the more he respected them.

She watched him walk down the hall to the front office, pause for a brief conversation with the receptionist, Betty Daniels, then return with a clipboard in his hand and a carefully bland expression on his face.

The feigned nonchalance didn't fool her. Sweeping back a lock of dark blond hair that had fallen across her eyes, she said, "You might as well hit me with the bad news."

He gave an upward thrust to the clipboard, managing to make it look like an obscene gesture. "We've got eighteen paternity cases this week. And almost as many clients who want genetic profiling before they consider having children."

Megan did a rapid calculation. That was going to suck up most of the workweek. Which meant that if she were going to do anything with her own project, she would be doing it after hours. Damn, what was wrong with Walter? Didn't he know that if she succeeded in her treatment protocol, Bio Gen would have plenty of money? Not to mention credit for a major medical breakthrough?

Hank rolled back the top sheet of paper and stabbed his long finger at a line on the second page. "There's a notation on this one—about a client who lives in Lisbon. Apparently he wants someone from the lab to go out there and get a blood sample."

"Lisbon, Howard County? Or Lisbon, Portugal?"

He laughed, apparently giving her points for the quick comeback. "Howard County."

"That's an hour's ride from here."

"Maybe he's got some nasty genetic defect that

causes warts all over his body, so he doesn't go out in public."

"Sure."

"Or he could have a sick kid who can't be left alone."

Megan felt her stomach clench in that old familiar way. She didn't even know the man, but she could imagine what his life might be like. If he were taking care of a critically ill youngster with a serious genetic defect, he might well have trouble getting to the lab.

"Whatever it is, you can bet Walter is charging him through the nose for the house call." Hank let the top sheet fall back into place, set down the clipboard on the edge of her desk, and pulled a quarter out of his pocket. "I'll flip you for it."

"Sure. Why not?" she agreed, wishing she could be as blasé as he was. She called heads. And lost, of course. Her luck hadn't been particularly good lately.

"I'll cover the next house call," Hank offered as he took in her gloomy expression.

"Like we're going to get another one anytime soon," Megan answered, picking up the clipboard.

The conversation came to a halt when the outer door slammed open with enough force to shake the walls.

"What the hell was that?" Hank muttered as they exchanged glances.

In the reception area, a man was bellowing at Betty.

The administrative assistant's voice was unnaturally high as she responded—and hardly anything usually disturbed her equanimity. She was a veteran office manager whom Walter had enticed away from NIH. He liked having her in the front office for the combination of motherly warmth and polished efficiency she projected. And her word processing skills were nothing to sneeze at, either.

By unspoken mutual agreement, Megan and Hank started down the hall, bent on rescuing the poor woman.

They both stopped dead when they saw that the person bellowing at Betty was Walter Galveston. Ordinarily their boss looked like he'd just sauntered out of a photo session for *GQ*. This morning, his charcoal gray suit was rumpled, his expensively cut hair was mussed, and Megan thought his face appeared to have aged five years since she'd seen him Friday afternoon.

Her own features contorted. "Walter, what is it? What's wrong?"

He flapped his arm in an angry gesture. "Some bastard ran me off the road on the way here. Then he sped away before I could get his license number."

"Oh, my God. Are you all right? What about your car?"

His jaw trembled with emotion. "I'm just shaken up. But there's a gouge on the side of the Mercedes where I sideswiped a traffic barrier."

"Did you see what kind of car it was?" Hank asked.

Walter shook his head. "It all happened too fast, and I was busy staying out of that ditch where they're laying sewer pipes on Montrose Road."

Megan pictured the intersection he meant. "Were there any witnesses?"

"Probably, but everybody just kept driving by. You know—the usual behavior these days. People don't want to get involved. And no wonder. If you stop to break up an argument between two motorists, you could get your head blown off."

As she nodded in agreement, Hank asked, "What exactly happened?"

"The car came up behind me, nudged me to the side, then sped away."

"You think it was an accident?" Hank asked. "Or road rage? Did you do something to yank his chain? Cut him off or something?"

A guarded expression crossed Walter's sharp features. "I don't know."

Megan wondered if he *had* cut the other guy off— or done something else he wasn't going to admit.

Before they could ask any more questions, he was shoving open the front door. "Come see what the bastard did to me."

Bio Gen was in an industrial park, near the end of a one-story building of buff-colored brick strung out along a parking lot. Separating the entrance and the paved area was a five-foot strip of crabgrass. Walter's only concession to charm was a couple of conical evergreens in fancy cement pots on either side of the front door.

As Megan and Hank followed Walter down the short sidewalk and across the blacktop to the parking spaces, she braced against the late March wind. Betty trailed behind them, clutching a baby blue cardigan closed across her ample breasts.

Walter's gold Mercedes was parked in a reserved spot next to the handicapped space.

Her lab coat whipping around her legs, Megan followed Walter's gesturing hand and squinted, trying to locate the damage to the vehicle. Finally her gaze lit upon a hardly noticeable scrape in the gold metallic paint.

Behind Walter's back, Hank raised his eyes toward the heavens. "It shouldn't take too much to fix that," he commented.

"Yeah, well, it's not just the paint. There's a dent underneath you can feel if you run your hand along it. I'm going to start making calls to body shops right now."

As he strode back inside the building, his bemused audience followed.

Walter paused to grab a phone book from the drawer in Betty's desk and then stalked down the hall to his plush, private office, leaving his three employees in the reception area.

Standing with the others, Megan felt the awkwardness of the moment. Obviously nobody knew what to say about the boss's uncharacteristic behavior. The clipboard was still in Megan's hand. To give herself something to do, she looked at the name and the phone number of the guy in Lisbon. "Ross Marshall," she murmured.

Betty responded almost instantly. "The guy who doesn't want to come in to the lab."

"Right. I guess you talked to him."

"Uh-huh." She paused for a moment, taking a pencil from the holder on her desk and fiddling with it. "He's got a very . . . compelling voice."

Perhaps Hank was worried that the Ross Marshall job was still up for discussion, because he turned and hurried out of the room.

Megan stood where she was, studying the secretary's unfocused expression and the fingers she ran up and down the pencil shaft. It wasn't like Betty to react to clients in anything but a professional way.

"Walter confirmed an appointment for this afternoon," the assistant informed her. "Mr. Marshall said he'd be home. So you or Hank just need to set the time."

"I'm doing it."

"I keep wondering what he looks like. Since I'm not going to see him, I expect a full report."

Megan blinked. "Okay," she agreed, as much to end the conversation as anything else.

Her curiosity piqued, she returned to her desk and dialed the phone number on the sheet. On the fifth ring, an answering machine picked up. Five seconds into the recorded message, she understood what Betty had been reacting to in the man's voice. It was assured, compellingly masculine. But there was something more. An inviting quality that set off a subtle vibration deep within her.

"This is Ross Marshall. I'm out of the office right now. Please leave your name and number, and I'll get back to you as soon as possible."

When he finished speaking, she looked again at the sheet in front of her. According to the notation, she was supposed to be calling a home number. Well, maybe the guy worked from home.

She'd hoped to get directions to his place. So she asked if he'd call her back, then added that she planned to be at his house around four-thirty. What she didn't say was that she was going to be really pissed off if she drove all the way to western Howard County for nothing.

A couple of miles away at the Second District police station, Detective Jack Thornton stared down at the thick file in front of him as he rubbed his thumb against his lean jaw.

Inside the file was a name he hadn't expected to encounter: Ross Marshall. One of his most useful contacts.

He'd met Marshall three years ago. Jack had just been promoted to detective and was working a seemingly unsolvable homicide case. A woman named Helen Dawson had disappeared from a car later found pulled into a patch of weeds along Falls Road. There were no suspects—except the estranged husband who was the beneficiary of an insurance policy that the woman had neglected to alter when they'd separated. The man had an alibi, though, that stood up to extensive investigation.

With no police leads, the woman's distraught parents had hired Marshall to find out what happened to their daughter. A week later, the PI contacted the department, saying he had some pertinent information. Jack had been skeptical at first, but he'd agreed to a meeting with Marshall at a coffee shop on Rockville Pike.

He remembered their first encounter with vivid clarity. The PI had been tall, athletic, intelligent looking, and reserved in a way that made it hard to get a handle on him.

Telling himself not to make any judgments until he heard the whole story, Jack had listened to the tale

Marshall had to tell: that Dawson had been abducted, raped, and killed by a man named Billy Preston, a mechanic who had done some work on her car several weeks before and who had become obsessed with her. When she'd stopped for gas on the night she'd disappeared, Preston had asked for a ride to a nearby shopping center. But they had never reached that destination.

Jack remembered asking Marshall how he'd come up with that kind of detailed scenario. The PI had declined to reveal his methods, but the look on his face dared Jack to ignore the information. Still figuring it was a long shot, he had pursued the lead, using an outstanding traffic violation as an excuse to search Preston's car. He'd hit pay dirt when he'd found Dawson's bloodstained sweater stuffed in a gym bag.

Marshall never had explained how he'd fingered Preston, but the Dawson case had been the start of a working relationship between the two of them. On his end of it, Jack ran license plates for Ross, checked outstanding warrants, and meted out inside information available only to the department. In exchange, Ross provided leads that could have been obtained only by illegal means—or magic.

Jack didn't believe in methods impossible to verify. Which meant that Ross was collecting information through clandestine searches and other questionable procedures. The assumption put a barrier between him and the PI, a barrier that neither one of them had been able to breach.

Yet Ross kept coming to him when he had something he thought the police department could use. Although Jack admitted to himself that he still had suspicions about the guy, he continued to accept his help.

He stared across the squad room, his blue eyes unfocused. Then the phone rang on a nearby desk, and his attention snapped back to the file on his blotter—a five-year-old missing persons case, a man named Edward Crawford.

There was more in the folder than simply information on Crawford's disappearance. The man had been a suspect in the killings of several young women from the Baltimore-Washington corridor. Then his sister had reported him missing—and the murders had stopped.

That was the end of it—a Stone Who Done It. An unsolvable case. Until three weeks ago when torrential rains had washed a skeleton out of the ground in a rural area near Sugar Loaf Mountain. It had been identified by dental records as Crawford.

It hadn't been Jack's problem five years ago. The dead man's folder had ended up on his desk because the primary investigator, Ken Winston, was now retired.

Jack had started by going over everything in the file: pages from Ken's notebook, a couple of Post-it notes, an old envelope with the sister's address, a couple of business cards, and neatly typed official paperwork.

One of the notebook entries had yielded a very interesting piece of information. A private detective named Ross Marshall had been hired to find out who murdered one of the missing women, Lisa Blake.

Jack paged to the medical examiner's report. Because of the deterioration of Crawford's body, the cause of death was undetermined. If the man had been shot, the bullet hadn't shattered any bones. If he'd been strangled, the hyoid bone hadn't been crushed. And there was no skull-crushing trauma to the head.

But a soil sample estimating the decay placed the burial at about the time of Crawford's disappearance.

The Frederick County officers who'd been called to the scene had searched for evidence. Things like old cigarette butts, a lighter, buttons—anything that might provide clues. But there was nothing useful. Either physical evidence had been covered by falling leaves, or someone had carefully cleaned up the burial site.

Next Jack studied the pictures of the grave, then of the skeleton, along with a few shreds of clothing that still remained. Also included was a close-up that showed the victim's neck and one shoulder. Accompanying text noted that these areas had been gnawed by a predator. And there had been some dog hairs near the body.

As he looked at the photo, an unaccustomed sensation of cold traveled across his skin. He had certainly seen far more gruesome bodies—like jerks who went up in the attic in the middle of summer to hang themselves and weren't discovered until several days later. So he wasn't sure why he was having such a reaction to the pictures of Crawford's remains.

Still, he had learned to pay attention to his hunches, and he had the feeling that Ross Marshall could tell him something about this case.

He went back to the folder, spreading out several sheets of Ken Winston's cramped handwriting. One cited a meeting requested by PI Ross Marshall to talk about Lisa Blake. Marshall had pointed the finger at Crawford, but Winston hadn't followed up on the tip. Well, that fit what Jack remembered about Winston, a tight-assed type unlikely to act on information he couldn't verify for himself.

A week after the meeting, another woman had been found murdered, although, again, there was no proof to link her to Crawford. Two days after that, the man had vanished off the face of the earth.

Winston had gone back to Marshall with some questions. Ross had no alibi. He'd been home alone in his house in Lisbon, he said. But there was no evidence that linked him to Crawford's disappearance, and Winston had been forced to give up on that angle.

Yet as Jack sat at his desk now, he couldn't stop his mind from playing out an interesting scenario:

Marshall goes to Detective Winston with evidence he's sure will nail Crawford. When Winston presses him for details on his sources, Marshall clams up. So Winston blows him off. Marshall stews over the lack of police cooperation. Then Crawford kills again, and Marshall takes the law into his own hands.

Jack thought it a fascinating line of speculation, even if he did say so himself, but it didn't fit with the Ross Marshall he knew. Marshall was calm, controlled. Had he been a hotdog five years ago? Angry and outraged enough at another woman's death to put Crawford away?

Jack drummed the blunt-cut nails of his left hand against the papers.

There were no other leads in the case besides the tie-in to Ross Marshall. If the media had known Crawford was a murder suspect, then the families of the victims might be possibilities. But the investigation hadn't gotten far enough to go public.

Which led him back to Marshall.

He'd never run a background investigation on the PI beyond checking to see that he didn't have a police record and that he wasn't a former cop who'd washed out and had to settle for the next best thing. Thinking about it, he realized how little he knew about the man—and how little he'd wanted to know. Because Ross had been a good contact, he hadn't wanted to rock the boat.

That might have been a mistake.

He'd gotten the impression from the Jeep Grand Cherokee Laredo Sport that Ross drove and his clothing that he lived a reasonably upscale life. And from their talks, he'd assumed he was a serious, career PI.

But working as a private investigator didn't usually bring in big bucks. Was freelance investigation Ross's main source of income? Was there something hiding in his background? A child custody battle? A lawsuit?

Mentally Jack checked off other sources of information. Utility bills. Cable and phone company records. The man's credit report.

Then, flipping open a notebook, he reached for the phone.

*   *   *

ROSS'S body was burning up. His mouth felt like a desert wasteland. And it took a major effort of will to distinguish reality from the fevered imaginings swirling in his brain.

Crawford. Arnott. His family. Father, mother, brothers—and all the children who had never had a chance.

In his lucid moments, he knew that if he didn't get to the bottle of antibiotics in the kitchen cabinet, he was going to die from the infection spreading from his leg to the rest of his body.

He'd arrived home yesterday—or was it the day before? He wasn't sure anymore because the hours had blended into each other like watercolor paint splotched by an unexpected spill.

He remembered sitting in the truck, gathering his strength for the drive home. He remembered the pain in his leg when he'd pressed on the accelerator. The rest of the trip came to him in nightmare snatches. Then he'd staggered into the house and down the hall to the bathroom, where he'd dug the bullet out, working in the oversize bathtub so that he could wash the blood down the drain. And he'd sloshed antiseptic onto the wound before tying on another bandage. If he'd been thinking more clearly, he'd have started antibiotics, too.

Too bad the disinfectant hadn't done the trick. Or perhaps the infection was just more of the bad luck dogging the Crawford case.

No. Not Crawford. Arnott.

Keep them straight, he ordered himself.

Crawford had died a long time ago. Or maybe he was coming back to get him. In his present condition Ross wasn't sure.

Yet he knew he needed to get out of bed, get to the antibiotics. Because an enemy might come charging through the door. And he suspected the pain of trying to change to wolf form now might finish him off. So he pulled open the drawer in the bedside table, got out his Sig .40, and slid in a clip.

Wrapping his hand in a death grip around the weapon, he heaved himself off the mattress and stood swaying on his feet, gritting his teeth with the effort to remain erect. By the time he reached the hall, his vision was blurring. Moving to the wall, he slid his shoulder against the vertical surface, willing himself to stay erect.

Every step was agony, but he pushed himself along, even when his muzzy brain forgot where he was going and why.

Blackness gathered at the edges of his vision. He made it as far as the rug in front of the sofa before he went down, first to his knees, then flat on his face— consciousness slipping from his brain even as he tried to struggle to his feet again.

CHAPTER
THREE

MEGAN BRAKED THE car and stared through the windshield at the sign tacked to the gray bark of an oak tree at the foot of Ross Marshall's driveway.

NO TRESPASSING. THAT MEANS YOU.

The black letters were faded, and the white background had taken on a dirty gray tinge. But the aging appearance did nothing to diffuse the potency of the warning.

Marshall's voice might sound inviting, but the man didn't have the welcome mat out for company.

She felt her neck muscles tightening, felt the stirrings of pain at her temples, and made a deliberate effort to relax. She'd been stressed out almost from the moment she got to work that morning. No—stressed out since last night, since the phone call from Dory. Her sister had been drunk. Abusive. Angry.

And Megan had hung there on the end of the line, taking it. More than taking it. Abandoning her previous resolve, she'd ended up promising to write a check to cover Dory's rent so she wouldn't get kicked out of her apartment.

Megan stared unseeing at the dappled sunlight filtering through the trees. She and Dory both had inherited two hundred and fifty thousand dollars from their parents, a mind-boggling amount in light of their father's frugality. Megan had used part of her share on a down payment for a house. The rest was still in the bank.

Dory had gone through the money like a plague of locusts chomping through a wheat field.

Broke again inside of a year, she'd started working on her sister's feeling of guilt, and there was plenty of that. Enough so that this morning, even with time for second thoughts, Megan had put a check for nine hundred dollars in the mail.

Partial payment for sins she hadn't known she was committing.

She squeezed her eyes shut, struggling to push the painful memories out of her mind. Life had been tough for the Sheridan women—not because Dad had been into physical abuse. He'd known how to be careful of the law and nosy social service workers, how to deal out punishment that for the most part wouldn't leave any physical marks. Most of the damage had been psychological, and each of the Sheridan women had handled the pain differently. Mom had turned into a Stepford wife, terrified to do anything to set off her husband's derisive outbursts. To an outside observer, Megan admitted, her own demeanor must have appeared similar to her mother's. Being a good little girl was the easiest way to keep from setting off the man who seemingly lived to criticize and humiliate the women in his family.

But the surface had given no clue to what was inside her. Secretly she'd vowed to make something of herself—to prove to the tyrant who alternately belittled and lashed out in anger that she wasn't the fucked-up mess he wanted her to be.

Not like Dory—who had gone out of her way to prove the accusations true. Rotten grades. Shoplifting. Joyriding in stolen cars. A pregnancy when she was sixteen—ending in an abortion at Dad's insistence.

Last night, Dory had come back to a familiar theme—accusing Megan of abandoning her. And in a way it was true. A long time ago, she'd turned her back on everything familiar. Moved from Boston to Baltimore when she was still in college, because she'd had the strength to save only one person—herself.

Now it was too late for her to help her sister. About all she could do was try to stanch a bleeding artery with a Band-Aid.

Megan slumped down and rested her head against the steering wheel until a sudden puff of wind shook the leaves overhead and buffeted the car, bringing her back to present reality.

It was like some cosmic hand shaking her out of her lethargy. Raising her head, she looked around, then reminded herself that she couldn't afford the luxury of sitting here feeling sorry for herself—or anyone else.

She'd already wasted twenty minutes backtracking down Route 99 when her computer-generated directions had erroneously indicated a right turn instead of a left. On the other hand, now that she was finally at the entrance to Ross Marshall's property, she couldn't help wondering if this harebrained assignment from Walter was going to get her shot.

Thumbing through her purse, she pulled out the number she'd copied down that morning and reached for the phone she kept in the closed compartment below the dashboard. It was a portable phone—not attached to the car. But she wasn't the kind of dork who sat in a restaurant or strolled down the walkways of a mall while carrying on a loud private conversation that was going to annoy everybody within fifty feet of her. The car was where she was most likely to use the phone, so that was where she kept it, not weighing down her pocketbook.

After punching in the number, she listened to the ringing on the other end of the line, then the same recorded message she'd heard that morning.

"Mr. Marshall?" she asked, unable to keep her frustration from creeping into her voice. "Are you there? I'm at the end of your driveway. If you're home, pick up the phone."

Her plea met with silence, and she felt her anxiety level crank up a notch. Where was he? Hadn't he gotten her message? Or was something very wrong at the Marshall house?

She was normally a calm person. Methodical. Careful. And she ordered herself to settle down and think with the logical mind she knew she possessed. She was already late because of the map problem. What if Marshall had come outside to wait for her—and that's why he wasn't answering?

Or what if he'd called the lab after she'd left and canceled the appointment?

Clicking on the phone again, she dialed the Bio Gen number. Betty answered.

"Hi. It's Megan. I'm out on that house call. Did Mr. Marshall by any chance phone to say he wasn't going to be home?"

"I haven't heard from him. Isn't he there?"

"I don't know. I'm at the bottom of his driveway, facing a No Trespassing sign."

"Oh, dear."

There was no point in asking Betty what to do. She couldn't make a good judgment from her desk in Bethesda.

"Okay. I'll go on up there. But if you don't hear from me tomorrow, send the police," Megan quipped, speaking only half in jest.

Betty laughed nervously.

"Just kidding. I'll see you in the morning."

"Oh—before you hang up, I have a message for you from Dr. Stillwell."

Megan made a face, glad that Betty couldn't see her expression. "What did he want?" As if she didn't know.

"He wants to discuss that plan of action he proposed."

"Well, I can't do anything about it now. I'll have to call him later." Or never, she thought as she got off the line.

Carter Stillwell was turning into a nuisance. She'd been introduced to him at a medical conference in September by one of her fellow Hopkins interns. He'd invited her for a drink and questioned her about her research, then told her that he knew someone at NIH who could get her funding to work on Myer's disease without the backing of Bio Gen. At first she'd been interested in at least pursuing the alternative. But as she'd gotten to know him better, she'd decided that he was all talk and no action. At least on the medical front. Personally, there was too much action. He was the kind of guy who stood too close, touched too much. He made her uncomfortable, and she'd been trying to stay away from him for the past few months. But he wasn't taking the hint.

With a sigh, she put away the phone, eased her foot onto the accelerator again, and started up the narrow drive. It looked like the access road had once been covered by gravel, but most of the chippings had been ground into the dirt or washed away, leaving large ruts that practically swallowed the wheels of her Toyota. How did Marshall get up and down here? she wondered. In a tank? Or one of those SUVs that guys seemed to love?

The road wound uphill, through light forest, where the first delicate green buds of spring leaves were visible on the dark branches. A number of the tree trunks were adorned with signs similar to the one near the entrance, just in case she hadn't gotten the original message.

She left them behind, then crossed a creaking wooden bridge spanning a stream where dark water tumbled over rounded rocks. Along the banks, delicate pink flowers carpeted the forest floor. It was a beautiful little surprise. Captivated, she swept her eyes over the gurgling water and the pink blossoms, caught by the aura of the place. It was a magical spot. And if at that moment some mythical creature—an elf or a fairy— had come wandering out of the woods, she wouldn't have been shocked.

Blinking, she shook off the fantasy. Elves and fairies! Really. She had work to do.

The scenery changed abruptly just a dozen feet on the far side of the bridge. The woods ended in a small glade warmed by the late-afternoon sun. Diagonally across the clearing was a stunning one-story wood and stone house, so cleverly sited on the property that it almost looked like a natural feature of the landscape. It wasn't large, probably two or three bedrooms, she judged.

At the edge of the woods, on a three-foot-tall post, was another sign. Braking to look at it, she saw it was also white, also faded. It said DÍTHREABH.

She struggled with the unfamiliar syllables, carefully pronouncing the word aloud. Was it "No Trespassing" in some foreign language? Or maybe the name of the house?

Shaking her head, she drove toward the building, emerging into the sunshine. A Jeep Grand Cherokee was parked close to the front door. Apparently she'd guessed right about Marshall's choice of transportation.

Glad that she hadn't turned around prematurely, she parked, picked up the kit she'd brought to collect a blood sample, and stepped into the late-afternoon sunshine. Immediately she was struck by the isolation of the place. No traffic noises drifted up from the road, but the woods seemed alive with the sound of birds.

She had started up the walk to the front door when she stopped short as she spotted a trail of red droplets spattering the stone walkway. Stooping to get a better look, she decided they were dried blood.

Immediately all sorts of dire possibilities leaped into her mind.

But she shut off the speculation. Whatever had happened, she'd find out pretty quickly. Raising her hand, she knocked on a varnished panel of the front door.

There was no answer. After waiting a full minute, she closed her fingers around the knob and turned, feeling the latch click.

Long ago her family had been in an automobile accident, hit from the rear at a red light by a driver whose brakes had failed. She'd been in the backseat with Dory, and when the car had slammed into their vehicle, she'd felt herself being thrown forward, then yanked backward as the seat belt had caught and held her. The crash must have taken place in mere seconds. But time had slowed at the moment of impact—making her feel as if she'd stepped outside herself and was watching the action in a slow-motion film.

She felt that way now—as if she'd stepped out of ordinary time into a separate reality. In the long-ago accident, she'd been helpless to change the outcome of events. This time, though, she had the power to make a choice. She could turn around and back away. Or she could push the door open.

If she did the latter, some sixth sense told her that her life would never be the same again. On the face of it, that was a ludicrous notion. Still, the impulse to turn and run for the safety of her car almost overwhelmed her. Backing away from the door, she decided to hedge her bets.

The living room windows were huge. Surely she could find out what waited for her inside the house.

Stepping off the walk, she waded through the bushes that flanked the front of the house. They were low hollies, and the sharp leaves raked her stockings, pulling at the delicate nylon.

Suppressing a wince, she cupped her hands around her eyes to cut the glare, brought her face to the glass, and peered inside.

It took a moment for her vision to adjust to the dimmer interior light. She was looking into a large, comfortable room—a great room, she supposed it would be called—with furniture of leather and rich wood, a massive stone fireplace along the far wall, and a floor of wide planking covered in several places by wool scatter rugs.

It was expensively done. Nothing looked out of the ordinary—aside from the man lying sprawled on his stomach across one of the throw rugs. He was naked except for a blood-soaked bandage wrapped around his right thigh.

All thoughts of flight vanished from her mind. Tearing back through the bushes, heedless of the thorny leaves, Megan leaped to the front door, turned the knob again, and plowed inside.

"Mr. Marshall?"

"Wha . . . ?" The word sighed out of him, a shadow of the deep, rich tone he'd used on the answering machine, yet just as compelling in its own way.

Hunkering down, she touched his shoulder. Though his skin was hot and clammy, the feel of his naked flesh under her fingers sent a sudden and totally unexpected electric buzz through her hand and up her arm.

With a small involuntary sound, she snatched her hand back, even as impressions assaulted her. The stale sickroom smell. The barely conscious man—his physical perfection like the work of a Renaissance sculptor. He lay facing the door, one hand flung out to the side and hidden under the edge of the couch.

She stared down at his unclothed body, remembering her conversation with Hank. Both of them had assumed that some debilitating genetic illness had kept the client from coming to the lab. If so, the defect wasn't anything obvious. His arms and legs were muscular. His shoulders were broad, his hips narrow. Firm buttocks. Olive skin that was flawless, except where it was marred by several scars—the one on his shoulder quite recent.

He conveyed an impression of healthy, lean strength—but for the oozing bandage on his right thigh. The skin at the edge of the bloodstained gauze was an angry red. She was sure that if she removed the bandage, she would find an infected wound.

Megan felt her heartbeat quicken. She was a physician, but a physician who hadn't treated a sick patient in over three years.

Still, old lessons and the old sense of involvement came flooding back. She felt for the pulse at his neck, counted the beats. It was fast and rapid. Did he have a thermometer in the bathroom?

God, what did it matter? She could tell he had a raging fever just by touching his skin.

She started to stand, intent on looking for medical supplies, when he made a low moaning sound.

One moment he was motionless. In the next, he had lifted his head, pushed himself up on one elbow. As she watched, mesmerized, sooty black lashes fluttered against his cheeks. Then his lids snapped fully open, and his midnight gaze zeroed in on her. No, not on her. She was pretty certain he wasn't seeing Megan Sheridan, that his gaze had pierced through present reality to some other scene.

"Mr. Marshall. What happened to you?"

A harsh, guttural word welled in his throat. *"Namhaid."*

She had no idea what it meant or even what language he spoke.

Before she could ask what the strange-sounding word meant, the hand that was hidden under the sofa emerged. Holding a gun. Pointed in the general direction of her stomach.

Her gasp of fear was followed by a quick plea. "Don't shoot me!"

His eyes were bloodshot, haunted as they bored into her—or was it through her?

"Crawford." He spat out the word as if it were a curse.

"No." Violently she shook her head.

Marshall ignored the protest. "Did you come back

to even the score?" he demanded, struggling to push himself up farther and flopping down again with what must have been a painful thunk. But the weapon was still in his hand, the muzzle only a foot from her body.

God, if his finger twitched on the trigger, she was a dead woman.

She wanted to back away. Run. But instinct told her that was exactly the wrong thing to do. "Put the gun down before it goes off," she ordered, amazed that her voice held steady.

The weapon wavered, then came back with unerring accuracy to the center of her stomach.

"Crawford," he said again, then dragged a labored breath into his lungs.

"No. My name is Megan Sheridan," she answered in a kind of daze, wishing she'd had the sense to get off his property before she looked in the window. "Please, don't shoot," she begged. "You don't even know me."

He stared at her with narrowed, red-rimmed eyes that struggled to focus on her face. *"Namhaid,"* he said again, though this time he sounded less certain. "Enemy."

"I'm Megan Sheridan," she repeated desperately, wondering if he could hear her through his delirium. Apparently he had no idea who was in the room with him. Which would make no difference when he blew a hole in her abdomen.

He made a kind of growling noise in his throat that stirred the hairs on the back of her neck.

Then his body went slack, and the hand with the gun fell to the floor, the weapon clanking against the bare wood, as though holding it up had simply become too much effort.

Without giving herself time to think about the danger, she sprang forward, grabbed his wrist, and pushed the gun barrel away from both of them as she struggled to pry his fingers off the weapon.

He tried to hold on to the gun, to wrest his hand from her grip, but he was too weak to fight her. She got control of the pistol, scrambled to her feet, and backed away, setting the weapon on a low chest at the other side of the room.

God, now what?

Fear urged her to keep on going out the door, to get as far from this man as humanly possible. She made it to her car in a blur of motion, her lungs burning from lack of oxygen. She had to get out of here before she ended up dead. Or worse.

She couldn't say where that last thought had come from. She had no idea what worse might be. Just a sense of foreboding that was impossible to shake.

Locking the car doors on the chance that he'd come staggering naked from the house, she scrabbled in her purse for her keys.

But even as she reached toward the ignition, an invisible force seemed to stay her hand.

She might be frightened. He might be dangerous. But she couldn't leave an injured man who was burning up with fever. Couldn't leave *this* man.

Call 911. Get out of here while the getting's good.

Intelligent advice. She closed her eyes and pressed her fingers against her temples, suddenly aware that the pain she'd been trying to fight off all day had mushroomed into a full-blown headache.

Not just from the personal confrontation with Marshall, although that had been bad enough. The encounter with him had brought long-suppressed turmoil bubbling to the surface of her mind. Treating patients on a daily basis had been too emotionally draining for her to endure. Yet quitting the medical profession would have been an admission of failure—an admission that her father had won in the end. That he'd been right about her all along. So she'd made a compromise and found a more detached way to practice medicine.

Within the space of seconds, detachment had vaporized like early morning fog burning off in bright sunlight.

If she'd ever known anything in her life, she knew

that Ross Marshall needed her. She couldn't simply walk away from him. Not and live with herself. Not now.

Maybe when she got him stabilized. But certainly not when his life might depend on what she did in the next few minutes.

Still, her heart threatened to pound its way through the wall of her chest as she marched back into the house.

CHAPTER
FOUR

MARSHALL LAY WHERE she'd abandoned him, but he'd pushed himself onto his back.

He was a large man. Over six feet. Long limbed. With impressive male equipment.

Chagrined that she was staring at his genitals, she dragged her eyes upward to his face. The features were very masculine. A classic nose, a strong jaw. But purple smudges almost like bruises marred the skin below his closed eyes, and a sheen of moisture coated his broad brow. "Mr. Marshall? Ross?"

His mouth tightened when she called his name, but he made no other response. And she was painfully aware of his stillness, aside from the labored sound of his breathing. As she watched him struggle to fill his lungs, she felt a thick pain in her own chest.

The sensation was more than physical. The man, the wound, the strange circumstances made her feel as if she'd suddenly stepped into another world where the laws of the universe were different from her own. Where anything she could imagine might come to pass.

The notion caught her, held her the way the fantasy and science-fiction stories she'd read as a teenager had transported her away from her oppressive Boston existence. Only now it wasn't a story. It was real life. And she couldn't step away from the scary part by closing a book.

She shivered, then with an effort of will shook off the fanciful notion. She was in the home of a man who desperately needed her help, and she was wasting time. Lips compressed, she started making a mental list of what she needed to do.

There was a well-worn quilt draped over the back of the sofa. Unfolding it, she laid it over him. When she spotted the gun still lying on the chest, she grimaced. It was sitting out in full view. What in the world was wrong with her?

After shoving the weapon into a drawer, she returned to the unconscious man. Gingerly she knelt beside him—ready to spring back at the first sign of another attack. "Mr. Marshall? Ross?"

One moment, his face was immobile as granite. Then his eyes blinked open, fixing her with the intensity of a laser beam. She cringed as she remembered his delirium. But this time was different. This time she was sure he saw her—Megan Sheridan—not some phantom enemy springing up from his subconscious to trigger his aggressive instincts.

His dark gaze pinned her, making escape impossible. The breath stilled in her lungs as she felt the two of them make a sort of wordless contact—communication on some deep level that she only dimly understood.

For long seconds, she was incapable of speech, incapable of movement.

His voice broke through the spell. It was raspy now, the richness eroded by the ravages of pain he must be suffering. "Who are you? What are you doing here?"

"I'm Megan Sheridan. From Bio Gen Labs. You called us to make an appointment."

He closed his eyes, then opened them again.

"You called Bio Gen Labs," she repeated.

His head gave an almost imperceptible nod of understanding.

"What happened to you?"

He made a sound halfway between a laugh and a groan. "I was dumb enough to get shot."

"Shot? You have a bullet in your leg?"

"I dug it out. It was a flesh wound."

Lord, what kind of man could dig a bullet out of his own leg? When she tried to imagine inflicting that kind of torture on herself, a shudder went through her. "You should be in the hospital. I'll call an ambulance."

His fingers closed around her wrist, and his dark eyes focused on hers with a sudden fierceness that made her throat constrict. "Please . . . no hospital . . . no doctor."

"Why not?"

He heaved a deep sigh, seemed to gather his strength. "They'd have to . . . report it. Can't talk about what happened . . . with them. Have to talk to . . . Thornton."

"Who's Thornton?"

"The police."

"I don't understand."

He sucked in air, his gaze holding her again, and she decided his eyes were the most compelling she had ever seen. Dark and bottomless, full of depth that drew her toward him as no other man had ever drawn her. "I'm a private detective. . . ." he wheezed, then paused to take in more air. "Investigating . . . murders. Of . . . women. But . . . can't prove anything . . . yet. Can't risk a bunch of questions."

The short speech exhausted him, and he went limp against the rug.

"You'd risk your life for an investigation?"

The eyes hardened. "To put Crawford away." He stopped, blinked, began again. "To put Arnott away . . . yes."

"You won't put him away if you're dead."

He grimaced. "I won't be. I just need . . . antibiotics."

She opened her mouth to say he needed around the clock nursing care.

Before she could deliver the advice, he started speaking again, his words tumbling forth as if he were afraid that his stamina would give out before he delivered the message. "Keflex. In . . . kitchen cabinet nearest the door . . ."

The drug was probably the right choice. Where had he gotten it?

"Please."

The plea tore at her, partly because she sensed that he wasn't a man who needed to beg for anything under normal circumstances. He was a man who took charge of situations. Even wounded and half out of his head, he'd instinctively defended himself. He'd probably dragged himself out of bed to get the medicine. His iron will had carried him this far, but now he was at the end of his strength.

"Just get me . . . Keflex. Then you can go."

His lids drifted closed, and he lay very still, probably at the end of his strength.

She stared at his unmoving form, thinking that the biggest favor she could do him was call an ambulance and get him to the hospital. It was the logical thing to do. The right thing. Medically.

Emotionally, it felt more like betrayal. Because he'd trusted her to keep his gunshot wound between the two of them.

Hardly understanding her own motivation, she realized she'd made a decision. Standing, she looked around. The kitchen was on her immediate right.

To the left of the sink she found a mostly empty cabinet that held the plastic container of blue caplets. The prescription was eight months old. There were only six caplets, apparently left over from some other illness. She knew from her training that taking leftover antibiotics was a bad idea, but the medication hadn't reached its expiration date, and the supply in the bottle would be enough to get him started.

After filling a glass with water, she retraced her steps.

Marshall was lying where she'd left him. She thought he'd drifted into a fevered sleep, but his lids flicked open when he heard her footsteps approaching across the wood floor. She froze when she encountered the same dangerous glint in his eye that she'd seen just before he pulled the gun from beneath the edge of the couch.

God, was she a fool, spending another minute with a man who'd proven that he was dangerous?

"I'm Megan Sheridan from Bio Gen Labs." She repeated what she'd told him earlier, her fingers tightening on the glass of water, ready to throw it at him if she had to. "Do you remember? I'm here to help you."

He considered the question, the cloudy look in his eyes fading as he studied her. "Are you a doctor?"

"Yes."

"But you won't report you're treating a patient who's been shot?" he asked, his voice tense.

She gave a small laugh. "I'm treating you without a license. I think we're even."

He took that for agreement, and she set the water on the floor so she could open the medicine bottle. "Can you sit up?"

He tried, giving the project considerable attention, the strong muscles of his arms and chest straining with effort. When he couldn't raise himself enough to drink the water, she came down beside him and helped him up, propping his back against the base of the sofa. Then she handed him the caplet and the glass.

He managed to get the blue pill into his mouth, then grimaced as the bitter medication hit his tongue. With a jerky motion, he lifted the glass to his lips and gulped water, some of it spilling down his chest.

Before he could drench himself, she took the glass from his hand and eased him back against the rug.

"The bandage you wrapped around your leg probably needs changing."

"Yeah," he wheezed. "First-aid stuff . . . bathroom. Antiseptic. More bandages."

She might have told him to wait right there, but she knew he wasn't going anywhere.

UNTIL he'd found that big dog pawing at Charlotte's grave, Donald Arnott had thought he was safe.

The moment of discovery had sent terror shooting through him like the shaft of an arrow.

But his confidence hadn't been punctured for long. He had been scooping up women and doing what he wanted with them for the past eight years. And he was damned if some snoop with a dog was going to fuck him up.

Since he'd shot at the dog, he'd been too busy to worry. He had dug up Charlotte's body, and the rest of them, then taken the evidence to the mountains, where nobody would connect the dead women with him.

When the bodies were out of the way, he'd used a rototiller on the fresh earth and visited a garden center, buying twenty shrubs to landscape the newly plowed areas. Spring was supposed to be a good time to plant bushes. And he'd made it look like he was into a massive home improvement effort. That took care of the burial ground on his property.

The underground room wasn't a problem. He'd built it like a bunker, with a steel door hidden under what appeared to be the ruins of an old barn. Nobody was going to find it.

The morning after the break-in, he'd driven down to the road, checking out the area that was closest to his fence. There had been fresh tire tracks in the dirt beside the shoulder. From a pickup truck or an SUV, he judged, noting the size of the tires and the space between the wheels. Unfortunately, the information did him little good.

But he was absolutely safe for the moment, he told himself firmly. He'd shot the dog, scared the man away, and let him know that Donald Arnott was a formidable enemy.

Everything he'd picked up beside the fence was in a plastic storage box he'd bought at Kmart. Opening the door to his workshop, he lifted the box off a shelf and set it in the middle of the table.

In the merciless glow from the fluorescent light, he examined the contents once more, looking for something he had missed when he'd first inspected the haul.

Again he picked up the wire cutters. The adjustable wrench, the set of Craftsman screwdrivers. The flashlight that looked like it had come from Sunny Surplus. And a pair of Bausch & Lomb binoculars that must have cost the earth.

He turned them over in his hand. They were lightweight but powerful—with 200mm lenses. Setting them down, he picked up a running shoe, examined the treads, then fingered the soft fabric of the shirt.

Who the hell was this guy? Not a cop. The cops didn't have a clue about him. He'd been too careful for that. Still, he'd been going over and over it in his mind, and he couldn't come up with a scenario to explain why some guy would be sneaking around in the woods less than half dressed.

Unless he was some kind of pervert.

That brought a bark of laugher to his lips. A pervert stalking a pervert. Nice.

At least that was how the world would think of him. He preferred to style himself as a man whose level of existence was so far above the petty lives of normal human beings that he functioned like a god. A god with the privileges and obligations of ruling over ordinary mortals.

At least the women. They were all sluts. Like his mother. And that gave him the right to decide which of them would live, which would die, and which would gratify his sexual desires.

But he hadn't anticipated some guy interfering in his chosen pursuits. A man with a dog. A man who had cut his fence and then sent his dog searching for evidence. Because that was the only scenario that fit.

A sudden surge of anger flared inside him like hot lava shooting from a volcano. Picking up the wrench, he slammed it against the workbench, the thunk of metal against wood sending a shockwave up his arm.

The pain sobered him, set his mind working again. Because the worst thing he could do now was let this throw him off his stride.

He had to find the guy. Maybe the way to do it was through the dog. It had been injured. Shot high up in the right leg. Christ, the bullet should have slowed the beast down. But he'd kept running with a strength and speed that Donald would have admired—if the two of them hadn't been mortal enemies.

Still, the animal would need to be treated. And the bullet wound was something he could use to his advantage—the centerpiece of a story he could tell the local vets.

He chuckled as he imagined the conversation. *Have you found an injured dog? I saw somebody shoot it, but it ran away before I could catch it, and I'm worried about the animal.*

Yeah, that would work.

Methodically he replaced the man's possessions in the box, stowed it on the shelf, and then went in search of the telephone book.

MEGAN went looking for first-aid supplies and found them on the bathroom counter where Marshall had tossed them. Before returning to her patient, she wet a clean washcloth with warm water. After laying the cloth on a towel, she knelt beside Marshall again, fighting the unaccustomed sense of unreality that had crept up on her earlier.

His eyes were closed once more, and for a long moment she stared down at him, struck by the notion that there was something remarkable about this man. Something she didn't quite understand.

His voice had been compelling when she'd heard it on his answering machine. Even in his weakened state, his physical presence added to the impression of strength and power. Not just physical strength. Something more. Charisma? That didn't seem to be the right word. Cutting off the speculation, she bent to her task.

He was still covered by the quilt. With a firm hand, she moved it away from the right side of his long-limbed body. When she connected with his thigh, her fingers felt icy against his hot flesh.

Calling on rusty skills, she assessed the wound. The hole in his leg was red and oozing, ragged around the edges where he'd dug out the bullet. The surrounding skin was hot and swollen.

He groaned as she began to clean it, groaned again as she sloshed on antiseptic.

Next she replaced the bandage, praying that the antibiotic was going to take care of the infection. Otherwise they were looking at blood poisoning.

She sat there beside him, feeling overwhelmed. Then she shook herself, because she couldn't leave him on the floor.

Unfortunately, there wasn't a chance in hell that she could carry him to bed. What was the alternative? Getting a sheet under him and pulling him along the floorboards?

Grimacing at the prospect, she pushed herself up and retraced her steps down the hall—this time entering his bedroom. As she'd anticipated, the linens were stained with blood. First she stripped the bed and remade it with fresh sheets and pillowcases she found in the closet. After bundling the soiled laundry into the hamper in the bathroom, she returned to the man on the floor.

"I have to get you into bed. Can you help me?" she murmured, not really expecting an answer.

"Yeah."

She jumped, wondering how long he'd been with her again.

"Did I hurt you when I changed the dressing?"

"No."

She was sure he was lying.

Then he asked a question of his own. "Did I threaten you with a gun?"

"You remember that?"

"Well, it has a . . . dreamlike quality." Regret etched his chiseled features. "Sorry."

"You were pretty out of it."

"I'm . . . not in the habit of shooting visitors."

She nodded tightly. "Can you walk?"

"I hope so."

"How do I get you on your feet?" she asked, turning the problem over to him.

He thought about it for a moment. "Need to sit up." After taking several breaths, he heaved his torso to a vertical position, sweat breaking out on his forehead from the exertion. Moving close to him, she squatted and draped her arm around his waist, holding him up.

He took several more breaths, then said, "You . . . count to three. Then . . . I'll push . . . you lift."

"Wait." Realizing that he was going to be naked again when he got to his feet, she tugged at the edge of the quilt, pulled it away from his legs, and tucked the fabric over his shoulder like a sort of toga.

Then she started to count. As she reached three, she felt his muscles strain. She was pretty sure he couldn't have stood on his own, but working together—pushing and pulling—they managed to get him erect, where he stood swaying on his feet, leaning on her shoulder. She knew they weren't home free yet, and she wanted to urge him to hurry before he toppled back to the floor.

His progress down the hall was painfully slow, with his weight on her shoulder increasing and the quilt slipping immodestly off his body as they moved. Finally, when she thought one of them might trip over it, she kicked it away.

By the time they reached the bedroom, he was naked again, and they were both panting from the exertion of moving him thirty feet.

She eased him down onto the mattress, pulling the top sheet out of the way as he collapsed with a groan. When he was horizontal, she pulled the sheet back into place, covering the lower half of his body.

The trip down the hall had provided a fresh assessment of his condition—and of her ability to take care of him. "You should be in the hospital," she said again.

"No. I'm tough."

She didn't bother to argue, because she knew that much was true. Partly because she wasn't sure how a man in his condition had dragged himself down the hall before she'd arrived, and partly because she was sure that few men in his shape would have made it back to the bed on their own feet—even with help.

"More water," he said.

She left him, went back for the glass, and topped it off at the kitchen sink.

It seemed he was out of energy. Although he gave it a good try, he couldn't push himself up again, and she sat down beside him on the bed, lifting his shoulders, cradling his back against her front, feeling like she was invading his privacy as she felt his body trembling against her.

She wanted to tell him there was nothing humiliating in being weak from a high fever. She was pretty sure he wouldn't agree. So she simply held him as he took several swallows of water.

"Enough?"

"Yes." His voice was barely audible now.

She helped him lie back on the mattress, and he sank into sleep within seconds of his head coming down on the pillow. Instead of getting up, she remained beside him on the bed. With a tissue from the nightstand, she gently wiped the sweat from his brow, then brushed back a strand of his dark, wavy hair. It was fine textured and seemed to twine around her fingers of its own accord.

Her touch must have startled him, because those fathomless eyes blinked open again. Feeling as if she'd been caught doing something illegal, she scrambled for something to say.

"You need to sleep."

"You need to leave."

"I can't leave you like this. You and I both know you should be in the hospital."

"No hospital. I'm used to . . . being alone," he said through gritted teeth.

"Not in this condition."

"You . . . clear out."

She sensed danger in his dark eyes now. Danger to her, on some hidden level that she hardly understood. Yet he couldn't be a physical threat—not when he could hardly hold his head up.

Still, as she stood up, she knew it would be a good idea to take his advice. Clear out of his house before something happened—although she couldn't say what.

A sudden image flashed in her mind. The two of them. Herself and Marshall on the bed, their naked bodies tangled together, their breath coming in sharp gasps as searing heat swirled through every one of her nerve endings.

Momentarily dizzy, she swayed on her feet, her heart pounding and her breath rushing in and out of her lungs. She must have made some sound, because his eyes shot to her face, and she had the sudden conviction that he'd seen the same image as she. That they had unaccountably shared the same heated vision.

"No," he said thickly. "Get out of here."

"All right," she breathed, and this time she took a step back.

His features relaxed, and she turned and bolted from the room.

Standing in the dimly lit hallway, she felt her mind clear, her heart rate and breathing returning to normal. Resisting the impulse to look back over her shoulder, she wondered what had happened to her. The vision had been like a prophecy. A promise. A promise that she longed to keep.

Teeth clenched, she shook off the notion. God, had she ever been so unprofessional with a patient? Well, it certainly wasn't going to happen again.

The bottom line was, she needed to stay. To give him medical attention because she'd promised not to call an ambulance.

Deep within herself, though, she knew that she wasn't being entirely honest. There were other reasons for her reluctance to leave, reasons that had nothing to do with logic and everything to do with the way this enigmatic stranger made her feel.

CHAPTER
FIVE

JACK FINISHED THE note he was writing on Marshall, then rocked back in his chair, feeling a little surge of excitement flare in his chest. It was the old hunting instinct, he supposed. Not the primitive hunt of a man in the woods, stalking game with spear or a gun. But the modern variety—following a paper trail, adding bits and pieces of information until you had enough to take the measure of the man you were investigating.

He was still waiting for utility records, a credit report, and tax information. But he'd found out some fascinating—and unexpected—stuff as a result of checking through motor vehicles.

Not the two speeding tickets Marshall had acquired over the past five years. No, his interest had pricked up when he'd seen the long string of address changes, going back to when the PI was eighteen and had moved out of his parents' home.

Jack looked down at his notes on his interview with Rosa Lantana, who'd lived a couple of doors down from the Marshall family in Parkville, a working-class neighborhood north of Baltimore.

"I'm doing a credit check on Victor Marshall, and I was wondering if you're acquainted with the Marshall family," he'd begun.

"Is that no-good son of a bitch in trouble again?"

"I'm not at liberty to say."

That had led to an earful about the family. The senior Marshall was an auto mechanic by trade and a belligerent individual who had alienated everyone in the neighborhood. He'd also beat the hell out of his sons and finally driven them away—including the middle one, Ross.

"Alice, she's a saint," Lantana went on. "He kept her pregnant and barefoot until she got too old to have any more of his children."

"There are a lot of children in the family?"

"No. Most of them were stillborn. Let's see. There were four or five boys who lived into their teens. I think there are only two who are still alive. None of them are at home anymore. Troy got himself killed in a bar fight. Adam is out west somewhere. Ross is still in the area. I know 'cause he visits his mother sometimes when the old man isn't home."

Mrs. Lantana rambled on.

Two boys had keeled over from mysterious causes in their teens. Personally, she thought the old man had beaten them to death, although there was never any evidence against him.

She painted a picture of a classic dysfunctional family, if there was such a thing. And she also put forth the theory that the senior Marshall supplemented his mechanic's income through some kind of illegal means.

Long after they'd dispensed with any material that would be relevant to a credit check, he kept digging for information, recognizing pay dirt when he encountered it.

"Did Ross get in any trouble that you know of?"

"That boy? Oh my, no. I never saw a youngster more determined to make something of himself. Starting when he was fifteen, he worked as a carpenter's helper in the summers and after school. Then he started doing, you know, handyman projects on his own. He built the shelves under my stairs. And . . . let's see. He practically rebuilt my falling-down shed out back. He was in college—the University of Maryland—on a scholarship, when he bought a row house in the city. His mother told me. You should have seen her face; she was so proud of him."

Instantly alert, Jack asked, "Where did he get that kind of money?"

"I don't know. But I can tell you he came by it honestly. That boy was a real straight arrow. Not like his good-for-nothing father. He sold that first house he fixed up. And he bought another one. And then did it again."

Well, that accounted for the string of addresses in progressively more affluent neighborhoods around Baltimore and D.C. Apparently he'd made a career out of buying distressed properties, whipping them into shape, and investing the profits in more real estate.

Jack slipped the notes from Mrs. Lantana into the folder. It wasn't what he'd expected to find out about Ross. A young man from a troubled family who'd made good in the eyes of the world. It sounded like a real success story. Except for the violence factor. The father had pounded on his sons, taught them that might makes right. Had Ross learned that lesson too well? Or had he escaped that part of his heritage?

Standing, Jack went to the computer room to put Victor Marshall's name into the database and see what he got.

MEGAN headed down the hall to the bathroom, leaving the bedroom door ajar so she could hear her patient if he needed anything. She'd been in a hurry when she'd

stuffed the dirty sheets in the hamper and collected
medical supplies. Now she had time to look around.

The room had obviously been remodeled—with a
greenhouse wall totally exposed to the woods. There
were no blinds and no screening, except for the lush-
looking ferns hanging in the window over the large spa
tub. At least the toilet was behind a half wall, giving
some privacy. The remainder of the area was domi-
nated by the tub and the curving window wall. The
open vista and the indoor greenery gave the room the
effect of being in the middle of the woods.

After using the facilities, she washed her hands, then
cupped her palms under the faucet, scooped up some
cold water, and gulped it down.

She made her way back to the great room—and another bank of windows.

The house was as open to the natural environment
as it could be and still keep out the elements, she
thought as she stared at the meadow and the forest
beyond, the leaves taking on a golden hue where they
caught the last rays of the sun.

Then the sun disappeared, and darkness began to
swallow up the landscape, blurring the shapes of the
bushes and the trees.

When she'd stopped at the wooden bridge over the
stream, she'd imagined cunning little fairies and elves
gamboling among the ferns and flowers. Now the images that came to her were much darker: creatures of
the night, monsters you wouldn't want to meet in this
isolated location—or any other.

She stifled a nervous laugh. All kinds of amazing
images had been popping into her head since she arrived here.

Not just images, she reminded herself. There had
been one strikingly memorable incident, too. When
Marshall had pulled that gun on her.

Perhaps it would be smart to take his advice and get
out while the getting was good. Forget about imaginary
monsters in the woods. She was focusing her fears in

the wrong direction—like the heroine of a horror movie who goes around locking all the doors and windows only to find that the real threat is inside the house. It was folly to stay here with a man she didn't know. A man who had already proved himself to be dangerous. And who'd chosen to live in as secluded a spot as you could find in the Baltimore-Washington corridor.

She had told him she would leave.

On the other hand, she had also told him she wouldn't call an ambulance. And she couldn't possibly do both those things. So she chose to stay and make sure he didn't die.

As soon as she knew everything was all right, she would go home and stop obsessing about Ross Marshall. That was a promise she was making to herself.

She told herself she'd been acting in a perfectly rational manner since arriving here. And the decision to clear out as soon as it was safe to leave her patient lifted a weight off her shoulders. Feeling lighter, she moved around the living area, turning on lamps, the yellow pools of light shutting out the darkness beyond the windows.

The room had been made for nighttime. In the lamplight, the leather upholstery took on a soft, inviting patina, and the wood floor gleamed.

The massive stone fireplace was set about two feet from the floor, with a neat stack of wood piled underneath. It was an appealing, cozy environment, and she thought for a moment how nicely a roaring fire would chase away the evening's chill. Unfortunately, she had little experience with building fires. And trying to learn the skill with someone else's fireplace smacked too much of taking liberties.

Instead she drifted toward the custom-made bookcases that took up the rest of the fireplace wall. Reading had been a part of her life since she'd gotten old enough to ride her bike to the library on Saturdays to bring back a stack of books. Novels. Nonfiction. Her own parents hadn't been readers. In fact Dad had jeered at her for having her "nose stuck in a book" instead of doing something constructive. But reading had opened up a world for her that reached far beyond the confines of her middle-class Boston neighborhood. And she'd come to the conclusion that you could tell a lot about people by the kind of libraries they owned.

One thing she knew about Marshall: he was a collector. Books lined the wall from a foot above the floor to several feet above her head, with two wheeled ladders attached to tracks along the shelves giving access to the upper volumes.

She learned more as she began to study the titles—like the fact that Ross Marshall was a very organized man who arranged his books by subject matter and then alphabetically by author. With such a well-ordered collection, it was easy to see that his interests were wide, ranging from philosophy and psychology to genetic diseases and criminal investigation and animal husbandry.

Apparently he liked poetry. Particularly e. e. cummings, Emily Dickinson, and T. S. Eliot. Unusual reading material for a man who made his living as a detective. Well, it was more than simply making a living, she amended. When he'd spoken about investigating a killer, she'd caught a fervor in his voice that revealed he was on a personal mission to wipe a demon from the face of the earth.

Lord, what kind of man was he? she wondered. Dangerous. Powerful in ways she didn't understand. Idealistic. Intelligent. Stubborn. Macho. Sexy. *Let's not forget sexy.*

Resolutely pulling her mind away from that direction, she returned her attention to the bookcase.

He had a large section on mysticism, ancient history, early Christianity, and pagan religions—the biggest portion of which was on the Druids of pre-Roman Britain. He also had not one but three Gaelic-English dictionaries.

And his taste in fiction ranged from Mary Renault and C. S. Lewis to Robert Heinlein and E. B. White.

His fantasy collection was particularly impressive. She smiled when she saw the complete set of Lewis's Narnia books, her first foray into fantasy after a favorite teacher had lent her the first book in the series. Along with the Narnia books were Grimm's Fairy Tales and all sorts of stories of the supernatural—tales of witches, ghosts, vampires, and werewolves.

Dracula, Frankenstein, The Turn of the Screw, the complete works of Edgar Allan Poe, *Rosemary's Baby, The Exorcist.*

Her hand was drawn to a volume in that section that had obviously been read many times, judging from the condition of the dust jacket. It was called *Darker than You Think* by a writer named Jack Williamson—a tale of werewolves who preyed on the human race, she gathered from the cover copy.

The grim subject matter brought a tightness to her chest, and she quickly replaced the book in the shelves, lining it up with the volumes on either side so that he wouldn't know she'd taken it down.

When she realized what she was doing, she gave a tiny laugh. What did it matter if he found out she'd been thumbing through the volumes on his shelves? Except perhaps that he'd know she'd been poking through his stuff—after he'd told her to leave.

Well, she'd found out he had eclectic tastes in reading—much broader than her own. After her science fiction and fantasy phase, she'd consumed a lot of literary fiction and poetry in college. But these days her recreational reading was mostly confined to easily accessible fiction. When she came home from the lab, she was too worn out for anything taxing.

In truth, she was worn out now. And the panty hose she'd been wearing all day were starting to bind.

In the trunk of her car were a clean T-shirt and sweatpants that she'd been planning to wear to the gym that evening, although it looked like she wasn't going to manage to get there, again. Despite the extenuating circumstances, she felt a stab of guilt. Going to the gym was supposed to be one of her priorities. Like cooking dinner instead of grabbing something already prepared from Sutton Place Gourmet or Fresh Fields on the way home. Every morning she got up promising that she'd do forty minutes on the weight machines after work. But somehow those sessions got pushed back when she had too much to finish at the lab.

Well, putting the gym clothes on now would make sense, if she was planning to stay. Even for a little while.

Flipping on the porch light, she took a tentative step outside. Immediately she was struck by the quiet and the solitude. There wasn't another house in sight—or even a light winking through the trees. Again she noted that even the traffic sounds from the road were non-existent up here on Marshall's hill. She could be in the middle of the Maine woods.

Shivering in the evening chill, she hurried through the darkness to retrieve her gym bag, her eyes scanning the woods even as she told herself it was childish to be afraid of the dark. Still, she was back inside in under a minute and locked the door behind her with a firm click.

After changing in the office, she folded up her skirt and blouse, stuffed them in the bag, and headed into the kitchen to see what she could discover for dinner.

The freezer was stocked with steaks and chops. And there were few canned goods. The closest thing she found to fast food was a can of beef and barley soup. Warming that up shouldn't be too difficult, she decided as she eyed the microwave over the stove.

While the soup heated, she tiptoed down the hall and looked in on her patient. He seemed to be resting peacefully, so she didn't go in to pull up the sheet, which had slipped midway down his lean hips.

She also peeked behind the other doors along the hall. Next to the bathroom, there was a room set up as a home office with a desk, computer, and filing cabinet. Behind another door was a rack of barbells and one of those universal home gyms where you could do fifty different strength-training exercises. But she didn't see any aerobic equipment. Maybe Marshall was a runner or a jogger.

Another thing she didn't see was a guest bedroom.

Well, he'd said he was used to being alone. Apparently that meant he didn't encourage overnight company.

As she sat at the kitchen table sipping her soup, she pulled out the small writing tablet she always carried in her purse. She was a researcher, and she'd found she never knew when documentation was going to come in handy.

On a clean page she labeled "Ross Marshall" at the top, she began to write up detailed notes on what had happened so far, editing out the fact that the wound had come from a bullet.

In the middle of her case study, she found herself yawning. Maybe she'd better set a timer to make sure she gave Marshall his next dose of Keflex, she thought as she moved to the couch in the great room.

She knew she should keep her eyes open. But closing them was simply too tempting. And once she'd blocked out the world, she drifted into a light sleep—until a sound from somewhere nearby made her sit bolt upright.

She was still trying to figure out where it had come from when a low groan from the back of the house told her it was Marshall—and that he was in trouble.

He cried out again, the sound more like that of an animal in pain than a man.

Pushing herself up, she went running barefoot down the hall to the bedroom.

Marshall was thrashing around on the bed, the covers on the floor and his body glistening with a sheen of perspiration.

"Ross," she called, crossing to him, then jumping

back as his arm flailed, barely missing her leg.

Even semiconscious he was dangerous. Especially semiconscious.

"Ross, don't. It's Megan Sheridan. Remember?"

He didn't respond, and she sat down on the bed so that the flailing arm was trapped between his side and her hip. Leaning over, she pressed her hand to his reddened cheek. As she'd known it would be, his skin was hot and damp. Without a thermometer, she'd guess that his temperature was at least a hundred and five. Much too high.

His head rolled back and forth on the pillow, his dark hair plastered to his forehead.

"It's all right. You're going to be all right. The antibiotics will start working soon."

His eyes were closed. His fingers dug into the bottom sheet. Then his lips moved, shaping syllables she couldn't catch. The words were low, in some foreign language that had nothing in common with English.

At first she couldn't even distinguish the syllables sliding from his lips. Then his tone changed, becoming sharper, more distinct. More urgent.

"Taranis, Epona, Cerridwen," he intoned, then repeated the same phrase and went on to another.

"Gá. Feart. Cleas. Duais. Aithriocht. Go gcumhdaí is dtreoraí na déithe thú."

The low grating tone of his voice and the strange words raised goose bumps on her arms and stirred a deep primal fear in the marrow of her bones. The words were like nothing she had ever heard—a throwback to a time before written history, when the world was a savage place. They sounded like a chant or a prayer—incredibly ancient syllables passed down through the ages without benefit of written language. They roared through her, rooted her to the spot where she sat as surely as if Ross Marshall had reached out and circled her wrist with one of his strong hands.

She stared down at him, unable to take her eyes away. Unable to move or even speak.

The strange, sharp sounds echoed in her brain, rising and falling, distorting her senses so that all she heard now was a ringing in her ears that was below the level of perceived sound. And something was happening to her vision, as well.

For a moment out of time she could no longer clearly discern the man on the bed. His skin seemed to go a shade darker, grayer, the texture changing to something she couldn't name. And the very shape of his face and of his body wavered dangerously in her vision, turning fluid like a movie image of one familiar object morphing into another.

The rational part of her brain simply wasn't capable of dealing with what she was seeing. But the deep, primitive part responded, a stab of fear like the blade of an ancient dagger piercing through her chest. She wanted to run from him, run for her life. Run for her sanity. But she couldn't move, because she was caught in the grip of some terrible magic spell. It held her—and the man, too. Only he was the one doing it. He was the master magician working the transformation.

There was no way she could articulate what she was feeling. But a sound she hardly recognized welled in her throat. A sound that was part mind-numbing fear, part protest that came from the depths of her soul

His body stiffened. The outlines snapped back into his familiar male shape. And in the space of a heartbeat, the spell was broken.

She stared down at him, her eyes and her brain telling her that she had only imagined what she thought she saw. Her groggy mind had been playing tricks.

Somehow she had been in the grip of a weird hallucination, as if she were the one with the high fever and he were only a silent witness to the delusions wafting through her mind. Because that was the only way she dared explain to herself what had happened.

His eyes blinked open, focused on her. And a deep shudder went through him.

His lips moved. "No."

"What happened?" she gasped out.

"Nothing."

She waited for him to say more, to admit that he understood what she was talking about, but he only closed his eyes with profound weariness.

Caught in a tide of emotion she couldn't understand, she reached to cup his shoulder. As she did, she was jolted by the terrible heat radiating from his body. God, he was burning up. And she was sitting here like a dummy when the first priority was to bring his fever down. The best thing would be to get him into a cool bath. But she had no illusions about her ability to carry him down the hall. And she was pretty sure he'd gone past the point of being able to make it under his own power.

Instead she dashed to the bathroom, threw open the medicine cabinet, and sighed in relief when she found an almost full bottle of denatured alcohol.

On her way back to the bedroom, she grabbed a washcloth from the linen closet.

Her patient lay very still now, so still that her stomach twisted as she eased onto the bed beside him.

Quickly she poured alcohol onto the washcloth, then began to rub the pungent liquid on his face, his neck, his chest.

He coughed from the strong scent rising toward his nostrils. "Don't," he choked out, turning his head and trying to push her hand away.

It was obvious that the smell bothered him. But she ignored the protest, catching his arm as she had before and wedging it between her body and his. Then she poured more of the alcohol directly on his chest, feeling his strong muscles ripple beneath the cloth and sweeping dark hair first one way and then the other as she tried to cool him down.

He coughed again. "Are you trying to kill me?"

"I'm trying to bring down your fever."

His body jerked, but she held him in place with one

hand while she used her other to rub him with the damp cloth.

When he began to shiver, she breathed out a little sigh, relieved that the rapidly evaporating liquid was doing its work.

Reaching down, she pulled the sheet up to his waist, covering him again. When she looked up, his eyes were open, fever bright, their intensity pinning her anew.

"What's wrong with me?" he asked in a low voice that was almost a growl.

"You got shot. The wound is infected. I'm trying to get your temperature down," she told him, repeating earlier exchanges of information.

She watched his expression change as he looked down toward the bandage on his leg. Experimentally he flexed the leg, grimacing from the pain.

"Can you tell me why someone shot you?" she asked.

"I *found . . . one of the graves.*"

"What grave?"

"Of one of the women Crawford killed." He stopped, blinked. "Not Crawford. Crawford's dead."

She shuddered.

He had been speaking almost to himself. He focused on her again, looking startled, as if he had just realized she was in the room with him. "You can't stay here."

"Somebody has to take care of you."

"Not you."

"You think I don't know what I'm doing?"

He closed his eyes, lay motionless for several moments as though gathering enough energy for a long speech. Still, his next words, when they came, were so low that she had to lean closer to hear him.

"I know you don't. Or you'd have the sense to get out."

The way he questioned her competence had her lifting her chin and glaring down at him—a tough combination to manage, but she did it. "I have a medical degree. I may not have treated a patient in several years, but believe me, I know the right things to do for you."

He madc a low, dismissive sound more animal than human. "I'm not talking about your medical degree. . . . You and me. Not good."

"We don't even know each other."

"We know enough."

"I don't understand what you mean."

His eyes snapped open, drilled into her. "Don't lie to me." He dragged in a ragged breath and let it out slowly. "I wasn't going to let this happen. It can't happen." Agony mingled with a sense of purpose in his voice.

She leaned toward him, wanting him to explain. But his eyes took on a shuttered expression. "I called the lab, and they sent *you*. Jesus!"

She didn't understand what was upsetting him. Didn't understand what he meant.

She might have kept asking questions, but the exchange seemed to have used up all his energy. His eyelids fluttered closed, and the regular rise and fall of his chest told her he had sunk back into sleep. Leaving her with more questions than he had answered.

CHAPTER
SIX

ROSS DRIFTED IN and out of sleep, ambushed by nightmares that gripped his fevered imagination, scenes following one another in a jumbled order that made no sense in the way they filtered up from deep within his subconscious.

First he was in the kitchen at home, looking at his hollow-eyed mother, listening to her tell him about his father's latest scrape with the law. She looked so old and tired and worn out from years of living with Vic Marshall that he felt his heart turn over.

"Leave the bastard," he urged.

"Don't call him that. He's your father."

"Leave him."

"Where would I go?"

"You can live with me."

She snorted. "Live with you! He'll come to get me, and one of you will kill the other."

It was an old argument. One he had never won, and his hands squeezed in frustration.

Then he heard the sound of footsteps crossing the floor.

The Big Bad Wolf. Christ, if his father found he'd dared to come here, they were in for a hell of a fight.

Adrenaline surged through his body. Fight or flight, and he was spoiling for a brawl. His mother's pleading eyes stopped him.

He wanted to tell her he was sorry—for the things his father had done and for the grief he'd given her.

Before he could get the words out, the scene shifted abruptly. He was no longer in the house. Now he was a wolf, running through the woods, tree trunks rushing past him. Brambles reaching out to grab at his gray coat. But he kept moving, fleeing the footsteps behind him.

He dared not look to see who was back there. But he knew the pursuer was a blond, blue-eyed woman, her body naked, lithe, sexy, shimmering in the moonlight. Blood pounded in his veins. He wanted her with a strength that bordered on madness, yet he fled from what he wanted most. Because if she caught him, he would turn her into something sad and pitiful, old before her time. Like his mother.

So he kept running, each breath a sharp stab in his lungs, and finally she was no longer behind him. Instead he was the pursuer, chasing a demon named Crawford through a nighttime landscape thick with trees and rich with the new life of spring.

Energy flowed through his body. He felt the blood pumping in his arteries. Felt his own power.

The breeze riffled his thick coat, his predator's eyes pierced the moonless night, and he drank in the scent of his quarry. The scent of man. The scent of fear.

Crawford, ahead of him in the darkness. Running for his life. Stumbling over a tree root in his terror. Splashing through a stream, hoping to throw his pursuer off the trail.

But there was no shaking the chimera behind him, no escape from the yellow eyes and white fangs of the beast.

Because the wolf was on a sacred mission.

Now, in his dream, a hot fire sluiced through him as he followed the trail that his quarry was helpless to hide. This was no rabbit, no fox, no animal using instinct and cunning in a desperate attempt to escape. This was a man—a man with a gun.

It was a fair contest, Ross told himself as he deliberately closed the distance between them.

Crawford had stopped in a small clearing, gasping for breath, spinning in a circle as he pointed the gun first in one direction, then in another—unable to spot the enemy.

The wolf padded to a halt behind a tree, his body quivering, a low growl gathering in his throat.

Then he sprang.

Crawford fired at the gray shape—once, twice—but Ross dodged the deadly projectiles with canine grace, then leaped for the kill, sinking his fangs into the man's neck, cracking his larynx, gnawing through his carotid artery.

He was a hunter, and blood was a familiar taste in his mouth. Animal blood. But this liquid was different. It gushed over his muzzle and down his throat in a hot torrent, pumping through his brain with a white heat that made him dizzy. Licking his lips, he lifted his head and howled his triumph into the darkness.

In the dream he was human again, feeling a sense of horror sweep over him. Staring down at the chewed remains of his victim, he was struck by a sickening truth: He was no better than the killer he had stalked and slain.

He woke from the nightmare, drenched with sweat, feeling blood pounding in his ears like the thrumming of a primitive drum.

His body braced for an attack, he lay on the tangled sheets in darkness, struggling to draw in a full breath. But it was impossible to fill his lungs. The air around him was too hot and thick.

He had dreamed of Crawford. And before that? The first part was hazy in his mind. He remembered only the lust for blood. Remembered his vow five years ago—that the intoxicating pleasure of the manhunt and the kill were too dangerous to repeat.

It took several moments for him to comprehend that he was in his own bed. He felt the raw pain in his thigh and remembered the bullet.

Retribution, he thought. If he died from this wound, it would be justice coming full circle.

He had ripped out Crawford's throat. And Arnott had shot him.

Part of him welcomed the pain. He deserved the punishment. Yet in the end, he couldn't let the killer win. He had to stop him, and he had to do it through the rules of law, not the rules of the jungle. Because if he sank to that animal level, he would lose what humanity he could still claim.

A sound outside the bedroom made his throat tighten with tension. Then a light snapped on in the hallway, and every muscle of his body went rigid as he prepared to spring from the bed. His mind mixing reality with nightmare, he imagined Crawford or Arnott walking through the door. *Namhaid*. The enemy.

He needed his gun. He would fight with the weapons of a man. Not teeth and claws.

Where was his gun? he wondered as he felt frantically over the sheets.

Then he saw the figure in the doorway and recognized the woman. The woman who had come to take care of him, her hands moving over his body with a familiarity that he should never have permitted.

He knew the consequences of her touch.

As he stared at her, another part of the dream leaped back into his mind, and he felt a pulse jump in his belly.

He wanted to call to her, reach for her, pull her down to the bed with him. But he kept his hands locked at his sides.

In the dream she had been naked, moonlight washing over her skin. Now she was wearing a T-shirt and sweatpants. The knit clothing clung to her shape, molded her breasts as though forcing his attention to center there.

Desperately his mind struggled to separate reality from fantasy. She had been in his house. Ministered to him. Spoken to him. And he thought he had ordered her to leave. Apparently she hadn't followed directions.

The light from the hall illuminated her shoulder-length blond hair. Her delicate features were hidden from his view, but he remembered them with vivid clarity. The wide-set blue eyes, the dainty nose, the full, sensual lower lip. Even in his man shape he caught the delicate scent that clung to her. Lemon and soap and woman. And a thousand dreams he had never dared to bring into the light.

Her nighttime voice was soft and seductive. "You're awake."

"What arc you doing here?"

"It's time for your medicine."

He summoned strength he didn't know he possessed. "I told you to go."

"You're sick. You need me."

Part of him knew it was already too late. "Don't you know that a wolf mates for life?" he asked, wondering if he meant the words as a warning or an invitation. A warning, surely.

She cocked her head to one side as though considering the pronouncement, and he cursed himself for saying what had leaped into his mind.

Bending over him, she set a glass of water on the bedside table, then pressed her hand against his forehead. "You're still feverish."

"I think you woke me out of a nightmare."

"About wolves?"

"Yes," he answered, hoping that neither one of them would remember this encounter in the morning.

At least she took him at his word. Then she asked, "Can you sit up?"

Pride wouldn't allow him to say no. Gritting his

teeth, he pushed himself erect, and she shook a caplet into his hand. When he'd put it in his mouth, the sharp taste made him shudder.

Seeing his reaction, she quickly offered him the glass of water. He remembered sloshing the cold liquid down his chest when he'd taken the medication earlier. Now he took care not to spill any as he gulped several swallows, washing down the medicine and moistening his dry mouth and throat.

When he finished, she took the glass, and he felt a small shock as her hand brushed his. He knew she felt it too by the way she snatched the glass away and set it down with a thunk on the nightstand.

"I need to check your wound," she said, her voice businesslike now.

Silently, he slid down against the pillows. Getting prone was easier than sitting up.

The mattress shifted as she lowered herself to the edge of the bed. "I'm going to turn on the light."

Appreciating the warning, he closed his eyes against the sudden flare of brightness, then watched through his lashes as she eased the sheet away from his leg, being careful to uncover only as much of his flesh as she needed to see.

As she removed the bandage, her fingers on his thigh, he struggled not to react to the pressure of her hands on his flesh. She worked quickly and efficiently, yet he sensed she was fighting the same pull as he—that the intimate touch was binding him to her in ways he couldn't explain on any conscious level. And binding her to him.

Years ago, his father had told him what it would be like to be drawn to a woman by powers beyond his control. The need of the werewolf to take a mate—to perpetuate his kind.

Vic Marshall's crude, mocking words came back to him now. "You think you're better than me. Well, the same thing that happened to me will happen to you. Around when you turn thirty, sonny. Whether you like it or not. You'll see her. You'll know she's the one you've got to fuck or die. And when you touch each other, you'll be a goner, and so will she. She'll give herself to you on every possible level. Sexual, mental, emotional."

Like the way his mother had given herself to his father, and now she was trapped with a man who used her as he wanted. A man who didn't know the meaning of love.

"No!"

"Ross, are you all right?"

He blinked, realized he'd spoken aloud.

If he could have heaved himself off the bed, he would have jerked away from her—away from the intimacy binding them together as closely as a vine twined around the trunk of a tree.

The image in his mind sharpened. The vine covering the tree, sucking the life from the living plant even as the tree gave it a refuge.

Or perhaps it was all in his imagination—blown out of proportion by his fever. Nothing serious had happened, and nothing *would* happen because he wouldn't allow it.

He'd always known women were attracted to him, that he could have almost any one he wanted if he put out a little effort. Maybe that was part of the werewolf aura. A scent that drew the opposite sex? A fortuitous combination of physical characteristics? It wasn't something he'd tried to analyze.

But it had made him cautious.

He'd never allowed a woman to work her way past the defenses he'd built up. Never allowed his own control to slip.

Tonight he felt as if all choices had been yanked away from him by some ancient cosmic jester who had been waiting for aeons to spring this trap.

Striving for detachment, he watched his beautiful blond doctor replace the gauze. "How is it?" he asked, hearing the thickness in his voice.

"A little better."

"Turn off the light."

She did as he asked, and he felt more comfortable in the darkness, where it was easier to hide. It had been a long time since he'd been in a bedroom with a woman. And never here. He had never brought a sexual partner to his lair.

Before he could stop himself he reached for her wrist, circling it with his thumb and index finger.

There was no strength in his grip. And he knew she could have pulled away. Instead she simply sucked in a sharp breath, her hand resting in his grasp.

He stroked a finger over her knuckles, testing the feminine skin, then pressed his thumb to the pulse point at her wrist, feeling her heart rate accelerate. And his. Hearing a sound like wind roaring in his ears, he closed his eyes, the only contact point his hand on her wrist. A slender connection, yet it sent blood pounding through his veins.

"Did you help yourself to some of my clothes?" he asked imagining one of his T-shirts covering the soft swell of her breasts like a lover's palm, his pants cupping her feminine bottom—before he stripped the clothing off her and pulled her naked body beneath his on the bed.

It was only a fantasy. He was too weak to make it reality. But the very weakness drew him further into the tantalizing reverie.

Maybe she was following the direction of his thoughts. "They're my gym clothes. I keep them in the trunk," she hastened to inform him, tripping over the words as if she were having trouble controlling her tongue and lips. Snatching her hand away, she was off the bed in seconds, out of the room before he could catch his breath.

Maybe now she would take his advice and leave. If it wasn't already too late.

*   *   *

DONALD Arnott was awake, restless and on edge. He needed a woman. But he couldn't take one. Not until he learned the identity of the man who was stalking him and got rid of the bastard.

Heaving his body out of bed, he stood naked in the darkness, feeling blood swelling his cock. Still naked, he strode to the back door of his house and stepped outside. The night air was cold on his fevered skin as he made his way down the familiar path to the ruined barn.

Shoving aside hay bales, he heaved open the trapdoor, then switched on the overhead light as he descended into the underground chamber.

He stood in the middle of the brightly lit room, his breath quickening as he stroked the stained wooden table, the leather restraining cuffs, feeling his erection grow harder. By the time he ran his fingers across the metal instruments neatly arranged in racks along the wall, he was aching.

The videotapes were on shelves along the opposite wall. He walked past the camera on its tripod and read the titles on the neatly labeled boxes. Penny Delano. Charlotte Lawrence. Cindy Hamilton. Brenda Eckhart. And half a dozen more.

He went back to Cindy. One of his old favorites. A plump girl with big breasts and a thatch of silky pubic hair he had shaved off with a dull razor.

Sliding the tape into the machine, he took the remote control and relaxed into the easy chair in front of the large-screen TV.

He skipped the first part of the tape where he was showing her his knives and got right to the good part, stroking his cock as he watched himself work her over, climaxing with a hot shudder of pleasure as she begged him to let her go.

The second climax wasn't quite as good. It never was, not when he was alone. When he had a woman down here, he could come over and over from the strength of his response to her pain and fear. Only part of what he needed came through on the tape. But the self-gratification calmed him so that he was actually whistling a jaunty tune as he made his way back to the house and started getting ready for work.

He was on the ten-to-six shift this week, at Westfield Shoppingtown Montgomery, although nobody ever called the place anything besides its former name, Montgomery Mall. He'd worked there as a security guard for the past year. Before that, he'd been living in Pennsylvania and working at King of Prussia Mall.

A mall was a good place to meet women—sort of like combining work and play. But he couldn't stay too long in any one location, because it was imperative that he not establish a pattern that the police could pick up.

The last thought made his features contort and his hands squeeze so hard that his nails dug into his palms. A man with a dog had picked up on what he was doing. And he was going to either obliterate the bastard—or obliterate all evidence of this room, sell the property, and move on.

CHAPTER
SEVEN

"WHEN KEN SAID he was going to retire, I told him I didn't care how he spent his days, just so he was out of the house from nine to five," Mildred Winston had told Jack when he'd called and asked to speak to her husband. "There's no phone in the workshop," she continued. "If you want to talk to him, you can come over, or wait until lunchtime."

Jack elected to drop by around ten. Following Mildred's directions, he parked in the driveway behind a Chevy Suburban, bypassed the house, and took the gravel path around to the small, shingled workshop at the back of the property.

The sound of a power saw sliced through the morning quiet as Jack stepped onto the porch, and he waited until the cut was finished before knocking on the door.

Ken Winston, gray-haired and potbellied, was holding up a small pine rectangle, inspecting the cut he'd made.

"Hey, Jack!" he said, setting down the piece of wood and switching off the power on the saw. "What brings you around?"

"I wanted to get some input on one of your old cases."

The retired detective wiped his hands on the sides of his blue overalls. "You want some coffee? Coke? I got all the comforts of home out here. I only have to go inside when I need to take a leak."

Jack opted for coffee—black. As Winston poured them both a mugful, Jack looked around the workshop. On the shelves lining the wall were fifteen or twenty precisely made, identical bird feeders.

"You going into the bird feeder business?" he asked.

"Nope. They're for the PTA fair at my grandson's school."

"Nice job."

Ken beamed. "Thanks. I like it. You can see what you're doing. Get the same results every time. I got the design and the measurements down pat now. So what case did you want to talk about?"

Jack took a sip of coffee. "Edward Crawford."

Winston thought for a moment. "The murder suspect who disappeared?"

"Um-hum. His body—well, his skeleton—turned up at Sugar Loaf Mountain."

"Cause of death?"

"Undetermined."

"Yeah, well, I wasn't too broken up when the guy evaporated. He probably abducted and murdered five or six women."

Jack set down his coffee mug on the worktable and slipped his hands into his pants pockets. "It says in the case file that you were working with a PI named Ross Marshall."

The older man's eyes narrowed. "That slippery bastard still around?"

"You didn't like him?"

Winston's jaw tightened. "He came to me with some cock-and-bull story about Crawford's hanging around across the street from the Damascus High School campus where that girl Cherry Phelps went to school.

When I asked him where he got his information, he clammed up, wouldn't tell me a damn thing."

"Maybe he saw him there."

"How'd he know to look?" Winston demanded, obviously reliving his reaction at the time. "Nobody else saw anybody who fit Crawford's description."

"He could have been in disguise."

"Then how did Marshall figure out it was him? All I wanted was a simple answer to my questions about his investigative techniques, and he got this closed look on his face. Just acted superior, like he knew things I didn't."

Jack wouldn't have put it quite that way. Ross was secretive, but he didn't act superior. At least with him.

"The guy wanted me to feel like I wasn't doing my job. Then the next thing you know, Crawford vanishes," the older man was saying. "And you better believe I pushed Marshall on that. He was real hostile. Guilty acting. You know what I mean? But I couldn't prove he'd been anywhere near the guy."

Jack didn't point out that another victim had been taken between the time Ross had tried to give information to Ken and Crawford's disappearance. What was the point?

It was obvious that Ken Winston and Ross Marshall hadn't hit it off—on a professional or a private level. And it was obvious that Winston was unable to deal with tips that he couldn't verify by other means.

"Anyway," Jack said, "the mystery of what happened to Crawford is solved."

"But we don't know who did it." Winston raised his voice. "I still like that Marshall guy. Why don't you see how he reacts when you tell him you found the body?"

"I might do that."

Winston shoved his hands into his overalls pockets, as he studied Jack. "I heard you were working with him on some stuff."

"Where'd you hear that?"

"Around. You trust his information?"

"He's given me some good leads. Helped me clear some cases."

Winston nodded tightly. "And what about that violent streak of his?"

"What violent streak?"

"Don't tell me you can't see it below the surface. That guy is a pressure cooker. And maybe the lid blew off with Crawford."

Jack sucked in a breath, held it in his lungs before exhaling. "He doesn't have a rap sheet."

"Yeah. So he's been lucky."

Jack nodded without bothering to add that he'd checked out the father, Vic Marshall, and found that he'd been arrested and convicted of a number of minor offenses—disorderly conduct, simple assault, battery. If a guy was prone to violence, you'd expect that kind of thing on his record. But, unlike his old man, Ross was clean.

Jack shifted his weight from one foot to the other. "Well, I appreciate the insights. It's always good to get the perspective of a guy with thirty years on the force."

Winston looked somewhat mollified. "Um. Right. But I should get back to work. The PTA is expecting me to deliver twenty-five of these feeders by the end of the month."

After an awkward exchange of good-byes, Jack left, knowing why Winston hadn't accepted any help from Ross Marshall. It had as much to do with his own prejudices as any vibes he'd picked up from Ross.

Still, Jack was thinking about violence as he climbed back in to his car. That hadn't been something he'd personally seen in Ross, and he considered himself pretty good at reading people. But there was the abusive background.

Had the man been different five years ago? Changed himself? Or was there really something below the surface ready to break out and strike again? Something dangerous that a police detective would be remiss if he ignored?

MEGAN stood with her shoulder propped against the doorjamb of the bedroom, looking at the sleeping man, studying his features—the slightly parted lips, the three days' growth of beard darkening the lower half of his face. She reached out a hand toward him, then let it fall back to her side, dropping her gaze to the steady rise and fall of his broad chest. The covers had slipped almost to his waist, exposing dark hair spread in a circular pattern around his flat nipples.

One foot splayed to the side, peeking out from the edge of the sheet, and she could see his toenails, blunt cut across long toes.

She had no excuse for standing here watching him sleep, yet she remained where she was, looking her fill.

She'd been in his room several times during the night, drawn by her need to take care of her patient— and by something more, some deeply buried compulsion that she was powerless to describe.

In the hours after the sun had set, she'd felt an invisible force gathering in the room around them, drawing them to each other on levels that existed below conscious thought.

Then, afterward, she couldn't be sure that anything had really happened.

Suddenly she found herself fighting the impulse to wake him and demand that he tell her if he'd felt the same disturbing pull. But she wasn't selfish enough to interrupt his rest. And she wasn't crazy enough to ask about feelings she couldn't articulate—feelings that she might have conjured up from some self-conscious need of her own.

Perhaps she was simply reacting the same way she had to previous patients—getting involved with them on a level beyond the professional. Getting her emotions mixed up with Marshall's. And the problem was worse than usual because she'd avoided this kind of situation for so long that her nurturing instincts were working overtime.

She folded her arms across her chest, reassured by rationalizations as she struggled to view her patient with professional detachment.

He had been sleeping for the past four hours, and he'd barely awakened when she'd changed his bandage again and given him another Keflex. But it seemed to be a normal sleep, not a fevered stupor.

Sometime during the night he'd dragged himself out of bed, put on a pair of white undershorts, and somehow made it to the bathroom without her help. She knew that because she'd been startled to find the toilet seat up in the morning.

She couldn't imagine how he'd managed to stagger down the hall—not in his condition. Apparently his determination and his stubbornness were formidable. Which meant he'd probably set his recovery back. The assumption gave her a good excuse for staying. That was better than admitting she was in the grip of a compulsion she couldn't explain—as if leaving had become somehow unthinkable.

And even if he'd heaved himself out of bed during the night, he wasn't going to be cooking any food. Or driving his car to the pharmacy. He was down to his last caplet, and he needed a lot more to finish the course of the medication.

Again she walked through the house, this time searching for the telephone she knew he owned, since she'd left a message on his answering machine.

She didn't find the machine. So he was probably using the phone company's answering service.

But where the heck was the phone that went with it? All she found was the charger for his portable.

Finally, she went outside, intending to use the one in her car. But she stopped to look around first, picking up details that she hadn't noticed on her way into the house the day before or in the dark.

Near the front door and extending along the side walls were natural looking plantings of ferns, violets, and other woodland vegetation that she couldn't identify this early in the season. Interspersed among them were bright blue, yellow, and red primroses, some of the earliest spring flowers. The plants could have grown there by accident, she supposed, but the arrangement was a little too artful to be accidental.

Apparently Ross Marshall was a talented gardener as well as a private detective. A strange combination. Thinking that the man was full of surprises, she walked around the side of the house, noting the way the garden blended with the edge of the woodland. After staring at it appreciatively for a while, she went back to her car.

Knowing she was stalling, she clasped her hands and stared at the holder below the dashboard where she kept her portable phone.

She'd never bothered to get a license to practice medicine in Maryland, so she needed Walter to write Ross a prescription for Keflex. Still, she knew instinctively that telling her boss a lot about Ross would be a mistake. Prevarication wasn't her strong suit. After hesitating for several more moments, she picked up the phone and switched it on.

The Bio Gen receptionist, Betty Daniels, answered.

"Can I speak to Walter?"

"Who's calling, please?" Megan asked.

"This is Megan Sheridan."

"Oh, Dr. Sheridan. I'm sorry I didn't recognize your voice. Where are you? We called your house, but nobody answered. We were starting to get worried."

"I'm fine. I'm with a client."

"You are? You don't mean the one from yesterday? Ross Marshall?"

"Yes."

"Oh, my. What are you still doing there? Was he as . . . sexy as he sounded over the phone?"

Megan blinked. For Betty, interjecting *that* into the

conversation was definitely out of character.

Ignoring the question, she said in a no-nonsense voice, "Mr. Marshall is sick. I've got the situation under control. But I need to speak to Dr. Galveston."

"Uh, you had a couple of other calls. One from Dr. Stillwell again. He says he needs to talk to you."

"Oh, shit," she blurted, and immediately wished she'd kept the reaction to herself.

"What?"

"Betty, I'm sorry. I don't want what Stillwell's selling."

"And your sister called."

"Dory called me at work?"

Betty made a throat-clearing noise. "She was quite . . . uh . . . forceful. She says you owe her a check."

Megan struggled to control her anger. She wanted to protest that she didn't owe her sister anything. Instead she said, "It's in the mail. You can tell her that if she calls again. And please put me through to Dr. Galveston."

"Certainly. Just a moment."

Walter came on the line, his voice querulous. "Megan, where are you?"

"With that client. Ross Marshall."

"I thought you went out there yesterday afternoon. What's going on?" he demanded.

"I did come out here yesterday. He's sick. I stayed to take care of him."

"That's not your job."

"Well, if he dies, you won't get a fee out of him."

"He's dying? What the hell is wrong with him?"

"He has an infection. He had some leftover Keflex. I gave that to him last night and early this morning. But he needs more."

"What's he got, some sort of immune deficiency that makes him susceptible to opportunistic infections?"

That was the last thing she'd ascribe to Ross Marshall, but she hedged. "I don't know. He hasn't been in shape to tell me much."

"How long are you going to be out there?" Walter demanded.

Megan closed her eyes, picturing her boss's stormy expression. Walter didn't like surprises, and he wouldn't like having to juggle the workload. Maybe he'd even have to do some of the lab tests himself. Too damn bad.

"Until tomorrow, at least," she answered.

"Well, if you're taking care of him like a private duty nurse, charge him at that rate. What is it, fifty dollars an hour? Seventy-five?"

"Walter . . ."

"Either charge him, or come back to town."

She sighed. "Okay."

"Okay what?"

"I'll charge him," she answered grudgingly, knowing that she was lying. It was getting to be a bad habit. "But I can't write a prescription. I need you to order him some more Keflex. He got the last bottle at the Giant Pharmacy in Lisbon," she added, giving Walter the phone number.

He asked more questions. She answered with evasions. And when she hung up, mission accomplished, she was shaking. Yet she found it impossible to share anything with Walter beyond the bare essentials. She'd been angry when she'd had to drop her work and come out here. Now her feelings had changed, although she wasn't willing to go into the reasons too deeply.

ROSS listened for the sound of her moving around the house. She'd been in his room earlier and thankfully hadn't come over to put her hands on him again. Now she was gone. He hoped she'd left. He should get up. Eat some meat. But he was too weary to move.

He dozed, then slipped deeper into sleep. As another dream dug its claws into his mind, a moan rose in his throat.

When he realized he was back in the terrible summer

of his fourteenth year, his whole body began to shake.
It was late at night in the room he shared with his
brother, sixteen-year-old Michael. A deep fear clogged
his chest, making it almost impossible to breathe.

He and Michael had always been best friends. Troy
was older. He'd moved out of the house two years ago.
Adam was five years younger—a pest. But he and Michael had stuck together. They'd played cops and rob-
bers. Sat next to each other at the dinner table. Climbed
the fence at the rich kids' pool and gone for a midnight
swim. Gotten sick trying cigarettes. And run away together—staying in the woods half the night until the
Big Bad Wolf had sniffed them out and nipped their
flesh all the way home.

Michael was the one who helped him with his math
homework. The one who had kept Thad Stevenson
from beating the crap out of him on the way home from
school.

But after tonight they were going to be separated
forever—one way or the other.

Michael's body was making the change from boy to
man. And with that change came another demanded of
the werewolf species. A demand that could not be denied.

His time had come. Tomorrow night he was going
to the forest alone with Dad for the ancient ceremony.
No one else could be there. Michael would say the
chant he had learned. And he would transform to a wolf
for the first time. Or he would die.

The scared, sick feeling in Ross's chest threatened
to overwhelm him. With every scrap of self-control he
could muster, he struggled to keep it from showing in
his voice as he and Michael talked long into the night.

They wouldn't have dared to stay up so late if Dad
had been in the house. But he was out, getting money.
Stealing money, although nobody was allowed to talk
about that secret. But Mom knew. And the boys knew.

"Are you worried about tomorrow night?" Ross
whispered.

"No."

Ross didn't believe the emphatic denial. And his stomach clenched painfully when Michael continued, "I've got fifty dollars saved. In the bottom drawer of my dresser. I want you to have it . . . if, you know . . ."

"You're gonna be fine!"

"I know. I memorized the words and all. And Dad coached me how to . . ." He swallowed. "How to ride above the pain. But just in case. Don't let Dad get his hands on the money. It's mine. I saved it up."

"I won't. I promise, Michael. I promise."

Desperation rose in his soul as he fought the need to climb out of bed, throw his arms around his brother, and hold on tight. But that would have embarrassed both of them, so he stayed where he was, because if he hugged his brother, then he might start to cry. And if Michael could be strong, then he could be, too.

In the way of dreams, the scene changed. Time compressed. He was standing at the front door in the twilight, feeling small and alone—watching Michael and Dad get into the car, seeing the rigid lines of his brother's face and knowing he was terrified.

And then, in the blink of an eye, the car was coming back. Not their real car but a long black hearse. Pulling slowly into the driveway.

Panic stabbed a dozen knives into his chest, choked off his breath.

Michael. Where was Michael?

Then his father was standing at the back door, holding Michael's body in his arms.

His mother was falling to her knees, weeping. And his father was staring at him over Michael's body— telling him with his eyes that it was his turn next.

WHEN Jack got back to the squad room, most of the reports he'd requested on Ross Marshall were sitting on his desk. The PI's credit record, his phone company records, his credit card statements. He didn't have cable

TV out where he lived in Howard County. Or a satellite dish, for that matter, so he apparently didn't watch much TV. He also didn't have a wife or an ex. Or any children that he acknowledged.

Ross's credit rating was excellent. He paid his mortgage on time every month, and he owned only the one piece of property—a twenty-four-acre plot off Route 99.

He kept a minimum credit card balance. Most of his purchases weren't extravagant, except for big orders of expensive meat from a place called Omaha Steaks. Apparently the man liked his beef.

In the past six months he'd acquired a state-of-the-art digital camera and a pair of expensive binoculars, both of which he undoubtedly used for surveillance. He'd bought ammunition for a .40-caliber gun a couple of months ago. And he had a license to carry a concealed weapon.

Interestingly, he didn't seem to own many of the other fancy toys Jack had expected a PI to acquire—nightscopes, listening devices, recorders, transponders—unless he'd bought the stuff several years ago. But then why hadn't he updated his equipment, when technology was changing so fast? Either he couldn't afford the newest and best—which the credit report belied—or he'd decided he didn't need all that fancy stuff.

So how did he come up with his amazing leads? Jack had the sudden image of a comic book superhero endowed with powers beyond those of mortal men. Ross Marshall could make himself invisible at will. Or he could see through walls.

With a shake of his head, Jack dismissed the absurd notions and shuffled the reports into the folder. Ross was the only lead in a case that had gone cold five years ago. But Jack had done his homework on the PI and couldn't find any evidence of criminal activity.

So why did he still have the feeling that there was something missing from the picture? Something he could figure out if he fit the pieces of the Ross Marshall puzzle together correctly.

CHAPTER
EIGHT

BUSINESS CLOTHING WAS an important part of the self-image Megan had created for herself over the years—another proof that she wasn't the "slob" Ray Sheridan had raised. This morning, however, she'd decided she'd look more presentable in her sweat clothes than her rumpled skirt and blouse from the night before.

But as soon as she stepped into the Giant Food outlet in Lisbon, she felt uncomfortable about appearing in public in sweats.

At the pharmacy counter, she struggled not to squirm under the clerk's scrutiny.

"Ross Marshall," the petite redhead behind the counter repeated, looking Megan up and down as she glanced from her to the name on the prescription Walter had called in.

The redhead flicked a glance at her left hand—which was absent of rings.

Megan could almost read her thoughts. *Who is this woman picking up medicine for Ross Marshall? His girlfriend? A nurse?*

Well, Lisbon was a small town. And Ross Marshall was a good-looking guy. So it wasn't strange that the women around here had noticed him—and would notice a woman who was doing errands for him.

Still, her relationship with Ross was none of the clerk's business.

Although words of explanation bubbled at the back of her throat, she kept her lips pressed together as she waited while the woman searched through the box of medications that were ready to be picked up.

"Does he have an insurance card registered?" the clerk asked.

"I don't know."

The woman went to a computer, called up a file. "Yes. He owes a ten-dollar copayment."

Megan had intended to pay for the antibiotics with a credit card. Instead she pulled a twenty-dollar bill from her wallet and waited for change.

Stuffing the envelope with the prescription bottle into her purse, she fled into the grocery aisles. She might have left the store at once, but there was hardly any food at Marshall's house. So she grabbed some chicken soup off the shelves, then bought eggs, milk, bread, and a few other staples. Because this was one of those big stores where you could buy almost anything except a hunting rifle, she put a three-pack of panties into her shopping cart and an orange-and-black Baltimore Orioles T-shirt. Then she went back to one of the drugstore aisles and grabbed a toothbrush.

She didn't have enough cash to pay for the groceries and other purchases. At the checkout counter, she was forced to fork over her credit card, repressing the urge to look over her shoulder to see if the pharmacy clerk was watching the transaction.

She was fully aware that she was acting paranoid. And out of character. What did it matter if the clerks at the grocery store knew the name of the woman who had come in to get medicine for Ross Marshall?

It didn't matter at all—unless her own emotional investment in the man was making her jumpy as a cat on thin ice.

Maybe it was hormonal, she told herself with a disgusted shake of her head as she clenched her hand around the strap of her purse. It had been a long time since she'd gone out with a man she was attracted to— let alone made love with anyone. That long dry spell had made her susceptible to Ross Marshall, and now she was feeling things that she had told herself could stay on hold until she met the right guy.

Her mind switched gears again. Did that mean Ross Marshall was the right guy?

It hardly seemed likely, yet from the moment she'd found him lying on the floor, she'd been on an emotional roller coaster.

So if the women in the Lisbon Giant Food store were looking at her speculatively, it was really no more speculatively than she was looking at herself.

Making a rapid exit from the store, she plucked the two bags from her shopping cart and headed for her car.

It had been sunny when she'd left in the morning. As she got into her car, she saw that heavy gray clouds had begun to gather in the sky. By the time she crossed the bridge leading to the meadow, the atmosphere had darkened, making her feel like the sky was pressing down on her shoulders.

Braking at the edge of the meadow, she stared at the sign she'd seen the first day. Not the ones that said NO TRESPASSING. The one that said DÍTHREABH. This time she pulled out her notebook and copied it down.

Inside, the house was dark. After stopping to turn on a lamp in the great room, she set the bags of groceries in the kitchen, then tiptoed down the hall to her patient's room.

Marshall was still sleeping, or perhaps he was feigning sleep to avoid interacting with her. She might have let him slumber, but she needed to assess his condition.

Gently she touched his shoulder, and his eyes

snapped open, regarding her with the intensity that had unnerved her the night before.

"How do you feel?" she asked, hearing the husky note in her voice as she set a glass of water down on the bedside table.

His gaze turned inward as if he were taking an inventory of muscle and sinew. "Better," he finally answered without elaborating.

"You got out of bed last night."

"Early in the morning."

"You should have asked me to help you."

"I made it down the hall and back again on my own."

"If you'd fallen, it wouldn't have been good for the wound."

"I didn't."

His clipped answers told her that the conversation was an imposition, and she felt a stab of disappointment tighten her chest.

With an inward sigh she acknowledged she'd been hoping that things would be different when he started getting better. That their communications would normalize.

Now, as she remembered her thoughts at the grocery store, she felt her face flush. As far as he was concerned, this was simply a doctor-patient relationship—and not a very cordial one, at that.

Cutting her losses, she changed the subject. "It's time for your medicine."

He pushed himself up and reached for the bottle she'd set on the night table, shaking out a caplet into his hand. When he picked up the water, she saw he was able to hold the glass steady. He was definitely getting better—and asserting his independence.

But there were still things he needed from her.

"I should check the wound," she reminded him.

Without commenting, he slid back to a prone position. As quickly as possible, she changed the dressing, more aware than ever of her hands on his flesh, aware that he was watching her from under his long, dark lashes.

"How is it?" he asked.

"Healing."

He accepted the information without comment.

"Do you think you could eat something?"

He reached for the second pillow on the bed, propped it behind his back. "There's meat in the freezer."

Her response to that suggestion was instantaneous. "You can't handle meat. You're still too sick."

He looked like he was about to argue, then shrugged. "What do you suggest?"

"Chicken soup is more like it."

He sniffed the air, looked puzzled. "I don't smell any."

His quizzical look made her laugh. "I'm not the domestic type. You have a choice of Campbell's Chicken Rice or Lipton's Chicken Noodle."

He debated, apparently weighing the merits of each. "Lipton's, I guess," he answered, sounding less than enthusiastic. "With lots of noodles."

She retreated to the kitchen and concentrated on fixing the soup, telling herself that investing any kind of emotional energy in the man was a mistake. When she returned to the bedroom, she saw he'd straightened the covers. His head was turned, and he was staring out the window.

She was pretty sure he knew she was standing in the doorway, yet he kept his gaze focused on the swaying tree branches thirty feet away.

The blur of motion brought back memories from her childhood—images that she'd thought she'd outgrown.

"Do you see animal shapes moving in the leaves?" she asked in a low voice.

"Do you?"

"Yes. I'd look out my window when I was a little girl and see them. They scared me."

"Do they still?"

She managed a laugh. "Unfortunately, yes."

He gave her a considering look. "It just means you're imaginative."

"Scientists aren't imaginative."

"Don't duck away from a compliment. Of course you are."

Before she could think of how to answer, his gaze moved back to the window, and he looked like he wanted to climb out of bed and disappear into the foliage.

"I'm sorry. It's going to be a few days before you can get out of the house."

"I need . . ."

"What?"

"Fresh air. Going outside won't hurt me. It will help me get better."

"You can barely walk."

"I'm at home in the woods."

She wasn't going to waste his strength arguing about it. Realizing she was still holding the mug of soup, she set it on the nightstand, along with some plain soda crackers she'd purchased at the grocery store.

He gave the meal a wry look. "Is this what the doctor ordered?"

"Yes."

He thought for a moment. "My memory's a little vague about the past couple of days."

"That's nothing to worry about. You were pretty sick."

"Yeah, well, did you tell me you were a doctor? That you work for Bio Gen?"

She nodded, wondering exactly how much of their previous exchanges he recalled. The words they'd spoken. And all the rest of it. Her holding him while he drank. Her looking at his naked body. His trapping her wrist in the circle of his thumb and finger. The sense of connection that defied explanation.

She felt her face warm and was glad he had turned

to reach for the soup. Picking up the mug, he blew on the hot liquid, then took a cautious sip.

After several swallows, he raised his head, looking at her with his unnerving dark gaze. "I should thank you," he said grudgingly. "I don't mean just for the soup. If you hadn't come along when you did, I would have been in trouble."

"Then I guess I should say you're welcome."

"Tell me you would have done it for anyone."

"Why?"

"Then it's nothing personal."

The curt observation stung. She was about to back out of the room when he asked, "Would you open a window so I can at least smell the outside?"

That was an odd way to put it, she thought. With a tight nod, she crossed to the window wall, which featured an enormous middle glass panel that was fixed in place. There were two side units, however, that could slide open and closed. She pushed open the one on the left, then watched as he dragged in a deep lungful of air and let it out as he relaxed against the pillows.

She stood there regarding him, her own breath quickening as she tried to understand what he was experiencing.

"Thank you," he said, his eyes fixed on the woods. He said nothing else, ignoring her as if she were no longer in the room. The night before, he'd ordered her to leave. This morning he was using a different tactic.

She opened her mouth to point that out, then closed it again. Wondering why she was staying to take care of a man who so obviously wished her out of his house, she exited the bedroom.

Her car was outside. She could collect the blood sample she needed for the genetic test he'd requested and clear out, but she couldn't bring herself to abandon him. Or to go back into the bedroom and confront him again, either.

After standing uncertainly in the hallway for several moments, she strode into the bathroom and locked the door. Again she hesitated, staring nervously at the expanse of unbroken glass and the windblown trees beyond.

Then, telling herself that no one would dare spy on Ross Marshall's house, she ripped her gaze away, turned her back, and pulled off her clothes. After she took a quick shower, she changed into the T-shirt and underpants she'd bought, using one of the plastic grocery bags for her dirty clothes. Too bad she didn't have another pair of sweatpants, too. But she wasn't about to borrow any of his.

In the great room she stood staring at the furniture, then the bookcases, finally focusing on the Gaelic dictionaries. With an odd sense of anticipation, she crossed the room and reached for the largest one, turning to the *D*'s.

The word *díthreabh* was there. It meant "wilderness, hermitage, isolated place of safety away from other human beings."

So that was how he thought of this property—this house. As his refuge. And she had invaded his territory. No wonder he wanted to get rid of her.

Yet he was attracted to her. All the feelings experienced over the time she'd been here had not been one-sided. She couldn't believe that. He might be fighting the pull, pretending it didn't exist, but he felt it, too.

That was *why* he was fighting it, she thought with sudden insight. Because he sensed what was happening, and he feared the intimacy.

Because of his illness? Not from the gunshot but the genetic problem that had caused him to call Bio Gen Labs in the first place. Despite his apparent physical health, there was something wrong with him. Some inherited defect he didn't want to discuss—and perhaps didn't plan to pass on to the next generation.

When she considered his situation in those terms, his reserve made perfect sense. Maybe he'd gotten close to a woman before. And maybe she'd run in the other direction because she'd decided the risk of bearing his children was simply too great.

Megan pressed her fist against her mouth, feeling a stab of anguish for him as she imagined that kind of rejection. Whatever he'd called the lab about wouldn't be something he'd want to reveal on the first date. But she was in a unique position. She already knew there was some genetic problem in his background. That was something to consider carefully before she got in any deeper.

Good advice. But was she capable of taking it?

After putting the dictionary back, Megan flopped onto the sofa and stared into space. Finally she pulled out her tablet and started to add to the notes she'd written the night before, intent on documenting how quickly her patient was recovering.

But fatigue pressed against her chest, her limbs. Succumbing to an unaccustomed lethargy, she swung her legs onto the couch, propped a cushion behind her head, and let her mind drift. For months she'd been working at breakneck speed, trying to make some progress on her gene therapy treatment for Myer's disease while getting through the increasingly heavy workload that Walter was demanding. Now her routine was totally disrupted. She had nothing to do, and the feeling was unsettling.

She intended to close her eyes for only a few moments.

Hours later, she woke with a start, disoriented and immediately on edge. When she realized where she was, her gaze flew to the window. The sky had been gunmetal gray when she'd fallen asleep. Now the sun had set.

Which meant that Marshall had missed a dose of medicine, unless he'd gotten it himself. A lot of good she was doing him, insisting on staying here.

Standing too quickly, she wobbled on her feet and reached out a hand to steady herself against the sofa back. Then she made her way down the darkened hallway to the bedroom.

The door was closed. She knocked. "Ross?"

No answer.

"Ross?"

A sensation of cold scraped at the back of her neck. Clenching the doorknob, she tried to make it turn. But it was locked from the inside.

"Ross. Are you all right in there?"

No answer.

"Ross, open the door."

Flicking on the hall light switch, she bent to examine the lock. It was similar to the ones in the house where she'd grown up, and she knew that if she found something slender enough to penetrate the small hole in the center of the knob, she could spring the locking mechanism.

An unbent hairpin was about the right size. But she didn't have a hairpin.

Again she rattled the knob. "Ross! Let me in."

When he failed to acknowledge her demand, she ran down the hall to the kitchen and started opening drawers. There was nothing she could use.

God, what if he'd had a relapse? What if some problem related to his genetic makeup had kicked in?

Frustrated and frightened, she pulled open the door to the utility room and looked wildly around. One wall housed a washer and dryer flanked by shelves of laundry supplies. The rest of the room appeared to be a well-stocked workshop. There was a large workbench, a table saw, and lumber neatly stacked in racks along the wall. Shelves held hand and power tools. On other shelves were cases of small plastic drawers containing various items such as washers, nails, and screws. All of them were too large in diameter to fit the hole in the doorknob. But she found a piece of wire that looked like it might do.

Back at the door of the bedroom, she called to her

patient one more time. "Ross, if you can hear me, open up!"

When he still didn't answer, she unwound the coiled wire and pushed the slender tip into the hole in the knob. After wiggling it around, she finally heard a soft click.

"I'm coming in," she informed him as she pushed the door open and charged into the room, almost tripping over something on the floor as she skidded to a stop beside the bed.

It appeared to be empty.

Lunging back to the door, she switched on the light so that she could see better.

There was still no one in the room, but she discovered what she had tripped over. The shorts Ross had been wearing lay on the floor beside the bed. She also saw that the side window panel she'd pushed partway up was fully open.

She stood there breathing hard, a combination of fear and anger making her stomach churn. Then, unable to cope with the empty room, she ran down the hall to the bathroom, hoping she'd find him there. But that room was empty, too.

The bedroom had been locked from the inside. But her brain didn't seem capable of processing the information. In a rising state of hysteria, she ran through the rest of the house, switching on lights, calling his name, thinking she was going to discover him sprawled on the floor the way he'd been yesterday afternoon. But there was no answer. And no body.

Nearly defeated, she made her way back to the bedroom, pulled open the closet door, and swept her hand behind the clothing hanging in a neat row. But he wasn't hiding there like a kid afraid of the dark.

Finally, inevitably, she switched off the light and moved to the window. Because if Ross wasn't in the house, the only place he could be was outside.

Staring into the gathering darkness, she strained her eyes for the sight of a naked man moving among the trees or spread-eagled and unconscious on the ground.

She saw branches swaying, heard the sighing of the wind, smelled the earthy scent of trees and soil, but she saw no one. She knew he had to be out there. And she had to bring him back.

The idea of leaving the house sent a wave of cold sweeping over her skin. But there seemed to be no other choice. Not when he had been burning up with fever the day before. Not when this stunt was going to set his recovery back days.

God, was the man crazy?

Her mouth compressed into a thin line, she eyed the window, picturing herself climbing out. But the opening was several feet from the floor, and her legs were not as long as her patient's. Retracing her steps down the hall, she crossed the great room, switched on the porch light, and opened the front door.

Silently she stepped out into the night and stood with her arms wrapped around her shoulders.

Although the sky had been overcast early in the evening, the clouds had blown away, making way for the radiance of a three-quarters-full moon. It bathed the meadow in cold light that did nothing to banish the goose bumps rising on her skin.

"Ross?" she called, feeling the wind take the word and hurl it from her.

She had never felt comfortable in the dark. But when Ross didn't answer, she stepped off the pad of cement at the front door and began to circle the house, keeping the solid bulk of the structure to her back and her gaze to the ground as she searched for his limp body.

She was facing the woods when a sudden burst of wind swished through the trees. In the light filtering like ghostly ribbons through the swaying branches, she saw a gray shape prowling the forest, its head bent to something on the ground.

For a moment she told herself it was simply her childhood fantasy of shapes moving in the trees. Then she sucked in a sharp breath as she saw it really was an animal.

A large dog. Maybe a German shepherd—or a husky-shepherd mix. But somewhere in the deep, primitive part of her mind she knew it was a true creature of the forest. A wolf.

As soon as the thought surfaced, she rejected it as impossible. There were no wolves in Maryland. At least she had never heard of any.

Yet her mind continued to shout the word *wolf*.

She stared at him. Him.

From where she was standing, she couldn't see the sex. But she had the absolute conviction he was a male from the way he held himself, his posture dangerous and aggressive. He was standing in the moonlight as if he had owned this patch of woodland since before man had tread upon the continent.

As she watched, he raised his head, surveyed his forest.

Details came to her with striking clarity. His pelt was silver gray. His ears alert, edged with black. His tail full and held at a downward angle, except where the black tip curved upward.

The bottom half of the face was light gray, in sharp contrast to the shiny black nose.

His eyes were his most striking feature. They were yellow—and glowing with an intelligence that seemed impossible for an animal to possess.

He bent again, and she saw what she hadn't noticed before—a limp furry form on the ground in front of him.

His teeth flashed. When she realized what he was doing, she made a small sound of protest in her throat. It looked like he had caught a small animal and was tearing at its bloody flesh with his sharp teeth.

The wolf must have heard her. Or more likely he had known she was there all along and had finally decided to acknowledge her presence.

Lifting his head, he pinned her with his gaze, a low

warning growl drifting to her on the wind. It was a sound that gave meaning to an old cliché—the feel of icy fingers walking themselves down her spine.

She had never known the sensation before. She felt it now, the quivers starting at the base of her spine and traveling to every nerve ending of her body. She wanted to run back the way she'd come, around the house and through the front door. But her legs refused to cooperate. Immobilized, she watched the animal abandon its prey and move toward her. His gaze burning into her, he closed the distance between them until he was standing a mere ten feet away and she could see the blood staining the fur of his muzzle.

Her heart was pounding so hard in her chest that she could barely draw in a full breath as she stood there, exposed and vulnerable, sure that his brilliant yellow eyes might be the last thing she saw on earth—before he ripped her throat out.

The wolf regarded her with a stare that seemed to penetrate to the depths of her soul. Then his lips pulled back over sharp white teeth.

She waited for him to spring, braced for the impact of his body slamming against hers, knocking her to the ground. Instead some emotion she couldn't read gathered in his face. For heartbeats she and the creature of the night stood facing each other. Then, as if he'd changed his mind about tearing her limb from limb, he turned abruptly and trotted into the woods, disappearing into the darkness under the trees.

Released from his spell, she sagged back against the wall of the house, breathing in jagged gasps, feeling as if she'd made a miraculous escape. Not just from physical danger. From something more basic that she was helpless to name.

Pushing herself up straighter, she made an effort to collect her scattered thoughts—then suddenly remembered why she had come out here in the first place.

"Ross! For God's sake, Ross," she croaked, her voice barely carrying above the sound of the wind.

She had come looking for him. But she was too terrified to continue now. When he didn't answer, she
turned and dashed for safety, slamming the door behind
her.

Closing her eyes against the sudden light, she leaned
against the solid barrier of the closed door, trying to
stop shaking.

When she was able to move again, she ran back to
the bedroom, staring at the empty bed, the open window.

"Ross!" she called once more, her voice high and
desperate.

She pushed the window closed far enough so that
she was sure a wolf couldn't slither through. Then she
dragged the heavy easy chair partway to the window
and sat, staring out into the night, her eyes trying to
penetrate the darkness under the trees.

But the wolf had vanished. And now that she was
alone and safe in the house, she wasn't even sure
whether she had imagined the whole strange incident.

She cursed Ross for going outside into the night.
Cursed her own cowardice. Her only comfort was what
he'd told her earlier. He was at home in the woods. He
craved the outdoors. And maybe he and the animal out
there had reached some kind of accommodation.

He must know it lived in his woods. He wouldn't
have left the house if it was a danger to him.

Her numbed mind tried to go back over the conversation they'd had earlier in the day. Had he been warning her that he was going out? Preparing her without
raising an alarm? Asking her not to worry? She
clutched at that, telling herself that he would be back
soon. And if he wasn't, it would eventually be light
and she'd go looking for him.

Because there was simply no way she could go out
into the darkness again and face the creature with the
yellow eyes and the sharp teeth.

CHAPTER
NINE

THE WOLF WAS as shaken by the midnight encounter as the woman. In the shadows under the trees, he stood with blood roaring in his ears.

Trying to cope with the human and animal emotions clashing inside him, he finally turned away from the house and prowled deeper into the woods. When he caught the scent of another rabbit, he gave chase, bringing down the creature and eating like a starving cur. He *was* starving—for protein. Raw and as close to its natural state as possible. His system demanded fresh meat to heal itself. One more wolf trait he was powerless to deny.

But even the urgency of the hunt couldn't stop his mind from circling back and back, frantically turning one way and then the other like a wounded animal trying to outrun its pain.

When he'd seen Megan come out of the house, a shockwave had rolled through him as he pictured the scene as she must—a wolf tearing his prey apart. The horror of it had seized him by the throat—even as he made the decision to stand his ground, to let her see what he really was. Then the fear in her eyes had slashed through him, the pain as hot and intense as the bullet that had mutilated his flesh.

Long after he was dizzy with fatigue, he stayed away from the house, afraid of what he would find when he went inside. Afraid to put a name to the emotions roiling inside him.

But finally there was nowhere else to go but home to Díthreabh. His refuge, until the woman with the silky blond hair and the wide blue eyes had stolen it from him.

When he saw her car still in the driveway, relief surged through him. It was followed quickly by regret. If she'd only taken his warning to heart and cleared out, he'd be free of her by now.

Still in the shadow of the woods, he changed back into human form, then propped his shoulders against a tree, gathering the strength to limp across the stretch of grass between the woods and the house. When he discovered the front door was locked, he retrieved the spare house key hidden under a rock and slipped back inside.

An almost frantic need grabbed him as he stepped across the threshold. Where was she? How was she?

On shaky legs, he made his way down the hall and found her slumped in a chair by the window—no doubt exhausted by the silent confrontation with the wolf and by the toll the past few days had taken on her. He wanted to go to her. Hunker down beside her. Touch her. Wake her. But he turned away lest she see the blood on his face and hands.

After grabbing a pair of jeans and a T-shirt from the laundry room, he stepped into a hot shower, washing away the evidence of the night's activities. Afterward, too exhausted for anything besides sleep, he went into the great room and collapsed on the sofa.

The first rays of the sun striking the windowpanes woke him. For long minutes, he lay with his eyes closed, his thoughts focused on the woman who had driven him from his bedroom.

Dreading what might come next, yet helpless to stop himself, he tiptoed down the hall, gritting his teeth against the pain in his leg.

Megan was still sleeping, sprawled against the corduroy chair cushions. On bare feet, he moved closer, stopping eight feet away, caught and held by the delicious scent of her body. Soap and woman and something personal that he couldn't name. But he would always know it was her scent, always react.

He stood in the early morning light, cataloguing physical details. Her legs were drawn up, her hair like spun gold was spread out around her face, and her head was tipped back. Her slightly parted lips gave her the look of a child who had begged to stay up late on New Year's Eve and had fallen asleep before the magic stroke of midnight.

But she was no child. He had learned over the past few days that she was a very resourceful, very stubborn, very appealing woman. Testing his reaction to her, he let his gaze slide over her face—the brows several shades darker than her hair, the high cheekbones, the small chin. From there it was a natural drop to the slender column of her throat, then lower to her breasts—small but tempting mounds, high and firm-looking, hidden by the barrier of her T-shirt.

She was wearing a shirt with a picture of the Baltimore Orioles mascot. And he caught himself watching the bird's beak move back and forth across the tip of one nipple as her chest rose and fell with each breath. It wasn't difficult to picture his finger there instead of the bird's rigid beak, caressing that delicate peak, bringing it to arousal with his touch. Tightening his jaw, he forbade his body to react. He reminded himself that he had been close to death two days ago. He was still weak. Yet it was impossible not to respond to her.

He told himself it was because he hadn't had a woman in a long time. Only half believing it, he clenched his teeth against the physiological response. When he found he had no control over the hot blood pooling in the lower part of his body, he whirled— welcoming the stab of pain in his injured leg as he strode back down the hall to the bathroom.

Naked, aroused, he turned on the water, adjusted the temperature to cold this time, and stepped into the shower enclosure. The needle-sharp spray cooled his hot skin.

He stayed there for a long time, leaning against the shower wall to steady his still-weakened leg. Cutting off the water, he shook droplets from his dark hair, then reached for the towel.

After shaving off four days' growth of beard, he pulled on his jeans and black T-shirt.

Finally, when he could no longer postpone the confrontation, he opened the door and started for his room, trying not to limp. He'd left Megan sleeping. Now she was staring fixedly toward the hallway, apparently having heard him approaching.

"You're awake," he said, feeling his voice clog. Remaining in the doorway where he could prop his weight on his good leg, he slipped his hands into the pockets of his jeans as he watched her eyes flash with a mixture of anger and something else. Relief?

Would she tell him about the wolf? What would she say? What would he answer? He waited, his breath shallow in his chest. He could force the issue, here and now. Tell her he was the animal she had seen outside. Send her screaming from the house.

Because there were only two possibilities he could imagine. She would understand that he was a monster, and leave. Or she would think that he was a dangerous lunatic—and leave.

He found he could face neither of those. So he stood very still, waiting.

She raised her chin. "What are you? Self-destructive? Going outside in your condition . . . I came in to check on you yesterday evening. You weren't in your bed. You weren't anywhere in the house. You think you're in shape to go tramping off into the woods?"

He had never been in quite this situation, and he wasn't sure what he was going to say until words came from his lips. "I'm not used to explaining my thinking . . . or my actions." By an effort of will, he kept the hands in his pockets from clenching. "But, okay, I'll give you a little pertinent background. My ancestors were Druid priests. For me, going into the woods—making myself one with nature—is part of the healing process," he said, managing to keep a straight face as he mouthed the touchy-feely explanation.

"You need to go outside in the dark, naked—"

"To revive my body and my spirit, yes," he finished calmly, omitting the part about needing to hunt for fresh meat.

He would have liked to stay where he was—twelve feet from the woman in the chair. A safe distance. But he didn't have the energy to stay on his feet much longer, so he moved into the room and lowered himself to the edge of the bed.

She looked torn between telling him that his explanation was bullshit and respecting his pagan beliefs.

"Nothing happened. I'm fine."

She sucked in a sharp breath and let it out in a rush. "I saw a . . . a big dog out there. It threatened me. It could have attacked you."

"That's not going to happen."

"How do you know?"

He pretended utter innocence. "Are you sure of what you saw?"

"I . . ." She looked uncertain, then lowered her gaze to the hands clasped in her lap. "I don't know."

"Are you sure it was a dog?"

"I . . . don't know," she said again, this time more uncertain.

"Well then," he answered mildly.

The wolf had confronted her, intent on burning the

encounter into her brain—and chasing her away. But she was still here. And the man was thankful that she wasn't ready to cope with the implications of the late-night meeting. He might have been surprised by her morning-after reality check, but he'd seen the phenomenon before. Human eyes saw a large menacing animal where no animal should be. And the mind behind those eyes turned away from the evidence because it was too disturbing to be real.

He helped along the process of denial—gave her a couple of other alternatives. "I take it you were pretty upset. Maybe you saw . . . what did you call them? Animal shapes in the leaves? Or maybe it was just a bad dream. A very vivid dream—brought on by the stress of the last few days."

He saw her swallow. "Maybe," she said in a doubtful voice. "But why would stress make me see a wolf?"

"A wolf? I thought you said you saw a large dog."

She closed her eyes for a moment, pressed her hand against her mouth. "I . . . don't think there are any wolves in Maryland. But it looked like a wolf."

"Have you ever seen one before?"

"I don't think so."

"Well, all the more reason why it must have been a dream." Before she could take away control of the conversation, he said, "You came here to get a blood sample. You can do it now."

She looked startled, as if she'd forgotten all about the original purpose of her visit. Then she rallied. "Yes. Right. But first I'm going to take a shower and brush my teeth, if you don't mind."

Ross was left staring at the swaying rear end of his uninvited guest. He'd thought he could get her out of the house immediately. But she'd just worked her way around his resolve. Cursing under his breath, he pushed himself off the bed and winced as his foot hit the floor. Still, he walked rapidly past the closed bathroom door so he didn't have to imagine any intimate details as he heard the water come on in the shower.

In the kitchen, he pulled one of his expensive shrink-wrapped steaks out of the freezer. After sticking the package in a pan of tepid water to thaw, he propped his hips against the counter and looked down the hall toward the bathroom, where he could hear water running.

MEGAN turned up the hot water a notch, tipping her face into the shower spray, then let it play over the tense muscles of her back and shoulders while she tried to sort through her memories of the night before.

What exactly had happened last night?

For starters, she had panicked when she'd found Ross's door locked. She'd torn through the house looking for him. And when she'd satisfied herself that he was absent, she'd gone outside.

That's what she remembered. Until Ross had questioned her memory.

Her jaw started to tremble. Gritting her teeth, she directed her mind back to the conversation they'd just had. When she'd confronted Ross, he hadn't denied going outside. So that made the first part real.

Didn't it?

Sometime during the night, she'd fallen asleep in the chair. She knew that much for sure. At least that was where she'd woken up when she'd heard the shower running this morning.

But the rest of it . . . *Could* it have been a dream?

As she stood under the water, clenching and unclenching her hands, a long-forgotten memory came surging back.

When she'd been a powerless little girl, afraid of Daddy, she'd invented a magic bear who would growl at her father when he got too mean.

That bear had been very real to her—a necessary ingredient in her young existence. She'd named him Mergatroid. He'd been her protector and her friend. And she'd fallen asleep every night, imagining he was crouched beside her bed as she whispered to him in the dark, telling him about her hopes and fears.

The memory had been buried for a long time. Now it was so vivid that she could clearly picture the large brown animal dressed in the checked vest he always wore. Back then when she'd needed emotional support, she might have mixed up dreams and reality, she silently conceded.

What if it was happening again?

What if she'd gone outside, seen something frightening that she couldn't explain—something so disturbing that she couldn't cope with it—and translated it into the scene with the wolf?

Another memory bobbed to the surface. This time it was from a book she'd read in her abnormal psychology class in college, *I Never Promised You a Rose Garden*. It was written by a former mental patient, a woman who had invented an imaginary land where she took refuge from the things in the world that disturbed and frightened her. At first her private refuge had been inhabited by friendly people, but gradually the land had taken on a life beyond her control. The population had turned nasty and started to dominate her—and she'd been helpless to escape. Finally she'd ended up in a mental hospital where a psychiatrist had helped her sort through fantasy and reality.

Was that happening now? Megan wondered with a shudder. To her? God, after two days and nights of private nursing duty, was she losing her mind?

The hot water turned gradually cold, and she started to shiver. Not just from the temperature—from her unwanted thoughts. Reluctantly she turned off the shower and reached for a towel, rubbing briskly. But the cold went deeper than her skin.

She'd told herself from the first that she should get out of Ross Marshall's house as fast as she could. Then he'd warned her to leave. Too bad she hadn't taken either her own or his advice.

With a grimace she looked at the clothes she'd worn

the day before—and then slept in. And too bad she hadn't thought about borrowing Marshall's washer and dryer. Just another example of how she wasn't thinking too clearly—on a lot of fronts.

ROSS had slapped the steak onto the stove-top grill when Megan came into the kitchen, her hair towel-dried but still damp.

He didn't look directly at her as he pretended to contemplate the meat. She seemed shaken, more fragile than she had been at any time since she'd arrived, even when he'd pulled that stunt with the wolf—and then given her reasons to question whether the whole episode had been a bad dream.

At the moment he was regretting his impulses. He wanted to apologize for frightening her and making her doubt her own senses. He wanted to reach out and catch her shoulder, pull her toward him and fold his arms around her, knowing the comfort would be as much for him as for her. But he sternly clamped down on the desire because he knew that touching her was a bad idea. For both of them.

She seemed to be working at control as much as he. Her pale lips were pressed together, and the skin around her eyes looked pinched. When she briskly filled the kettle at the sink and set it on a burner, he relaxed a fraction.

As she turned on the gas flame, she said in a slightly breathy voice, "I couldn't find any coffee yesterday."

"I don't drink it."

"Do you mind if I fix some instant I picked up at the grocery when I filled your prescription?"

Caffeine had always made him sick. Just the smell of coffee was enough to make him a little queasy, which was probably a good thing today since he was trying to keep his hands off the woman standing five feet away. So he shrugged and got down two mugs.

For himself, he also pulled out a packet of wild berry tea.

He and Megan moved stiffly around each other in the kitchen, he forking up the steak and turning it over, she waiting for the kettle to boil. As he watched her from the corner of his eye, he was vividly aware that no woman had had breakfast here.

"You take this nature stuff seriously," she said, eyeing the box of herbal tea.

He shrugged again, backed away from the pungent aroma that rose from her mug as she stirred hot water into the coffee crystals. While she poured milk into the coffee, he started steeping the tea bag.

The steak had a thin layer of brown on both sides, enough for cosmetic purposes, he decided. Transferring it to a plate, he took it to the table, sat down, and began to eat, aware that he was being rude.

"I bought some eggs at the store yesterday. Do you mind if I scramble a couple?"

He chewed and swallowed the piece of steak in his mouth. "There's a pan in the lower cabinet next to the stove."

"Do you want some?"

"The steak is enough for me."

As he ate, he watched her cracking eggs into a small bowl, stirring in a little milk, melting butter in the pan. For an unguarded moment he found himself fantasizing about having her here every morning.

When he realized what he was doing, he slammed the door on the pleasant mental picture and focused on the smell of the sizzling fat.

Clearing his throat, he said, "I wouldn't mind a couple of eggs."

She added two more to the bowl and stirred them in, along with more milk, salt, and pepper. Then she transferred everything to the pan.

As she watched the eggs cook, she said, "I realize you're anxious for me to collect my sample and clear out of your house."

He managed a little shrug.

"I'll get this over with as fast as I can. But when a client calls for a genetic workup, we need to get some background information."

He shifted in his chair. "Like what?"

"You told our secretary that you have a genetic disease in your family."

Was that what he'd said? He didn't remember being that direct.

"Have you had the condition evaluated?" she asked.

"No."

"Then how do you know it's a genetic disorder?" she asked.

"I know what happens to the children born in my family. Not just to my parents. My grandparents. Further back."

"Can you be more specific?" she asked, moving the eggs around in the pan.

He could be specific as hell. All he said in a clipped voice was "The girl babies die shortly after birth. The males hang on until puberty, at which time about half of them join their sisters. I'm one of the lucky survivors."

CHAPTER
TEN

HE SAW SOMETHING flash across her face. Pity? He didn't want pity from her or anybody else.

"Genetic disorders are my specialty. And I've never heard of anything like that," she said as she quickly scooped eggs onto two plates. "Has this disease ever been diagnosed?"

He cut a piece of meat, and chewed and swallowed as though he were enjoying the food, although the ability to taste anything other than his own tension had suddenly deserted him.

"It hasn't been diagnosed, because nobody's talked about it in public. It's been treated like a shameful family secret. But the evidence is there. For as many generations back as we have family records." *And further than that,* he silently added. *Back into the mists of antiquity.* Female babies died. Teenage boys died.

She kept her features neutral as she brought the plates of eggs to the table, along with a fork for herself.

"You're sure *all* girls die? And half the boys die in their teens?"

"Yes."

"For the boys, is it a degenerative process?"

"No."

"What then?"

"I don't know. It's a sudden event. A stroke maybe," he answered in a low voice, remembering the terrible burst of pain in his own head when he'd first changed. It had felt like a thousand daggers piercing his brain tissue, and he'd thought it was going to kill him. But somehow he'd conquered the pain.

He stole a quick glance at her to see if he'd given too much away. Her vision was turned inward, her eggs forgotten, cooling in front of her on the table.

"What you're describing—a sex-linked disease—sounds like it would have to be passed on through a recessive gene. In other words, a child would have to receive a defective copy from both the mother and the father."

"No, this is passed on only through the males. They're the only ones who survive."

"How do you know that for sure?"

"I can document it for four generations. My great-grandmother had twelve children," he recited in a flat voice. "Six girls died at birth. Four boys died before their sixteenth year. Two boys survived into adulthood. My grandmother had fifteen children. Eight girls died at birth. Four boys died in adolescence. Three boys survived—including my father. My own mother had nine children. Four girls died at birth. She was lucky with the boys. Three survived into adulthood. Including me. I think you can see the pattern."

"Yes. But it could still be a recessive gene."

He shook his head. "That's not what's happening."

"How do you know?"

"The men in my family share certain . . . characteristics that aren't found in the general population."

"What?"

He shifted·in his chair. "The reason that I didn't

come to the lab in the first place was that I didn't want to discuss it."

He saw her swallow, hesitate. "You seem perfectly healthy—apart from your recent infected wound. Which is healing faster than expected. Do the men have some defect that only shows up later in life? Have you heard of Huntington's disease? Is it something like that?"

"I've read about it. It's not like that."

She pushed a portion of egg around on the plate. "It would be helpful if you could tell me a little more."

Below the level of the table, he clenched his hands. He'd wanted to avoid this, although he hadn't really understood how painful it would be. "It's not an illness, but there are physical changes in the men who survive. Under certain circumstances I have heightened sensory perceptions. And you've already seen that my body has unusual recuperative powers." He sighed. "And there are some . . . social consequences. When the men in my family reach maturity, they find it impossible to live in any kind of proximity to one another. I have a brother who's a forest ranger in Texas. I haven't seen him since he left home ten years ago. I wouldn't try to stay in the same room with my father for more than half an hour. We'd end up slugging it out."

He watched her staring at him, waiting for more information. He had never spoken of these things with anyone, not even his mother, and it was agony to continue. But he forced the words out of his mouth.

"This is something that's been in my family forever. In the past, it was accepted as a curse or a blessing—depending on whether you were one of the ones who beat the odds. But with modern gene technology, I think there's a chance to change the outcome."

"You're looking for a cure?"

"I didn't ask for genetic testing because I thought it would solve any problems I have." He stopped, then forced himself to continue, speaking to her more directly than she probably realized. "I don't intend to put an innocent woman through the hell that was my mother's life. Bearing child after child. Knowing the girls will die at birth. Waiting to find out if the boys will survive beyond the age of fifteen or sixteen—then having them move away because they couldn't stay in the same room with their father. I've read about gene therapy. I've heard about using transfusions of fetal blood to cure sickle-cell anemia. I'm hoping there's a therapy that will do the same thing for my children. If not, then I won't be responsible for passing this genetic curse on to another generation." He sat there, amazed that he had said so much—and to this particular woman sitting across the breakfast table.

She looked shocked, and yet there was a kind of excitement glowing in her eyes. "All right. Yes. The first thing I want to do is a karyotype—a profile of your chromosomes. If I do an analysis of your DNA, I'd want to test your parents, too—and some of the other men in your family."

He gave a grim laugh. "My father would run you off with a shotgun if you came near him to try to get a blood sample." *Metaphorically speaking. More likely with his fangs. The way I tried to do last night. Only he won't hold anything back.*

"Do you ever go home?"

"Only when the Big—" He stopped abruptly, rephrased the answer. "Only when the old man isn't around."

"I don't need blood. I could use hair from his comb."

"I suppose I could get my mother to get some for me."

"You said two brothers lived into adulthood."

So she'd been paying attention to the details. "Yeah, well, getting into dangerous situations is one of our characteristics, I'm afraid. One of my brothers died as the result of a, uh, barroom brawl."

"I'm sorry."

He gave a small shrug.

"And you've channeled your aggressions into detective work?"

"Yeah. It's an excellent outlet."

When he didn't elaborate, she nodded. "Because of the family sensory talents you spoke of?"

"Yes."

Her expression had grown thoughtful. "There's something I was curious about. You work out of the office down the hall?"

He nodded, wondering where the conversation was going now.

"I left a message on your answering machine. Then when I saw all the No Trespassing signs along your driveway, I called you again. I assume you didn't get the message."

"No. I was too sick to call in for my messages."

"When I needed to get a prescription for more Keflex, I couldn't find your telephone."

"I don't have a hardwired phone. I use a cell phone. Part of the package is the answering service." As he listened to his own words, his mind streaked back to four nights ago when he'd grabbed his pants in his teeth and run like hell from Arnott.

As the scene leaped into his mind, a sudden feeling of panic crawled through his gut. "I'll be right back," he told her, pushing his chair away from the table and lurching to his feet.

Limping down the hall as fast as he could move, he surged into the bedroom and picked up the pants from where he'd kicked them into the corner. With icy fingers, he reached into the right front pocket. His keys were there, but no telephone. His wallet was in the back left pocket where he'd left it. There were a couple of pieces of loose change on the right.

Carefully he went through all of the pockets again. No telephone. Jesus!

He felt the hair on the back of his neck stir as he bent to search under the bed, under the dresser. Looking up, he saw Megan watching him.

"You're trying to find the phone?"

"Yes."

"Can I help?"

"It isn't in here!"

"In some other room? The office?"

"No. I came straight to the bedroom, took off my clothes, and fell into bed. When I felt like I could get up, I went into the bathroom, climbed into the tub, and cut out the bullet."

She winced, then came back with another suggestion. "Maybe the phone is in your SUV."

"Yeah." Hoping against hope, he reached for the running shoes under the bed and jammed his feet into them. Then he brushed past his guest and sprinted for the car, ignoring the throbbing in his leg.

A pool of dried blood had soaked into the driver's seat and dripped onto the floor mat. He ignored the mess and checked under the front seat, then wedged his fingers into the cracks where the seat cushions and backs met. Megan pulled open the rear door on the other side of the SUV and methodically went over the back, even feeling around under the front seat.

He followed suit on his side, pulling up the floor mat, sweeping his hand under the seat. The only things he found were a quarter and the ice scraper he hadn't used since February.

"It's not here," she said, her voice strained, her face reflecting the tension he felt.

He nodded tightly, knowing there was only one place where he could have dropped the damn thing. In the woods outside a serial killer's chain-link fence. Too bad he'd been too busy running for his life to check his pants pockets.

Straightening, he slammed the car door, feeling his facial muscles tighten.

"What?" she asked, closing the opposite door and coming around to his side of the vehicle.

"You have to get out of here," he said.

She raised her eyes to his. "You said that a number of times when you were sick."

"Yeah, and now I know the reason why. The guy I was investigating knows I was on his property. If he finds that phone, he can figure out who I am. And if he does, it's dangerous for you to be here."

Megan didn't move. "If it's dangerous for me, it's dangerous for you, too."

"I can handle him."

She cocked her head to one side, gave him a long look before speaking again. "I hate to contradict. But didn't he shoot you in the leg?"

His gaze drilled into her. He was accustomed to making men back off by giving them that look. But she stood her ground. And when he took a step forward, she stayed where she was, her hands clenched in front of her. He couldn't repress a flash of admiration, but standing her ground wasn't going to change anything.

"If he comes looking for me, he'll be on my turf. And I'm not going to discuss my plans with you. What you're going to do is clear out so I don't have to worry about defending you as well as myself," he said, punching out the words for emphasis.

She gave him a small nod, then reminded him they still had unfinished business. "Before or after I take the blood sample I came to collect?"

CHAPTER
ELEVEN

MEGAN WATCHED ROSS flap his hand in exasperation. "Take the damn sample. Then get out of here before we're both sorry."

"Okay. My kit's inside."

In the kitchen, she cleared the table and washed the white Formica surface with a soapy dishcloth because she was too obsessive a technician to work with half-eaten plates of food sitting in front of her. But there was another reason, too. She needed to give her hands enough time to stop shaking before she tried sticking a needle into Ross Marshall's vein.

He'd told her he'd dropped the phone at the house of the killer he was investigating and that the man might come after him. And he was ordering her to leave so she wouldn't get caught in the cross fire. If there was going to be any cross fire.

Calmly she dried the table with a paper towel, watching the smooth motion of her hand sweeping across the flat surface.

God—he was asking her to just walk away when he

might be in danger. She didn't like what he'd told her about the phone. She hated the idea of leaving him alone, yet she was pretty sure she didn't have a choice. She'd known from the beginning that he would have kicked her out if he'd had the strength. Now that he was capable of doing it, she wasn't going to make him waste his strength on her.

"You need to sit down," she said around the clogged feeling in her throat.

He sat, and she washed her hands at the sink. Then, turning back to the table, she opened her kit and took out a hypodermic, a Venoject tube with lithium heparin, and a piece of rubber tubing to wrap around his arm.

"Turn your arm over."

He obeyed, and she tapped the veins, finding one that looked promising.

After cutting off his circulation with the tubing, she swabbed his flesh with alcohol, watching his nose wrinkle.

"I guess you hate the smell of this stuff."

"Yeah."

"Then why did I find a bottle in your medicine cabinet?"

"Because when it stings, I know it's working."

"You like to punish yourself."

"No. I like to know the wound's being disinfected."

"You hurt yourself often?" she asked, aware that her shaky nerves were making her chatter.

"Yeah."

He was back in his laconic mode, so she cut her losses and concentrated on the procedure.

Some patients looked away before she pierced their flesh. He kept his gaze fixed on what she was doing.

She'd touched him far more intimately when she'd changed the dressing on his thigh. But he'd been half out of it then. Now she sensed that he was fully aware of her fingers sliding against his skin, of her hand releasing the rubber tubing.

She knew he was concentrating on staying very still as she took about eight milliliters of blood, withdrew the needle, and pressed a sterile piece of gauze to his arm.

Methodically she pushed the green stopper into the tube's mouth and then wrote his name on the label.

He watched her work. And when she lifted her eyes, their gazes collided.

For a charged moment, neither of them spoke. Then she cleared her throat, thinking she had nothing to lose by telling him what was on her mind. "If you were anybody else, I'd order you to bed. But I guess I've figured out that I can't order you to do anything."

"That's right. But you don't have to worry."

She knew he was saying the last part with as much reassurance as he could project, but she wasn't going to let him off that easily. "Tell me what you're going to do about the phone."

Sighing, he answered. "When it gets dark, I'll go back and look for it. If I find it, the problem's solved."

"And if you don't find it?"

"I'll cross that bridge when I have to."

She heard herself asking, "Will you call me—tell me what happened?"

She half expected him to refuse. Instead he nodded.

"Thank you." Reaching into her purse, she brought out a business card, then wrote on the back. "This is my home number. Call me as soon as you know anything."

He stood up. "In the middle of the night?"

She turned to him, raising her face to his. "I don't think I'll be able to sleep until I know you're okay."

When he didn't answer, she added softly, "You hate that, don't you? Someone staying up late at night, worrying about you."

She'd been here for two days, feeling like an intruder, feeling his resistance to any meaningful exchange of emotions between them. The barriers were still in place. His barriers. And she understood the reason—at least part of it.

But now that she was leaving, she was damned if she was going to let it end without some measure of honesty—on her part if not his.

The tight, warning expression on his face only spurred her on. She'd never been an impulsive woman. And her childhood had made her wary of men who took control of situations like a storm front blowing away all thought of opposition. Despite all logic, she found herself moving forward quickly, before she could change her mind. She saw his eyes darken, saw him glance behind himself and find that he was blocked from escape by the edge of the table.

Opening her arms, she reached for him, clasped her hands behind his back. For an instant he went rigid. Then she felt as well as heard the breath hiss out of his lungs. Her own breath was frozen inside her as she absorbed the impact of her body pressed to his. The contact was as potent as she'd known it would be. No, far more potent.

Stunned, she clung to him, knowing full well that he was strong enough to break her hold, wrench himself from her grasp. Instead she felt his arms rise, circle her shoulders, tighten, wedge her body more firmly to the length of his.

"Ross."

Earlier this morning she'd been badly off balance—torn between doubting her encounter with the wolf and doubting her own sanity. In his arms, she felt centered, secure. Eyes squeezed shut, she laid her cheek against his broad chest, drawing strength from him even as she felt him leaning into her.

She breathed in the fresh-washed scent of his skin and, below that, his unique scent, something like the tang of rain on the wind. Greedy for more, she moved her hands over the hard muscles of his back, pressed her face more tightly to his chest, feeling the deep steady thrumming of his heart beneath her cheek. He might be holding himself still, but she knew she was affecting him as powerfully as he was affecting her.

She had tried to deny the deep sense of connection to this man, but that had suddenly become impossible. Her heart leaped as she felt his hands move over her. He pulled her closer, aligning her body more perfectly with his, and she felt a tide of heat sweep across her skin, sink into her flesh, burn its way to the marrow of her bones. It felt good, right. It felt like something she had secretly craved for a long time, yet the need hadn't been there until she'd met him.

"Ross." She said his name again, lifted her face, and saw his eyes burning hot and bright. Time had stopped. The world had contracted to the circle of his arms clasping her to him. For a charged moment, she stared up at him, as though the two of them were shipwreck survivors who had miraculously washed up on the same beach after fearing each other lost. Her mouth opened slightly, anticipating the feel of his lips coming down on hers. Anticipating the jolt of heat.

But it didn't happen.

Gently but firmly he cupped his hands on her shoulders, moved her body back and away from his.

She felt abashed. Light-headed. Confused.

And the look on his face told her he was experiencing all those things, too.

"Are you feeling sorry for me?" he asked, his voice gritty.

"No."

"Then what?"

She struggled for honesty. "I . . . I like you."

"Didn't you listen to anything I told you?" he asked, his voice thick.

"I listened to everything."

"Then you know the consequences of getting mixed up with me."

"Is hugging a man getting mixed up with him?" she asked quickly.

"You can't argue it both ways."

"I—"

"If you're smart, you'll back off before . . ."

"Before what?"

He didn't answer. But the image she'd had that first evening—the image of the two of them naked on a bed, hot and wanting—came back to her. The bed down the hall.

In her mind she understood that he was little more than a stranger. A man with secrets and sorrows. Yet the feelings building inside her defied logic. As she stood there staring at him, she knew that she longed to feel connected to him. Physically, emotionally.

Before she could tell him what was in her heart, he turned away and rested his elbows on the counter, and she knew he was calling on more strength than she possessed at the moment. She saw it in the rigid set of his shoulders, heard it in the rasp of his breath.

He uttered a fierce oath, then said, "You'd better go."

Torn, she stood beside him for seconds that felt like an eternity. Every female impulse inside her urged her to reach out and touch him. If she did, he would turn. He would take her in his arms again. It was what they both wanted. But she understood that this was the wrong time. Because he had asked her to do it, she backed away. Perhaps that was the only thing she could do for him now.

Later was another matter.

But she didn't allow herself to think about later.

Turning, she grabbed up the kit with the blood sample and her purse and fled the house.

She was in the car when she saw him stride outside.

Feeling a reckless surge of hope, she rolled down the window as he came toward her, anxious to hear what he had to say.

It was, "Where's my gun?"

She struggled to keep hurt and disappointment out of her eyes. "In the chest near the front door."

He nodded and turned, and she watched the door close behind him with a sense of defeat.

In the car, driving home, she had ample time to reflect on the pain and confusion she was feeling.

She had always been cautious with the opposite sex. It took a long time before she let herself risk getting close. And she'd always picked men who weren't like her father—men who weren't harsh, dominating, aggressive, strong. In the two days she'd known Ross Marshall, he'd been all those things. And yet she'd put her arms around him and held him close as though he were precious to her.

A shiver rippled across her skin. She was attracted to him on some deep level where no man had ever moved her before. Yet at the same time she was afraid of him. A little while ago she had blocked the latter out. Now she didn't know what to do about it—or the attraction.

Always before, relationships with men had been on her terms. And they went no further than she wanted them to go. She had been to bed with a few of the men she'd dated and enjoyed the experience on a superficial level. But she knew that with Ross Marshall making love would be different. More powerful. More meaningful.

She blinked, brought herself up short. She was still thinking about making love with the man. And he had done everything possible to put distance between them—until this morning when she'd forced him to confront the powerful emotions building between them.

Even then he had been compelled to fight the attraction. Earlier she'd wondered if his genetic problem was the reason he was putting up barriers between them. After what he'd told her this morning, she was sure it was the case. That and his tragic family background. He hadn't spelled out that last part. But it didn't take much imagination to picture the grief his mother had gone through—losing so many daughters at birth, then half her sons.

God, what a sad life. Why was she even thinking about getting mixed up with a man who had told her his heritage was grief and suffering?

By the time she reached her house, she had made what she considered a smart decision. She would turn the blood sample over to Hank and let him proceed with the tests.

By the time she'd discarded her sweat clothes and put on a crisp skirt and blouse, she had changed her mind. As she put on lipstick and a bit of blusher, she told herself she wasn't going to take the coward's route. She would do the tests herself, report back to Ross on what she found, and see where things went from there.

WHEN she arrived at the lab, however, she abruptly abandoned all work plans. Betty was sitting at the reception desk, looking distraught. And Walter, his face pinched and his skin gray, was talking to a couple of uniformed police officers who had apparently been there for a while. Barlow and Sandler, their name tags said.

Completely disoriented, she stared at the unaccustomed scene. For a terrible moment, her mind leaped to the conclusion that this had to do with Ross—with the lost phone. The killer had found it, come after him. And now the police were at the lab to tell them that their client was in the hospital—or worse.

"What happened?" she wheezed, reaching out a hand to steady herself against the wall.

"A burglary," Betty said.

It took another moment for the words to sink in. "A break-in? Where?"

It was Walter who stepped away from the cops to answer. "Here. Somebody forced the lock on the door early this morning. Betty found the door open when she came to work. She was afraid to go inside so she left a note on the door and went to call the police. We all stayed outside for over an hour, waiting for the police to come," he said, an accusing note in his voice as he glanced toward the two detectives.

Megan took in the overview, then zeroed in on the personal ramifications. "My project," she gasped, and dashed into the lab area. Quickly she inspected her laminar flow hoods, her virus cultures. Her genetic material.

The officer named Sandler followed her. "You're Dr. Sheridan?"

"Yes."

"Was your work disturbed?"

She did a more careful inspection, then breathed out a small sigh. "Not as far as I can see."

He wrote that down in a notebook. When the microphone clipped to his collar sputtered, he pressed a button and conferred with some unseen dispatcher. After completing the call, Sandler turned back to Megan. "Would you take a look at your desk area?"

She retraced her steps and walked into the office she shared with Hank, who had evidently gotten the assignment to check the file drawers.

He glanced up when she entered and rolled his eyes. "Welcome back. Your timing is impeccable."

"Right." She sank into her desk chair, opened drawers, shuffled through the contents. Nothing seemed to be disturbed. Then she booted up her computer and brought up her main directory, scanning the entries.

There was no problem accessing her directories. And when she opened some of her files at random, the information was intact.

"I'm not finding anything missing," she reported.

Sandler asked, "Can you tell me where you were this morning?"

She might have taken offense, but she realized he probably had asked everyone the same question

"Getting a blood sample from a client of the lab," she answered. "You can check with him if you like."

"His name?"

"Ross Marshall," she answered, then fumbled in her purse for the slip of paper with his address, which she read off to the detective.

Sandler copied it down before returning to the hall, where Walter was still standing, giving his report to Barlow. When her boss finally wound down, the officer handed him a business card.

"If you have anything else to report, give me a call," he said.

When they had departed, she joined a scowling Dr. Galveston in the hall. "Yeah, and if we do think of something, good luck in getting you to call back," he muttered.

"Did anything turn up missing?" Megan asked.

"It looks like the alarm scared them off. But the officers took some fingerprints from the door."

"It's strange that someone went to the trouble of breaking in, then took off," she mused.

Walter's expression turned darker.

"What?" she asked.

"Nothing."

"Something's bothering you."

His mouth tightened. "Maybe there's a pattern here."

"A pattern of what? Did you tell that to the police?" When he didn't reply, she prompted, "Walter?"

He glanced toward the office, where Hank was still thumbing through files, then lowered his voice before saying, "Let's go where we can talk."

Wondering what he wanted to keep so close to his vest, she followed him to his office, a room that was twice the size of the area where she and Hank worked. He pulled the door shut, then rounded his oversized rosewood desk and lowered himself into the executive leather chair.

Uneasily she took one of the comfortable guest chairs, waiting for him to speak.

When he finally did, his voice was pitched low. "Six months ago, there was an incident."

"What kind of incident?"

"A couple came in for genetic testing. It turned out that the test results were erroneous."

The word hung between them.

As the implications sank in, a wave of cold swept over her skin. "A test I did? Is that why you called me in here?"

"I think it was one of Hank's."

"You don't know for sure?"

"The records have disappeared."

She stared at him. "Disappeared? How?"

He shrugged.

"You've spoken to Hank?"

"No. And I don't want you to, either. Anyone can make a mistake." He looked down at his desk blotter, then up again. "Or maybe what I'm trying to say is that it was really my fault. I'd piled too much work on him, and he was rushed."

"You're piling too much work on both of us," she answered, then wondered why she couldn't simply keep her mouth shut. But this time he was the one who'd brought it up. Maybe he was feeling guilty.

She saw him swallow hard and glance toward the closed door. "I got an angry call from the client threatening me. That was several weeks ago and nothing happened, so I figured the guy was just blowing off steam. Then there was the incident Monday on the way to work."

She was thrown completely off track. So much had happened since Monday morning that it took several moments for her to recall what he was talking about. When she remembered the way he'd come in all upset, her eyes widened.

"You said somebody ran you off the road."

"Yes. And I thought I recognized the guy."

"You didn't mention that!"

"I was hoping I was wrong. Then this morning, after I discovered the break-in, I checked my case files. Some of them are gone."

"Did you tell that to the police?"

"No."

"You have to."

"And have an article impugning the reputation of the lab in the *Washington Post* tomorrow? No thank you. I don't need news like that spread across the headlines. Not when I'm expecting a big contract to come through."

"What contract?"

"That's confidential information."

"But, Walter, you're already giving me confidential information," she argued.

He glared at her, then made an effort to relax his features. "Let's wait and see what happens. Waiting a few days isn't going to hurt anything."

"You're not thinking this through logically."

"I want to handle it in my own way."

"Walter—"

"I'm trusting you to let me deal with the problem. And to keep this conversation between the two of us. Do I have your word on that?"

"I guess so," she answered reluctantly.

"I need to know you won't blab to Hank or Betty."

"All right."

"Thank you."

"Why are you telling *me*?"

"I just want you to know the background, in case something happens to me."

"And then what?"

"Then you can tell the police. Until then, I expect you to keep your mouth shut."

CHAPTER
TWELVE

SINCE THERE DIDN'T seem to be anything more to say, Megan got up and started down the hall to her own office. But she stopped short before she reached the door. Hank was probably there, and she couldn't face him after Walter's accusation, so she switched directions and stepped into the ladies' room. Locking herself in one of the stalls she sat down on the closed toilet seat and pressed her palms against her forehead, trying to dispel the sudden throbbing in her temples.

God, what a mess. Walter was telling her the lab was under attack from a crazed client. And that it was Hank's fault. Or was that really true?

She pressed harder as the pain in her head reached Anvil Chorus proportions.

Could Walter have done something he wasn't prepared to talk about? And was now blaming it on Hank?

She and Hank had a good, solid working relationship. She wanted to ask him if he remembered the test. But she'd promised Walter she'd keep the information confidential.

Damn him. He'd boxed her into a corner. The way Ross Marshall had boxed her into a corner.

Two different men, with two completely different styles, and they both had her flummoxed.

A year ago, when her parents had died, she'd made the mistake of mentioning her inheritance to Walter, and he'd urged her to invest in the lab. It was a topic he brought up every few months—but so far the money she hadn't used for a down payment on her house was still in the bank.

Now she was grateful that she hadn't leaped to invest in Bio Gen. Because it looked like the business was falling apart in front of her eyes.

The idea of bailing out was becoming more appealing by the minute. But if she found another job, would she be able to take her research with her? Or would her boss claim it was the property of the lab?

She sat there for a long time, wondering what the hell she was going to do.

Since she couldn't come up with a long-term answer, she decided to start the test on Ross Marshall's cells.

ROSS sat with three pillows propped behind his back, his notes on Donald Arnott spread across his lap and on the bed. His eyes were fixed on a line of type. But his mind was far away. Megan had said she wanted samples of genetic material from his parents. And he pictured himself standing in the house where he'd grown up, broaching the subject to his mother.

Only he wasn't seeing himself as the Ross Marshall of today. He was an eighteen-year-old kid, home from his freshman year of college, leaning against the cracked and stained kitchen counter.

He'd been telling Mom he could replace the work surface for her. Replace the cabinets.

Apparently his dad had been standing in the dining room listening, for he'd come charging into the kitchen, his eyes blazing.

"So you think you're better than me, because you've got a big-deal scholarship to the University of Maryland and you've got some money saved from your pissing little construction jobs."

"No," he answered automatically as his mother slipped out of the room.

"Don't lie to me, sonny. You blame me for the tragedy of your mother's life. 'Cause I picked her for my mate. And now you're gonna make everything nice for her."

He'd started to turn away, but his father's words held him, words he'd heard in some form or another many times before.

"You dare to blame me, you shit-head moron? Wait till it happens to you. They call it chemistry." His father gave a harsh laugh. "They hardly understand the meaning of the word. They don't know the burning need. The lust. The pain. Wait until you're old enough to start searching for a mate. When you meet her, you'll *know*. Fucking her once won't get her out of your system. Because a wolf mates for life, sonny.

"The good part is that she'll want to fuck you as much as you want to fuck her. When you catch her scent, when you touch her, you'll understand what it's like for one of us, you sanctimonious bastard. So if you want to have some fun with the gals, do it now. 'Cause when you meet your mate, your cock just won't go in any other hole."

He'd heard it all before, more times than he could count. This time his hands balled into fists, and he struck out, caught his father on the chin. One minute they were standing; the next minute they were rolling on the worn vinyl tile, snarling, hands at each other's throats.

It was his mother who had dashed back into the kitchen and stopped the fight by dousing them with a pan of cold water. It was his mother who had fixed the cut on his cheek, hugged him fiercely, and said he'd better leave. She'd tried to give him money. He told her he didn't need it, but he'd promised to call her when he found a place to live. He'd clung to her for long moments, the way he had when he was a little boy and he'd scraped the skin off his knee. Then he'd gone, because he knew what would happen if he stayed. But his father's words were still ringing in his ears.

He'd studied genetics and social biology, and he knew that bonding with one female was counter to the usual male survival tactic. In most species, the male scattered his seed as far and wide as possible. He'd come to the conclusion that the male werewolf needed to be around for the transition of his sons from boy to wolf. He needed to teach them the ritual and coach them on surviving the pain of transition.

The werewolf was unique in that. And unique among wolves, too. Ross had also studied wolf behavior and had learned that in a wolf pack, there was only one alpha male, and all the others were subservient to him. Apparently werewolves didn't conform to the same social order. Every adult male was an alpha male. And if they stayed in one another's company for long, they would fight for supremacy. He'd explained that to Megan this morning, but not in such concrete terms.

Once again, he found his thoughts wandering to her. Cursing under his breath, he pulled his attention back to the notes spread across his lap. His life depended on thinking through his options, on not making another mistake with Arnott tonight. And instead of planning his return to the scene of the disaster, he was thinking about Megan and his father.

Of course, it didn't take a genius to figure out why. He was scared shitless. Not about Arnott. About what had already happened with Megan in the two days she'd been here.

He wanted her—wanted her in a way he had never wanted another woman. Wanted her with a bone-deep hunger that clawed at his insides. And in the kitchen this morning she'd let him know in no uncertain terms that the feelings weren't all one-sided.

Squeezing his eyes shut, he shook his head in denial. He wasn't going to let hormones or chemistry or genes rule his life. He wasn't Vic Marshall. He was in control of himself.

He wasn't a selfish bastard like his father, incapable of real love, only interested in fulfilling his own needs—and to hell with anyone else he hurt in the process.

He wasn't a hostage to his genetic heritage. He—

Another scene leaped into his mind. The woods at night. Crawford. The wolf following the scent of his prey. The blood lust of the kill. It had been the night of the full moon. Was that a coincidence? Or did the moon really affect werewolves—the way the old myths said?

He made a strangled sound in his throat. When he realized he was mangling the sheet of paper in his hand, he loosened his grip.

He had been younger then. Unaware of the danger that came from within. But he'd learned to handle his aggressions, channel them in an acceptable direction. And now he was damn well in control of himself. Ross Marshall, private eye.

Who had dropped his phone in the woods where a serial killer could find it. And if he wanted to stay healthy, he had better get that phone back.

Then there was the rest of the stuff he'd abandoned beside the fence. His brain had been too muzzy to think about that earlier. Now he closed his eyes, picturing the knapsack. He hadn't been stupid enough to stick a name tag on it, of course. Inside he'd stowed his wire cutters, the adjustable wrench, the set of Craftsman screwdrivers. The flashlight. And the big-ticket item: a top of the line pair of B & L binoculars.

Arnott had probably pored over the contents, trying to figure out who had lost the pack. But there was nothing to tie any of that to a PI named Ross Marshall.

The phone was another matter.

A knock on Megan's office door had her looking up. She was startled to see Dr. Carter Stillwell standing there.

She stared at his thin face, mop of curly hair, and deep-set brown eyes. When they'd first met, she'd thought he was handsome. Then she'd stopped liking the way the pieces fit together. Now she saw he was working to keep his features composed.

"Carter?"

He stepped into the room, glided toward her desk on silent feet. "I was in the neighborhood. Since I don't seem to be able to get you on the phone, I was hoping to catch you in."

"I've been out of the office for a few days. I'm just getting back. And we had some problems here this morning. A break-in."

He kept his unnerving gaze fixed on her. "The secretary gave me an earful."

"We're all kind of upset."

He waited a beat, then lowered his voice before saying, "I've got some new information that could be very helpful to you on your gene therapy project. Get you funding that won't have to rely on . . . a boss who's lost interest in your research."

It was so completely inappropriate for him to be saying that *here,* she felt her jaw drop. Recovering, she said, "Carter, I'm afraid . . . I'm too busy right now. I've got a whole bunch of work to catch up on."

His eyes narrowed. "I was hoping we could get together to discuss it. But you seem to be too busy all of the time lately."

"What can I say?"

"Really, Megan, it's a mistake to brush me off like this."

"I'm not."

"Then when can we talk? What about lunch today?"

"I, uh—"

Before she could finish, he stepped into the room.

A few minutes ago, he had put her on the spot. Now relief flooded through her. "Uh . . . Walter. This is Carter Stillwell. Carter, this is my boss, Walter Galveston."

They shook hands stiffly, made the appropriate noises.

"Megan and I have a meeting," Walter said. "I was just coming to look for her."

She glanced down at her hands to hide the expression on her face, since this was the first she'd heard of any meeting.

"Well, then, I'll get out of your way." Stillwell pushed past the other man and exited the room.

"Thanks for rescuing me," Megan breathed.

"I could see you wanted to get rid of him. Who is he?"

She thought about how to answer, then settled on, "I met him at a convention. He keeps making up excuses to get together with me."

Walter looked down the hallway. "He has some nerve barging in here." Turning, he left Megan sitting at her desk. She stayed there for several moments, collecting herself, then pushed away from the desk and headed for the lab. After donning a white lab coat and rubber gloves, she reached into the refrigerator and pulled out the tube with Ross's blood.

No, not Ross's blood. It was the wrong sample, she realized with a start as she stared at the label. Putting it back, she carefully retrieved the correct tube. She'd done hundreds of karyotypes and couldn't remember making a mistake like that before, yet this time she felt a sense of personal involvement that had always been missing in the past. Lord, was she trying to prove there was nothing wrong with him by testing the wrong sample?

Don't think about the man, she ordered herself. It was impossible to completely shut him out of her mind. Still, the scientist in her was able to focus on the tasks she had to accomplish. The first step was to break apart the double strands of Ross's DNA and the probe DNA being used by heating them in a solution of formamide at seventy degrees Celsius so that they could bind to each other.

Working on autopilot, she finished the procedure, then placed the sample on a glass slide, set a cover slip on top, and sealed the edges. Next the slide went into an incubator at thirty-seven degrees Celsius, where it would have to remain overnight for the probe to hybridize with the sample chromosomes.

Wishing she could go on to the next steps right away, she stared at the incubator. But there was no way to speed up the process. So she went back to the load of tests their boss had piled on her and Hank. Hank had already completed some of the procedures. She started on the next one, glancing over at his work area, wondering if he were making some vital mistake that was going to get them in trouble.

But that didn't sound like Hank. He was always meticulous in the lab. In fact, the way things were going today, *she* was more likely to screw something up, since only half her mind was on what she was supposed to be doing.

When she looked up and found Walter standing beside her workstation, she jumped.

"Sorry," he apologized. "Do you have a minute?"

Since the automatic equipment was now handling a polymerase chain reaction test, she nodded and stepped to the door.

"In all the excitement, I forgot to ask you about that guy out in Lisbon. Ross Marshall. I thought you said he was really sick and you wanted to stay with him."

"He got better pretty quickly."

Her boss raised a questioning eyebrow.

"Apparently he has remarkable recuperative powers."

Walter's eyes flashed with interest. "I thought he had some sort of genetic defect. Is it something that affects him personally, or is he a carrier?"

"He didn't want to give me much information."

"This isn't supposed to be a guessing game. Have you started any tests on him yet?"

Megan could have kicked herself as she recognized the eager look in his eyes. If she'd been less distracted, she would have thought of something more noncommital. "I've started the karyotyping," she answered.

"Well, let me know what you find."

"You really want a report on a routine case?"

"From the way he approached us—and from what you're telling me—it doesn't sound routine."

She shrugged, trying to look casual though her heart had started pounding like a trip-hammer inside her chest. She didn't want to discuss Ross Marshall with Dr. Galveston. She didn't want her boss poking into his business. But she forced a light tone into her voice when she said, "I'll let you know if I find anything interesting."

ROSS washed the bloodstains out of the car seat as best he could, threw away the floor mat, then ate a couple of raw steaks for lunch. Pulling the blackout draperies in the bedroom, he slept until eleven-thirty that night and woke feeling almost normal. After warming up and doing a half hour of weights, he showered and dressed in a black sweatshirt and pants. He was out of the house by twelve-thirty, hoping the late hour would provide some protection from Arnott. His *namhaid*, he thought, using the ancient Gaelic word.

He had studied the language. He could probably hold a conversation in ancient Gaelic. If there was anyone to speak it with. Certainly not with his father. Vic Marshall had laughed at him when he'd first caught him studying a book on the ancient Druids, called it crap. He'd been interested in present results. Not his ancient heritage.

Amadán. Fool, he warned himself.

Keep your mind focused on the killer. But as he took the back roads to upper Montgomery County, he realized he was thinking about his own life. How it had worked out since the day he'd left home and never returned, except for brief visits to his mother when he knew the Big Bad Wolf was out of the house.

He'd found himself a cheap room to rent in Cheverly, not too far from the university. Found a construction job for the summer, and lucked into his first detective case. The owner of the construction company, Phil Laniard, had been losing materials from one of his building sites. And Ross had said he could tell him who was doing it, if Laniard seeded a delivery of new lumber with wintergreen oil.

The boss had been skeptical. But he was willing to give anything a try. Two days later, Ross led him to a garage in Dundalk where the lumber was being stored.

That earned him a five-hundred-dollar bonus. And a referral to a guy who thought his wife was having an affair with one of their friends, only he didn't know which one.

That time, Ross had negotiated a two-thousand-dollar fee—and earned it within the week.

Other jobs had followed with increasing regularity as it became known that the Marshall boy could find missing objects and track people with uncanny accuracy.

He'd banked as much of his earnings as he could spare all through college. Before he graduated, he had enough for a down payment on a run-down row house in the city. The bank had only been willing to give him a short-term loan. But that didn't matter. With his construction skills, he'd rehabbed it himself, sold it at a nice profit, and picked up another property in Ellicott City. All the time continuing his detective work.

The two sources of income had allowed him to sock away enough to buy a twenty-four-acre tract in western Howard County with a house he could remodel to his liking.

He'd been satisfied with his life. Until Arnott had shot him in the leg and Megan Sheridan had found him lying naked on the living room floor.

Megan. Inevitably his thoughts had circled back to her. He tried to wrench his mind away. Tried not to think of her in the same breath with the crude language his father had used when he talked about the werewolf and his mate. But Ross was under no illusions about what he wanted to do with Megan.

He didn't know how much of what his father had said to him over the years was true. Some of it, certainly, although he'd learned the bastard was capable of lying for effect.

But he'd taken the warning to heart. His sexual partners had been few and far between. He'd never stayed with anyone long enough to get attached. And as he'd gotten closer to the age at which his father had married his mother, he'd stayed away from sexual liaisons altogether. Which was probably why he'd reacted like a stallion scenting a mare in heat when he'd encountered Megan. It was a plausible explanation. He wanted it to be true.

More than that, he wanted her to stop haunting him. Her face, the touch of her hands, the way her breasts filled out the front of her T-shirt. Her sweet feminine scent, like a meadow in the sunshine.

As the memory of her essence flooded his senses, he found himself hard and aching for her again.

Cursing, he deliberately turned his mind to graves and bullets and the hot pain in his leg that had almost led to his death. The effect was sobering enough to drive thoughts of sex from his mind for the time being.

After passing the spot where he'd parked last time, he drifted farther down the road, pulled onto the shoulder, and eased the SUV under some low-hanging tree branches.

The last time he'd been here, he'd been energized—eager for the hunt. Tonight he felt subdued as he walked two dozen yards into the woods, where a thick tangle of brambles hid him from any motorists who might happen to pass by at this late hour.

Discarding his clothing, he stood in the darkness, naked, mentally preparing himself for the pain that always came with transformation—and thinking about the words he was about to speak.

He knew the meaning of them all. Taranis, the Lord of Thunder. Cerridwen, the Goddess of Darkness. Epona, the Goddess of Horses. Although the texts didn't say so, he was sure her influence extended to other animals as well.

The familiar syllables flowed from his mouth.

"Taranis, Epona, Cerridwen," he intoned, then repeated the same phrase and went on to another.

"Gá. Feart. Cleas. Duais. Aithriocht. Go gcumhdaí is dtreoraí na déithe thú."

His damn ancestor had asked for a miracle, a great feat of prowess, a gift from the gods. And he'd even dared to be specific—to ask for the power to change his shape.

Ross repeated the words, felt the change—felt his jaw elongate, his teeth sharpen, his body contort as muscles and limbs transformed into the shape of his other self. Dropping to all fours, he endured the sensations of bones crunching, muscles jerking, fur sprouting from naked skin.

In seconds it was over, and the world was a different place—rich with promise. A shiver of anticipation rippled through him as he breathed in the odors of the night. Damp soil. Rotting leaves. Insects. Tree bark. A rabbit in its burrow. All of it coming to him in layers, each scent separate and distinct and exciting.

As always, he wanted to throw back his head and howl for the pleasure of it. But his human brain kept the words locked in his throat—kept him focused on the night's purpose.

Ignoring the tantalizing rustling sounds in the underbrush and the scents of the animals around him, he trotted through the woods, heading for the place where he'd cut the fence.

As he drew closer, he breathed in his own scent from four days earlier. It was still clinging to leaves and the debris on the ground but overpowered by the stench of another man, stronger, more recent, more pervasive. It could only be Arnott's. He must have come out here more than once, compulsively searching the woods for something besides the knapsack.

Had he found the phone? Ross didn't allow himself to contemplate the possibility as he padded through the darkness.

He was so intent on his purpose that he didn't see the glint of metal until almost too late.

Recognition filtered into his brain, and he pulled back his right front paw. Hair rose along his spine as he stared down into the jagged teeth of the animal trap that had almost closed around his leg.

A deep animal growl of anger welled in his throat.

Arnott had been doing more out here than looking. He'd been busy setting traps for the animal he'd shot. The animal that had gotten away.

For a split second, it flashed into his mind that somehow Arnott had figured out what kind of creature was stalking him. Then he dismissed the notion as beyond the realm of possibility. The killer had shot at and wounded a large dog, maybe even a wolf. Then he'd found a knapsack and clothing. That added up to a man and an animal. A K-9 unit.

Sternly he reminded himself of what kind of man he was dealing with. Arnott fantasized about the brutal acts he wanted to carry out on the bodies of young women—and followed through with the scenario. But his type didn't go around imagining paranormal creatures in his backyard.

Still, that didn't mean the danger was less. He knew Arnott was deadly and resourceful. The trap was only another demonstration of his ingenuity.

All Ross's senses were on alert as he padded past oaks and poplars, wild cherry and dogwood, their newly budded branches swaying slightly as the wind picked up. He was a hundred yards closer to the fence when a more disturbing thought slammed into him.

If Arnott had gone to the trouble of setting out traps, he could also have set out alarms—which had already been tripped. If so, the bastard could be on his way out here, with an Uzi instead of the hunting rifle he'd been armed with four nights ago.

The wolf's mouth drew back in a snarl. He had his animal senses. The hunter had modern technology on his side.

Yeah, modern technology. He was sure he hadn't left the phone on. But all he needed now was for the damn thing to somehow ring. Then he'd be in big trouble.

DONALD woke to the sound of a bell ringing. For a moment he was disoriented, thinking it was the phone, blinking as he stared at the green numbers on the alarm clock.

One-twenty in the morning.

Who the hell was calling him in the middle of the night?

Anger warred with a flash of fear as he snatched the receiver from the cradle—and heard nothing but a dial tone. But the ringing persisted. Then he realized it was the alarm system he'd installed the day before.

Jesus Christ. He'd hit pay dirt. Already.

Leaping out of bed, he pulled on his clothes, grabbed some serious firepower, and pounded down to the gate.

His fingers were clumsy on the lock, and he cursed as he forced himself to slow down, get the numbers of the combination right.

The lock clicked, and he snapped it open, slipping

outside into the night, the excitement of the hunt pumping through his veins. This time the bastard wasn't going to take him by surprise. This time when he saw the damn dog, he was gonna be ready. Or maybe it wasn't the dog—maybe it was the man. Well, that was even better.

THE need for caution warring with the need for speed, Ross continued on a course through the darkened woods that would take him near the spot where he'd dropped the knapsack. He kept his nose to the ground and all his senses tuned for trouble. His bad leg was throbbing dully now, but he ignored the pain.

To his right was another trap. Then another on the left, the metal cold and deadly in the darkness. How many of the fucking things did Arnott think he needed? He'd spent a lot of money on setting out a defensive perimeter. That was one more indication that the bastard wasn't living on his salary as a security guard.

The wolf paused, sucked in a deep breath. The scent of the killer was stronger here. But so was the Ross Marshall scent.

MEGAN stared at the clock on the bedside table. One-thirty in the morning. Ross had promised to call and tell her he was all right. But she hadn't heard from him, and she'd been lying in bed, feeling her pulse pounding in her temples, thinking that her blood pressure had probably climbed to one-fifty over ninety as she waited to hear from him.

More and more edgy by the minute, she slapped her fist against her palm. Damn Ross Marshall for making her care about him! Was he home safely? Had something bad happened?

Or was he even going to bother with a call?

Plumping up the pillow behind her head, she made

an effort to relax. But it was impossible to let go of
the tension.

Then, because she couldn't stand to lie in the dark
another minute, she heaved herself out of bed, turned
on the hall light, and padded down the hall to the
kitchen. Picking up her purse from a chair where she'd
set it when she brought in groceries, she opened the
side compartment and felt for the slip of paper that had
Ross's phone number. In the light from the hall, she
read the numbers.

Again she glanced at the clock. One forty-five. By
now he was probably home, fast asleep in his wide bed,
while she was standing here in the kitchen with her
teeth on edge.

The image of him lying in his bed made her fingers
crumple the piece of paper. Carefully she smoothed it
out again.

Damn him for doing this to her. Damn him for making her crazy with worry. Well, she knew how to pay
him back.

Crossing to the counter, she lifted the receiver of the
wall phone and reached toward the keypad.

THE wolf moved more slowly now, closing in on the
strongest source of the Ross Marshall scent. When he
came to a swirl of fallen leaves, he was sure that was
the place. Although he couldn't see the phone, he could
detect it nonetheless—either the instrument or something else he had carried close to his body. He was
darting forward, ready to snatch it from the leaves,
when he heard the sound of booted feet crunching on
the dry ground. Coming toward him fast and eager.

Animal instinct briefly took over. Coherent thought
fled from his brain. There was only fear. And searing
pain—the remembered pain of the rifle bullet tearing
into his flesh.

His breath was coming in sharp pants. The animal
part of him wanted to turn and run for his life. The

part that was human forced him to stay where he was, pawing at the leaves, struggling not to work too fast and screw it up.

The scent grew stronger. Then a slender rectangle of black plastic appeared among the leaves—a man-made intrusion on the forest floor. He lowered his mouth, caught the object in his teeth, then bolted for safety as a spray of bullets hit a tree trunk inches from his body.

Changing directions, he twisted through a tangle of wild roses and blackberries, lowering his head to avoid the sharp thorns. The man couldn't follow without getting badly scratched, but he sprayed the thicket with a hail of bullets.

The frightened animal part of him would have dashed straight for the safety of the truck. The human part knew that would be a fatal mistake. Making a wide circle around the vehicle, he ducked through more brambles and emerged, breathing hard.

He was in no shape to run for his life. But he had no choice, so he sprang ahead, outdistancing the man with the gun. Behind him, he could hear Arnott pelting through the forest, but he sensed he was out of danger now. The man could never catch him.

He slowed his pace as a tantalizing thought wafted into his mind. He could circle back, get behind the man, spring on his shoulders, and bring him down before he even knew what had hit him.

On a surge of adrenaline, he imagined pinning his quarry to the ground, sinking his fangs into the column of the neck.

The sweet, hot taste of blood welled in him, and a vivid image of the kill filled his mind like a bright light that blotted out all conscious human thought.

He was pure animal now as he turned and raised his head, sniffing the air, drinking in the scent of the man with the gun.

Body quivering with renewed purpose, he started back the way he'd come, eager for the feel of his teeth punching through soft tissue, crunching through bone.

CHAPTER
THIRTEEN

THE WIND SANG a hunting song in his blood. A song without words. A song that drew him forward, primed him for the kill.

But he had taken only a few eager steps when the screech of an owl above the treetops broke the stillness of the night. The bird dived toward some small animal on the ground. In that instant, reason came flooding back through the wolf's brain cells, and he stopped in his tracks.

His jaw snapped around the phone he still carried in his mouth, and his right front foot pawed the ground. For long moments he stood with his body trembling and his breath rushing hotly in and out of his lungs as he forced himself to stand in place. Forced himself to forgo the unholy pleasure of showing his enemy who was hunter and who was prey. Of wreaking vengeance for the bullet that had almost killed him.

Silent, subdued, he turned and started for the place where he'd left the truck.

Minutes later he had transformed to human shape,

welcoming the pain that came with the change. Dressing quickly in his pants and shirt, shoving his feet into his shoes, he climbed behind the wheel. His skin was covered by a film of perspiration from the pain in his leg and from the effort of controlling his instincts. His motions were jerky as he started the engine and pulled off the shoulder of the road, his back wheels spinning on gravel as he roared away into the night, the beat of his pulse drumming in his temples.

DONALD heard the car engine and sprinted toward the road, heedless of the brambles tearing at his pants legs. Breathing hard, he broke through the cover of trees and saw the bulk of a large vehicle—an SUV moving rapidly away. Red taillights mocked him. He zeroed in on the pool of light between them where the license plate rode low over the bumper.

Straining his eyes, he picked up the first two letters—DE. But that was all he could get. And he couldn't see the color or figure out the model in the dark. He was aiming at the bastard when headlights came blazing around a curve in the road, and he froze, a stream of curses tumbling from his mouth. He couldn't risk a shot, not when he might hit another vehicle. He waited until the other car had passed. Then, in frustration, he lifted the Uzi and squeezed the trigger, letting loose a hale of bullets into the trunk of an oak tree, bark flying as the projectiles hit.

His finger didn't loosen until the clip was empty.

"Fucker," he spat. "Fucker."

He was talking about the man, not the big dog he'd shot at again. The man had been back here in the SUV, waiting for the animal—ready to peel rubber the moment the animal appeared.

He stared in the direction in which the vehicle had disappeared. DE. How many license plates began with those letters? A couple of thousand, he was sure.

Anger bubbling inside him, he walked slowly back

through the woods, kicking at debris on the ground. But he didn't let his anger get the better of him. Methodically he illuminated the path in front of him, being careful not to step in any of the steel-jawed traps he'd set out.

The dog had been lucky. Or smart. Or something. An involuntary shiver traveled down his spine, and for a moment he allowed his brain to conjure up an image of a devil dog. Satan's spawn. Come to punish him on earth for his sins.

He shook off the ridiculous notion. That dog out there was no supernatural apparition. It had come in a truck with its master. And it was just a very well-trained animal. He'd shot it, hadn't he? And followed a trail of its blood.

Shot it four nights ago, he realized with a start.

Shit, he hadn't even been able to locate the vet that had treated it. And now it seemed to be good as new.

Well, animals healed faster than people, didn't they? Or maybe it was another dog. Maybe the fucker stalking him had a whole kennel full of the yapping bastards primed and ready to go. Maybe he was some kind of K-9 nut.

Still cursing, he started off again in the direction of the gate, swinging the light in an arc across the forest floor. When he hit a spot where the ground covering had been disturbed, he paused and squatted down.

It looked like the animal had pawed into the leaves.

Jesus. Had the man dropped something else, something besides the knapsack and his clothes? He sifted his fingers through the ground cover, feeling nothing. Standing again, he gave a savage kick at the dirt, imagining he was kicking the man in the head or the guts, thinking about all the things he was going to do to the guy when he finally caught up with him.

DRENCHED in sweat, Ross drove as if furies were pursuing him. Tonight he'd almost done it again. He'd almost lost control and ripped out his enemy's throat. At the last minute, sanity had returned.

Human sanity. Not the primitive instincts that ruled the wolf.

Those instincts had almost overwhelmed him. Yet somehow intellect had won out tonight.

Was it only the screech of the owl that had saved him? Or would he have stopped himself before he leaped for the man's throat, jaws snapping?

He didn't know. But he wasn't going to give himself the benefit of the doubt. Not when he remembered the hot joy of the hunt.

He felt a tight, choking sensation in his throat. Pushing the accelerator to the floor, he tried to outrun the wolf. But the creature kept pace with him—a part of himself that he could never cast away. The dangerous, primitive part that most men never encountered on a conscious level.

It was different for him. But he had never been under the illusion that he was like most men. He was the outsider. The man who could never completely trust the humans around him—because they would turn against him if they learned his secret. Even Jack Thornton, his friend. Or as close to a friend as he'd ever hoped to have. After Michael had died, Adam had tried to get close to him. But he hadn't responded to his younger brother's overtures. He'd been too depressed, he realized now. Then he'd decided that there was no use in establishing a relationship, when one or both of them was likely to die.

He thought of his father. Another loner, hiding his true self from the world. Was the need for secrecy what had transformed Vic Marshall into a hard, cynical man focused on his own needs and his own pleasure?

In all the years that Ross had hated the man, he'd never thought of his father in those terms. Never felt any sympathy for him. Now he wondered if his judgment had been too harsh. He'd taken care of his own—his wife and his children—in his fashion. He'd even let the boys stay home until they got old enough to challenge his authority, Ross thought with a snort, remembering Troy's and his own battles with the Big Bad Wolf.

His mind scrambled to escape from the thought of his home—lost to him forever—and came winging back to Megan.

He'd promised to call her.

His eyes flicked to the clock on the dashboard. Two-thirty. She couldn't be up now, waiting to hear from him. Could she?

She'd forced the promise from him at a vulnerable moment. Which canceled out any obligation, as far as he was concerned.

Pulling to a stop in front of his house, he cut the engine and sat in the darkness, staring out at the familiar landscape. His home.

He had named it Díthreabh. His refuge. As a wolf he could roam his property, letting go of all the human problems that plagued him.

Tonight he had already prowled through the woods— hunting for human prey. And the outcome had brought him to the brink of disaster.

Moving slowly, his body worn out from the physical and emotional turmoil of the night, he limped into the house and found himself gravitating toward the kitchen counter, where he'd tossed Megan's business card. He stared at the white rectangle, remembering the way they'd stood in the kitchen early this morning. She'd hastened across the floor toward him, and he'd taken her in his arms. She'd wanted to kiss him. And more. He had seen it in her eyes, felt it in his blood.

An hour ago he had felt something else in his blood. The killer lust of the wolf. The animal that lived in the same body with the rational man. He'd sworn to control the animal, keep it on a tight leash. Tonight it had broken that leash—leaped out of control with a savage fury that had frightened him to the depths of his soul. If he had a soul.

Was he human—or animal?

Despair choked him, cutting off his breath. He didn't know how to find his humanity. Not tonight.

Not tonight. When he felt as if he were standing alone on a desert island in the middle of an endless ocean.

Then, from somewhere in the depths of his consciousness, an old Simon and Garfunkel song floated into his mind: "Bridge over Troubled Water." He thought of the words, then thought of that bridge—stretching, stretching across a wind-tossed ocean to the lonely island where he stood alone. Megan was on that bridge, running toward him the way she'd come to him in the kitchen, her eyes so large and beautiful, looking at him. Ross Marshall.

She'd reached for him, and he'd clasped her in his arms. A man holding a woman. As simple as that.

With a sound of pain that rose from deep inside him, he snatched up the card, then pulled the phone from his pocket. Feeling a need, a desperation that was almost beyond control, he lifted the receiver to his ear and punched the On button.

After four days of lying in a pile of leaves in the woods, the phone was stone-cold dead, and a curse rose to his lips.

Striding down the hall to the office, he dropped into the desk chair and reached for the charger—with its extra battery. When his fingers closed around the spare, he breathed a sigh of relief. Inserting it into the phone, he listened for the dial tone, then punched in Megan's number. After switching the light off again, he leaned back in the comfortable chair and closed his eyes.

She answered on the first ring, and a feeling of warmth and gratitude flooded through him when he heard her voice. "Ross. Thank God."

She sounded relieved, the relief tinged with other emotions that brought a painful pressure to the region of his heart. She was worried and angry, and he longed to soothe her. "How did you know it was me?" he asked softly.

"Who else would keep me awake, waiting for him, until . . . almost three in the morning?"

"You're angry."

A breath sighed out of her. "Well, I was worried. I thought of calling you. Then I realized that would be a bad idea."

The way she said it increased the painful pressure in his chest. "I just got back. I told you I was going to be late."

"Did you run into a problem?" she asked anxiously.

"No," he lied, because he hadn't called to worry her. He had called because she was the only person in the world who could ease the aching knot of tension in his chest.

"You have the phone? You're all right?"

"Fine," he answered automatically. He was far from fine, on a number of different counts, but he wasn't going in to them. "You should get some sleep."

"I'm okay."

He'd fulfilled his obligation. He ought to let her go to bed. Instead he sat there, his hand tightening around the phone, held captive by his own blind, selfish needs. He couldn't hang up. And he couldn't handle the depths of his feelings, either. So he pretended to himself that the needs he felt were on some safe, superficial level. The same needs he'd felt with other women. "What are you wearing?" he heard himself asking.

"What?"

"Never mind." Bad idea.

"A T-shirt and . . . panties."

"I was picturing you in a gown. Something sexy," he said into the darkness of his familiar surroundings. He was miles away from her. That made this conversation okay. There was no harm in staying on the line. At least that was what he told himself. "Are you in bed?"

"No, I'm in the living room. On the couch. Where are you?"

"In my office. Are you lying down or sitting up?"

"Lying down."

He imagined the knit fabric stretched across her breasts, her long legs bare and smooth. He didn't know why he was torturing himself with the vivid picture. Again he started to speak before his brain had a chance to consider the consequences. "I wanted to kiss you this morning in the kitchen."

"Yes. It was in your eyes." Her voice hitched. "Then you turned away from me—and I felt . . . desolate."

He made a low, incoherent sound, the words and her voice tearing at him.

For long moments there was only silence on the phone line. He pictured her now. And pictured the look on her face when she'd been standing there with her lips parted. Suddenly being separated from her was more than he could bear. He wanted to touch her. Wanted to hold her. Wanted to get as close to her as possible.

Eyes closed, he pressed his fingers to his mouth, the touch sending tingling sensations through his body as he imagined the sweetness of kissing her. "Do something for me now. Touch your fingers to your lips. Rub them for me," he asked, his voice thickening even as he wondered if she would do it.

On the other end of the phone line, he heard her breathing accelerate. Or maybe it was his own breath rasping in and out of his throat. After several endless seconds he asked, "Did you do it?"

"Yes."

"Your soft lips," he murmured, imagining the feel of them against his.

She gave a shaky laugh. "Not soft. Chapped."

Her laugh only increased the tension coursing through him. He had told himself he needed to feel connected to her. He was feeling that, all right.

"If I touch my lips, you have to do that, too," she whispered.

"I already did."

"Oh!" Then, "Did it feel good?"

"Yes." He drew in a gasp of air, let it out in a rush. It felt intoxicating. So much better than the pain he'd felt earlier in the evening.

"Is this something you like to do with women? I mean have phone conversations like this?" she questioned, her tone a bit shaky.

"I've never had a phone conversation like this."

"Neither have I."

"Good. That's good."

"You have a very sexy voice."

"Do I?"

"Don't you know? Your voice turned the fifty-year-old administrative assistant at Bio Gen into a quivering mass of marshmallow cream."

He laughed.

Silence stretched again. Then she asked, "Ross, what are we doing, exactly?"

He considered the question. "Getting as close as we can to each other without being together. Don't try to distract me with the fifty-year-old secretary at Bio Gen. Are your eyes opened or closed?"

"Closed," she whispered.

The image in his mind had changed. Now her neck was arched up, pale and vulnerable for his pleasure. "If I were there, I would nibble my way along your jaw, your neck."

"Oh."

"Nip you with my sharp teeth," he said in a low growl, waiting to hear her response. She drew in her breath, quick and piercing.

His voice turned to honey in the darkness. "Touch your fingers there for me—stroke your neck."

"Oh!" she said again, this time with more force.

"You like that?"

"Yes."

He was reckless now. Somewhere along the line, the conversation had gone out of control like a train with no brakes speeding down the tracks. "I want to touch your breasts. I want to cup them. Feel their weight in my hands." Again her little gasp egged him on. "I want to rub my hands back and forth across your nipples. Make them hard so that they stab against my palms," he said, his body clenching from the intensely tactile images he'd painted.

He heard a high sound escape from her, part arousal, part protest. "I shouldn't be letting you do this."

"Do what?"

"You know what you're doing to me."

"Do I? Tell me."

"No."

"Arousing you?"

"You know the answer to that."

Unable to stop, he pushed a little further. "I want to touch you, but I can't. You have to do the touching for me."

"Don't ask me to do that."

"Why not?"

"It's indecent," she said in a whispery voice that feathered along his nerve endings like fire.

"You've never touched your own breasts? I mean, because it felt good?"

Her voice quavered. "Don't ask questions like that. And don't ask me to do anything else now."

"Are you embarrassed that I'm turning you on like this?"

"Yes."

The admission fueled his reckless need. Heedless of the consequences, he demanded more from her. "All right, but I don't have to ask, do I? You can feel it anyway. In your breasts. Between your legs."

"Please . . ." He heard a desperate note in the plea.

"What do you want? Do you want me inside you?"

He needed to hear her say it. Needed to know she was as hot and wanting as he.

She made a strangled sound. He heard her suck in a shaky breath, then let it out in a rush. "You have to stop."

"Say it."

"Ross, I can't handle this."

He blew out air, shifted in the chair, trying to ease the ache in his groin as he imagined his body covering hers, imagined himself plunging into her.

There was a roaring in his ears—the sound of her breath coming hard and fast, matching his.

When she spoke again, her voice was low, barely above a whisper. "Why did you start this?"

Because I'm frightened of what I might do to Arnott. Because I'd rather play games with you than think about wanting to rip his throat out.

"Because it feels good," he growled.

"Yes. But it's . . . bad."

"Does it feel bad?"

"It feels wicked."

"No."

She was silent for several moments; when she spoke again, there was a measure of control in her voice. "You said what we were doing was getting close."

"Um-hum."

"You meant you wanted to create physical sensations. You didn't mean you were going to tell me any more about yourself than you already had."

It was his turn for silence. She was right. He hadn't been thinking in terms of revealing his secrets. He had only thought about how talking intimately to her on the phone had eased his pain. Turned his thoughts away from the fears that haunted him.

"Ross?"

"I shouldn't have started this."

"All you want from me is sex?"

"Yes," he lied, closing his fingers around the phone so hard that the knuckles whitened. He refused to let her glimpse his vulnerability, but he couldn't stop his mind from spinning back to what he'd been feeling when he'd dialed her number.

"Then I'm going to hang up now."

"Wait." The plea rose to his lips before he could call it back.

He heard silence on the other end of the line and felt a stark panic at the thought of her severing the connection. "Are you there?"

"Yes."

Relief sighed out of him.

"Tell me something about Ross Marshall."

He held back a laugh, knowing she would run screaming in the other direction if he gave her what she thought she wanted. Still, he scrambled for something to say, something that would keep her on the line without giving too much of himself away. "I make my living as a private detective."

"I know that. Are you the one who remodeled your house?"

"What makes you think so?"

"I was in your workroom when I was looking for something to unlock the bedroom door. I saw all your tools. And a lot of wood and stuff."

"Okay, yeah. I remodeled the house."

Her voice turned warm. "I love what you did with it. The bookshelves in the great room are wonderful. Do you call it a great room?"

"Yes."

"And the kitchen. I love the kitchen."

"Thanks."

"The bathroom is the only thing I'd change."

He gave a small laugh. "You don't like soaking tubs?"

"Those big windows with no shades are a little disconcerting."

"I like soaking in the tub and looking out at the woods."

"Are you the one who plants the flowers? Or do you have a gardener?"

"You noticed a lot of stuff."

"Um-hum."

"I do it. It relaxes me." Then, "Now I get to ask some questions. How did you get into medical research?"

"I found out I'm not all that good with patients."

"You were good with me."

She hesitated for a moment. "I get too . . . involved."

"Like with me."

"No. With you it was something more."

She was giving him an opportunity to take the conversation in a different direction. Instead he asked, "Where did you grow up?"

"I grew up in Boston. My sister still lives there."

"What about your folks?"

"My parents were killed in a car crash about a year ago."

"I'm sorry."

"I miss Mom."

"But not your dad?"

"He was the kind of guy who had to get his way." She paused, then went on. "And when the least little thing was out of his control, he . . . made life hell for Mom."

He sucked in a breath. "That sounds like my old man."

"Does it?"

"Yeah. I warned you to stay away from me."

"You're not your father," she murmured.

"I'm more like him than I want to be," he admitted in the darkness.

"Don't beat yourself up."

"Why not? I came within a hairbreadth of . . ."

"Of what?"

"Killing the bastard who was shooting at me again," he admitted.

"He was shooting at you! Oh, God, Ross. You said you didn't have any problems."

"Well, I was lying. I almost killed him."

"In self-defense."

He sighed, feeling as if he were back where he'd started. "We'd better hang up. You have to go to work in the morning."

"Ross . . ."

"What?"

"You're a good man."

He gave a hollow laugh. "You don't know me."

"I learned a lot about you in the past few days."

"Didn't I pull a gun on you five minutes after we met?"

She came back with an immediate excuse. "You were delirious."

"Okay. Right. See what happens when I can't control my impulses?"

"You risked your life tonight going after a very bad man."

"How do you know he's so bad?"

"He runs around shooting people. And you told me he's murdered women."

"Did I?"

"Yes."

"What else did I say?"

"Nothing."

He wondered if she was telling the truth. He might have pressed her, but the emotions churning inside him had become too raw for him to continue the conversation. "You need to get some sleep."

"I don't want to get off."

The way she said it started an ache deep in the pit of his stomach. "Get some sleep," he repeated, then said, "Good night, Megan." Before she could answer, he broke the connection. For the second time tonight, he'd been out of control.

The first time the sound of an owl screeching had snatched him back to sanity. The second time . . .

The second time, it was Megan who had taken control.

CHAPTER

FOURTEEN

WHEN THE ALARM buzzed at seven, Megan turned it off and gave herself an extra half hour to doze, then lay in the gray light of morning, taking a physical and mental inventory.

Physically she felt better than she had any right to feel after staying up so late and worrying. Mentally, she wasn't so sure.

In the smug little world she'd occupied until a few days ago, she'd never understood why people would engage in phone sex. The idea had always seemed perverted. But she'd certainly let Ross turn her on over the phone. Maybe because she'd allowed physical attraction to a man she didn't really know overwhelm her. A man who was as mysterious and frightening as he was sexy. A man who had told her he thought he had some strange genetic disease that she suspected she wasn't going to find in the medical books.

That alone should send her running in the other direction. But she'd found running away wasn't as easy as it should have been. Whether either one of them wanted to admit it or not, they were involved. On a level that was more intimate than anything she'd felt before.

That was scary. Pulling back from the thought, she deliberately started thinking about the blood sample that she'd been incubating overnight. This afternoon she could get to the next phase of the test—looking at his chromosomes, she thought with a mixture of anticipation and dread.

She was glad that Walter wasn't around when she arrived at the lab, glad that she had routine stuff to do until she could get to the next step in the karyotype.

JACK was working his way through a stack of reports when the phone on his desk rang.

"Thornton," he answered.

"This is Ross Marshall."

"How's it going?" he asked, feeling a small pang of guilt. He'd been investigating the man all week and now knew a great deal more about him than he had the last time they'd talked.

"I'd like to meet you for lunch."

Interesting. Marshall hadn't contacted him in at least six weeks. Now, in the middle of the Crawford investigation, the PI was making a point of getting in touch. Of course, unless Marshall was clairvoyant or had some hidden source of information in the department, there was no way he could know about the body that had washed out of the ground up at Sugar Loaf Mountain.

"Sure. Where and when?"

"How about that Middle Eastern restaurant where we met last time? Across from Congressional Plaza."

He remembered the place. Not one of the glitzy eateries that paid for an address on Rockville Pike but a more modest establishment where the decor ran to travel posters from Jordan. But the food was plentiful and good.

"Sure. I can be there at twelve-thirty."

In fact, he made a point of arriving early and settling himself in a booth at the back of the smoking section where he could study Marshall as he arrived. Outwardly, he was confident that he looked relaxed. But his nerves were jumping.

The PI walked into the restaurant at the appointed time, wearing jeans, a dark T-shirt, a leather jacket, and a tight look around his eyes and mouth. He was limping slightly, too.

He spotted Jack and started toward him, favoring his right leg. Before he'd taken ten steps, he stopped and rubbed his eyes. By the time he drew abreast of the table Jack had taken, he was coughing.

Casting a glance at a guy two tables away who had left a cigarette smoldering in an ashtray while he ate his baba ganoush, Ross asked, "Do you mind changing tables?"

"Right. You're allergic to smoke," Jack said, as if he'd forgotten. The choice of tables had been deliberate, since he'd wanted to watch the effect of a little stress on Marshall. Sliding out of the booth, he pointed toward a corner table on the opposite side of the room. "What about over there?"

"Fine."

When they were settled, he gave his luncheon companion a closer look. In addition to the red eyes, the limp, and the tight features, his complexion was pale.

"You okay?"

"I picked up something on an investigation—in the woods at night. How are you?"

"Good. Haven't heard from you in a while," he answered conversationally.

"I've been busy."

Jack didn't· bother to ask for clarification. He'd learned long ago that Marshall only gave out the information he chose to share.

"So what have *you* been up to?" the PI asked.

"Well, you remember the case of the hidden videocamera in the ladies' dressing room at the YMCA? A couple of county councilwomen use the place, so we've had a lot of R, J, and F A on that one." R, J, and F A was running, jumping, and fucking around. In other words, outward signs of great activity where nothing is really accomplished.

Marshall laughed. "Yeah. I was feeling sorry for you when that hit the papers. I take it you haven't caught the enterprising voyeur?"

"Well, we figure the camera was installed when the building was remodeled. There were workmen and contractors in and out for nine months. So we've narrowed it down to about three hundred suspects."

Marshall shook his head, then opened his menu and studied the selections. When the waiter came over, he ordered a combination lamb and chicken shish kebab, rare, with rice pilaf.

Jack ordered a beef kebab, medium, still thinking about how to play the interview. The element of calculation made him feel guilty. He hated wondering if Marshall had had something to do with the death of a scumbag serial killer five years ago. What did it matter how Crawford had died, really? Eliminating him had been a public service.

Still, there was a nagging voice in the back of his mind as he took a sip of water. The file had landed on his desk. And his job was to close as many cases as possible.

Marshall glanced up and caught Jack's speculative gaze. His shoulders tightened. "What?" he asked.

"I was just thinking that whatever you picked up on that investigation must have been a doozy."

"Yeah, it's hanging on."

Jack shifted in his seat. "You've got something for me?"

Before Marshall could answer, the waiter brought their food, and they were both silent until the man had left them alone again.

Marshall cut a piece of rare, marinated beef in half and forked up a piece.

Jack tucked into his own meal.

After finishing several pieces of meat, Marshall reached into his jacket pocket, brought out a folded piece of paper, and pushed it across the table.

When Jack unfolded it, he found a man's name at the top.

Donald Arnott, 5962 Newcut Road. Security guard, Montgomery Mall. White male. Thirty-five. Brown and brown. Five eleven. One hundred seventy-five pounds. Owns several guns, including a hunting rifle and a compact machine gun.

Underneath Arnott's description were the names of five women. Two, Penny Delano and Charlotte Lawrence, he recognized as missing persons cases. One recent, another from about five months back. The three others were unfamiliar. Lisa Patterson. Cindy Hamilton. Mary Beth Nixon.

"Arnott moved here about eight months ago," Marshall said. "Before that, he was living in Paoli, Pennsylvania. You'll find missing persons reports on three of the victims up there. There are probably others."

"You're telling me Arnott is responsible for Delano and Lawrence?"

"Yeah."

"But you can't prove it?"

"I was on his property a few nights ago. There were shallow graves. They're probably gone by now."

"He spotted you prowling around?" Jack asked, his cop's mind making rapid connections. Marshall was limping. He said he'd caught something on an investigation. The implication was that he'd caught a cold or the flu. But what if he'd caught a bullet and managed to patch himself up without medical attention? Was that what had happened? A bullet in the leg? A shot low on the body. Maybe Arnott had come upon him down on the ground, digging for evidence. And somehow he'd gotten away. As he debated proffering the hypothesis, Marshall started speaking again, his voice hard.

"He knows somebody's on to him. Which is why you have to act quickly, before he decides to pull up stakes and try his luck somewhere else."

"You've got a personal interest in this?"

"I was hired to find one of the women, Penny Delano. When the police drew a blank."

"She disappeared after work at Montgomery Mall one evening. Nobody saw her leave. There was no evidence to go on. She'd broken up with her boyfriend a few weeks earlier, but he had a rock solid alibi for that night. And we don't have any other leads."

"Arnott is a security guard at Montgomery Mall. I know she was in his vehicle."

"How?"

"I have my methods."

"Which you aren't going to share."

"I don't have the same constraints that you do. He's got a Land Rover with a ring bolted to the back of a fold-down rear seat. My guess is that he uses it to restrain his victims when he carts them home. He's probably got handcuffs to go with it."

Jack winced. "We can't search without probable cause."

"I know. I'm hoping that if you tail him, you'll come up with something. I'm also hoping you can stop him before he does it again."

"Not like Edward Crawford." Until the moment he mentioned the man's name, he hadn't been sure he was going to bring up the unsolved murder.

Marshall didn't move, but the blood drained from his face. "What about Edward Crawford?"

"You were investigating him five years ago."

"What about him?" Marshall repeated.

"His body turned up at Sugar Loaf Mountain."

The PI shifted his legs under the table. "I always wondered what happened to that bastard. What was the cause of death?"

"Undetermined."

Marshall nodded.

"You gave Ken Winston some information—but he didn't use it. Then another woman was killed. That must have been frustrating."

"Winston made it clear he didn't want any help from me."

"So what would you do if I didn't act on this tip you're giving me now?"

"I'd be disappointed, because I think we have a good working relationship. And I'd be angry when Arnott took another victim."

"Will he?"

"You know he will."

"You told me you're not bound by the same rules I am. Would you try to stop him if I can't?"

"If you mean, would I try to get evidence that you can use, the answer is yes. If you mean, would I kill him to stop him, the answer is no, because that would put me on his level," Marshall said, his voice low and firm. His eyes bored into Jack's as he sat there on the other side of the table, waiting for the next question.

Jack elected not to ask it, and Marshall picked up his knife and fork and cut another piece of marinated lamb.

After he'd chewed and swallowed, he came back with a question of his own. "So what kind of condition was the body in?"

"Skeletal remains. Apparently mauled by some large animal."

"How long has he been dead?"

"The ME thinks about five years."

"So he died right after he disappeared."

"Yeah."

Marshall leaned back in his chair. "Interesting," he said, both his tone and his hand steady as he took a drink of water.

*   *   *

MEGAN'S hand shook slightly as she washed the slide of Ross's tissue with a salt-detergent solution.

Get a grip, she ordered herself. *You've done this a hundred times.* But she hadn't done this analysis on genetic material from someone she'd gotten to know personally, someone whose deep, sexy voice had aroused her over the phone the night before.

Someone she would be speaking to again after she finished this analysis—unless she chickened out and gave the job to Hank.

Lips pressed together, she added a series of dyes designed to make the details of each chromosome stand out. There were two basic classes of chromosome aberrations, numerical and structural, one or the other found in association with many abnormalities of development: Turner's syndrome, Klinefelter's syndrome, fragile X syndrome, complex malformation syndromes.

With the advent of chromosome banding techniques in the 1970s, it was possible to identify with certainty all chromosome pairs and to characterize more accurately abnormalities of number and structure. She was looking for either or both, although Ross had told her she wasn't going to find anything that had already been described. But she'd check that out for herself.

While the traditional method of analysis was very labor intensive, she had access to an automated system that used an interferometer similar to ones employed by astronomers for measuring light spectra emitted by stars, with the results analyzed by a computer program and displayed on a monitor.

Afraid of what she was going to find, she waited for the computer to complete the analysis, then looked at the screen, prepared to settle down to the process of checking for any of the known abnormalities. What she saw made her jaw drop open.

After glancing over her shoulder to make sure nobody was standing behind her, she looked at the screen again, touching each set of chromosomes with her finger, counting carefully to verify what she thought she was viewing. The correct number of human chromosome pairs was twenty-three. Ross Marshall had an extra twenty-fourth chromosome. Impossible.

Yet there it was on the monitor. Once more, she made sure that her eyes weren't playing tricks on her. But the results were the same. No mistake in her counting.

Had the computer program made some kind of error? Carefully she went through the steps of the procedure again, waiting with her pulse pounding in her temples for the analysis to finish. The picture on the screen was the same one she'd viewed a few minutes earlier.

She knew of abnormalities caused by an extra chromosome, but the anomaly was always an extra one of the known chromosomes, like the extra Y chromosome responsible for a documented type of violent-aggressive male personality. She had never heard of a case of a totally undocumented twenty-fourth chromosome.

After saving the analysis onto a disk, she exited the program, went back to her desk, and sat down. Glancing at Hank, she saw he was bent over his computer. Ordinarily she wouldn't hesitate to confide in her colleague when she found something as startling as what she'd just seen. But this was different. Walter had given her reason to worry about Hank's research skills. And even if he hadn't, what she'd found out about Ross was something she didn't want to advertise.

Still, she needed confirmation that her results weren't out of whack. "Can I ask you a question?"

Hank looked up, blinked as though coming out of a fog.

"Sorry to interrupt you."

"It's okay. What do you need?"

"The cytogenetic analysis equipment—have you used it this morning?"

"Yeah. I did a couple of workups."

"And you didn't have any difficulties with the computer system?"

"Uh-uh. You got problems?"

"Not really. I was just checking," she said lamely.

He gave her a considering look, and she thought he was going back to his work. Instead he said, "Are you mad at me or something?"

"What?"

"You've kind of been avoiding me since yesterday."

"Have I?"

"We usually joke around about stuff. You've been . . ." He shrugged. "I don't know. It's like you've withdrawn or something."

He was right, of course. But she didn't know what to say—couldn't tell him that Walter's accusation had tainted her image of him.

"I'm sorry," she murmured. "I guess I'm kind of preoccupied with some personal stuff."

He nodded, stared at her for a few more seconds, then went back to his computer. She looked at the phone, thinking that her next step was to call Ross. But not in front of Hank. She'd wait until he left for lunch.

ROSS slid behind the wheel of his Grand Cherokee, turned the key in the ignition, and looked behind him before easing out of his parking space. His movements were slow and careful, as if he were afraid that he would make a mistake and Jack Thornton would come running out of the restaurant to give him a traffic ticket.

Thornton was still inside. In the men's room. And Ross was making his escape.

There hadn't been a great deal of conversation after the detective had asked how far Ross might go in his quest to stop a man like Arnott—or Crawford. Somehow Ross had forced himself to keep sitting in his chair and calmly finish his lunch—while he felt the walls of the restaurant close in on him.

Now that he was outside, he was feeling a bit less claustrophobic, but the lunch he'd eaten was as heavy as a bag of sand in his stomach. He'd told Thornton in no uncertain terms that he wasn't going to kill Arnott to put a stop to his activities. But he'd come within a hairbreadth of doing just that last night.

And if he'd come that close, well . . .

Ignoring the pain in his gut, he deliberately went back to the conversation with Thornton—the other part, about Crawford.

With as much objectivity as he could manage, he analyzed the exchange of information and the probable consequences. The detective had let him know that Crawford had died five years ago, that his body had been found, that the cause of death was unknown—and then watched him for reactions.

After that, the police detective had answered questions about the body and the crime scene. The killer's flesh had decomposed, so there was no evidence that his throat had been ripped out. No fiber or trace evidence on the body, if there ever had been any. That is, if Thornton was telling the truth. Which he might not be. Because when a cop was interrogating a suspect, he was likely to lie like hell.

But what would knowing the cause of death prove? Only that a large animal with sharp teeth had killed Crawford. Not a man.

And not a man who could change himself into a wolf. Because any police detective who tried to pin the crime on a werewolf was in for a long session with the department shrink.

The chain of logic made Ross relax a little. Finally able to think of something else besides the meeting with Thornton, he reached into the pocket of his jacket, took out the phone that he'd turned off before going into the restaurant, and checked for messages.

There was one. From Arthur Delano, Penny Delano's father—the man who'd hired him to find his daughter. What timing!

"I don't want to keep pestering you," the man had told the answering machine. "But I haven't heard from you in a couple of weeks, and my wife and I were wondering if you've found out anything new about our daughter. So if you could give me a call, I'd appreciate it. Our phone number is 301-555-4976."

He stabbed the brake pedal, pulling up short at a red light. He was sure Penny was dead. But there was no proof yet, and he didn't want to give the parents that kind of news without being positive. Confirmation would have to come from Thornton—if he trusted the information Ross had given him.

He scrubbed his hand over his face, then punched in the numbers.

Arthur Delano answered immediately. "Hello?"

"This is Ross Marshall. I have a message to call you."

"Thank you for getting back to me. At least you return phone calls."

Hating to leave the man twisting in the wind, he said, "I'm sorry that I don't have any definite information for you, sir."

"Definite information?"

Ross sighed. "I'm hoping to have something for you in the next few weeks."

"We've already been waiting weeks."

"I know. And I wish I could alleviate your anxiety." The words sounded hollow in own ears. He wanted to do something more for this man, but his hands were tied.

"We were assured that if anyone could find our daughter, you were the one. I guess we were being optimistic when we hired you."

A horn honked behind him, and he jerked across the intersection. "I've been working on the case. I've given information to the police that I hope will have some positive results. If you'd like, I can return the retainer you've given me."

Delano thought it over for several seconds. "No. You

might as well keep the money. You might as well keep working for us."

"I'm sorry, sir. I wish I had more I could give you at this time."

There was another hesitation on the other end of the line. "Will you just tell me one thing? Please? Do you think there's any chance that Penny will be found alive?"

Ross debated for a moment, then answered, "Honestly, no."

"I won't tell that to my wife. But I appreciate your being straight with me."

"I wish I could give you better news."

"Please tell us the moment you know anything definite."

"I will, sir."

He hung up, driving automatically. When he almost smashed into the back of the Honda in front of him, he decided it was time to get off the road. Pulling into one of the shopping centers that lined the pike, he found a parking space and sat with his eyes fixed on a furniture display window.

Christ, there were things about this job that he utterly detested. It was gratifying when you could come back to a family with the good news that you'd located their missing relative. It was hell when the only thing you could give them was confirmation of a death. Which was what he was going to have to give the Delanos eventually—but not until Jack came through for him.

While he was still sitting in the parking lot, the phone rang again. Pushing the Receive button, he found himself talking to Megan.

All she had to do was say his name in a slightly breathy voice and he felt his heart speed up as he remembered the previous night's conversation.

"What can I do for you?" he managed.

"I need to talk to you about the chromosome analysis."

Of course. There'd been so much else on his mind that he hadn't been thinking about that at all.

"You've got some information for me?" he asked, striving to mask his sudden tension.

"I'd rather not go into it over the phone. Uh . . . could we talk in person? Can you meet me at the lab?"

He felt a fine sheen of perspiration bloom on his skin. "You remember I didn't want to come to the lab in the first place?"

"Right." She was silent for several seconds. "Uh . . . my house?"

That wasn't a great alternative. But where? Not a public place like the restaurant where he'd just talked to Thornton. Not when she had some very personal information.

"The lab's better," he answered grudgingly. "But could we make it after hours?"

"All right. What about six o'clock?"

"Okay."

They hung up, and he sat there, feeling a pulse pounding in his temple. She'd found something. Something abnormal.

But why was he surprised? He'd known that all along, hadn't he?

CHAPTER
FIFTEEN

NERVOUSLY MEGAN CHECKED her hair in the ladies' room mirror, then applied a touch of lipstick,
powder, and blusher.

Peering at her reflection, she saw the brightness of
her eyes, the slight flush of her skin.

Despite what she might have told herself in the
morning, she was excited about seeing Ross Marshall
again. And worried. Partly because their relationship
was strangely tangled on a personal and professional
level, and partly because she wondered how he would
react to the news she had to give him. Would he tell
her any more about the effect of the syndrome or the
men in his family? Or was he going to clam up?

And why should she care so much?

Opening the door to the ladies' room, she stepped
into the hall and started decisively toward her office.
Before she'd taken half a dozen steps, she heard the
drumming of rain on the roof of the building. And suddenly she remembered stopping to fill the car with gas
on the way to work, spilling some on the pavement,

and tracking it into the car. She'd rolled the window on the passenger side partway down to get rid of the smell. And she was pretty sure she hadn't remembered to roll it back up again.

Damn.

It wasn't supposed to rain today. Just her luck.

She took a quick look at her watch. Ross wasn't due for another ten minutes. She probably had time to dash outside and close the window before he came.

The rain was coming down pretty fast, and thunder rumbled in the distance. Stepping into the lounge, she snatched up the umbrella that she'd forgotten to take home the week before.

The front door was still unlocked, and as she turned the knob, the wind snatched the door away from her and flung it wide.

The lights in the parking lot must be out, she thought, fumbling with the umbrella as she stood in the doorway, the rain coming down in sheets so thick that she couldn't see more than a couple of feet in front of her face.

She was considering going back for the flashlight on her desk when a dart of movement caught her eye. Turning her head, she saw a man materialize out of the rain and darkness—a man hurtling purposefully toward her.

There was hardly any warning before he crashed into her, almost knocking her to the wet ground. The still-unopened umbrella sailed out of her hand and onto the grass, and she gasped, stumbling on the water-slick sidewalk, numb with shock as arms fastened around her body, pulling her close in a parody of an embrace.

He was taller than she, and too close for her to see anything. But she felt him, solid and menacing in the darkness.

Rain pelted against them, drenching her hair before he pushed her against the wall where the overhang gave some protection from the torrent of water.

She began to pound at him with her fists, trying to

make him loosen his hold. But he was wearing something slick like shiny rubber or plastic so that her hands slid off of him, unable to get a grip on the wet surface.

When she finally landed a heavy blow, he grunted. Raising her hands, she tried to claw at his face, his eyes, but his head was covered by some sort of knit fabric—a ski mask, from the feel of it.

He had deliberately hidden his face, and that simple fact spurred her terror. Sensing there was no point in wasting her breath on pleading with him, she simply fought him as he wrestled her to the wet pavement.

Desperately her fingers scrabbled under the edge of the ski mask, and she raked her nails across his neck.

With an angry roar, he slapped a hand across her face so hard her ears rang. Coming down on top of her, he tore at her clothing, his hands on her body in intimate places—high up on her legs, her breasts.

And the scream that had been frozen inside her tore from her throat.

A woman's scream pierced the downpour. Ross had been sitting behind the steering wheel of his car, eyes closed as he waited for the rain to let up enough so that he could dash to the door of the lab. He was still tired from the night before, still weak from the leg wound, and he was half dozing, lulled by the drumming of the rain on the roof of the SUV.

But the scream snapped him to instant attention.

Megan. God, that was Megan. In trouble.

He didn't stop to think, because thought had become impossible. He was already kicking off his shoes, tearing off his jacket and shirt and throwing them onto the seat of the car. Then, leaping onto the rain-slick pavement, he pulled his pants and underwear off and kicked them under the car even as the words of transformation rose in his throat.

"Taranis, Epona, Cerridwen. *Gá. Feart. Cleas. Duais. Aithriocht. Go gcumhdaí is dtreoraí na déithe thú,"* he shouted into the deluge then repeated the phrase.

He could see nothing through the driving rain. But the wolf would know. The wolf would find her.

He had never felt this urgency, never tried to hurry the transformation. But tonight he pushed the process, the pain searing him as he forced muscle and sinew to respond to his commands.

He picked up Megan's scent even before he was down on all fours and streaking across the strip of blacktop.

MEGAN fought as the assailant dragged her skirt over her hips and clawed at her panty hose.

Dimly, in the back of her mind, she thought she heard the sound of a car door opening and strange words drifting toward her above the pounding rain.

She couldn't understand them, and yet she had the feeling she'd heard them before.

Thunder rumbled in the distance as if nature were providing background music for the attack. The next sound that reached her ears was an animal snarl, deep and dangerous in the darkness. It sent a jolt of awareness through her system, and all she could think was that a hound from hell had come to tear her to pieces.

The attacker must have heard it, too, because his whole body stiffened.

Claws clicked against the pavement. She could still see nothing through the pouring rain, nothing from her position on the ground. But she felt a heavy body crashing into the man on top of her—heard more growling, snapping, snarling, the scraping of claws.

MEGAN'S scent had led him to the struggling figures. She was on the ground. A man was on top of her. Rage coursing through his mind and body, the wolf leaped onto the man's back, jaws snapping, claws digging through slick vinyl to contact flesh.

The assailant gave a cry of pain and terror and sprang away from Megan, his face strange and grotesque in the darkness.

Not a human face at all.

Before the wolf could puzzle it out, the man raised his hand to protect his eyes as he skittered away across the wet pavement.

With a growl the wolf started to leap after him—to finish him off.

Then the woman on the ground moaned, and he knew his first thought must be of her.

Words clawed their way to the surface of his brain. But there was no way to force them from his mouth.

Megan. Talk to me.

Are you all right?

He couldn't speak, couldn't ask the question. He could only stand there in the rain, staring down at her with anxious eyes as she pushed herself up and cringed away from him.

A car door slammed, an engine started, and a car skidded off through the pelting rain. Dimly he realized that he had let the man escape. But that was good, wasn't it? He hadn't killed him. He had gone to Megan instead.

He stood for a moment, choked with a swirl of emotions. Then, backing away, he turned and fled to his own vehicle, shielding himself behind the open door as the words of transformation echoed in his head again. Once more he pushed the process. Once more he intensified the pain, his head spinning with it, his vision blurring.

Then he was standing on two feet—a man, naked in the slackening rain. Reaching under the car, he found his jeans and shoved his legs into the legs before grabbing his shirt and pulling it over his head.

*   *   *

DIZZY, disoriented, Megan scooted back under the shelter of the roof overhang, out of the rain, her hand grasping at the rough surface of the brick wall. Her mind was focused on standing—running. But when she tried to shove herself up, her legs were like rubber, and she flopped back to the pavement with a sob of frustration.

She was making another attempt to coordinate her limbs and her brain when the light in the reception area snapped on, casting a dim glow into the rain and darkness. It was enough for her to see a man's shape filling the doorway.

"No." The cry tore from her throat just as the man came down beside her on the pavement, looming over her.

She was still cringing away when the sound of his voice, his words, penetrated her fear.

"Megan. Megan, are you all right? Megan," he said over and over.

When she realized who it was, a sob welled in her throat. "Ross?"

"Yes. I'm here. I'll take care of you."

She pressed against him, and he scooped her up, carrying her inside the building. Leaning back against the wall, he set her gently down, but he didn't let her go. His arms embraced her, cradling her close, protective and possessive. She burrowed into his warmth, the familiar scent of him, the strength.

"God, Ross," she gasped out, clinging to him, her face burried in his shoulder.

He moved them to the reception room couch, holding her on his lap, stroking the wet hair out of her face. Then his hand touched the sleeve of her blouse, and she realized it was ripped.

"Did he hurt you?" he asked, his voice hoarse.

"No. The dog stopped him. Or was it the wolf?" Unable to meet his gaze, she kept her face pressed against his chest as she asked, "Did I dream that, too?"

She heard him make a low sound in his throat. "Do you want it to be a dream?"

"Yes."

"Then it is."

The confirmation soothed her. Something had happened. Something strange that she had no way to explain. But she didn't want to think about the details. They were far too threatening.

Instead she nestled closer to him. Ross. Ross was here. Not the wolf. Seeming to know exactly what she needed, he rocked her in his arms, leaning back so that her body rested against his. She felt his lips skim her damp hair.

"He was on top of me, tearing at my clothes," she said, gulping.

"He won't hurt you. He's gone," he said, repeating the reassurance, probably because he knew she needed to hear it again.

She nodded, but the thought of what had almost happened stabbed at her, and she made a small sound of protest.

As Ross's arms tightened around her, she lifted her face, stared up into his dark eyes. She could lose herself in those eyes, she thought. Lose herself in him.

For long moments, he didn't move, didn't speak. Then he cleared his throat. "We have to call the police."

She started to protest that she didn't want to talk about it with the police, then realized he was right. "You'll stay with me?"

"Of course."

Pushing herself up, she tried to straighten her clothing and found that the front of her blouse was hopelessly torn and her skirt was sopping. Quickly she walked to the lab and grabbed a white coat and a pair of scrub pants that she sometimes wore when she was working with chemicals that might ruin her clothing.

Ross stood guard at the door, then escorted her to the ladies' room where she changed into the coat and pants and stuffed her ruined clothing inside a plastic bag from the supply closet.

When she came out, he was there, although she'd thought she heard him run down the hall while she was in the bathroom. He stayed beside her as she returned to Betty's desk and stared at the phone, her hand suddenly shaking.

"You want me to do it?" he asked.

"Would you?"

He picked up the receiver, made the call to 911.

"A patrol car is on the way," he said after he hung up.

She nodded, then thought about Walter. "I should call my boss."

"I can take care of it."

She pictured Walter's reaction to yet another disturbance in his ordered way of life. "No. It's better if I do it."

Ross handed her the phone, and she struggled to control her trembling fingers as she punched in Walter's number.

She got his answering machine and was relieved that she wouldn't have to talk to him right away. Instead, she left a message saying that there had been another incident at the lab and to call her as soon as he could.

As she sat on the couch in the reception area, her eyes lifted to Ross, who was pacing back and forth.

She studied him, thinking that he'd been barefoot when they'd first come in. Or was she remembering that right? Because now he was wearing his shoes again.

Her eyes flicked to his jeans and shirt. His clothing was damp, but not as wet as hers had been.

Why not? she wondered, an uneasy feeling gathering in the pit of her stomach.

"What should I tell the police when they get here?" she asked.

"Tell them what happened."

"That you chased him away?"

She saw him swallow. "Yes."

Even as she nodded her agreement, some part of her knew that she was treading on dangerous ground. Unstable ground that could open up and swallow her whole. Instinct urged her to back away, back to where the surface under her feet was firmer.

The wolf . . .

He had stood there, staring at her.

No. *Forget the wolf,* her mind ordered. *You were scared spitless, and you made him up. That's all.* It had to be all, because there was no other way her mind could cope.

ROSS forced himself to stop pacing, forced himself to sit quietly on the couch in the reception area with his arm around Megan. While she'd been in the bathroom, he'd retrieved his shoes from where he'd dropped them before he changed. The underwear he'd shucked off was in the pocket of his coat. Presumably the police weren't going to search him, so there'd be no reason to explain why his underclothes were in his pocket instead of covering his butt.

Now that he had time to think things through, he knew that he'd had no real reason to change into a wolf. Private detective Ross Marshall could have gone after the man who'd attacked Megan. But when he'd heard her scream, animal instinct had taken over. He'd torn off his clothing, changed into wolf form, and leaped on top of the bastard.

Instinct again. The curse of the werewolf. And now he had to deal with the consequences—whatever they were going to be.

At least he hadn't ripped out the man's throat. That was something.

Before he could wander any further down that line of thinking, two uniforms came through the door, introduced themselves as Officer Brant and Officer Martinez, and began taking information from Megan.

They were in the middle of taking her initial state-ment when a detective joined the proceedings. It was Jack Thornton, and Ross's first thought was *Oh, shit*.

CHAPTER
SIXTEEN

JACK STARED AT the bedraggled couple sitting on the sofa in the reception area, Ross Marshall and a woman who had apparently been assaulted outside her office. He was wearing rain-spattered jeans, his leather jacket, and a shirt—the same clothes he'd had on earlier in the day. Her hair was wet and mussed, and she was clutching the front of a white lab coat.

He'd responded to the call because he was working the late shift. From the expression on the PI's face, it looked like he wasn't pleased to see Detective Thornton.

After telling the uniforms they could leave, he studied the couple's posture. Marshall had his arm around her. And she was leaning into him as though she were seeking comfort and protection. Maybe more than that, he thought with sudden insight.

He introduced himself to the woman. "I'm Detective Jack Thornton,"

"Dr. Megan Sheridan," she replied. "And this is Ross Marshall."

"We know each other," Ross interjected.

She looked from one of them to the other. "Professionally?"

"Yeah," Marshall answered.

Jack cleared his throat, addressed her again. "You work here?"

"Yes."

"You're a medical doctor?"

"Yes, but I don't treat patients. My job is research oriented."

"You want to tell me what happened?"

"No. But I will." She pressed closer to Marshall, and his arm tightened around her. "I was working after hours. When I realized the window of my car was open—" She stopped, made a face. "It's still open! Anyway, I got an umbrella and went outside."

"You're not wearing the clothes you had on during the attack?"

She looked down at the lab coat. "No. I put this on because my blouse was torn and my skirt was wet."

"Where are they?"

"In my office."

"I'd like to send them to the lab."

"For what?"

"Trace evidence. Hair. Fibers. Something to help us identify the guy."

She got up, swaying a little on her feet. Marshall was about to jump up and steady her when she lurched away and walked stiffly down the hall.

Jack watched Marshall keep his eyes trained on her until she disappeared through a doorway. "How is she?"

"Shaken up. Not hurt," the PI answered.

Before he could ask about Marshall's role in the incident, she was back carrying a plastic bag, which she set down beside Jack.

"Okay. Sorry for the interruption," he said. "You grabbed an umbrella and went outside."

"Yes, I opened the front door, and it was raining

really hard. I couldn't see more than a couple of feet in front of me. I was thinking about getting a flashlight when a man came out of the darkness and attacked me."

"What did he do exactly?"

She shivered, and Marshall stroked his hand up and down her arm. "He grabbed me, threw me to the ground, and started ripping at my clothes." She stopped, glanced at Marshall, and a look passed between them that Jack wished he could read. "Then Ross got the guy off me."

"Did you pursue him?" Jack asked Marshall.

"He got away."

"Were you in the building?"

Marshall shook his head. "No. I was in the parking lot and heard Megan scream. I came running toward the door, and I could dimly see her struggling with someone on the pavement outside."

"You pulled the guy off of her?"

Marshall's mouth tightened. "Yes."

There was something odd about Marshall's answers. Something that he wanted to understand. But he decided to come back to that later. "Can either of you tell me anything more about the man?"

"He had a ski mask over his face," Dr. Sheridan said. "I know because I tried to claw him, and my hand hit the fabric."

"It was dark. I can't give you many details," Marshall added. "I guess he was something over medium height. Medium weight. I couldn't see his features, of course."

Jack wrote it down, then asked, "What kind of work does Bio Gen do?"

Dr. Sheridan replied, "Genetic testing—mostly for couples who want to know if planning a family is a good idea. Also testing in paternity cases. And I have my own research."

"On what?"

"Myer's disease, a genetic form of macular degeneration that strikes certain individuals in their thirties. The macula is the part of the eye where the vision is sharpest. I'm working on a gene therapy that I hope will arrest further deterioration."

"Gene therapy? Isn't that dangerous?"

"It's gotten some bad press. But what I'm doing is different. I'm using an adenovirus—a modified cold virus—to deliver a normal copy of the gene to the back of the eye. But I haven't gotten to clinical trials, if you're thinking that someone I damaged with my wild experiments came after me."

Again her expression shifted subtly. He waited for her to elaborate, but she apparently didn't have any more to say on the subject.

He turned to Marshall, "And what were you doing at the lab?"

"I was here to meet Megan," the PI answered.

"You mean, for a date?"

"Business."

"Which was?"

"Why is that relevant?"

"Everything's relevant."

"I had asked the lab for genetic testing."

Jack stared at the arm that Marshall kept firmly around the woman's shoulder. "And you and Dr. Sheridan have gotten to know each other well during the course of your professional relationship?"

Marshall was silent.

Sheridan answered. "He and I have gotten close."

Jack burned to explore that simple statement, since he'd doubted that Ross Marshall was close to anyone. It was another thread he had to drop for the moment. "What kind of genetic testing?"

Marshall hesitated, then answered in a low voice. "A family trait that causes high infant mortality."

"And you recently got the test results?"

"No. That was why I came over here."

So was that why he'd been uptight at lunch? Jack wondered, suddenly revising his assessment of their recent conversation. Marshall had been anticipating some bad news from Dr. Sheridan. From a woman he was romantically interested in, of all people. Switching his attention back to the doctor, he saw something was bothering her. Something about his questions? Something about Marshall?

"What else do you want to tell me about?" he asked gently.

She sucked in a breath of air and let it out. "Can we talk off the record?"

"Yeah," he answered, knowing he'd decide when he heard it whether to press her.

"Okay. There was a break-in at the lab yesterday morning."

Marshall's head swung toward her. Apparently this was the first he'd heard of it.

"My boss told me in confidence that someone had been harassing him. A former client who claimed that he'd gotten incorrect test results from us. He said he thought the man had run him off the road a couple of days before that."

"So that's why you wanted me to know it wasn't one of your, uh"—he flipped back through his notes— "macular degeneration patients who came after you."

"Yes."

"Is the information about the former client on record with the officers who investigated the break-in?"

"I don't think so. Walter said he didn't want bad publicity for the lab, so it was better to keep that aspect of it quiet."

Beside her Marshall made an explosive noise. "So he didn't say anything—and tonight something happens to you!"

"It might not be connected," she said in a shaky voice.

"And it might!"

Jack watched the exchange, sure now that whatever else was true, Marshall cared a lot about this woman.

And from the way she was glued to his side, it looked like the feeling was mutual.

She raised her eyes to Jack's. "Please, don't tell Walter that I said anything to you."

"This is bullshit!" Marshall spat out. "You could have been raped because your jerk of a boss is trying to protect the lab's reputation."

"Your boss—Walter what?"

"Walter Galveston."

Jack wrote it down, then asked, "Did he tell you the name of the client?"

"He said some of our records were missing."

"Oh, great," Marshall said, his voice sarcastic.

"Ross—" she murmured.

"Okay, I'll shut up." He stood, paced to the far wall, then came back to the couch, leaving several inches between himself and Dr. Sheridan. She immediately closed the distance separating them.

Marshall gave Jack a direct look. "Do you need anything else from her tonight? Or can she go home?"

"I . . . I don't want to go home alone," she said in a small voice.

Marshall hesitated for a beat before saying, "I'll follow you in my Jeep."

"Will you stay with me?"

Jack saw him swallow, saw his features tighten. He wanted her, but he didn't want to be alone with her? Because of what he'd found out from the tests? Was he lying about not having gotten the results? Or was he just anticipating bad news?

Marshall dipped his head toward her. "I'll stay with you."

Her fingers knit with his, clung. "I'm sorry I'm acting like a wuss."

"You've been through a bad experience," Jack answered. "And Ross will make sure nothing happens to you."

He saw the flash of surprise in Marshall's eyes, then turned his attention back to Dr. Sheridan.

"I've just got a couple more questions. Is the door normally locked after hours?"

She thought about that for a moment. "I assume so."

"And there's no alarm?"

"There is. But it wasn't set, because I was waiting for Ross."

Marshall's jaw muscles tightened. "Which means the guy could have come in here and gotten you—and I wouldn't have known about it."

She acknowledged the observation with a quick nod.

Jack stood, wishing the perp had gotten into the building. Instead he'd caught her outside in the rain—which was going to make the crime scene a nightmare for the techs. "Can you show me the place where the attack occurred?"

She stood, glanced at Marshall, then grabbed his hand as she moved toward the door. In the darkness, she pointed to a spot that was partially protected by an overhang. Which was better than nothing. Maybe there was still some evidence that hadn't been washed away.

"Okay. Thanks. I'll wait for the lab technicians," Jack said.

"Thanks," she answered, sounding grateful that she was being allowed to leave. Then, "Do you think you can catch him?"

"I hope so."

She nodded. "I have to get my purse."

Marshall stayed with her as she retreated down the hallway, then returned. "Who else works here?" Jack asked.

"Our receptionist, Betty Daniels." Sheridan stopped and pressed a hand against her lips. "What if she came in here tomorrow morning and got raped? And Hank—Henry—Lancaster. Dr. Lancaster. He's the other researcher on our team."

"Write down their names and numbers, so I can interview them. And Dr. . . . . Galveston's."

She opened a Rolodex in the receptionist's desk and copied down the information, which she handed to him.

When they'd concluded their business, he watched Marshall checking out the parking lot before allowing Dr. Sheridan outside and escorting her to her car.

Over the three years they'd been working together, Jack had made a lot of assumptions about the PI. All week he'd been rethinking those conclusions. And tonight had given him a lot more to consider.

ROSS followed Megan home, sticking close behind her as she headed toward Gaithersburg. She turned on to a road called Walnut Lane and drove through an older neighborhood with mature trees and enormous lots by today's standards. When she pulled into the driveway of a small, redbrick ranch, he parked several feet behind her.

By the time he joined her in the kitchen, she'd taken off her coat and hung it on a rack near the back door.

Looking at the wide moldings and real plaster walls, he judged the house to be about sixty years old. Somebody had remodeled the kitchen, a bare minimum job, with dark green Formica counters, white appliances, inexpensive white cabinets, and a white tile floor that was probably hell to keep clean.

She'd relieved the monotony with pot holders and tea towels decorated with black-and-white cows. The cow motif was repeated on the salt and pepper shakers and the teakettle. And the wallpaper between the cabinets and the countertop was of a green meadow.

A lot of men probably wouldn't have given the room much notice. But with his remodeling experience, he found the effect both whimsical and charming.

However, he didn't bother to say so as he carefully kept his distance from her. The way she looked—disoriented, bedraggled, haunted—tore at him. He wanted to reach for her, hold her, comfort her, as much to ease the tight feeling in his chest as anything else. But now they were alone, and it wasn't safe to touch her. Especially after last night's phone call. So he kept his arms stiffly at his sides.

"You want some coffee?" Megan asked in a voice that was barely above a whisper.

"I don't drink coffee."

"Right. I forgot. I've got some herbal tea." She turned toward a cabinet near the stove, opened it, and stood staring blindly at boxes of tea. Tonight had been the most terrible of her life, and here she was preparing to make tea, while the man who could help her get through till morning was standing a few feet away.

He had put his arms around her. Soothed her. She needed more than that from him. More than he was willing to give?

The flood of emotions sweeping through her was dangerous. But she disregarded the danger. With a small sound, she swung back around and faced him, unashamed of the naked need on her face.

"Ross. Please. Hold me."

Only a few feet separated them.

She saw the stiff way he stood, as though powerful forces warred inside him. She had come to understand what they were. His need for her—and his silent vow to resist that need.

Last night, when she had been safely out of his reach, he had allowed himself to give rein to his feelings. She understood that. Distance had made him feel safe.

Now . . . the buried fire in his eyes made her bold enough to take a step closer.

When she moved, so did he, step by step, until she could feel his warm breath, then his flesh. At the moment his lips touched hers, the world contracted to the feel of his mouth, his hands on her body.

Last night she had touched her own lips, imagined his kiss—and come alive with wanting him.

But tonight the reality of the flesh and blood man was more potent than the game they'd been playing.

She opened her mouth under his, drinking in the taste of him—the taste of woodlands and dark shadows where magic lurked. Magic she could only dimly imagine. She'd sensed hidden powers within him. Now she knew they came from the earth and the forest.

She made a small, wanting sound, captivated by the feel of his hands on her shoulders, her back, her ribs. When she said his name again, the syllable was lost in the pressure of her lips against his. He shifted her in his arms, eased back against the countertop, splaying his legs to equalize their heights. A strangled exclamation rose in his throat as he pulled her to him so that his chest pressed against her breasts.

Her tongue met his, retreated, came back again to stroke and slide, the contact sending alternately hot and cold shivers over her skin.

She wanted him. Wanted him to drive everything from her mind but what was happening between the two of them.

Her heart raced at a feverish pace, the beat frantic— as frantic as her need to get close to him and closer still.

She wrapped her arms around him, sealed his body to hers, only half aware of the their surroundings. The only thing of importance was the man whose physical presence had imprinted itself on her.

She felt all of him. Hard muscles. Corded arms. Long legs. And the rigid pressure of his erection against her thigh. That wasn't where she wanted him. Squirming against him, she eased into a more intimate position so that his sex was pressed to hers, with only scant layers of fabric separating their heated flesh.

"God, Megan," he groaned, his hips moving rhythmically against hers, his body like a furnace, heating her.

He shifted her in his arms, found her breast with his hand, stroking and pressing through the fabric. Her nipples were already stiff and aching. The touch of his hand sent a quivering wave of need surging downward through her body, and she arched against him.

The clothing had become an intolerable barrier. Her fingers tangled with his as she reached for the buttons on the front of her lab coat.

Her fingers stopped. She caught her breath as a shaft of reality stabbed through her, and she suddenly remembered why she was wearing her lab clothes at home.

Perhaps he felt the change in her. Perhaps he was struck by the same realization, because he moved her away, putting inches of space between them.

She grabbed for his arm, but he was already turning her so that she was standing next to him, pressed to the countertop.

She stared at him, saw his breath coming hard and fast as he stood with his head thrown back and his hands thrust behind him, gripping the counter.

"Ross—"

"No," he said between gasps of air.

"Why not?"

"Because this is the wrong thing for you."

"Ross, let me decide what I want."

"No. You're vulnerable. I'd be taking advantage of you."

Maybe he was right, but she'd wanted him with a desperation that bordered on madness. She stretched out her hand, then let it fall back, keeping her eyes on his face. His features were contorted, and she saw him struggle to relax them.

"Fix the tea," he said in a raw voice.

The strangled sound and the tight look on his face were enough to make her obey. That and her own embarrassment.

She'd started something he wasn't prepared to finish, and she wanted to duck out of the kitchen and flee down the hall. Instead she mechanically filled the kettle, got two tea bags from the box, and put them into black-and-white mugs.

"Sugar?"

"No thanks." He looked like he wished he were anywhere else as he pulled out the chair farthest from her and sat.

The kettle whistled and she busied herself getting their tea.

Then she scraped out a chair on the other side of the table and sat down, cupping her hands around the mug but not drinking.

"Are you angry with me for asking you to hold me?" she asked, her breath frozen inside her as she waited for the answer.

"No."

"Then what?"

"I'm trying to keep my hands off you," he answered, clamping his fingers around his own mug.

"I thought I made it clear you don't have to do that."

"You've been through a terrible experience tonight. You're not in any shape to make sexual decisions."

"Sexual decisions," she repeated, struggling to keep her voice steady. "That sounds so cold."

When he said nothing, she shifted in her seat. "You and I . . . want each other." That was only a shadow of what she was feeling.

Wanting. Not just sexual wanting. So much more. Needs she was powerless to articulate because she'd never imagined them before.

She saw her own needs mirrored in his eyes. But he kept his hands firmly on the mug of tea.

"I told you that getting mixed up with me was a bad idea. Didn't you call me this afternoon because you had some results of the, uh, karyotyping?"

She sighed, recognizing that he was determined to change the subject—to shift the two of them away from the out-of-control passion of a few moments ago. "Yes, I called about the tests."

He'd been slumped in his seat. He sat up straighter, leaned toward her. "And you found something abnormal?"

"Something strange."

When he sat there, still as a statue, waiting, she went on. "You probably know that the correct number of human chromosomes is twenty-three pairs?"

"Yes."

"You have a twenty-fourth chromosome."

"What the hell does that mean?"

"There are two kinds of chromosome abnormalities, and each can cause major problems," she began, striving for detachment. "There can be defects in the structure of the chromosomes. Or there can be an incorrect number. Each kind of abnormality can result in spontaneous abortions, children who die shortly after birth, mental retardation, abnormalities of sexual development. Down's syndrome is caused by an extra twenty-first chromosome."

"What does a twenty-fourth chromosome do?"

"There are no documented cases of a twenty-fourth chromosome like yours. It simply doesn't happen."

"Except in my family."

"It would seem so."

"And it kills the girl babies."

"Apparently. But the males have some kind of protection against the effects. Which must mean there's some interaction between the protein from the Y chromosome and this twenty-fourth one."

When he nodded, she went on. "But with some males, the protection only holds until sexual development begins."

His eyes were alert, and she could see that he was taking it all in.

"Can you do something about it?" he asked.

"I don't know. I'd love to have a fertilized egg to work with, see what happens if we remove that extra chromosome."

When she realized what she'd said, she pressed her fingers to her lips, looked away.

*   *   *

ON the way home Jack thought about discussing the events of the evening with Laura. Then he remembered Laura wasn't waiting for him on the couch in the living room. Two years, and he still felt like a limb had been amputated. She'd been his wife, his partner. She was the mother of his children, and she would never be waiting for him at home again because some damn drunk driver on I-270 had crossed the median and slammed into her car with enough force to ram the engine block into the front seat.

He gritted his teeth, pushed the awful image out of his mind. There was no point in thinking about it, because it wasn't going to do him any good.

Instead of Laura, his housekeeper, Emily Anderson, was in the living room watching a classic movie channel when he came through the front door. But she switched off the set when he walked in.

Thank God for Mrs. Anderson. She was a sixty-year-old widow with steel gray hair, warm brown eyes, and more energy than a lot of women half her age. For the past eighteen months, she'd occupied the spare bedroom at the end of the hall. She was wonderful with the kids, eight-year-old Craig and his six-year-old sister, Lilly.

Jack tried to spend as much time as he could with his children. But sometimes the job interfered. Having Mrs. Anderson made him feel less guilty.

"Another long day," she said, as she bustled into the kitchen and lifted the lid on the pot that sat on a back burner of the stove.

"Yeah." He sniffed appreciatively. "Your Hungarian goulash?"

"Yes. The rice is in the oven."

It was the kind of meal she could serve herself and the kids early in the evening and keep warm for him. The woman would have made a damn good cop's wife if she hadn't been married to an electrician for thirty years.

He opened the fridge, took out the salad she'd set

there, and also pulled out a beer. Popping the cap, he took a long swallow.

A place was set at the kitchen table for him. He dropped into a chair, watching her move about the kitchen, getting his dinner. At sixty, she still kept herself trim. If he squinted through half-closed lids and mentally changed her hair color, he could almost make himself believe it was Laura.

"Do you want some company?" she asked, breaking the spell.

"I'd like that."

She set a mug in the microwave, waited for the water to heat, then added a tea bag and joined him at the table.

"So did Craig get into any more trouble with that Dawson kid he was fighting with at school?" he asked after gulping a couple of mouthfuls of stew.

"Not that I know of."

"And what about the math test?"

"He got a B."

"Great."

"He's really working at his grades this semester."

"I know."

They exchanged a meaningful glance. Last semester Craig had been in trouble almost every week—both for academic and social problems. This semester, he seemed to be settling down.

"Lilly was picked as one of the painters on the new mural in the school lobby," Mrs. Anderson said.

"I'll bet she's pleased."

"Pleased as punch."

She gave him more information about the kids' day, then he gradually slipped into the old routine of talking about his work—because he still needed an outlet, and Mrs. Anderson was willing to listen.

"I had lunch today with Ross Marshall."

"The guy you call the Lone Wolf? The PI who feeds you information?"

He was surprised she remembered, because he

hadn't mentioned Marshall in a couple of months.

"Right. He wanted to talk about a guy he thinks murdered several women in the county."

"And you're going to follow up on it?"

"When he gives me a lead, it's usually solid."

She studied him over the rim of her mug. "But this time you're wondering about it?"

"No." He shifted in his seat. "I went out to take a report from a woman who was almost raped at the biotech lab where she works. Marshall was there."

Her eyes widened. "You mean he attacked her?"

Jack shook his head quickly. "No, he chased the perp away. And it was pretty obvious he and the victim have a relationship."

"You told me he was a loner."

"That's what I thought. But I could see he cares about this woman—and she returns his feelings."

"So why are you still looking so grim?"

There were a lot of reasons. All of them should remain confidential. But he was sure that Mrs. Anderson never talked about his cases, unless the information was already splashed across the front page of the *Washington Post* metro section.

Still, he had to say, "This can't go any further."

"I'm not going to blab to my bridge group—or anybody else."

"I know. The woman's a doctor who does genetic testing. It seems Marshall came to her because he's got some sort of disease or condition. I don't know what."

"Does he seem healthy?"

"Yes. So maybe he's just a carrier." He cleared his throat. "I was doing a background check on his family. Apparently he had a lot of sisters who died at birth. And some brothers who only lived into their teens."

The lines in Mrs. Anderson's face deepened. "That's sad. It would make a man think twice about starting a family."

Jack nodded.

"How did you happen to be looking into his background?"

"His name came up in another context."

"And you're not going to tell me about it."

He wanted to talk about it. He wanted to lay it all out for her and see what she thought because she sometimes came up with surprising insights. But this time there were simply too many factors, too many variables. More than that, it wasn't ethical to tell his housekeeper that Ross was a suspect in a five-year-old murder. So what he said was "No."

She took another sip of her tea, stared at him assessingly.

"You know I hate it when you give me that look," he said, smiling.

"Well, you've piqued my curiosity. But I suppose that if it's anything significant, I'll end up reading about it in the papers," she said primly.

"Yeah, you will."

CHAPTER
SEVENTEEN

MAYBE HE HAD slept sometime during the night, Ross thought as he heaved himself off the couch and folded up the blanket Megan had given him.

He'd lain on the narrow sofa, his body radiating heat and tension. But at least he'd kept himself from going down the hall and opening Megan's door and crawling into bed with her. That had to be some kind of moral victory.

He padded past her door to the bathroom, looked at his hollow-eyed face in the mirror, and rubbed a hand over the stubble on his chin. Although he could see a disposable razor and a can of shaving cream sitting on the edge of the bathtub, he decided it would be presumptuous to use them. Not to mention too intimate, he thought, imagining dragging a razor across his face that had swept up and down the soft, feminine skin of her legs.

But the lure of the shower was too great to ignore. So he found the linen closet, grabbed a towel, and turned on the taps.

The hot water made him feel marginally better. Pulling on jeans and a shirt that were definitely worse for wear canceled out the effect.

Back in the kitchen, he leaned over the sink and peered out the window. It looked onto the street, but he couldn't see much because fog blanketed the area.

Picking up his mug from the table, he used the microwave to warm up the tea he hadn't drunk the night before.

He could hear Megan moving around in the back of the house as he sat at the kitchen table, sipping from the mug.

When the phone rang, she answered in the bedroom. A few minutes later she came into the kitchen, dressed for work and looking upset.

He wanted to hold her again, slide his lips across her hair again. Somehow he managed to keep sitting there at the table as he asked, "How are you?"

"Not great."

He hoped it was because of the phone call—not the attack. "Was that your boss on the line?"

She nodded. "He was in a hideous mood."

"Yeah. Another incident at the lab would do it."

"That. And what I said to the detective. Jack Thornton."

"You mean because you told Thornton somebody had a grudge against the lab?"

She looked down at her hands clasped in front of her. "Walter said he'd talked to me in confidence—that I had no right to bring it up with the police."

"Did you tell him Thornton asked if you could think of any reason for the attack?"

Her hands clenched until the knuckles were white. "I tried to explain what happened. He didn't want to listen."

Her obvious distress tore at him. "The hell with Walter, then."

"Ross, I work for him. It's a small office. It's going

to be impossible to do my job if we're having another conflict."

"What other conflict are you having?"

She sighed. "About the way he's distributing the workload. He wants us to concentrate on jobs that will bring in fees. I want to devote more time to my research project."

"You mean the macular degeneration study? Myer's disease?"

"You remembered the name of it?"

"I'm good at details."

"So am I. I don't have any steak in the freezer. But I can give you eggs."

"Eggs would be good."

"Scrambled."

"Fine. Tell me about your project," he requested, partly because he was interested in anything about her and partly because he wanted to keep the conversation impersonal.

For the next five minutes, as she made the scrambled eggs, she filled him in on her progress so far. He sat at the table, enjoying listening to her enthusiasm when she talked about her research, enjoying the efficient way she worked.

"It sounds like you're close to a breakthrough," he said.

"Yes. Are you keeping me talking because the subject is interesting or so we don't have to deal with anything personal?"

He shifted in his chair, sorry she was so perceptive. "Both."

A little smile flickered around her lips, a smile he couldn't read.

She set down the eggs, several pieces of toast, and a jar of blackberry preserves.

He noted that she'd picked his favorite jam without even asking, then cautioned himself not to make anything of it.

They both reached for a piece of toast at the same

time, both snatched their hands back, but not before he felt a jolt like an electric shock where his flesh touched hers.

She glanced quickly at him, then back at her plate. In the next few minutes of silence, they both managed to eat some of the food she'd prepared.

"Walter asked me if I was going to stay home today."

"Are you?"

"I'm better off keeping busy." Standing, she scraped the rest of her breakfast into the trash, then put the plate in the dishwasher.

He watched the rigid set of her shoulders, knew she was going to say something he didn't want to hear.

"So when I walk out the door, am I ever going to see you again?" she asked.

"I don't know."

"I want to." She moved to his side, laid her hand over his. No pressure, just a gentle touch, but it was enough to make him instantly hard.

She fixed her blue gaze on him, the color seeming to deepen and intensify.

"I've never felt anything like this," she said in a husky voice.

"Like what?"

"Are you going to pretend you don't know what I'm talking about?"

"I guess that would be a waste of time."

"Yes."

"Why are you interested in a man you know has a genetic defect?" he asked.

"Maybe I can cure him."

"It's too late for me. You can't send a virus to the backs of my eyes and make any significant changes."

"No. But the answer could be just as obvious."

"I doubt it. Besides, I can't change what I am."

Her hand pressed his more firmly. "Ross—"

"Why are you interested in a man who frightens you?"

Her chin jutted up. "You don't."

"That's a lie."

"Okay. Maybe I'm tired of playing it safe."

"Don't be in a hurry to sacrifice yourself to the wolves."

He saw a shiver travel over her skin, but she managed to keep her voice steady. "Don't be in a hurry to throw away something that you know is going to be spectacularly good."

He felt his nostrils flare. Somehow he managed to keep from pulling her body tight against his.

She lifted her hand away, took a step back. "If you're not going to communicate with me, I might as well go."

He ignored the editorial comment and said, "I should leave, too."

She shook her head. "You don't have to clear out because I'm going to work. Just make sure the door's locked."

"You shouldn't trust a stranger alone in your house."

"You're not a stranger." She paused, then said, "There's a package of disposable razors in the medicine cabinet and some toothbrushes I got from a drug company, if you want to use them."

"Okay. Thanks." Although he sat back and stared down at his plate, he was aware of her every move as she gathered up her purse and exited.

When she'd left, he felt more relaxed and at the same time more restless now that she was no longer with him.

He was rinsing off his mug when he heard a car slow down in front of the house.

Had she forgotten something and come back? Anticipation leaped inside him as he leaned toward the window and looked out. It was still foggy, but down by the street, twenty-five yards away, he could see a car had pulled to a stop.

Too big and solid-looking to be Megan's, he decided, and the color was wrong—although it was hard to tell exactly what the color was due to the fog and due to the distance.

The mist also made it impossible for him to see who was behind the wheel. The reverse was apparently not true. Almost as soon as he leaned forward to look out the lighted window, the car started up and sped away.

Had the driver been going to knock on Megan's front door—and changed his mind when he saw a man inside?

Or was the explanation something more sinister? Had someone been waiting for Megan to leave the house, waited until she'd driven away, and then planned to come inside—until he'd seen someone at the window?

All this could be a big coincidence, of course, except that Ross had learned to discount coincidences a long time ago.

His eyes narrowed. He didn't like the implications. Yet there was nothing he could do except turn off the light and sit in the darkened kitchen for a half hour longer, hoping whoever was out there would come back. But no cars pulled up in front of the house. So he went to the bathroom and used the toothbrush and razor Megan had offered him.

DRESSED in his gray uniform, Donald Arnott strolled down the marble walkway at Montgomery Mall. He knew he looked good in the outfit—not like some guys who let their muscles go and their guts hang out. There was even one bozo so pudgy that fat oozed over the top of his belt all the way around his considerable circumference. The jerk needed a new uniform. Or, more likely, a new job. But the mall, like every other public place in Montgomery County, had increased its security staff since the World Trade Center and the D.C.-area sniper case. And it needed every guy it could get.

Really, it was easy work. And the threat of a terrorist attack gave him the excuse to come down hard on anybody he wanted. Still, the most action he'd seen all week was a couple of girls shoplifting and a woman nursing her baby on a bench. The mother had pulled her blouse up, exposing her big boob for everyone walking by to see. He'd glared at her, letting her know that nursing babies in public was disgusting.

The incident had made him feel energized enough to volunteer for an extra shift when another guard called in sick at the last minute.

He didn't need the money, of course. He'd lucked out on that score six years ago when Arden Mitchner had tried to buy her freedom with money stolen from her drug dealer boyfriend. While Donald waited in the car Arden had hoisted $500,000 of the guy's lean green. Then Donald had taken her home and killed her.

He'd also cleared out of the Fair Hills area and bought his place near Paoli.

When he'd moved to Maryland, he'd made enough profit on the Paoli house sale for a nice down payment on his present property. So he was sitting pretty. Or he had been, until the bastard with the big dog had showed up to try to ruin his life.

He knew the strong emotions churning through him were showing on his face, but he didn't glance around at the mall's lunchtime crowd. Instead he pulled out his walkie-talkie and pretended that he'd gotten an urgent call while he brought himself under control. Then he moved rapidly down to the second-level balcony. When he reached Indulge Yourself, he slowed, feeling his mood lighten. Sandy Knight worked here, and the thought of what he was going to do to her did wonders for him.

Indulge Yourself. What a wimpy name, he thought as he walked through the door. It sounded like a beauty shop or a cosmetics store. But since this was Montgomery County, where the income was one of the highest in the nation, the shop sold expensive toys for adults. Choice items like three-hundred-dollar leather carry-on bags, briefcases, key rings with real gold golf tees. Miniature electronics.

There were three or four saleswomen who worked there on a regular basis and a couple of part-timers. Sandy Knight was full time. She came out of the back room when she saw him and smiled warmly at him. She was a bleached blonde who'd probably had her boobs surgically augmented. But the effect wasn't bad, if you liked your women stacked. She was twenty pounds overweight, but her ass was tight. Sandy had told him she worked out a few nights a week at a local gym.

Which made her a challenge. He wanted her. But he'd never taken a weight lifter before. Would she turn out to be so strong that he would have trouble restraining her?

He thought not. But he'd get the cuffs on her right away, just to make sure.

He favored her with an ironic grin. "Sold any ridiculously expensive stuff this morning?" he asked.

She laughed conspiratorially. "One of those overprivileged housewives from Potomac came in looking for something to get her CEO husband for his birthday. I sold her a battery-operated mug that reheats the coffee every fifteen minutes and gives stock market quotations."

He rolled his eyes, shook his head.

"And yesterday evening I showed a guy that five-hundred-dollar watch that does everything but pilot your car. He snapped it up. And he also bought one of those phones where you can download music to a little disk and listen all day. Really, people around here have more money than they know what to do with."

"That's the truth," Donald agreed.

When a customer came in, he moved to the side, then out the doorway, sorry to cut his visit with Sandy short. He was going to take her. But not until he solved his problem.

*   *   *

AS Megan drove to work, breathing in the moldy smell from the rain, she felt sweat pooling in her armpits.

When she'd been a little girl and her father had driven her to school on foggy mornings, she'd sat in the car imagining that the school building might have disappeared into the mist. She played the same game now—imagining that the lab might have disappeared. Because she didn't want to go there.

Last night and this morning with Ross, she'd succeeded in blocking out memories of the attack. But the closer she got to work, the more on edge she became.

By the time she pulled into the parking lot, the freshly dry-cleaned blouse she was wearing felt damp and sticky under her coat.

After shutting off the engine, she sat for a long time, unwanted details coming back to her.

It had been dark and wet. The actual physical encounter had caused a rush of confused sensations. Although she hadn't been able to see her assailant's face or take in many details, there had been something familiar about him. Something. She couldn't say what. Yet she had the feeling she knew him.

Was he the angry client who had come in for genetic testing? Had he been waiting for someone—anyone—to come outside? Or was Walter wrong? Had *she* been the one who'd done the interview, handled the test? And was he now out to get revenge on her as well as the lab?

She tried to tell herself that couldn't possibly be true. Still, doubt tore at her as she sat behind the wheel, swallowing to moisten her dry mouth.

It was too much to cope with—that and the wolf that had haunted her since the last night at Ross's house, she finally admitted with a little inward shiver.

The wolf that had come back to haunt her last night.

When an image of the animal leaped into her mind, she lowered her head into her hands and pressed hard against her eyes, trying to wipe away the picture of the animal. But it stayed firmly in her consciousness.

Ripples of cold traveled over her skin, and she rubbed her hands up and down her arms.

The wolf. The symbol that she was coming unglued.

At Ross's house, the wolf had threatened her. And she'd let herself be convinced that the confrontation had taken place in a dream.

But last night had been different. She'd been attacked. And she'd told that cop, Jack Thornton, that Ross had rescued her, although the image in her mind was of the wolf. Snarling, teeth snapping, chasing away the attacker.

In unguarded moments since the assault, memories of the wolf had nipped at *her* heels. So she'd carefully constructed a cage in her mind to keep him trapped. But she couldn't always keep the door closed. And when it sprang open, the way it had just now, the wild animal leaped out, ready to dig his claws into her mind.

Although she struggled to keep him from prowling through her thoughts, his will was stronger than hers.

The wolf had saved her. Then the animal had disappeared into the darkness of the storm. There was a strange, unreal quality to the way he had appeared and the way he had disappeared that left her dizzy—and terrified.

The rational part of her mind wanted to understand what had happened. But the rational part wasn't in control. Because every time she thought about the lithe gray animal with the bright yellow eyes, she had no choice but to make him go away.

Teeth gritted and eyes squeezed tightly closed, she finally succeeded. Briskly she opened the car door and got out. But she knew the simple act of walking from her vehicle to the lab was never going to feel the same. Her body was strung as tight as a wire by the time she reached the roof overhang. She wanted to rush past. But her legs stopped moving, and she stood stock-still—stared at the place where the man had thrown her to the ground.

Her breath caught. Then she moved on, feeling as if she'd passed some kind of invisible barrier.

Stepping through the door was a relief—until she saw that Betty was staring at her, wide eyed.

She stopped in her tracks, fighting the impulse to back away.

"Oh, God, Megan, the police called last night. Are you okay?"

"Yes," she answered, knowing the high, thin tone of her voice made it sound like a lie.

The receptionist continued to study her as if she were trying to determine the truth of the statement for herself. "I'm so sorry."

"I'm fine."

"You stayed late to work?"

"Yes," she clipped out, hoping to cut the conversation short. She'd never liked being the center of attention, and in this context she liked it even less.

"Do you want to talk about it?"

"I had to talk to the police. I don't want to go over it again," she answered, hoping Betty would drop the subject.

"Is there anything I can do?"

"Let's just get things back to normal."

Betty glanced over her shoulder, lowered her voice to a whisper. "With all the bad stuff happening lately, I'm thinking about looking for a new job."

Megan nodded but didn't say she'd been having the same thoughts.

The receptionist prolonged her agony a moment longer by repeating one of her previous statements. "If there's anything I can do, let me know."

"I will," Megan promised, moving past, wishing she could turn the clock back a day and live the last twenty-four hours differently.

Steeling herself for an even more painful confrontation, she made her way down the hall. To her vast relief, Walter's door was closed. Apparently he was inside licking his wounds. Or he'd gotten his wrath out of the way over the phone this morning.

Like Betty, Hank gave her a long look as she came into their office. But after their conversation the previous day, he didn't press for details she didn't want to give. Thankfully, he went into the lab and left her alone.

Which didn't mean she could concentrate on what she was supposed to be doing. Because she couldn't get her mind off Ross, she got out her notebook and wrote down some of the details of yesterday's test.

Then a kind of numbing lethargy blanketed her. Realizing that she'd never had a cup of coffee that morning, she went to the coffee room and poured a mug.

When she returned to her desk, Walter was standing beside her chair, her notebook in his hand, as he thumbed through the notations she'd been keeping on Ross.

Her little gasp of dismay made him turn and look up.

"What are you doing?" she asked.

"I wanted to have a chat with you about last night's incident," he said, his voice cold and hard and his eyes focused directly on her. He sounded angry. Or was he afraid of something?

She swallowed as he continued to stare, as if trying to pick up some hidden cue.

He didn't say, "I'm sorry you were attacked." He didn't ask how she was feeling. God, was he worried that she was going to sue the lab or something?

After several seconds of nerve-racking scrutiny, he continued. "Then I saw this."

Her eyes flicked back to the notebook. "That's confidential. . . ."

"It's not confidential. It's information about the guy from Lisbon—Ross Marshall. Pretty interesting."

"I wasn't prepared to share it with you yet."

"So I gather."

She set the mug down on her desk, sloshing coffee onto the fake wood surface. Reaching for a tissue, she dabbed at the brown liquid.

"It looks like this guy is pretty amazing," Walter went on. "An undocumented extra chromosome. And he's in good physical and mental health? Why the hell didn't you tell me about it?"

"I haven't exactly had time," she hedged.

"Well, you've got the time now. Give me your impressions. If he's got something that other people might want, like accelerated healing, that could mean big money for the lab."

"He's a private citizen. In the first place, you can't appropriate genetic material from him. And in the second place, it's not something people would want. It causes female offspring in his family to die at birth. And only about half the boys survive puberty."

"But if you could alter the unfortunate aspects, you might have something salable."

"He's not a commodity."

"He came to us. The genetic material we tested is our property."

She had no idea if that was true, legally, but she pretended to know what she was talking about. "I don't think so."

He gave her a hard stare. "I want to see the full report on the cytogenetic analysis you did."

"And if I don't want to give it to you?"

"You don't have a choice. You work for me, and anything you do in this lab is my property."

She wanted to protest, but she knew she was already in trouble over what she'd said last night to the police detective. So she silently cursed her stupidity for leaving the notebook where Walter could see it.

Apparently he considered the matter settled. Turning on his heel, he exited the office, leaving her feeling a mixture of relief, anger, and guilt.

When Walter had seen her notes, he'd gotten off track. He hadn't blasted her for the information she'd given Thornton. But now his interest was focused on Ross, and it was her damn stupid fault.

CHAPTER
EIGHTEEN

JACK WAITED UNTIL almost noon before bugging Stan Murray, one of the technicians who had showed up last night. Stan worked for an independent lab that handled a lot of the Montgomery County workload. Which made for quicker results than going through the government bureaucracy.

He'd cultivated a friendly relationship with Stan. Still, he knew he was pushing when he asked, "You got anything for me on that attack outside Bio Gen Labs yet?"

"Jesus, it was raining pretty hard out there, you know. If there was any fiber, saliva, skin cells, or hairs from the perp, they're probably in a storm drain on their way to the Chesapeake Bay by now."

"What about the bag of her clothing I gave you?"

"I was waiting for you to ask me that. If I had to guess, I'd say the perp was wearing a raincoat. I do have a little bit of wool fiber."

"From his ski mask."

"There was one thing we picked up from the spot

where he threw her to the ground. Dog hairs over near the edge of the building, where the overhang kept some of the rain off. Maybe she was attacked by a German shepherd."

"She said it was a guy."

"Yeah, I guess it would be hard to mistake a dog for a guy. Maybe she was rescued by a Saint Bernard."

"Or she owns a dog."

"The hairs weren't on her clothing. They were on the ground."

"There's a wooded area near the lab. Maybe the dog's a stray, and it was sleeping next to the building sometime in the near past. Or maybe someone who came to the lab for testing left his dog outside. Are you kidding about German shepherds? Saint Bernards? Or do you know what kind of dog hairs?"

"Well, it is something like a shepherd, or a shepherd mix. They're dark gray with light tips. Want me to send them to the FBI?"

"No. Thanks for getting right on this. Let me know if you come up with anything else."

After hanging up, he sat drumming his fingers on the desk, thinking about the attack on Dr. Sheridan. There was something at the edge of his mind. Something that he couldn't quite pull into focus.

Shrugging, he went back to the paperwork on some other cases, sure that if he let the Sheridan thing roll around in his mind for a while, he'd make the connection he was looking for.

HOME again, Ross changed his clothes and fixed himself another rare steak. As he ate, he decided that his leg was almost back to normal. Good news. In contrast to his worries about Megan.

He couldn't stop thinking about the car that had pulled up in front of her house after she'd left for work. Couldn't stop wondering if the attack the night before wasn't what it had appeared to be—a rapist picking a random victim, a woman working late at a lab in an industrial park. What if it had been personal?

He tried to shake that notion. Tried to shake all thoughts of her completely out of his head. After going down the hall to his gym, he picked up a couple of forty-pound dumbbells and started doing arm curls.

When he finished with them, he set the universal gym for leg presses and started on those. Then he went on to push-ups, working until a sheen of perspiration covered his body and his arms were too shaky to lift his weight one more time.

After an hour workout, he showered, then flopped into his office chair, thinking that he was going to catch up on the paperwork he'd promised himself he'd do. After half an hour of staring into space, he decided he might as well go back to Bethesda because it was clear he wasn't going to accomplish anything at home.

JACK pulled out his cell phone and dialed.

"Dr. Sheridan?" he asked when a woman came on the line.

"Speaking."

"This is Detective Thornton. I interviewed you last night after the attack."

"Yes."

"I'm about a mile from your office at the moment, and I was hoping to catch you in."

He heard her voice hitch. "Why?"

"I'd like to ask you a few more questions."

"I wasn't expecting to see you again—I mean, unless you had some information for me."

"Well, what I've found in the past is that when I interview a victim of a violent crime right after it's happened, he or she is usually confused, upset, and running on pure adrenaline."

She gave a nervous laugh. "I guess that's a good description of me last night."

"So I'd like to go over a few details with you now that you've had time to get a little distance. Is there somewhere at the office we can talk?"

She hesitated a minute before answering. "I don't want to talk about it in front of the people here. They've been asking questions, and I just don't want to get into it. Plus . . ."

When she didn't finish the sentence, he said, "Plus your boss said something to you this morning about our previous conversation."

"How do you know?"

"From his attitude last night."

He heard her suck in a breath, then let it out. "Well, I'm not getting any work done." She paused for another moment. "I might as well stop and have some lunch."

He looked at his watch. One-thirty. He hadn't eaten either.

"Do you know the Two Brothers Deli on Rockville Pike?" she asked.

"Yes."

"Could we meet there? In about fifteen minutes?"

He thought about it. A restaurant had its good and bad points for interviewing victims. There were a lot of distractions, although it was past the lunchtime crunch. On the other hand, the setting might help put her at ease.

"Fine." Hanging up, he turned right at the next intersection and started in the opposite direction down the pike, thinking this was his second luncheon meeting in as many days.

As with Ross Marshall, he got there first, found a table in an out-of-the-way spot, and waited for Dr. Sheridan to arrive.

She was prompt. As she came toward him, he noted that she was neatly dressed but frazzled looking. And she hadn't bothered to put on much makeup that morning.

"How are you?" he asked as she took the seat across from him.

"Not great," she answered, picking up the menu and scanning the offerings.

He let her hide behind the lunch selections. "How's the corned beef here?" he asked.

"Good. Lean."

The waitress came to take their orders, and he decided to indulge in a Reuben sandwich. When Dr. Sheridan ordered a bowl of matzo ball soup, he got a cup for himself, as well.

"You like matzo balls?" she asked as the waitress poured them each a cup of coffee.

"They remind me of Mom's dumplings. Where did you acquire the taste?"

"From some of the guys in medical school. I figured today I needed the curative powers of chicken soup." She took a swallow of coffee, as if she also needed fortification before she could talk to him about anything substantive.

"You should watch the caffeine."

"I missed my first cup of the day. Ross doesn't drink it."

"He stayed at your house last night?"

Her color deepened. "On the couch," she said quickly.

He wondered by whose choice. His? Hers? Or were they not as close as they'd looked to be last night? What he said was "I'm not trying to pry into your personal life."

"I hope not."

He'd give a lot to know about her relationship with Ross Marshall.

He reached in his pocket for a notebook, wondering exactly how to play this. Not Spenser for Hire. Maybe he could pull off Detective Marcus Welby.

"If you don't mind, I'd like to go back over the questions I asked you last night and see if you remember any additional details."

"I wish we didn't have to. I'd like to forget about it."

"I understand. But the more you tell me, the more likely we are to catch the guy."

She nodded, looked embarrassed. "There's something I forgot to tell you the other night. You were asking if anyone had a grudge against me or something. Well, it's not a grudge. But there's a doctor from NIH who's been coming on pretty strong to me. He started out acting as if he could help get my project past the roadblock on patient trials of gene therapy. Then I began thinking that his interest was more personal."

"He's threatened you?"

"Not exactly. But he said it would be a mistake to keep avoiding him."

Jack picked up his pen. "What's his name?"

"Dr. Carter Stillwell." She pulled a piece of paper out of her purse and handed it across the table. "I feel bad about making him a suspect."

"Do you think it could have been him?"

"I don't know. I told you the guy wore a mask."

"Could Stillwell have been sitting in his car outside, waiting for you?"

"I guess he could have been. He came to the lab the other day."

"Oh?"

"He'd been trying to get me on the phone—and I hadn't returned his calls."

"He sounds persistent. Thanks for filling me in."

"Please, could you be discreet in your investigation of him? I'd feel terrible if I got him into trouble," she emphasized again.

"You'd feel worse if he turned out to be the perp and he got away with it."

The food came, and they paused for a few minutes to eat.

"Do you remember anything else about the guy last night?" he asked.

She hesitated for a moment. "Nothing specific. But I keep having the feeling that I know him." She shifted in her seat.

"Something that makes you think it's Stillwell?"

She deliberately took another bite of matzo ball before answering, and he was sorry that she could use the food as an excuse for staring down into her plate. "Not specifically Stillwell." She looked uncomfortable, then said in a tentative voice, "Um . . . there's something else I keep thinking about. When Walter said there had been some kind of mistake in a test. I started wondering if it was a mistake I'd made. If it was one of *my* clients."

"Do you often make mistakes?"

"No. But I almost grabbed the wrong tube of blood when I started working on Ross's test," she said as though making a confession.

"So you care about him, and it flustered you."

"I didn't come here to talk about me and Ross."

This time he was the one who flushed. "Sorry."

He thought she was going to switch topics until she cleared her throat and said, "You know each other."

"He and I have worked together on a number of cases. He comes to me with useful information."

She might not have come here to talk about Ross, but she was hanging on his words, so he went on. "We had a meeting about a case yesterday at lunch. He'd called me. So I was surprised to see him again the same evening—in a completely different context."

"A meeting about the killer?"

"What do you know about that?"

"Ross dropped his phone near the killer's place and had to go back for it."

"How did he happen to tell you that?"

"He said that if the guy found the phone, I was in danger, being at his house."

"You mean when you were taking care of him—after he got shot," he said, without missing a beat.

"How did you know that?"

"A lucky guess, actually."

She squeezed her eyes closed. "Damn."

"I'm not going to tell anyone. At lunch he didn't

look his usual robust self. I asked what was wrong, and he said he'd picked up something when he was scoping out ... the killer's place. I got to wondering if he'd picked up a bullet. Did you remove it?"

"He did."

"Ouch."

"The wound got infected."

"And ..."

"I shouldn't be telling you all this."

"He won't know you did."

"That doesn't make me feel any better about it."

"Do you want to tell me why he came to the lab?"

"No. That's confidential." She spread her hands in front of her. "Please, I'd rather talk about getting attacked—strange as that might seem."

He shifted in his seat, shifted back to the topic that should be the focus of the conversation.

"Okay, let's go over the sequence of events."

She nodded, thought for a moment, and began to speak in a mechanical voice, as if trying to keep her distance from the events of the night before. "I was waiting for Ross after hours at the lab. I heard rain on the roof and realized I needed to close my car window. I grabbed an umbrella and went out. A man attacked me. Ross was outside in his car, waiting for the rain to stop, saw what was happening, and got the guy off of me. I ... I guess the man escaped because Ross came back to me instead of giving chase."

"That's all of it?"

"Yes."

The response was a little tentative. "What else did you want to add?" he asked.

She hesitated for a second. "I was thinking about the motivation for the attack. At first, it didn't seem sexual. It only got that way after I tried to hurt him. Does that make sense?"

"Can you explain a little more?"

"First he was just hitting me. When I fought back,

he threw me to the ground and started pulling at my clothing."

Suddenly she looked as if a lightbulb had gone off in her head. "I scratched him on the neck! I forgot about that part."

"That's a good detail. Something I can look for when I interview Stillwell. Anything else?"

She thought about it—shook her head.

"Okay, after Ross got him off you, then what happened?"

Her gaze turned inward. "I heard a car start. Then Ross was there beside me."

There was something else, something she wasn't telling him. "And Ross couldn't have been the one who attacked you?" he suddenly asked.

Shock and anger flared in her eyes. "My God. No! Why would you even ask that?"

"Some guys like to play hero."

"Ross doesn't play hero. He *is* a hero. As far as I can see, he's risking his life going after a killer. When he went back there the other night to get the phone he'd dropped, he got shot at again."

"He told you that?"

"Yes. And he's had incidents like that before. With some guy named Crawford."

Jack leaned forward. "He told you about Crawford, too?"

"Not much."

"What did he say—exactly?"

"When I got to his house, he was passed out on the floor. He came to and started talking about someone named Crawford. Asking if he'd come back to kill him. He was delirious. I think for a few moments he thought Crawford was there with him in the room."

He'd come back to that astonishing revelation later. For the moment, he asked, "So you're sure Ross wouldn't pretend to ward off an attack to impress you?"

"Are you crazy? Ross doesn't want to impress me. He wishes he'd never met me."

"Why?"

She looked down at her hands. When she spoke, her voice was low and strained. "Because it's obvious we're attracted to each other, and he's fighting the attraction because he's worried about his genetic heritage. And you're taking advantage of my vulnerability to ask me a bunch of questions that are none of your business."

"Yeah."

"So do you have what you need? Because I don't think I can take much more of this."

"I have what I need for the moment."

"Good. Then let me know if you figure out who came after me." She took some bills out of her wallet, dropped them on the table, and walked away—leaving him sitting there flat-footed. There was a lot more he'd wanted to cover. Like asking her about the dog hairs, for example. But now he'd missed the chance.

CHAPTER
NINETEEN

THE FOG HAD burned off, giving Ross an excellent view of the Bio Gen lab as he sat in the Jeep Cherokee. The Sig Sauer .40 that he rarely wore was in a shoulder holster under his arm. When he saw Megan's car come past him, he raised his hand to shield his features under the baseball cap jammed on his head.

He caught only a glimpse of her face as she hurried into the building, but he could tell that she was upset about something.

A deep protective surge of energy flowed through him. He wanted to leap out of his vehicle and go to her, find out what was wrong, and make it right for her But he forced himself to stay where he was, his eyes glued to the door of the lab.

No one else came in or out until forty-five minutes later, when he was surprised to see her emerge again. As she drove out of the parking lot, he followed her back to Old Georgetown Road, then felt his chest tighten when she turned into the parking lot at Montgomery Mall.

Montgomery Mall—where Donold Arnott worked as
a security guard.

Megan found a parking spot near Hecht's. He
thought about pulling up behind her and yelling at her
not to go in. Then a space opened up in the next aisle,
and he took it.

When he strode inside, he didn't see her at first, and
his heart started to pound. Then he spotted her approaching the fountain.

Quickening his pace, he came up behind her. She
must have heard his rapid footsteps, because she
stopped short and snapped her head around, her face
registering alarm. Then she focused on him, and her
features lit up in a smile that burned away whatever
resolve he still possessed not to let her get any closer
to him.

As he closed the distance between them, he forgot
utterly that he'd wanted to tell her a murder suspect
was working at the mall. Instead an inane question
tumbled from his lips. "Hey. What are you doing
here?"

Her smile was still in place. But it had become
mixed with an underlying tension. "Ross! I was too . . .
restless to stay at work. I decided some recreational
shopping might lift my spirits."

"What's recreational shopping?"

"What women do when they want to give themselves
a treat."

He continued to watch her face. "Your boss get on
you about your conversation with Thornton?"

"That and some other stuff," she said, her eyes telling him she didn't want to talk about it. "What are you
doing here?"

He scrambled for an answer. "I . . . uh . . . lost a pair
of binoculars. They're from a store called Indulge
Yourself. I thought I'd try to replace them."

"Indulge Yourself. That's out of my price range."

"Yeah. Out of mine, too. Most of the time. But in
this case, I'm going for a tax deduction."

He could see her mind working, making connections. "You lost them the night you"—she lowered her voice—"got shot."

He nodded, realizing he had the perfect opening to warn her about Arnott. After making sure that nobody was close enough to hear what he was saying, he took a step nearer to her. "Something I should tell you. The guy . . . uh . . . the guy you're referring to works here. He's a security guard."

Alarm contorted her face and she looked around quickly before focusing on him again. "Here? You mean he might recognize you?"

Ross managed to hold back a grim laugh. "He won't recognize me. He never saw my face," he said, knowing that Arnott had only encountered him as a wolf. "I was thinking about you coming here alone."

"Should . . . should I leave?"

He thought about that, thought about the women Arnott had killed. They were all similar to each other—and not Megan's type.

"I think you're safe with me. But maybe after this you should, you know, stay away until the case is closed."

She nodded.

"You could come with me to get the binoculars. Then we can have an early dinner," he heard himself saying, because the thought of breaking the contact with her now was simply beyond his power.

Her answer was immediate. "Yes. I'd like that."

They walked along, not touching, but he was very conscious of his hand swinging near hers. He would only have to reach out a few inches to wrap his fingers around hers. Simply thinking about the brush of his flesh on hers sent a bolt of heat surging through him. He kept his eyes directed into the distance so that he would have walked right past the shop if she hadn't stopped.

"Isn't this it?"

He looked at the window. "Yeah."

He let Megan precede him through the doorway. Over her shoulder he saw that the small, dark-haired saleswoman who'd sold him the original pair of light-weight, variable magnification binoculars was behind the counter.

She seemed to know the store's stock, and she'd been helpful with the original selection.

Today her gaze slid from him to Megan and back again, as though she were disappointed that he'd brought another woman into her territory.

Still, her smile was friendly as she asked, "What can I do for you?"

Megan had gone off to examine some of the merchandise featured on Lucite display shelves around the store. While she looked at a phone that was also a portable computer, he turned his attention back to the saleswoman. "Remember those binoculars you sold me a few months ago?"

"The Bausch and Lomb ones? They're top quality. Don't tell me you're having a problem with them."

He felt a sheepish expression creep onto his face. "They were fine. Unfortunately, I lost them."

She gave a small shake of her head. "You lost a five-hundred-dollar pair of binoculars?"

"Yeah. And I want a replacement. Do you still have the same model?"

"We certainly do."

She brought out a pair; he picked them up, turning to look through the lenses at the hand-knit sweaters in the store window across the way. As he adjusted the focus, the knit stitches leaped toward him like they were only a few feet away.

"Yes, these are the ones."

He handed over his credit card and waited while she ran it through the machine.

Five minutes later, he and Megan walked out of the store.

"Did you know they sell a thousand-dollar toilet seat?" she asked in a whisper.

"What's it made out of—gold?"

"Plastic. But the seat's heated. And there are a couple of special . . . attachments. Two different water sprays and something like one of those blow-dryers they have for your hands in some rest rooms."

He laughed. "You're kidding. Right?"

"I couldn't have made it up. My mind isn't that inventive."

"If you say so."

They walked along the second-floor corridor. "We could go to the food court," she said. "That way you can have meat, and I can have a baked potato with cheddar cheese and broccoli."

"Sure."

It was early for dinner, so there were plenty of tables. They each went off to buy food. Megan finished first and was standing by a table partially screened by a bank of greenery, waving her hand, when he stepped away from the counter with his own tray.

He sat, eyed her potato.

"I should buy you dinner."

"Why?"

"You stocked my refrigerator."

A shadow passed across her face. She chewed and swallowed before saying, "You don't owe me anything."

He kept his eyes focused on her until she dropped her gaze.

"Are you worrying about the security guard?"

"No."

"Then what's wrong?" he asked.

She dragged in a breath and let it out in a rush. "I guess you can read me pretty well."

"Reading people is part of the job description."

"Okay," she sighed. "Two things happened today before we met up here. Both of them are my fault. First there was Walter. I was making some notes about your tests. When I came back from getting coffee this morning, he was reading them."

"And?"

"He got excited about writing you up."

Anger flashed through him. "Shit."

Her face contorted. "It's worse than that. He can't decide the best way to exploit the situation. The alternative to fame and glory is keeping you secret and bottling your extra chromosome."

"For what?"

"An extra chromosome usually causes some sort of defect. He could see from my notes that I was impressed with your physique. So he's wondering if there's any advantage to your genetic makeup."

"You told him it kills three-fourths of the children?" he asked.

"I tried to tell him that. He thinks he can work around the problem."

Ross swore again.

"I'm sorry."

"You didn't know."

"I should have been more careful, but I was pretty shaken up this morning." She cleared her throat. "Walter is going through a bad spell because of the break-ins—and because he's looking for ways to bring in more money. When I was out at your house, I had to promise to charge you for private duty nursing. Thank God he seems to have forgotten about that." Looking down at her plate, she picked up her fork and poked at her potato.

"He's likely to be going through a worse spell."

She raised her eyes to his. "What do you mean?"

"I mean, I'm going to have a talk with him and make sure he understands there will be no write-up about my chromosomes. And no exploitation of them, either."

"He—"

"Will follow my advice. I can be pretty effective," he said, his voice low but very firm.

She breathed out a little sigh. "Yes."

He cut off a piece of his cooling steak, chewed, and

swallowed. "How the hell did you get mixed up with a bastard like him, anyway?"

"For one thing, I thought he was offering me a good job. And I guess I was looking for a boss who seemed like the complete opposite of my father. I already told you about him."

"Yeah."

"Walter seemed pretty nonthreatening. But since I got to Bio Gen, I've found out there are all sorts of ways to dominate people. I guess Walter uses passive-aggressive techniques. Or he used to. Lately he's skipped the passive mode."

"You could get another job."

"I've thought about it. But there's a catch-22. I don't know whether I can take my research with me. I mean, I've used his equipment. In a way, the lab's been sponsoring me. He told me that work I've done there is his lab's property."

"Was that in your contract?"

"I didn't sign a contract."

"Maybe you need to see a lawyer. Maybe we both do."

SO far it had been a good day for Donald. He'd hassled some kids who were obviously hooking school and made a black guy conform to the no-smoking regulation. The highlight of the afternoon had been hauling a dim-witted fifteen-year-old cunt accused of shoplifting to the mall office and keeping her in custody until the cops arrived—crowding her so that he could feel her breast tremble against his arm as she stood there shaking, waiting for the Montgomery County Police.

He'd gone into a little fantasy, imagining taking her to his secret room, making her confess all the dumb things she'd done, then telling her that what he was going to do to her was punishment for her sins.

Then the police had taken her away. After that he'd

amused himself by picking out women and thinking about whether he wanted them.

Now it was his dinner break, which he'd timed to coincide with Sandy's. From a distance she looked so much like his mother that he felt his stomach muscles clench.

Brassy blonde. Too heavy because she loved to stuff her face. He concentrated on arranging his features into a delighted smile as she came out the door of Indulge Yourself.

"You on your dinner break?" he asked.

She looked pleased to see him. "Yes. Cathy is holding down the fort," she said, referring to the little brunette behind the counter.

"It's my break, too. Want to join me?"

"Sure."

They made their way toward the food court, where he got a couple of burgers and she ordered rabbit food—a salad with a few shreds of meat on top. When she caught him staring at her meal with distaste, she hurried to explain. "I'm on a diet."

"Aw, you don't look like you need to be."

"I've been a bad girl."

"You mean in the eating department? Or do you have other vices?"

She flushed. "I was referring to eating."

He tore into his burger. "I like a woman with a few vices."

"Oh?"

He deliberately took another bite of his burger before answering. "I've been wanting to get together with you for a while."

"I'd like that," she answered, making her voice low and sexy before taking a few bites of her salad.

MEGAN leaned toward Ross. "There's something else I should tell you," she said in a resigned voice.

He waited for more bad news.

"Detective Thornton called to ask me some more questions. I didn't want to meet with him in the lab, so I suggested a deli on the pike."

"He'd want to get back to you for details you might not have given him right after the attack."

"He got me talking about you. I probably said too much."

He sat up straighter. "Like what?"

"Like that you'd been shot."

"Shit!"

"He tricked me into it. I'm sorry."

"Tricked you how?"

"Acted like he knew about it."

He nodded tightly. "He's a smart guy. Maybe I underestimated him."

"I'm sorry," she repeated.

"It's his job to get information out of people—any way he can."

Megan still looked so miserable, and he couldn't stand being the cause of the distress. Not when she was already going through a pretty bad time. Reaching across the table, he touched her hand. He should have been prepared for the effect. Or perhaps nothing could have prepared him for the heat that leaped between them.

"Ross," she breathed, turning her palm up, stroking her hand against his. Just his hand on hers, and he was so hard he didn't know whether he was experiencing pleasure or pain.

For long moments, speech was impossible. Whatever he might have been going to ask her about Thornton totally went out of his head. When his brain finally engaged again, he said, "I need to know something else."

She lifted questioning eyes to his, her expression dreamy; he wondered if she was as aroused as he.

With an effort, he managed to ask, "Were you expecting anyone this morning?"

"Expecting anyone? Where?"

"At your house."

"No. What are you getting at?"

"After you left, a car stopped at the curb. When I looked out the kitchen window, it sped away."

She sucked in a breath. "Who was it?"

"I couldn't tell in the fog."

He saw a little shiver go over her shoulders.

"I'm sorry. I wouldn't have mentioned it, but I didn't want to keep you in the dark."

"I appreciate that." Her fingers clamped themselves onto his. "But it doesn't make me want to go home alone tonight."

"Do you want me to come back with you?"

"Yes."

The way she said it, just that one syllable, tightened his body again. He'd stopped kidding himself. Both of them knew what going back to her house would mean.

It was an effort to pull his hand away. They ate in silence then, but he felt the need to hear her voice, to learn everything he could about her. "You said you have a sister?"

"Yes. Dory. She's a couple years younger than I am, and she's still in Boston, where we grew up."

"Is she a doctor, too?"

Megan laughed. "No. She's had a succession of jobs, cocktail waitress being the latest." Her expression sobered again. "And she's gotten mixed up with a succession of men who remind me of our father. I guess the difference between her and my mother is that Dory's prepared to leave them when things get really bad."

"And what kind of men have you gotten mixed up with?"

She flushed. "Not too many. I never had a relationship that went very far. I've always looked for non-threatening guys. Then it turns out there's not enough substance to make them interesting." She said it forcefully, as if offering him a challenge.

"So I'm not exactly your type," he heard himself saying.

"I told myself you weren't." She raised her eyes to him. "You know how far that got me."

About as far as he'd gotten warning himself away from her.

"Do you want to leave?" he asked, giving her another chance to back away.

She didn't take it. "Yes. Where are you parked?"

"Near Hecht's."

"That's convenient. I'm over there, too."

DONALD took a sip of his Coke.

"Speaking of vices, it's amazing what people come into the shop to spend their money on," Sandy chirped.

He gave her an indulgent smile. "Yeah, you've told me about some of them."

"The guy this afternoon takes the cake. Cathy was waiting on him, but I was in the stock room, and I could see him and his girlfriend. After they left, Cathy told me all about him.

"She said a couple of months ago he bought an expensive pair of Bausch and Lomb binoculars. Top of the line. Five hundred dollars. Then this afternoon, he comes back and tells her he lost them. So he pulls out his credit card and buys a replacement pair. Just like that."

He felt the hairs on the back of his neck prickle. The binoculars he'd found in the knapsack outside the fence were Bausch & Lomb. And he knew they were a damn expensive pair.

Sandy broke into his thoughts. "In fact, there he is over there eating dinner. Him and the girlfriend."

Donald went rigid. "Where?"

"Over there. Behind that bank of plants. It looks like they're getting ready to leave." She inclined her head.

He swiveled around in his seat and saw a good-looking couple—a dark-haired guy and a little blonde.

They got up and walked through the court, their total attention focused on each other. Still, he bent over his hamburger, hiding his face under his cap. Then he looked at his watch. "Hey, sorry, I just remembered, I've got to check on a car that broke down in the parking lot this afternoon. I'll be back in a few minutes."

"No, that's okay. I'll see you later."

He stood, turned, and started down the aisle after the couple, keeping far enough behind them so that they didn't know they were being followed.

They walked through Hecht's and into the parking lot, where they separated.

Pulse pounding, he followed the guy, who headed up a lane and opened the door of an SUV. A Jeep Cherokee.

The license number was DEK 782.

DE—the same fucking first two letters as the SUV that had driven away from his house two nights ago. The same fucking binoculars.

Christ! He felt his heart literally stop—then start up again in double time. He had the bastard—if he could just get a little more information out of Sandy. And if he couldn't, there was always the DMV. Somehow he'd figure out how to get the guy's name out of them.

He went back into the mall and sprinted toward the food court. When he found that Sandy had already left, he bolted up the escalator to Indulge Yourself. She was behind the counter.

"Sorry about that," he said. "I figured I'd better take care of it before the mall closed."

She nodded, looking like she believed him.

He leaned toward her across the counter. "I've been wanting a pair of binoculars like the ones you were talking about. For bird watching."

"They're pretty pricey for bird watching." She reached into the case and brought them out.

He took them from her and turned to look at a sign in the store across the aisle, not really paying much attention to the focus. "Nothing's too good for my hobby."

"I know what you mean. I try not to spend too much on jewelry. But it's such a temptation when you see a piece you want. There's this diamond and ruby pin in Katz's that's just calling to me," she said, like she thought he might jump at the chance to buy it for her.

He managed a noncommital response, then put the binoculars back and looked around the shop and asked, "Where's, uh, Cathy?"

"She went home when I got back from dinner. Why?"

He gestured toward the binoculars. "These seem okay. But I'd like to ask that guy if he thinks they're worth it. Can you look at the credit slip and give me his name?"

She glanced toward the door, then back at him. "Oh, I couldn't do that. It's confidential information."

He gave her his most boyish smile. "It would be a big help—before I spend that kind of money. I mean, I'm not some fat cat. I have to live on my salary."

When her expression softened, he added, "Please." Jesus, he hated to beg, but he'd make her pay for that later. "I'd really appreciate it."

She hesitated a beat, making him sweat. "Okay. You can stop by tomorrow morning and look."

"Why not right now?" he asked, somehow managing not to shout.

She shot another glance toward the door. "Because my boss comes in sometimes in the evenings, and if he caught me letting someone look at the charge slips, I'd be in big trouble."

He gave her a conspiratorial wink. "I'm mall security," he reminded her. "There's been some credit fraud in the mall, and I need to look at your records."

She managed a nervous smile. "Tomorrow."

He could see that pressing her would be a bad idea. But he was sure of her now. Sure he could get the name. Feeling expansive, he said, "What are you doing after you get off?"

Her face brightened. "I don't have any particular plans."

"What about if we go down to Brennan's? There's a nice crowd there. Music."

"I'd like that. But I'd like to go home and change first. Why don't I meet you around ten-thirty?"

"Great!" He looked at his watch. "I'll see you later, then."

"Yes."

He exited the shop, feeling better than he had in days.

CHAPTER
TWENTY

ROSS PARKED IN the same spot as the night before, then walked through the darkness to Megan's kitchen door. If someone had leaped out of the bushes and assaulted him, he would have had no warning. The scenery around him was a blur—just the way the mall had been. There was a buzzing inside his head, and his vision had narrowed to the dim triangle of light beyond the doorway.

He stepped inside and saw that she'd turned on the fluorescent light over the sink, so that most of the room was in shadow.

Somehow he remembered to slam the door closed with his foot before reaching for her.

She came into his arms with a sound that was a cross between a sigh and a sob.

"Ross."

He folded her close, held on, trying to bring himself back to sanity. Apparently there was still enough blood in his brain for some of the cells to function.

"I've got to check the house," he managed to say.

Her face was flushed as she lifted it toward him. "Check for what?"

"To make sure nobody's broken in. I think you asked me back here because you were worried about that."

"Partly. And partly it was an excuse." Her voice was high and thick.

He made himself turn her loose, forced his mind to focus on his surroundings as he pulled the Sig .40 from the holster under his arm.

Her eyes widened when she saw the automatic. "Why do you have that?"

"Because I'm supposed to be prepared for trouble."

When he moved toward the dining room, she followed.

"Stay here."

She stopped in her tracks, swaying slightly, and he exited the kitchen, checking rooms and closets before coming back to her.

"Everything's okay." He brushed past her, turned the lock on the back door.

The trip through the house had given him a chance to cool down. "Megan—"

She didn't allow him to finish. "I'm in perfect shape to make sexual decisions."

The buzz was back in his head. Sexual decisions.

"Could you put down the gun?"

"Yeah." He laid it on the kitchen table as if it were a piece of crockery, and she came back to him, holding out her arms.

He walked into her embrace, and everything became sharp, vivid. The scent of her in his nostrils, the scent he remembered from the morning. The feel of her in his arms. The taste of her as he lowered his mouth to hers.

Their lips touched, fused, sealed with heat.

With a small sound she opened for him, and he swept into the warmth of her mouth, his tongue investigating the inside of her lips, the serrated edges of her teeth, the sensitive tissue beyond.

She moaned into his mouth, her tongue no less bold as it found his, then stroked the inner surface of his lips.

A whirlwind coalesced around him, pressing him more tightly to her as his hands swept up and down her back, cupped her bottom, lifting her against his erection.

His mouth never left her. But, finally, like a diver too long below the surface, he was forced to come up for air, his breath rasping in and out of his lungs.

"Come to my bedroom."

He nodded, took a step toward the doorway. The gun registered in his peripheral vision. "Wait a minute."

Her eyes were wide as he snatched it up.

"Can't leave it here," he said, his throat so constricted he could hardly get the words out.

He didn't know whether she was following his logic, whether she understood that anyone looking in the window could see the weapon—use it on them.

PI and lover shot with his own gun.

He abandoned that thought as they stepped into the bedroom. Again the weapon clunked onto a flat surface, this time the dresser, and then he reached for her, clasped her to him, the length of her body pressed to his.

The roaring in his head increased to hurricane force, sweeping away everything in its path but the woman in his arms.

He wanted to see her, wanted everything. Reaching toward the lamp on the dresser, he pressed the switch, sending golden light over her hair, her face, her shoulders.

Mad to feel her satin skin against his, he yanked his shirt over his head, fumbled with the buttons on her blouse. She seemed to be caught in the same wild surge of need as she dispatched the hook at the back of her bra and pulled it out of the way. He tore away the button at her waistband, hearing it ping against the floor.

"Sorry."

She shook her head, helped him shuck off the skirt, her panty hose, and panties.

Naked, she came back to him with a strangled cry that rose to a kind of desperate moan as he clasped her by the shoulders, moving her body so that her breasts swept back and forth across his chest.

He felt the softness of the mounds, the twin points of her nipples. His hands trailed down her back, over her rounded bottom, touching her everywhere he could reach.

Needing to taste as well as feel, he shifted her away from him. Her little exclamation of protest turned into a gasp of pleasure as his mouth closed over one distended nipple.

He drew on her, his body responding to the taste, the texture, the pleasure of her response.

"Ross. Ross. Oh, God, Ross." She chanted his name as she fumbled to open his belt buckle, opened the metal snap at the top of his jeans, lowered the zipper so she could push the jeans away along with his shorts.

When her hand closed around his taut, aching flesh, his brain momentarily shut down. He wasn't conscious of moving. All he knew was that one minute they were standing near the dresser. The next, they were stretched the wrong way across the bed, touching, kissing, exploring each other with a freedom and a passion that overwhelmed him.

He had never needed a woman more than he needed this one. And at the same time, it had never been more important to please his lover as well as himself.

He worshiped her breasts with his hands, his mouth, his teeth, the taste of her driving him close to madness. As his fingers stroked the hot, slick folds of her sex, he watched the tautness of her face, listened to the breath rasp in and out of her lungs.

"Ross . . . now . . . please." She reached for him, her hand firm on his penis as she guided him to her.

His body sank into hers, and he felt completed.

"Oh, Ross," she breathed, her hand lifting to touch his face, her head angling so that her lips could capture his at the moment they became one flesh.

He knew in that instant that he had been alone all his life, and now he had found his mate.

A kind of fierce joy rose in his breast as he lifted his head and gazed down at her.

Her face was radiant, glowing, suffused by passion as he began to thrust himself into her.

She matched his rhythm, clung to his shoulders, climbed toward orgasm with him. The pleasure of it was almost unbearable as he held himself back, waiting for her to reach her climax. And when he felt her start to contract around him, the all-consuming tension exploded into a release that rocked his body, rocked him to his soul.

He didn't have to ask how it had been for her. He had felt it. Sensed it.

He had been made for this woman—and she for him.

She moved her lips against his cheek, clasped him tightly when he tried to shift his weight away from her.

"Stay," she whispered, her hands settling into the place where his spine met his hips as she nibbled her lips against his face. And he felt himself responding to her touch, growing hard again while his body was still joined to hers.

When he raised his head and stared down at her, she grinned, then cupped the back of his head and brought his mouth back to hers, kissed him deeply.

It was incredibly erotic to feel her arousal building again, to feel the small tremors that contracted her inner muscles around him. Incredibly erotic to move his hips just enough to feed the tension building in his own body. Slowly, sweetly until the languid pace suddenly accelerated, and they were racing toward another shattering climax.

Afterward, when he shifted to his side, she let him leave her, but she didn't break their contact completely.

Her hand stroked the damp hair back from his forehead.

"You're exhausted," she murmured. "I should have my head examined, taking that much from a man who got shot a few days ago."

"You weren't taking anything. You were giving."

"And taking." She squeezed his shoulder, then slipped out of bed. "Come on, we need to swing around and get under the covers."

The room came back into focus, and he realized they were lying the wrong way across the bed.

While she pulled the bedspread down, he maneuvered his head toward the pillows, then let her cover him. She turned off the light on the dresser but left on the one in the hall.

He listened to sounds from the bathroom, then watched her come back into the room and open a drawer. When she took out a T-shirt, he roused himself enough to say, "Don't. I want to feel your skin next to me."

Silently she put down the shirt, then came back to the warmth of the bed. He pulled her close, needing to feel the length of her body tight against his.

She rolled to her side, her breast pressed against his arm, and he reached out in the darkness, stroking her, feeling her respond to his touch once more. He grew hard again. Wanting her even now.

But he had enough sanity left not to do more than hold her in the darkness as he drifted off to sleep.

CHAPTER
TWENTY-ONE

IT WAS LATE. Mrs. Anderson had long since gone to bed, giving Jack a look that said she thought he was working too hard.

He'd told her he'd come upstairs shortly. Instead he'd sunk into the worn leather chair in his office. His thinking chair.

It was the place where he settled when he needed to put together the pieces of a puzzle. Usually that meant he was mulling over a case, trying to fit together motive, means, and opportunity. Tonight he was working on the puzzle of Ross Marshall.

Until the beginning of this week, he'd thought he had a handle on Marshall.

Christ, had it really been only Monday when he'd picked up Ken Winston's old case file from his desk?

It seemed incredible. But there it was.

Purely as a ploy, he'd told Dr. Sheridan that some guys might attack a woman and pretend to rescue her to make themselves look like a hero. She'd been outraged by that suggestion and had told him heatedly that Ross *was* a hero.

He hadn't exactly thought about Marshall in those terms. Now he leaned back, closed his eyes, and mentally catalogued the kinds of individuals who fed information to the cops.

The reasons varied. Sometimes guilt was the motivating factor. Those were the men and women who came to him on the assumption that providing information in some way atoned for their own sins against society.

Then there were the ones who were greedy for money—who would sell you pieces of other people's lives on a cash and carry basis.

Others were driven by vengeance. They were smarting from some real or perceived wrong, and they wanted to "get even" by ratting out their enemies.

The hardest to deal with were the nuts with a cloak and dagger fantasy who saw themselves as supersleuths fighting crime, corruption, and terrorists, making the world safe for women and small children all by themselves.

They were dangerous—not just to the bad guys but to the public—because there was no telling what they might do to feed their inflated egos.

Another big category consisted of informers he thought of as John Q. Citizen. They wanted to do the right thing, but they were scared to get involved. So when they heard screams outside their window, they were likely to run in the other direction instead of coming to the rescue.

The good news was that they might come forward if pressed—or if their anonymity could be guaranteed.

Ross Marshall was none of the above. Jack pursed his lips, wondering if he'd describe the man as a hero.

One thing was for sure: Marshall believed in what he was doing. He believed in truth, justice, and that "the system" did actually work.

He was every detective's dream source. Knowledgeable, intelligent, professional, completely trustworthy—

at least in the dealings they'd had. Although Jack was pretty sure Ken Winston wouldn't agree.

Ross would have probably been a great cop. But there was something that had kept him from taking that route. Something in his background that made him choose to work alone, unless he determined that the only way to clear a case was to give information to the police.

So what had turned him into a loner? His deprived family background? The violent father? His relationship with the long-suffering mother?

Or some defect he saw in his own personality? Something that had caused him to take the law into his own hands five years ago and kill Edward Crawford.

Jack sighed. He was about ready to officially label the Crawford file as a Stone Who Done It—a case that couldn't be solved. Nobody would fault him for that. The evidence suggested that Crawford had been abducting and killing young women. Now he was dead. And there was no proof leading to Ross Marshall as the man who'd put him in the ground—other than that he'd tried to get Ken Winston to take a closer look at the guy.

But what about the current situation? Ross Marshall and Megan Sheridan cared about each other. She'd been attacked.

What would Marshall do if the police—if Jack Thornton—couldn't find the guy who had done it?

Take the law into his own hands again?

He hoped not.

Then there was the tip Ross had given him on Donald Arnott that he'd barely had time to pursue yet. His mind switched gears, and he started thinking about the process he needed to start in the morning. The first thing he'd do was talk with the police in Paoli, Pennsylvania, and find out if the series of abductions and killings up there had stopped when Arnott had moved to the D.C. suburbs.

He was just making a note about that on the pad he

carried in his pocket when a noise in the doorway made him look up.

A small figure in a white nightgown stood with one hand clutching the doorjamb. "Daddy."

Lilly's face was pale. Tears streaked her cheek.

"Honey, are you sick? What's wrong?"

Her lower lip trembled. "I had a bad dream."

"Come here."

She scurried across the room toward him; he scooped her up, cradling her in his lap.

Her head rested against his chest, and he stroked the soft blond hair that he loved so much. Her mother's hair.

"Can you tell me about it?" he murmured.

"A bad man was chasing me," she whispered, the last word breaking on a sob.

He stroked his hands through her hair, over her shoulders, rocking her. "It's okay. Daddy has you."

She pressed her face against his shirt, turning the fabric damp with her tears. When the flood subsided, he murmured, "Do you want to tell me any more about it?"

"I was running through the hallways at school, trying to get away from him; and every time I thought I got away, there he was again—in front of me." She gulped. "Then I woke up, and I was scared to be in my bed alone. I looked for you in your bed, but you weren't there."

"I'm sorry. I was working late. I'm glad you came downstairs and found me," he answered, continuing to rock her.

"I miss Mommy," she said in a small voice that stabbed at him.

"I do too, honey."

"If Mommy were still here, you would have been upstairs in bed with her. And I could have gotten in the middle, the way I used to do."

His throat clogged. "Yeah," he answered.

"Can I get in bed with you now?"

He ran a hand through his hair. Christ, was it okay to let a six-year-old girl get in bed with her daddy? Some psychology book would probably give him the answer. Or the family counselor they'd all seen after Laura had been killed.

The answer was probably no. But right now he knew that his daughter needed to know he was there for her.

"I'll come up and lie in your bed with you for a while," he said, standing and shifting her weight so he could carry her up the stairs.

She pressed her face into his neck. "You won't ever go away," she whispered. "The way Mommy did."

"No, I'll never go away," he said, clutching her to him as he climbed the stairs. "Tell me about that painting you're doing in the school hallway."

She snuggled against him. "It's really neat. One thing I get to paint is a cat. Any cat I want. I want to do a gray one—like Mrs. Williams has."

DONALD Arnott leaned against the bar, pretending not to watch the door. But he knew the moment Sandy walked in. Once again it struck him: she could be a carbon copy of his mother, the whore who would spread her legs for any guy, as long as he had the money to pay. When he was a kid, there'd been too many nights when he'd lain on the sofa in the living room, listening to her with some john in the bedroom, both of them so loud it was a wonder the neighbors didn't start banging on the walls.

That had ended abruptly when he was eleven, when one of her low-life fucks had climbed out of her bed and come after him in the morning, thinking he was going to have a little dessert—of the kiddy variety.

Donald had brained the bastard with a lamp. And good old Mom had turned him over to the juvenile authorities. He'd gotten even with her by blabbing about her lifestyle to anyone who would listen. That had kept him out of the detention center—and put him in the foster care program. Which wasn't great. But it was better than life with his slut of a mother.

They'd told him she died of cancer of the liver. He hadn't given a shit about it.

Sandy crossed the floor. In the dim light he could see that she'd frizzed out her hair, put on too much makeup, and wiggled into a red dress that looked like a second skin.

Jesus. What a sight. The first thing he was going to do when he strapped her to the wooden table in his secret room was wash the makeup off her face with paint thinner.

But he wasn't going to get a chance to do that tonight. Tonight he was going to have to be on his best behavior.

So he gave her a wide smile. "You look sensational."

She smiled back, patted that Day-Glo hair. "Why, thank you."

"So what can I get you to drink?" he asked expansively.

"White wine."

Woman's wimp drink. He signaled the bartender and inquired about the house wines. She picked a chablis. When it arrived, he suggested that they repair to a table in the corner.

"So are you from around here?" he asked.

"No. I'm from Michigan."

"What brings you to the D.C. area?"

"There was nothing to hold me in Kalamazoo."

"No boyfriend?"

Her face contorted. "I was married to a real jerk. But that's all in the past."

"Well, I'm glad you're free, white, and over twenty-one."

She took a sip of her wine. "You're the most interesting man I've met in a long time."

"Oh, yeah? How come?"

"You're not what you seem."

That brought a little spurt of alarm. "What do you mean?"

"You've got hidden depths. I know there are things below the surface that you don't show to everyone."

"Good things?"

"Of course."

He relaxed a little.

"You told me about your bird watching."

"Yeah," he improvised. "I have lots of different types of feeders—to attract the different species."

"Oh—which kinds?"

"Uh, robins, cardinals, sparrows."

"I didn't think robins came to feeders."

"Well, I've got special stuff for them. From the Wild Bird Center." He dredged up the name from an ad he'd seen in the local paper. What a waste of time, spending money on birdseed. But Sandy seemed enthralled. "But I'd rather talk about you."

"I'm not that interesting."

"Oh, don't be modest. You're a very charming woman." He lifted her arm, played with the gold and diamond bracelet around her wrist. "This is so pretty," he gushed, trying not to throw up as he said it. "I love your taste in jewelry. Where did you get it?"

He got her talking about clothes and jewelry while his hand dropped to her knee under the table. Smiling at her, he caressed the knee, her leg, working upward to her thigh. That wasn't difficult under the short tight skirt. The problem was the damn panty hose. He hated panty hose.

He would have liked to rip them off. Instead he smiled and made appropriate responses to her inane chatter.

"Let's go back to your apartment," he finally said in a husky whisper.

Her eyes turned cautious. "I don't know you well enough for that."

"Yeah. I guess you're right," he said immediately.

"Come sit with me in my car for a little while before we both have to go home."

She hesitated for a moment, then agreed.

He led her to the Land Rover he'd parked in a dark corner of the lot, opened the back door so they could sit on one of the bench seats.

He reached for her, kissed her, turning himself on by thinking about the metal ring riveted to the back of the seat—and what he was going to do to her after he got her where he really wanted her.

He amused himself by seeing how far he could get with the slut, pawing her breasts, reaching under her skirt. Getting her to shuck off the panty hose so he could stroke her cunt.

Because he still needed that credit slip, he made her come with his fingers, gritting his teeth at the disgusting sounds of pleasure she was making, keeping himself hard by focusing on his power over her. Then he told her that if she cared anything for him the way he cared for her, she wouldn't leave him hot and bothered.

When he opened his fly and took out his swollen cock, she reached for him, probably thinking she was going to get away with a hand job. But he took her head between his palms, pulled her mouth down to his rod, and got her to suck him off. Then he watched in amusement as she fumbled in her purse for a wad of tissue so she could spit out the cum.

When he got her back to his underground room, she was going to swallow it. For now he was satisfied that he'd gotten her to suck him off in the backseat of a car in the parking lot of a bar—proving what he'd known about her all the time. She was a slut. Just like all the women he'd punished.

But he kept a sincere look in his face as he thanked her. Acted tender and appreciative. Told her how much he wanted to see her again.

And when they went their separate ways that evening, he was feeling better than he had since he'd shot the dog.

CHAPTER
TWENTY-TWO

IN THE MORNING, reaction set in. Ross knew what he had done. Knew that at least some of what his father had told him had been right—about the selfish greed of the mature werewolf.

He had come to Megan's house with no other thought in his head besides fucking her. He had done the deed—twice. And the thought hadn't even entered his mind that protecting her from pregnancy would be a smart idea.

Jesus—what if he'd started a baby growing in her last night when he'd been thinking about nothing but his own pleasure? What if she were carrying a girl child?

He felt as if a raw, hollow place had opened up in the center of his chest, the pain seeping outward to every part of his body. Megan could soothe the terrible ache. Only Megan.

Last night . . .

Last night had been incredible. Thinking about it made him long to reach for her and see that smoldering look in her eyes again. But instead of letting his own needs take control, he eased away, made it down the hall to the bathroom and stood staring at himself in the bathroom mirror.

The face that looked back sickened him. He'd been kidding himself for the past five years—following some kind of half-baked moral code to make himself feel better about Crawford. But he had no right to think of himself as a moral person.

A werewolf had no morality. He was an animal—who followed his own selfish impulses. And maybe phases of the moon. Or maybe he could shift the responsibility to his genes, he thought with a snort. Maybe the things he did were only what his genes commanded him to do.

He turned on the water, stepped under spray hot enough to sting his skin. But a shower couldn't wash away the feeling of disgust, although he stood under the hot water for a long time.

Then he dressed and quietly slipped back into the bedroom to retrieve his gun and jam it back into his shoulder holster.

The blinds were closed, and the room was still dark. Standing a few feet from the bed, he looked at Megan, feeling his heart turn over in his chest. She looked so peaceful, so trusting. But what if someone had come into the house last night and attacked her?

He wouldn't have been able to do a damn thing about it because he'd been too focused on what they were doing in bed.

His nerves strung as tight as piano wire, he backed out of the room and walked to the sliding glass door in the living room. The need to escape building in his chest like a bomb about to explode, he shed the clothing he'd just put on, leaving everything in a heap on the floor as he unlocked the door and stepped into the gray light.

He was a wolf. That was his true nature.

He had the presence of mind to glance around, note

that the houses on either side of Megan's were screened by tall trees and that the back of her property bordered a wide stretch of greenery—perhaps a park.

But checking to see that he wasn't being observed was only perfunctory as the words of transformation sprang to his lips. This morning he welcomed the pain of bones crunching, muscles jerking, cells transforming from one shape to another.

Dropping to all fours, he streaked away, heading toward the trees that bordered the backyard.

MEGAN woke, then smiled as she remembered the incredible night with Ross. Sleepily she reached out to touch the man who had transported her to another plane of existence.

Until last night, he had resisted her. Resisted the sense of connection growing between them. But when they'd finally come together, their union had been glorious. Not just sex. Something more that she'd never believed could exist. Her essence merging with his while they danced together in a magic world where only the very lucky were admitted.

A small pang gripped her when she found the bed empty. Her eyes blinking fully open, she turned to stare at the impression his head had left in the pillow. He had been here. It wasn't a dream. He was gone now.

Gone away? Impossible. Not after last night. He must be somewhere else in the house.

Struggling to contain the feeling of uneasiness that tugged at her as she slung her legs over the side of the bed, she crossed to the closet and slid into the bathrobe hanging on the back of the door.

In the bathroom, she saw that he'd taken a shower not very long ago.

"Ross?" she called.

When he didn't answer, she headed down the hall toward the living room.

The drapes were still closed, but she could see them

blowing back and forth, telling her the window must be open. She never left the sliding glass door unlocked. So he must have stepped outside.

In the dim light she saw something on the floor by the window. A pile of clothing. The clothing Ross had worn the night before. And his gun.

Her brow wrinkled. He'd gotten dressed this morning, then taken off his clothing by the back door. And gone outside.

Against her will, her mind streaked back to another time when she'd found an open window, an empty room. His white shorts on the floor of his bedroom.

And outside . . .

Her body went stock-still, and a terrible wave of cold swept through her, all the way to the marrow of her bones. She didn't want to discover what was out there. But an invisible force had grabbed hold of her and was pulling her toward the window. On legs that felt like wood, she stumbled forward, her movements jerky as she pushed aside the drapes and stepped onto the patio.

For a brief moment, she saw nothing but her back-yard looking just the way it had looked the day before, and some of the terrible tension eased out of her. It was all in her imagination. All the smoldering anxiety that she was terrified to put into words.

In the next instant the feeling of relief was ripped apart. She saw a flicker of movement at the edge of the trees. Against her will, her gaze riveted to the spot. And as if she'd stumbled from sleep into a nightmare, she saw the gray wolf emerging from the woods, his silvery pelt catching the first rays of the sun, his ears alert and pricked toward her.

The wolf was *here*, her mind screamed.

Immobilized by a soul-deep fear, she watched the animal move toward her. Eyes fixed on her, he closed the distance between them until he was standing less than six feet away.

Her heart was pounding so hard in her chest that she could barely breathe as she stared into his brilliant yellow eyes—eyes that she'd thought held intelligence beyond that of a mere animal.

Human intelligence.

And in that one shattering moment, she knew what her mind had shut away—what her intellect had refused to believe when reality was too terrible to contemplate.

The wolf was Ross!

Even as the thought grabbed her by the throat, she rejected it.

Impossible.

But it came slamming back with a force that physically knocked the breath from her lungs.

Ross was the wolf.

The man who had made incredible love with her last night.

Ross. The wolf.

The first time she had seen the animal, he had threatened her, his muzzle smeared with blood from the kill. He didn't threaten her now. Not physically. He only threatened her sanity.

A sob rose in her throat as she turned and stumbled back through the door.

Shaken, feeling as if she'd been torn into shreds, she backed away from the door, crashed into a low table, and cried out as pain shot through her leg.

Making it no farther than the couch, she collapsed and huddled into herself, her thoughts scattered, fragmented.

She wanted to look away, but her eyes were drawn to the curtains.

Maybe she had been mistaken. Maybe she had somehow made it up. Just the way she'd made up the other two encounters. Then the curtains moved, and a shaft of sunlight pierced the darkness of the room.

He was coming in. But who? The wolf or the man?

Her breath heaving in jagged gasps, her arms wrapped around her shoulders, she waited.

Then Ross, the man, walked back inside. Naked.

A kind of frozen calm came over her as she stared at him. She should be frightened. She should be angry. But all she could feel was a thousand-pound block of ice compressing her lungs.

The terrible cold held her fast, froze her emotions, leaving her rigid as a statue carved from snow.

Ross stared at her with the same rigid calm, and she sensed that he was working to contain emotions as searing as the ones she felt.

Mechanically he pulled his clothes on. Strapped on his shoulder holster. Afraid that he might come closer, she watched him warily. But he stayed where he was by the wall, regarding her with his dark eyes. Eyes so like the yellow eyes of the wolf.

Why hadn't she seen that before?

Because she hadn't wanted to. Perhaps that was her fault. But he was the one who had hidden the truth.

"You lied to me," she whispered, feeling as if the two of them were confronting each other in the eye of a hurricane. In a little while, the storm would rage again. For the moment, the air around them was clear and calm.

"I never lied. I told you there was a genetic problem in my heritage. You told me I have an extra chromosome. Now you know what it does."

"You let me think that I was going crazy. You let me think I imagined the wolf."

"Are you better off now that you know?" he asked with maddening calm, then continued in the same flat voice. "I was trying to save you. My father told me that by the time I was thirty, I'd start looking for a mate—that I'd bond with a woman, and neither one of us would be able to resist the other—because the were-wolf is programed to perpetuate his genes. I told myself that wasn't going to happen to me. To make sure it didn't happen, I started keeping to myself. Then you found me naked and wounded. And I had no control over the situation. You touched me, took care of me, and you're seeing the results." His Adam's apple bobbed. "But maybe it's not too late for you. Maybe if I just walk away now, you can go on with your life and forget about last night."

She tried to take in what he was saying, even as he gave her one last regretful look. Then he turned and exited through the door where he'd come in.

In that moment, the ice that held her fast shattered. She fought for breath, felt the searing pain in her chest—in the very depths of her soul.

A cry welled in her throat, a cry of loss and rage. Curling into herself, she raised her arms and cupped them over her head, trying to protect something inside herself that was weak and vulnerable. Yet deep within her she knew that it was already too late.

HER cry of anguish pursued Ross as he staggered toward his car, wrenched open the door, slid inside, then fumbled with the key, his hands so numb he could barely push it into the ignition. He had held himself together long enough to say a few words to her. Then he'd fled, trying to escape pain greater than any he could have imagined.

Finally he succeeded in starting the car. Yanking the vehicle into reverse, he lurched backward down the driveway, almost plowing into a tree near the street.

Hardly knowing what he was doing, he whipped into first gear and roared down the road.

The blacktop in front of him was a blur, overshadowed by the picture in his mind of the horror on Megan's face when she'd finally figured it out. Figured out that the man she had made love with last night was a monster.

A monster who felt as if his heart had been ripped from his body. Because until he had seen that look on her face, he hadn't truly understood what it was to suffer the tortures of the damned.

His hands fused to the wheel, he drove on. He was several miles from Megan's house when he realized he was driving home. To his refuge. Díthreabh. Where he could lick his wounds.

What had happened was for the best. She'd stumbled upon the wolf when she'd been unprepared and vulnerable. And now she was in shock. But in some deep, unselfish part of himself, he knew she would come to understand what she had escaped. She had saved herself. The woman he loved.

The woman he loved. The phrase played over and over in his mind, and he understood what had eluded him until this moment.

If a man like him could love—then he loved her. But it didn't change anything. His love was tainted by his nature—by the genetic heritage he could never escape. He was a werewolf, helpless to stop himself from repeating the cruel behavior patterns of his kind. To keep his mate pregnant, bearing a succession of children who were doomed to die—or doomed to live the savage life they could never escape.

Rationally he knew that Megan was infinitely better off without him. In his heart he was sick unto death.

MEGAN tried to stand, found her legs were still too wobbly, and simply collapsed back against the cushions.

Lowering her head, she buried her face in her hands, her brain too stunned to cope with reality.

Last night, making love with Ross had been the most wondrous experience of her life. This morning, he had shattered her world.

"Ross." Megan spoke his name, not knowing if it was a plea or a prayer or perhaps a curse.

She wanted to cry. She wanted to scream. She wanted to pound the walls with her fists. She did none of those things, only huddled on the sofa, her mind in turmoil as bits and pieces of the past few days came back in flashes.

The books on his shelves. Fairy tales. Myths of night stalkers—vampires and werewolves.

His love of the woods.

His extraordinary recuperative powers.

His secrecy. The way he'd warned her to leave. The way he'd struggled to distance himself from her.

She should have been smart enough to listen to him.

A sound bubbled in her throat—something between a sob and a hysterical laugh.

She'd thought she was going crazy. Seeing the wolf. Having no explanation besides the phantoms of her own mind.

There had been no rational interpretation. Nothing she could have accepted until she'd seen it for herself.

FROM a doorway down the aisle, Donald watched Sandy open the shop. She was dressed for business again, in one of her outfits that looked only slightly less trashy than what she'd worn the night before.

On the drive home, he conceded that he'd made a mistake. He shouldn't have had any sexual contact with her until he'd resolved the problem with the binoculars guy. Now he was going to have to tread carefully.

So he did a couple of circuits of the mall before coming back to the shop.

She was alone in the store and behind the counter when he stepped through the door. Her head shot up when she saw him, and he could see her expression was guarded.

"Hi," he said. "I've been thinking about you since we parted. Wishing we hadn't been in a car, wishing I could have cuddled more and showed my feelings better."

She gave a little nod, and her features relaxed somewhat.

"I want to see a lot more of you."

"I don't exactly feel great about last night."

"I know, baby. And I'm trying to apologize for rushing you into stuff you weren't ready for."

"I wasn't."

Sure, he thought. *Wait till I rush you into something you're really not expecting.*

"So I was hoping you'd let me buy you lunch," he said. That hadn't been on his mind at all, but he figured it couldn't hurt.

"Okay."

He cleared his throat. "Do you have that credit slip for me to look at?"

She looked toward the door. "No."

He struggled to keep the anger out of his voice. "What do you mean, no?"

"I can't let you see the slip. That's against company policy."

Before he could reach across the counter and shake her, she said, "But I can tell you his name. It's Ross Marshall."

He felt the awful tightness ease in his chest. "Ross Marshall. There probably aren't a lot of guys with that name."

"Yeah."

"Sandy, I really appreciate this. I really appreciate you," he added for good measure.

"I just hope my boss doesn't find out."

"How could he—unless you tell him."

"You're right." She pressed her hands against the counter. "I'm off at eleven-thirty for lunch."

He made his features register disappointment. "I'm working until one. So that's not gonna work. We'll have to do it another day."

"Yes. Okay."

"I'd better get back to work, before I lose my job."

She nodded, and he left—then headed straight for the hallway with the telephones and the rest rooms. Choked with excitement, he looked up Ross Marshall in the phone book.

He wasn't listed in the white pages, and Donald's heart plummeted.

Shit!

Ordering himself to calm down, he tried information. This part was tricky, now that the system was more automated. So he told the recorded message that he was from out of the area and looking up an old school friend. In the middle of the explanation, a real live operator came on the line; he told her that he wanted to make sure he'd located the right Ross Marshall.

"I have a listing for a Ross Marshall, private detective."

A private detective! Jesus. It was several seconds before he could drag in breath enough to speak. "Could you just read me the address so I can see if it's familiar?"

"Eighty-five seventy-two Stony Brook Lane," she told him.

"Yeah. That sounds right. Thanks." He wrote it down and hung up, feeling light-headed.

A private detective. With a dog. Investigating him!

Well, so fucking what? He didn't have any proof of anything. The dog hadn't come back with a report about the grave.

It was his word against the bastard's. Now.

Soon the bastard was going to be dead.

His next stop was the bookstore, where he consulted one of those detailed street maps. Stony Brook Lane wasn't in Montgomery County. It turned out to be in Howard County, off Route 99.

Was it really him? It had to be. He'd seen the guy's SUV last night, with the same first two license-plate letters as on the SUV from the second time the bastard had come visiting with his damn dog.

He made another circuit of the mall, his mind whirling. When he passed a guy lighting up a cigarette, he didn't even stop to chew him out.

He couldn't keep his thoughts off Ross Marshall. Couldn't suppress the excitement surging through him with the hum of an electric current. It was almost like the way he felt when he got a woman in his car, handcuffed and scared shitless. Almost sexual.

He was breathing hard. His face was flushed. And he knew he couldn't spend the next five hours prowling the walkways of this stupid mall.

Changing directions, he went down to the office, told the dippy little secretary he must have picked up a stomach virus and that he was taking sick leave. Then he went to his locker, got out his coat, and started for his car.

MEGAN sat on the sofa for a long time, unable to rouse herself. Finally, to escape the pain and misery, she pushed herself up and staggered down the hall and got dressed. But once she'd slipped into the car, she wasn't sure where she was going.

Work?

A sound of denial bubbled in her throat. Betty would see she was still upset and try to get her to talk about it.

Another hysterical laugh bubbled up. She couldn't talk about this with Betty. Or anyone else.

Hank would still be wondering what was wrong. He'd slide her questioning looks, but he wouldn't say anything. Walter would still be angry. And God knows where that would lead.

Because if she told any of them what had happened this morning, they would think she had lost her mind. Funny, that's what she'd been thinking herself. Now she knew she was completely sane. As sane as she could be after last night and this morning.

At first she drove aimlessly. But when she found herself near an entrance to Montgomery Mall, she pulled into the parking lot.

She wasn't sure what she was doing there. But she didn't have any better ideas, so she found a parking space and started toward the main entrance.

She was marching up the aisle toward the door when

she stopped in her tracks, suddenly remembering what Ross had told her yesterday.

Yesterday, before he'd shattered her life.

She shook her head, refocusing her thoughts. Ross had told her the killer worked here. That he was a security guard. Which meant that hanging around the mall was probably a bad idea.

BECAUSE he couldn't bear the four walls of the house pressing in upon him, Ross fled into the woods. Not as a wolf. Not after the encounter with Megan that morning.

Stopping beside an oak tree, he ran his fingers over the rich brown bark of the trunk, pressing his flesh against the narrow ridges.

Even in his human body, this place always had the power to calm him. But today the pain was simply too great.

Once again he saw the look on Megan's face—the look when she understood that he was the wolf. His whole body ached from the horror he had seen in her eyes. Suddenly unable to stand erect, he folded in the middle, wrapping his arms across his stomach to hold back the pain.

He stayed that way for a long time—unable to do more than fight the sense of loss. He didn't know how he would get through the next few minutes, let alone all the long lonely years that stretched ahead of him.

Jaw clenched, he forced his mind away from his own misery. At least there was one good thing that had come out of the meeting of wolf and woman this morning. It had saved her from a future of sorrow. A future with a man who would take out his savage nature on his family as surely as he would on his enemies.

But there was still the present to deal with. He had managed to save her when she'd been attacked. Yet she might still be in danger—and that possibility twisted like a dull blade into his guts.

Infused with a sense of purpose, he began to think about the car that had stopped in front of her house the other morning. What if the bastard was coming back?

But why had he been there in the first place?

Because he was planning to search for something? Or because he'd found out her address and was stalking her?

He looked at his watch. She should be at work—if she'd managed to make it to work after the scene in her backyard this morning.

Trotting back to the house, he changed into fresh jeans and a T-shirt and made a few quick preparations. Then he jumped into the SUV and headed back toward Megan's house.

DONALD was about to push open the door when he stopped short.

It was *her*. Coming toward the mall. The little blonde who'd been having dinner with the Ross Marshall guy in the food court the night before.

About twenty yards from the doorway, she abruptly stopped walking. Jesus, had she seen him? Did she know who he was? The questions swirled in his head as she turned and rushed back through the parking lot.

It wasn't because of him, his mind screamed, even as he felt sweat break out on his forehead.

Should he go after her? Get back inside? What?

Opting for action, he bolted through the door, then hung back as she got into her car, a cheap little green Toyota.

Because he couldn't risk her spotting him, he couldn't get close enough to read her license plate. Too bad his Land Rover was half a block away. He jogged over to it, and by the time he made it back to the area where she'd parked, she was nowhere in sight.

Shit!

Making a split-second decision, he took a guess at what exit she was using and roared up a row of cars.

At the Democracy Boulevard light, he spied her stuck in a line of cars.

Dodging around a Volkswagen, he joined the line, slipping past a dumb as mud woman who was trying to make a left turn. By the time the woman in the Toyota was a quarter mile down Democracy, he'd caught up.

Yes! This was his day. Nothing could go wrong.

Being careful to hang well back, he followed her toward Bethesda. Before she reached the downtown area, she turned onto Conway Street, and then into an industrial park. He stayed several car lengths behind, waiting for her to get out of her car. But the bitch was just sitting there. What the hell was she doing anyway? Eyes narrowed, he pulled into a parking slot a dozen yards down the row.

CHAPTER
TWENTY-THREE

JACK HUNG UP the phone, made some notations on a lined pad, and put them in the new folder that he'd started.

He'd already ascertained that a Donald Arnott had worked at King of Prussia Mall in Pennsylvania for four years and that he'd resigned eighteen months ago.

According to his performance evaluations, his work had been satisfactory but not outstanding.

Then, pretending to be doing a credit check, Jack verified that Arnott had joined the security force at Montgomery Mall twelve months ago.

With the man's employment established, he put in a call to the Paoli police department. After identifying himself as a Montgomery County, Maryland, detective working on a local murder investigation that might dovetail with women missing from the Paoli–Valley Forge area, he was put through to one of the guys in the squad room, a detective named Paul Carmichael. Carmichael confirmed that a number of women had disappeared from the area without a trace, at three- or four-month intervals. Luckily, the abductions seemed to have stopped—indicating that the perp was either dead or had moved away or had been jailed for another crime. The detective couldn't, however, give Jack an exact time frame without checking back through old case files. But he promised to call back after he had a chance to check.

Jack added Carmichael's name and number to the file.

There was still nothing concrete to link Arnott to the Pennsylvania disappearances or to any in Maryland, for that matter. But the local problem had started after he'd moved here.

His next step was to check out the case files of the women whose names Ross had given him.

Penny Delano. Charlotte Lawrence. Lisa Patterson. Cindy Hamilton. Mary Beth Nixon.

Apparently nobody had studied the cases with an eye toward determining whether one man had abducted and murdered them all. But as soon as Jack saw their pictures, he started getting excited. They were all blondes with flashy clothes. All a little overweight. All between the ages of twenty-five and thirty-five. All from working-class backgrounds. And their addresses made it likely that they had frequented Montgomery Mall.

He had just closed the Arnott folder when his mind made a leap to another subject and served up a connection he'd been unable to make the day before. Reaching for the stack of case files on his desk, he shuffled to the bottom and found the Crawford file. Inside, he turned to the crime scene report from Frederick County.

He found what he was looking for near the bottom of the text. There hadn't been much physical evidence found with the body. But the technician had noted the presence of dog hairs. From a shepherd or a shepherd mix—dark gray hairs with light tips.

Like the dog hairs that had turned up where Megan Sheridan had been attacked.

When he'd first looked through this folder, he'd felt an unaccustomed sensation of cold travel across his skin. He felt it again. Christ, maybe he should have Stan send the dog hairs to the FBI after all. And see if he could get Frederick County to do the same.

And what did he expect to find? That the hairs were from the same animal?

Which would mean what—exactly?

ROSS slowed as he approached Megan's house. There was no car in the driveway.

Good. She'd gone to work after their confrontation this morning. And if there was any way in hell he could help Thornton find out who had gone after her, he was going to do it. Including invading her privacy, searching her house.

He drove at a moderate pace down the street, taking a look at the neighborhood. The houses were wildly spaced, and judging from the lack of cars, it appeared that most people were at work. Anybody taking note of him would see a man delivering a package. He pulled in front of her house and set a brown-visored hat on his head that matched the bomber jacket he was wearing.

Retrieving a cardboard box wrapped in brown craft paper from the passenger seat, he pretended to check her address, then walked up the driveway to the side door. Pulling a set of burglary picks from his pack, he went to work on the lock.

It took almost no effort to get inside.

Christ, he'd have to talk to Megan about getting a new lock, he thought, until he remembered he'd committed himself to not communicating with her again.

With a grimace, he brought in the box, set it on the counter, then stood looking around the darkened kitchen, thinking about how he'd stood there last night holding Megan.

*   *   *

JACK got into his unmarked car behind the station house. He had a lot of checking to do, of course. But so far it looked like Marshall had done his homework.

His first impulse was to scope out Donald Arnott's property, at least from the road. Was it secluded? The kind of place where he could keep a victim captive, and then dispose of the body? But Jack didn't want to go there unless he was sure Arnott was at work.

So he headed toward Montgomery Mall, thinking that there were several advantages to that approach. He might be able to get a look at the guy.

As he pulled into the vast parking lot, he thought about his quarry, tried to see the job of a mall security officer from Arnott's point of view. The man probably liked exercising authority over other people. Plus the mall was a wonderful place to watch women and decide which ones he wanted to cull from the herd— which was doubtless the way he thought about it.

At this stage in the investigation, Jack didn't want it to get back to Arnott that the police were interested in him. So he pulled out one of the fake Provident Credit business cards that he'd had printed up with his name and a phone number that was out of service.

He found the hallway with the mall office and pushed open the door. When the secretary looked up inquiringly, he showed her the Provident card and asked if Donald Arnott was on duty.

"I'm sorry," the receptionist told him. "He went home sick today."

"He did?" *Lucky I didn't go out to his house.* "Hmm. Can I see his work schedule?"

"What's this about?" the young woman asked.

"He's applied for a loan. It's our policy to personally verify his employment."

The girl nodded and handed over the schedule. When he asked if he could have a photocopy so he'd be more likely to catch Arnott at the mall, she willingly obliged.

The look on her face suggested that she didn't much care for Mr. Arnott.

"So what can you tell me about him?" Jack asked conversationally.

"When he came in here a little while ago and said he was going home sick, he didn't look like he felt bad. He seemed excited—like he was going somewhere fun, not home."

"You're very observant," Jack remarked.

She shrugged. "He gives me the creeps. So I kind of started paying attention to him. Yesterday, there was this girl who got caught shoplifting at the drugstore. He brought her in here to wait for the police, and you could see how much he was enjoying himself."

"Like how?"

"Like giving her this mean look that made her cry. Like standing real close to her so his arm was against her breast." The receptionist made a face. "I mean, maybe she deserved to be scared 'cause of what she did. But he was overdoing it; you know what I mean?"

"Yeah."

"I guess I shouldn't have said all that," she murmured, but he could tell that now that she'd gotten started, there was more she wanted to say.

So he stood there looking receptive, giving her a chance to spill it. After another thirty seconds she came out with "I don't know what that woman from Indulge Yourself sees in him."

Jack had passed the store. It was full of gadgets that were way out of his price range. "You mean one of the sales clerks?" he asked.

"Yeah. She's got big blond hair. Wears flashy clothes. I saw them having dinner in the food court last night. She looked like she thought he was pretty special. Yuck. She must be desperate for a guy."

Christ. The receptionist had practically described the other women on Marshall's list of victims. "Well, you've been very helpful," he said. "But I would appreciate it if you don't mention to Mr. Arnott that I stopped by. We like to make our visits a surprise."

Apparently she bought it, because she nodded in agreement.

Jack left the mall office, wondering where Arnott had gone. From the receptionist's description of his behavior, it sounded like he was up to something. But what?

Hell, maybe he was just going to pick up a new television set or a hunting rifle, and he'd decided to call it sick leave.

Still thinking about that, Jack headed for Indulge Yourself.

ROSS'S chest tightened painfully, and he closed his eyes. But it was impossible to wipe out all the potent memories assaulting him as he stood in Megan's kitchen. Maybe it was a mistake to have come here. Maybe he couldn't handle it.

Then he gave himself a mental shake. He was in her house, and he was going to do what he could to ensure her safety.

There was a spare bedroom that she used as a den or a home office. He'd check that out—after he looked through the bedroom.

It wasn't the most logical place to start, but he didn't seem to be operating on logic as he made his way down the hall.

Her scent filled his nostrils, filled his entire head like a cloud of perfumed fog. He stood there, breathing hard. Trying to keep his body from shaking.

When he could manage some measure of control, he stepped through the bedroom door.

He'd conducted searches before. But never when he could barely think.

He raked his nails across the back of his hand, the pain bringing his mind back into focus. Standing very still, he studied the room, taking in details that he hadn't noticed the night before. There were books and magazines on her bed stand. But little clutter in the room.

Bitterly conscious that he was violating her privacy, he turned to the bureau, poking through the drawers, the silky fabric of her undergarments abrading his nerve endings. But he found nothing hidden under the intimate apparel, and nothing of significance in the drawer where she obviously tossed things that she didn't know what to do with.

His next stop was the home office, where he started going through the papers on the desk.

In addition to the usual bills and bank statements, he found a family photo album. Leaning back in the chair, he smiled as he studied pictures of Megan as a baby, a toddler. A kindergartner. Megan with her sister, Dory. He could have spent the day wallowing in the images.

He had no family snapshots from his own childhood. Apart from the portraits taken every year at school, there were no cute little pictures of the Marshalls because Vic hadn't wanted any reminders of the children he'd lost.

His mother had saved the school pictures in the bottom of a bedroom drawer. He knew because one day he'd come home unexpectedly and found her looking at them. Michael. Himself. Adam. Jonathan. Troy. Only two of them were still alive. Himself and Adam. And he hadn't seen his brother in years.

Her eyes had been red, and she'd tried to hide the pictures. But he'd seen—and he'd backed away from the terrible look of sadness on her face.

He sat staring into space for several moments. Then gently laying the album back where he'd found it, he turned to the papers in the desk. When he finished searching, he was no closer to knowing who had attacked Megan than when he'd picked the lock on the door.

* * *

AS he stepped through the door of the upscale shop, Jack worked to keep his features neutral.

He'd just been looking at pictures of Penny Delano, Charlotte Lawrence, Lisa Patterson, Cindy Hamilton, and Mary Beth Nixon.

And this woman could have been one of their sisters. Probably at the upper end of the age limit, but definitely a candidate.

"Hi," he said, checking out her name tag. "I'm from Provident Credit, Miss Knight."

As soon as he said the word *credit*, a look of alarm crossed her face.

"I wanted to talk to you," he said, waiting a beat to see if she'd reveal anything more.

"About what?" she asked cautiously, her eyes flicking to what must be a drawer behind the counter.

"Credit," he said again, watching her knit her hands together. She stood there, her skin pale, her eyes guilty.

He gave her a little smile, let her worry for a few more seconds, then said, "One of our customers gave you for a reference."

She let out a shaky breath. "A reference."

"Is that a problem?"

"Oh, no. Of course not."

"Donald . . ." He paused, watching her expression grow expectant. "Samperson."

The punch line left her looking disoriented. "Donald Samperson?" she repeated.

"Yes. He listed you as a reference."

"He did? Well, I don't know anybody by that name."

"Hmm." He took out his notebook, flipped several pages, pretended to consult a previous notation. "Well, Donald Samperson definitely put your name down. Perhaps he was thinking we wouldn't check his reference."

"Yes. Well, I'm sorry."

He wanted to tell her that getting out of town for a couple of days would be a good idea. But that might send her running to her security guard friend for protection.

He left, wondering if she was into something illegal. Something with Donald Arnott?

He'd like to find out what. And he'd also like to make sure she didn't end up in a grave on the Arnott property.

As soon as he got back to the station house, he was going to run Arnott's license plate and arrange for patrols to keep an eye on his car when it was in the mall lot—and on Ms. Knight as well.

CHAPTER
TWENTY-FOUR

SHE WAS A creature of habit. Or maybe she just didn't have any imagination after all, Megan thought as she sat in the parking lot outside the Bio Gen office.

She'd told herself that she didn't want to go back to work this morning. Now here she was. Back at the scene of the crime. The spot where she'd been assaulted two days ago.

And as she sat again in the car, a few feet from where the man had grabbed her, her mind went back to the details of those terrifying few minutes.

The wolf. Ross. He'd known damn well who had rescued her. But he'd let her think it was some kind of fantasy.

She couldn't deal with that part, with his implicit lies and her own complicity. The evidence had been there. She just hadn't wanted to believe her own senses. Deliberately, she turned her thoughts back to the man who had jumped her. He hadn't spoken. He'd been wearing a ski mask. He'd given her very few clues to his identity. But she'd managed to scratch her nails across the skin of his neck. For all the good it was going to do her.

She made a muffled sound in her throat. She couldn't deal with that either. She would go crazy if she kept thinking about that night. Or about Ross.

Opening the car door, she marched into the lab, snatched up the assignment sheet, and silently dared Betty to engage her in conversation as she looked at the next test on the schedule.

In the lab, she started the procedure, working slowly and carefully, focusing on each detail so she wouldn't make any mistakes and she wouldn't have to think about anything else.

DONALD waited several minutes to make sure the little blonde wasn't coming back. Then he eased into gear again and drove past the door where she'd entered the building. A sign attached to the brick wall said BIO GEN LABORATORIES.

Did she work there? Was she going for lab tests or something?

He wasn't going to sit here all day wondering.

Knowing he was taking a chance, he slipped out of his car and walked back to the office.

There was a window in front with venetian blinds cranked partway open. He could see a plump secretary inside sitting at a desk, typing at a computer. Taking a twenty-dollar bill out of his pocket, he folded it into his hand, then opened the door.

The secretary looked up.

"Pardon me, I thought I saw a blond woman come in here a few minutes ago."

"Dr. Sheridan?"

"I don't know her name. But she dropped this in the parking lot." He held up the twenty.

"Oh, my."

Now that he'd established himself as a Good Samaritan, he figured he could ask a question. "Does she work here?"

"Why, yes, she does. Do you want to tell her you found the money?"

"Oh, no. I don't want to bother her at work. Just return it to her."

He stepped back out the door, hurried to the Land Rover, and slipped behind the wheel. There was a smile on his face as he pulled out of the parking lot. Jesus, what a day. He'd gotten the name of the guy—and his girlfriend, too. And he could feel an exquisite tension building in his chest. Things were coming together. He was making them come together. Because now he'd turned the tables on the guy.

Ross Marshall had been stalking him. Now he was stalking Ross Marshall.

ROSS wandered into Megan's living room, sank into one of the chairs, and closed his eyes. He should leave. Now that he'd searched the place and found nothing significant, he had no excuse for being in Megan's house.

The temptation to simply sit here for a few minutes was overwhelming.

He took a deep breath of her scent into his lungs, held it inside himself, exhaled and drew in again, his fingers stroking the fabric of the chair arms.

She had touched that fabric, sat here, he thought, sinking deeper into the cushions.

His eyes blinked open, and he looked around.

Lord, this was crazy. What was he planning to do, sit in her house until she came home? Explain why he'd broken in?

He ordered himself to stand up. Ordered himself back to the kitchen door.

He had just opened it when he saw a car pull away from the curb.

The bulk. The shape. The metallic color. He hadn't
been able to see the details in the fog. But he thought
this was the same vehicle that had been here the morning after the attack.

Leaving the door open, the box inside, he pelted
back to the Cherokee, jumped behind the wheel. But it
was already too late. The bastard had gotten away.

Cursing under his breath, he returned to Megan's
house, slipped inside, and checked to make sure nobody had come through the open door. Then he picked
up the box and locked the door behind him.

DONALD took a ride in the country, to western Howard County to be exact. He could see that it had once
been rural, much like the area where he lived. Now
there were mansions and small developments sprouting
among the cornfields and patches of woodland that still
remained. Stony Brook Lane was off Route 99. The
mailbox at 8572 said MARSHALL. It was at the head of
a long drive that wound upward through a largely
wooded plot. He slowed, seeing a rutted track where a
number of the trees were posted with No Trespassing
signs.

Apparently Ross Marshall didn't like visitors any
better than he did. His detective job was probably just
a cover for something else, the way Donald used his
security guard job at Montgomery Mall.

That made sense. He imagined Marshall was a man
much like himself. A man who had his solitary pursuits, who had discovered a rival in the area, and who
was bent on eliminating that rival.

Donald's mouth cracked into a parody of a grin. He
knew where Marshall lived now. And the more he
could find out about the man, the better off he'd be.

He wanted to take the road into the woods and see
what was at the end of that driveway. But he had no
way of knowing whether Marshall was home.

Considering his strategy, he decided that the best thing to do was hang around for a while. Maybe his luck would hold, and the bastard would leave. If not, he'd come back after dark with a nightscope.

He continued up Stony Brook for several hundred yards, looking for a sheltered place to pull off the road. Finally he backed into a neighboring driveway and cut the engine. Opening the map, he laid it on the seat beside him so he could pretend he was lost if someone came down the drive behind him.

Christ, he was burning to go up and poke around Marshall's place. The dog must be up there. If he was in a pen, it would be like shooting fish in a barrel. But it was too dangerous to do it now.

Maybe the best way to get rid of Marshall was to plant a bomb with a pressure trigger up there. He'd studied up on stuff like that. And although he'd never used one, he had every confidence that he could master the simple techniques.

He smiled as he pictured the man and the dog being blown into such minute pieces that the police would have to scrape the two of them off the trees and nobody could tell which was which. The scenario warmed his heart. But a bomb would raise questions with the police. Why had someone picked such a dramatic way to get rid of Ross Marshall?

Better to come up with something more subtle. Some kind of poetic justice. But what?

He was about to start the engine and pull away when he saw a blue Grand Cherokee come sailing up the road. It braked, turned in at the drive. And he saw Marshall behind the wheel—big as life.

Jesus. Scrunching down in his seat, he watched the SUV disappear into the woods.

As he sat and stared after the vehicle, an elegant but simple plan started coming together for him. A way to get rid of Marshall. Using the woman.

*   *   *

MEGAN found she could work through the day's tests if she concentrated on each step, keeping everything else out of her mind.

By late in the afternoon, she was feeling numb and hoping that when she got home she could fall into bed and sleep.

God. Not into bed. She and Ross had been in her bed. And there was no way she'd get to sleep there. Not now. Not after what she knew about him.

A wave of emotion ripped through her. She wasn't exactly sure which emotion. Fear? Was she afraid of him? Afraid of a man who could turn himself into a wolf? She should be.

But that wasn't what she was feeling.

It was more like longing. Did she still want him? Or was she aching for what she knew could never be?

That was probably it.

As she stood in front of the lab table, she squeezed her eyes shut, trying to block out last night and everything after that. When she opened them, she found Walter standing in the doorway, watching her with unnerving intensity. She'd been so preoccupied with her own problems that she hadn't taken a good look at him in days. Now she saw that he'd lost weight. His face was thinner and his collar gaped away from his pale flesh.

"How are you doing?" he asked, watching her carefully.

The scrutiny made her skin prickle. But she answered "Fine" automatically.

"You're sure? You don't look so good," he pressed.

"Boyfriend trouble," she replied.

He stared at her for another few seconds as if trying to ascertain whether she was telling the truth, then turned away. And it was then that she saw what she hadn't noticed before, because his collar had been tighter. Now, where it gaped away from his flesh, she could see a narrow bandage on the back of his neck.

A gasp rose in her throat. But she managed to choke

it back, managed to keep standing there as if the world hadn't turned upside down. Once again she remembered being thrown to the wet pavement, remembered raking her nails across a man's neck.

Frozen in place, she watched her boss stride down the hall and vanish into his office.

Stunned, her head spinning, she grasped the edge of the desk, reliving the attack. She'd thought there was something familiar about the man who'd knocked her to the ground, ripped at her clothing.

Until now she hadn't figured out who he was.

Now here were the scratches on Walter's neck. Scratches she'd put there.

Could it really be true? Walter?

She glanced in the direction in which he'd disappeared, feeling the walls of the lab pressing in around her. It was hard to draw a full breath as she tiptoed down the hall to her office and closed the door.

Fumbling in her purse, she found the number of the police detective who had interviewed her, Jack Thornton.

With shaky fingers, keeping one eye on the office door in case Walter came back, she dialed his number.

The phone rang three times, four, five. Finally a woman said, "Montgomery County Police, Detective Division."

"I'd like to speak to Detective Jack Thornton, please."

"I'm sorry, ma'am. Could you speak up? I can't hear you."

"Is Detective Thornton there?"

"I'm sorry, he's left for the day. Do you want me to page him and have him call you back?"

Megan felt her throat clog. "Okay." She gave her home number because there was no way she was staying at the lab.

But leaving a message wasn't enough. She wanted to talk to him now. She wanted *help* now.

Grabbing her coat, she ran down the hall, past Wal-

ter's office, seeing him in the corner of her vision. He
was at his desk. Looking normal. Looking like everything was okay, when everything was all wrong.

The reception area was empty. Betty must have left
for the day. Thank God. Because Megan wasn't planning to blurt anything to her.

Stepping into the twilight, she crossed the blacktop
at a run. Reaching the safety of her car, she pulled the
phone from the cradle and dialed the only other person
she could think of who could help her.

Ross.

*Oh, God, Ross. Please. Please answer your damn
phone. Please be there.*

One ring. Two. Three. She waited with the blood
roaring in her ears, silently begging him to be there.

But he didn't pick up. And when she got his answering machine, she wanted to scream.

When she'd called the police and hadn't gotten
Thornton, she'd left her number. Now that wasn't good
enough. She had to tell *somebody* what she knew.
"Ross, I figured it out," she gasped. "I tried to call
Detective Thornton, but he wasn't in. It was Walter.
The man who attacked me was Walter. He was just in
my lab and I saw a bandage on his neck. And I—"

She gasped as somebody flung the car door open.

"No," she screamed, the phone dropping from her
fingers as she was yanked from the car. "No—"

His hand clamped over her mouth as he wrestled her
to a big white SUV parked a few cars away. He opened
the door, and she tried to brace her arms, clawing at
the opening with her fingernails to keep him from shoving her inside. But he was too strong.

"No, you don't," he panted, tearing her nails as he
flung her into the back. The seats had been folded
down, making a flat cargo area.

Breathing hard, he hovered over her, blocking the
view of anyone who might walk by.

He took his hand away from her mouth, pulled off

a piece of duct tape that had been dangling from the far door, and slapped it into place.

Next she heard metal clink, felt cold bracelets circle her wrists. Handcuffs.

He pulled her arms up and attached the cuffs to a metal ring that was fixed to the flat surface of the seat back.

Terrified, arms stretched above her head, she stared up at him as he loomed over her, a frightening look of satisfaction playing over his thin lips.

"Well, now I've got you," he said with a smirk. "I've rescued you from that Ross Marshall guy. I know what he is. I know what he's up to. Stalking me. Him and his damn trained dog. Only I've got you now. And you've got the honor of helping me get him. They'll find your grave on his property and they'll think he's the one who did it. But first we're going to have a good time together. Well, at least I am."

He reached out, covered one breast with his hand. She tried to shrink away, tried to kick at him. But he only slapped her hard across the face, then brought his hand back to her breast, finding her nipple through the fabric of her blouse and twisting so hard that she screamed, the sound a choked gurgle behind the gag.

His muddy brown eyes bored into hers. "Don't worry," he said. "When I get you to my place, I'll pull the tape off. Then you can make all the noise you want. I like to hear my women scream. And you'll scream plenty. Because that's just a little taste of what you're going to get from me. And this."

Pulling out a penknife, he opened the blade and pressed it against her cheek, pressed into her flesh, drawing the blade up along her skin, not deeply but enough to leave a trail of fire that brought tears to her eyes.

He looked at the blood on the blade, pulled out a tissue, and smiled as he wiped it off. "That's just skimming the surface. Before I've finished with you, there won't be any part of your body I haven't invaded."

Slamming the back door shut, he moved to the front and climbed in behind the wheel. Moments later the vehicle lurched forward, twisting Megan's arms as the man drove out of the parking lot.

CHAPTER
TWENTY-FIVE

THE CAR ROCKED, and pain jolted through Megan's arms. If she stayed in this position, her bones were going to snap.

Using her feet, she pushed herself up so there was less pressure on her arms. Then, carefully, she maneuvered to the side, working her wrists in the cuffs so that her hands were in front of her. It wasn't an ideal way to travel, but it was less agonizing.

Cautiously she twisted her head and looked at the man behind the wheel, trying to contain the bolt of fear that shot through her. She could feel her mind shutting down as she stared at him. All she wanted was to disappear into some deep, dark, buried part of her brain where he couldn't reach her.

Hide.

But he was probably counting on that. He wanted her scared, powerless, unable to fight him.

So he could get her in his house and kill her.

Kill her slowly, she thought, feeling the sting on her cheek where he'd cut her.

Fear clawed inside her belly. Behind the gag, she felt her breath choking off, felt her brain filling with fog. He didn't need to kill her. She would suffocate in the back of his car if she didn't control her panic.

Deliberately she bit down on her lower lip, the self-inflicted pain jolting through her, bringing the danger into sharp focus.

Don't lose control. Don't hide. Keep functioning, she ordered herself as she tried to breathe slowly and evenly through her nose.

When she had some control of the fear, she went to the next step—thinking. What did she know already? she asked herself, forcing her mind to focus.

Ross had told her a security guard from the mall was the killer who had shot him. Somehow the killer had figured out who Ross was—who she was. He was going to kill her and pin it on Ross, she realized with a jolt.

God, no.

Again her breath threatened to choke off. Again she kept air moving in and out through her nose.

He'd killed more than one woman. She knew that from Ross. And he was going to kill her, too—unless she could stop him.

But how?

As the car jounced along, she fought a wave of nausea. Ross had said he'd found women's graves on this guy's property. He hadn't told her the man got a thrill from killing.

She squeezed her eyes shut. Not just killing. Terror. Torture.

How long did he keep his victims around? Hours? Days?

A white-hot jolt of terror threatened to overwhelm her. But she managed to contain it.

Nobody was coming to her rescue. Nobody knew where she was. If she was going to escape, she had to do it herself.

She was on her own. She had to get away from him

or die trying. Because she had no doubt that a quick bullet in the back was better than what he had planned for her.

ROSS was in his office when he remembered he'd turned off the phone before he'd gone into Megan's house.

Dialing his message number, he leaned back in his chair.

The chair bounced when he heard her voice.

"Ross, I figured it out," she gasped. "I tried to call Detective Thornton, but he wasn't in. It was Walter. The man who attacked me was Walter. He was just in my lab and I saw a bandage on his neck. And I—"

Her voice cut off in a choked gasp. Then she screamed, "No!" as the phone apparently clattered to the floor.

"Jesus! No. Oh, God, Megan," he shouted, even as his mind tried to process what he'd just heard.

It was her boss, Walter. The guy who had attacked her was her boss. And now the bastard had her.

Playing the message back, he listened for details. She'd said he was just in her lab. Praying that they were still there, that the bastard hadn't taken her anywhere else, he jumped back into his car and sped back toward Bethesda.

The trip should have taken an hour. He made it in forty minutes.

Teeth clenched, hands fused to the wheel, he spun into the Bio Gen parking lot.

It was dark when he arrived but he could see Megan's car was still there, thank God. And one other. The Mercedes.

Son of a bitch.

He strode to the door, tried the knob. It was locked. Without bothering to knock and give the bastard any warning, he went back for the picks that were still in his bag, found the right one, and manipulated the lock until he heard it click.

Once inside he sped past the darkened reception room and down the hall, then surged through the door of a plush-looking office where a slender man in a tweed sport coat was taking handfuls of files from a cabinet.

"Walter Galveston?"

The man whirled, goggled at him as he strode forward.

"Galveston! Where the hell is Megan? What have you done with her?"

Utter confusion suffused the man's features. "Megan? I haven't done anything with her."

Ross grabbed the man by the shoulder with one hand. With the other, he yanked the collar away from Galveston's neck, exposing the bandage.

"Stop that! What the hell do you think you're doing?"

Ignoring the protest, Ross pulled the bastard's arms from his sport coat, tossing the garment on the floor before yanking his shirttails from his pants and ripping the fabric up the middle of the back.

As he'd anticipated, Galveston's back was covered with claw marks. "The wolf did that to you," Ross spat. "Now tell me what you've done with Megan or I'll have the wolf rip out your throat." The words were half human, half animal growl.

"Please. I beg you. I don't know where Megan is. She went home."

"Sure."

"That's the truth. I swear."

Ignoring the words, Ross raised a hand, wrapped it around the scrawny throat, squeezed.

The man's eyes bulged; his face turned red.

Ross eased up the pressure. "Where is Megan?"

"I swear I don't know," he gasped.

"You were at her house the other morning. And this afternoon. You saw me at the window."

"I . . . please . . ."

"Convince me you haven't got her now. Tell me why you attacked her in the first place."

A desperate flow of words poured out of the man. "The lab is in financial trouble. I'm going bankrupt. But I've got money stashed in a safe place. Not the bank. I've been making it look like bad things were happening around here. The car accident. The break-in. When Megan was there that night, I got the idea that attacking her would add to the pattern of bad stuff happening at the lab. It would make it look like I didn't have any option besides killing myself when I staged my own death. Please. I went to her house that morning looking for my lapel pin. It's missing. I thought it might have gotten stuck to her clothes or something. You've got to believe that."

Ross peered into the wide, pleading eyes. And he did believe. Oh, Christ, he did believe. But then where was Megan?

"When did you see her last?" he spat out.

"She was here an hour ago. I think that's right. I saw her go past my door. She was in a hurry."

"You bastard." Ross tossed the frightened man against the wall like a sack of trash and ran back the way he'd come.

Reaching her car, he realized that the door wasn't quite shut. And when he pulled it open, he almost choked on a smell that had been burned into his consciousness. Arnott.

Arnott had been in Megan's car.

In the dim light of the overhead bulb he looked wildly around the interior, saw the phone on the floor. Her purse.

One of her shoes.

"God, no!" he roared. *God, no.* Somehow Arnott had found her—and taken her away. Somehow—

A sick dread gathered in the pit of his stomach. Had Arnott seen them together at the mall? And somehow figured out who was stalking him?

But how? How in the hell had he done it? Not because he'd recognized the wolf.

It didn't matter how he'd figured it out. All that mattered was getting Megan out of the bastard's clutches.

He was back in his car, heading into the country as he dialed the police.

"Jack Thornton, please."

"He's gone home for the day. I can have him paged."

"Yes. Tell him to call Ross Marshall at 301-555-9876. Tell him it's urgent. Tell him Arnott has Megan. Tell him I'm on my way out there."

"Spell that name, please."

"A-R-N-O-T-T."

Hanging up, he dialed information and got Jack Thornton's home number.

An older-sounding woman answered. "Hello?"

"Is Thornton there?" he asked, hearing the panic in his own voice.

"He's out. May I take a message?"

"This is Ross Marshall."

"Oh. Yes. Ross Marshall, the PI. He's spoken about you. This is his housekeeper, Mrs. Anderson."

"I've got to reach him. It's a matter of life or death."

"He's at a soccer game with his son. He won't be home for a couple of hours. Did you have him paged?"

"I already did that. But I'll give you the message in case he calls home. Tell him Arnott has Megan. Tell him to meet me there with backup."

He clicked off, concentrating his efforts on driving, praying that he wasn't going to be too late.

MEGAN felt her heart rate speed up as the car came to a stop in front of a gated fence. Arnott got out, unlocked it, drove through, then relocked it behind the car.

God, they were trapped inside a fence. But she could climb over, she told herself. If she could get away from

him. And she had to get away. There were no other
options.

He pulled the car to a stop and looked back at her,
his expression smug. "Wait right here. I've got to get
things ready."

The words sent a sliver of cold piercing through her.
After he got out, she started pulling at the handcuffs,
trying to slip her hands through the rings. But all she
got for her trouble was a pair of chafed wrists.

He returned, looking even more pleased with himself. Opening the back door, he climbed inside and
pulled her around so that she was lying on her back
again.

Her heart leaped into her throat. Was he going to
kill her here in the car?

No, she told herself. He'd mess up the car, and he
didn't want to do that, did he?

She could see the bulge at the front of his pants,
knew that her helplessness and her terror were turning
him on. Good—maybe with some of the blood drained
from his brain, he wouldn't be thinking as clearly.

He had done this before. He had been successful.
That would make him feel confident. Powerful. And
he'd think of her as one of the dumb women he could
use and discard as he pleased.

That gave her a tremendous advantage. He'd assume
that she was just one more terrified woman he could
control.

When his hand shot out to yank off her remaining
shoe, her body gave an involuntary jump. He tossed
the shoe to the side, then reached under her skirt,
grasped the elastic of her panty hose and panties, and
pulled them both down and off.

She closed her eyes, turned her head away.

"Look at me."

She swallowed, lay unmoving as she felt his eyes
traveling over her body.

"You'll be sorry if you don't do what I say."

She turned her head back, watched the satisfaction

spread across his face as he held her gaze with his for a long moment. Then he reached out and ripped the tape from her mouth, making her gasp from the pain.

"You look like a slut with your privates hanging out like that. Like my mom. She was always showing what she had to the guys."

She wanted to say that he'd been the one who'd exposed her. Wanted to ask if that's what this was all about—his mother. But she kept her lips pressed together.

Feeling his fingers stroke the skin of her hips, her belly, she cringed. When he reached down to rake his hand through her pubic hair, thrust his hand between her labia, she couldn't hold back a little moan.

He took out the knife again, and she stared at him wide-eyed, terrified of what he was going to do. He knew she was scared, and he was enjoying it. Bringing the blade down slowly, he cut an almost delicate line in the crease at the top of her right thigh.

She knew he wanted her to cry out. To beg. She didn't know which was worse—giving him what he wanted or keeping silent. So she opted for silence.

When he scooted forward, reached across her, and unlocked the bolt that held the handcuffs to the car, she tried to hold back her sigh of relief.

"Time to come into my playroom," he rasped. "We'll cut the rest of your clothes off when I get you on the table."

JACK looked at Craig and grinned. His son grinned back, and Jack felt a surge of love—and gratitude. Last year, after Laura had died, Craig had been eaten up with grief and rage. He'd had problems in school, problems with his friends, problems with the law.

That part was the worst to take. A cop whose son was caught shoplifting.

But the family therapy had helped Craig—helped them all. His kids were doing okay now—except for the occasional times like Lilly's nightmare.

"Great game, Dad."

"Yeah." Jack chomped on his hot dog, swallowed a swig of Coke. Before his mouth was entirely clear of food, he started shouting again. "Go for it, Martinez. Go for it."

Craig joined him, jumping to his feet in his excitement.

The moment was spoiled when Jack heard the beeping of his pager. Looking down at the number, he saw that it was his office.

Son of a bitch. Couldn't he even have an evening out with his kid? Was he supposed to be on duty 24/7?

"Craig, I'll be right back."

Trying to ignore his son's look of disappointment, he climbed out of his seat and went to find a quiet spot where he could see what was so urgent.

In the aisle, he almost collided with Emily Anderson. Jesus, what was she doing here?

"What is it? What's wrong? Is it Lilly?" he asked, his eyes searching hers.

Emily was quick to reassure him. "No. She's fine. I left her at the Wilsons'."

A sigh of relief rushed out of him. It wasn't his daughter. But then what was wrong?

They huddled against the wall, but it was impossible to block out the noise of the game.

He waited until another round of encouragement from the crowd had subsided before asking again, "What's wrong?"

"Ross Marshall called. He said he paged you."

"Yeah, I just got a page. He called the house, too?"

"Yes. He sounded upset. He told me to tell you that Arnott has Megan."

He stared at her in disbelief. "You're sure that's what he said? Arnott has Megan?"

"Yes."

"Jesus." Dr. Sheridan had paged him earlier and he'd

tried to call her back. But he'd only gotten an answering machine.

"He said he was going out to his place. He said for you to come and bring backup."

He looked at his son, who was once again happily immersed in the soccer game, and hated to drag him away.

But Mrs. Anderson had followed the direction of his thoughts. "You go on. I'll stay with Craig. That's why I came here."

His hand gripped her forearm. "Emily, thanks."

"Go on."

"Yeah." He ran down the steps, his phone already in his hand. First he called dispatch and got the same message from Ross. Then he called the station house and asked for patrol cars to meet him at the property of Donald Arnott, 5962 Newcut Road.

MEGAN stumbled, trying to stay on her feet as the killer pulled her after him into a ruined building and then down a flight of rough wooden steps and through a low doorway into a chamber where the air was fetid with the smell of old blood and other things.

It was brightly lit, and she gagged as she saw the racks of knives and other instruments on the wall. In front of it was a wooden table with leather straps. And at the foot of the table was a videocamera on a tripod.

Mouth dry, heart hammering in her chest, Megan knew that if he got her onto that table, she was a dead woman.

She took a few steps forward, then made a terrified sound as she sank to the floor beside the camera, going limp, pretending that the place was too much for her.

"Get up, cunt."

She stayed where she was, limp and unmoving, silently urging him closer.

When she didn't respond, he bent over her.

Bringing up her clasped hands, she smashed the metal handcuffs into his face

He made a grunting sound, and she pushed him aside, slamming the videocamera down on his head, then sprinting up the steps, the rough wood tearing at the bottoms of her feet as she ran.

Behind her she heard him bellow, "Fucking bitch!" The angry exclamation only fueled her sense of purpose as she ran through the building, her cuffed hands making her movements awkward.

DONALD scrambled up, crashed into one of the tripod legs, and went down again. Anger boiling inside him, he pushed himself erect.

"Fucking bitch," he spat out again. She'd gotten the drop on him. And now he was going to even the score. She might have gotten out of the room, but she wasn't going far. Not when the place was fenced and her hands were cuffed.

His guns were in the house. He'd never needed them in this room, never needed them to control the stupid, frightened women he brought here. With a grunt he rubbed his face where she'd clunked him. That bitch was going to be sorry when he caught up with her.

He'd get her, all right. Get her good.

He wasn't going to kill her with the gun, just shoot her in some fleshy part of her body to make sure she was under control. Then he'd bring her back in here for a session she'd never forget.

JACK turned on the radio, listened to the scanner traffic as he headed for Newcut Road.

Satisfied that a patrol car was on the way, he pulled his notebook from his pocket, found Marshall's, number and dialed.

"Hello?"

"Ross, this is Jack. What happened?"

"Are you on your way to Arnott's?"

"Yes."

"Thank . . . G- . . ." the PI breathed, his voice break-ing up from interference.

"How do you know he has Megan?"

The transmission was still flaky, but it sounded like Marshall said, "I smelled . . . in her car! All over . . . like rotten . . ."

"What? I don't understand."

"I can smell people. That's how . . . how I . . ."

Doubt shot through Jack. "You're not making any sense."

"Jesus. It doesn't matter . . . how . . . I know he's got . . . I thought it was Walter Galveston. But it wasn't . . . -im. And then I went out to her car and . . ." The transmission choked off. Marshall was probably in a pocket where his cellular service couldn't reach.

"Ross, Ross, can you hear me? Ross."

There was no answer. The line was dead.

Jack set the phone on the seat. The conversation hadn't made a great deal of sense. Was Marshall drunk? Out of his head?

The only thing he knew for sure was that the ur-gency—the fear—in his voice had been real.

CHAPTER
TWENTY-SIX

THE ANGER HAD boiled off, leaving him relaxed, enjoying the hunt on this fine moonlit night—although it was hardly a fair contest. A man with a gun stalking a handcuffed woman. In a big cage.

He knew where she was. He knew there was no possibility of her escaping from this locked compound. So he'd slowed down, letting her think that maybe she had a chance to get away from him before he moved in for the good part.

Now he stood very still in the darkness, imagining he could hear the breath hissing in and out of her tortured lungs as she cowered behind a tree. He'd run her pretty good. She was tired.

Alone, defenseless, and scared shitless.

The bitch had thought she was so smart, whacking him with the cuffs like that. But she was going to learn the consequences of her actions pretty damn soon.

With a grin he started moving forward again, making sure she could hear his booted feet crunching through the dry leaves, playing the flashlight on the foliage, bringing the light closer and closer to the tree where he knew she was hiding.

ROSS eased up on the gas pedal, pulled off Newcut Road, and screeched to a halt in front of the gate, weighing his options.

He could change into wolf form and go under the fence the way he had on the night Arnott had shot him. But he wanted Jack to be able to get inside—if he made it out here in time to do any good.

Snatching the burglary kit from the seat beside him, he leaped out of the SUV and started working on the hasp with a hacksaw. It took effort—and precious minutes—to cut through the steel, but finally he snapped the hasp, tossed the lock to the ground, and pulled the gates wide.

Jumping behind the wheel again, he started up the road—unsure of where he should be going and angry that he hadn't had more time to explore inside the fenced area before Arnott had found him that first time.

The bastard had brought her in here. He knew that. But then what? Was there a room in the house where he took his victims? Or did he take them somewhere else?

That would be the safe bet. Somewhere hard to find. But where the hell was it?

Well, maybe he didn't have a clue where to look, but the wolf would know.

Ahead was a white Land Rover gleaming in the moonlight. Stopping well behind it, he pulled off into the woods, then jumped out and trotted over to the vehicle. When he yanked the door open, he could see that the backseat had been folded down to make a cargo area.

Pushed to the side of the flat surface were a woman's shoe, panty hose, and underpants.

The blood froze in his veins as he stared in horror at the undergarments. The son of a bitch had started undressing her out here. What else had he done?

Keeping the panic at bay, he started tearing off his own clothes even as the words of transformation tumbled from his mouth.

He felt his muscles popping, his shape changing as he kicked his pants away, then he leaped into the vehicle, breathing in Megan's wonderful scent, mixed with the stench of the monster—and blood.

Oh, Lord—blood.

The combination made him gag. Jumping out again, he put his nose to the ground, finding the trail easily. Megan was wounded. But she'd been on her feet and able to walk. At least he knew that much.

He followed the combination of scents along a dirt path toward a ruined barn, moving cautiously lest the bastard lunge out and pop him again. Because if he got shot this time, he'd be no damn good to Megan.

JACK arrived at the entrance to Arnott's property, knowing backup wasn't coming anytime soon.

Two hotshot rookies had been on their way—but they'd been so excited, they'd crashed into a station wagon at Georgia Avenue and Damascus Road.

He called for another patrol car as he rolled through the open gate. A sawed-off padlock was lying on the ground.

Which must mean Ross was already here—and inside. Jesus, he hoped the two of them were going to be enough.

He spotted a Grand Cherokee pulled off the road and Arnott's Land Rover a couple of dozen yards farther on. He'd run the plate, so he knew the make and model.

Stopping behind Ross's vehicle, he unholstered his Sig P228 and cautiously approached the Cherokee. It was empty.

Proceeding to the second vehicle, he found the door was open, the backseat folded down, and what he assumed was Megan Sheridan's underwear lying in a discarded heap across from the restraining ring that Ross had described.

Beside the car was an untidy pile of men's clothing. Damn—had Arnott already stripped for action? And where the hell had he taken Dr. Sheridan?

Ahead he could see the lighted windows of a house. His best choice was to assume the bastard had taken her there—and that Ross was on the scene.

NOSE to the ground, the wolf sniffed the doorway of the barn. They had definitely come this way, Megan and Arnott—both still on foot.

Cautiously he slipped through the door, his claws scratching across the rough floorboards.

Ahead he could see a bright light coming from somewhere below ground level.

Ears pricked, body tense, he edged toward the illumination and came to a short flight of rough steps.

A shiver traveled over his body. If Arnott was at the bottom of those steps with a gun, anybody coming down was going to be an excellent target—particularly a four-legged animal who would have to negotiate the stairs carefully. But if Arnott was holding Megan down there, then going down was the only way to save her.

He thought about changing back to human form. But then he'd only be a naked man—without a weapon. At least this way he had his teeth and claws, he thought as he set his right forepaw on the steps, listening intently for sounds from below. There were none. But Megan's scent was strong here. So was Arnott's. And other odors overwhelming both their scents. Blood. Tortured flesh. Human waste.

Hugging the wall, he made his way down the stairs. The room was empty but he goggled in horror at the wooden table, racks of instruments, and overturned videocamera. Thank God Megan wasn't here now.

But she *had* been here. Very recently. Now she was

gone. So was Arnott. He'd brought her here. And somehow she'd gotten away from the bastard.

A good hypothesis. He prayed that it was true.

But, God, where was she now? She must have gone back up the stairs.

Climbing the steps, he reentered the barn, then stood breathing the night air, trying to catch Megan's scent. He had followed her trail from the Land Rover. He had to figure out where she had gone now.

MEGAN crouched behind a tree, watching the beam of a high-powered lantern play across the foliage, hearing the killer's footsteps crunching on dry leaves. She cowered down, afraid to run, afraid to move, feeling twigs and leaves digging into her bare legs, her bare bottom.

The tree was a barrier between her and the killer. But he was coming closer, relentlessly closer. And if she stayed where she was, he was sure to find her. So she gathered herself together, stood, and ran for a tangle of brambles, her breath burning in her lungs.

When bullets sprayed the ground only yards behind her, she screamed and sprinted faster, the air searing her lungs.

In the distance she could make out the chain links of the fence. But there was no question of climbing it now. She'd be a target perfectly poised for the killing shot.

She dodged to the right, trying to lose herself in the underbrush. Desperately she pressed on, gasping for air, each breath close to a sob as she came to the end of her strength.

Her mind almost paralyzed by terror, she kept moving, her only goal to put distance between herself and the man with the gun.

Then she felt her blood turn to ice in her veins as she realized what she'd done. The fence was directly ahead of her and her only options were to turn and sprint along the barrier, or try to dodge back the way she'd come, making a circle around the killer.

Liking neither choice, she opted to circle back. And then suddenly Arnott was looming in front of her, the gun in his hand and a satisfied expression on his beefy face.

"You bitch. You're going to pay for that little trick," he spat as he pulled the trigger, firing more bullets into the dry leaves before raising the weapon.

Her jaw clenched tight, she braced for the pain of a slug tearing into her flesh.

THE house lights were on, but there were no sounds from inside that Jack could detect. No screams. No pleas for mercy.

He was cautiously peering through a ground-floor window when the sound of a machine gun firing shattered the silence of the night.

Behind him and to the right. In the woods.

Turning, he bolted for the stand of trees, his feet sinking into newly tilled ground, then pounding across the firmer surface of the forest floor.

The sight that greeted him was like a blow to the chest. A man with an Uzi. Arnott.

A woman cowering in front of him, trapped. Dr. Sheridan.

THE sound of machine-gun fire ripped through the air. Digging his paws into the debris on the forest floor, Ross stopped in his tracks.

He was going in the wrong direction. He'd followed Megan's scent into the woods but she must have circled back through the trees, tried to hide in the underbrush. But the killer had tracked her—found her.

Changing direction, he lowered his head and hurtled through a tangle of bramble, the thorns tearing at his fur as he pelted toward the sounds of gunfire, running at top speed but closing the distance with agonizing slowness.

His only thought was *Save Megan*. He had to save Megan. His mate. His woman. That was the one essential idea his brain had room to hold.

A savage snarl tore from his throat as he sprang from a thicket and focused on the man with the gun turning toward Megan, his weapon raised.

With no regard for his own safety, the wolf gave a mighty leap, springing toward the killer.

"Ross, watch out! Ross!"

Dimly, in some part of his mind, he heard Megan scream a warning. But it rolled off him as he hurtled forward, bringing Arnott down in one graceful leap. As they hit the ground, the gun discharged, sending a hail of bullets into the underbrush.

The noise mixed with the scream of terror that welled in the man's throat.

Ignoring the bullets, Ross sank his teeth into Arnott's gun arm, wringing another scream from the man—this time of pain. Frantically Arnott beat at the wolf's head and back with his free hand.

But there was no dislodging the animal. Blind rage made him hold fast, shaking the arm, biting down until the man's fingers went limp and the gun fell to the ground.

Then a knife materialized in the killer's free hand. It arced downward, slicing a gash in the wolf's shoulder.

With a growl deep in his throat, Ross dodged away, then sprang again, straddling the man, pinning the knife arm to his side as he went for the throat, crunching down through flesh and bone with a savage snap of his jaw.

A sound of horror rose from the killer's vocal cords—choked off in a rattling gurgle.

The wolf held on for a moment longer, shaking the limp body, then let it fall backward to the ground.

His muzzle dripping with blood, he lifted his head.

As he stared at the woman who cowered away from the scene of carnage, he felt a sharp mixture of triumph and sorrow.

Megan was safe—and he was lost.

A noise penetrated his consciousness, footsteps crunching on dry leaves. Turning, he saw Jack Thornton staring at him wide-eyed.

Throwing back his head, he howled for his victory and his loss, his voice mingling with the man-made wail of approaching sirens. Then he turned and raced away into the darkness.

BESIDE the white Land Rover, Ross changed back to his man form, then bent and pulled on his jeans. His upper arm was stinging from the knife wound, but the cut wasn't deep. Returning to his own vehicle, he pulled his first-aid kit from the glove compartment and tied several gauze pads around the arm before pulling on his shirt and stuffing his feet into his shoes.

After wiping the blood off his mouth, he dashed back to where he'd left Megan and found Thornton on the ground beside her, speaking to her in a low voice.

When he closed the distance between them, she raised her head and stared at him, all the horror of what she'd just seen shimmering in her eyes.

Pain squeezed his heart as he stopped five feet away, because he dared go no closer. "It's okay. I won't touch you," he managed to say in a gritty voice, then demanded urgently, "But you've got to tell me. Are you all right?"

Her lips moved, but no words came out.

He backed up a step. Kneeling on the ground, his face at her level, he focused on her pale, bruised face. But he kept his hands rigidly at his sides to show her he wasn't going to reach for her no matter how much he wanted to fold her into his arms and cling for dear life. "Megan. For God's sake, Megan. Did he hurt you?"

She lifted her hands across her chest, and he saw that she was handcuffed.

Rage and pain welled inside him. "He cuffed you. Oh, Christ. Did he do anything else? Hurt you?"

"He cut me." The words were thin, barely above a whisper, but they slashed through his own flesh.

"Where?"

She raised the cuffed hands toward her cheek. "Here. And at the top of my leg."

"The son of a bitch."

"It's not bad." Her eyes were dazed, and he knew she was in shock. "I got away before he . . . before he . . ."

"Thank God!" Turning to the police detective, he asked, "Can you get her out of those damn cuffs?"

"I don't have the key."

Pushing himself up, Ross went to the ruined body and hunkered down again, his eyes dispassionately assessing the damage the wolf had inflicted. Then, calmly, he searched the pockets and found the key, which he handed to Thornton.

Moments later the restraints clicked open, and Megan rubbed her wrists. "Is he dead?" she whispered.

"Yes," Ross answered.

"Good," she choked out. Then her eyes went to Ross's arm, where blood stained his shirt.

"He cut you, too."

"It's not deep."

He saw Thornton's head swing around, focus on the bloody shirt.

The detective opened his mouth, but before he could comment, uniformed officers came charging through the underbrush, their guns drawn.

Quickly Thornton stood, held out his badge. "I'm Detective Thornton," he called out. "The situation's under control. The suspect's dead."

"What happened?" the lead officer asked. "Did one of you shoot him?" His questioning gaze swung between Ross and the detective.

It was Thornton who answered. "I was too far away to shoot. An animal killed him. A large dog or a . . ." He didn't finish the sentence.

The officer stared at him as if he couldn't believe what he was hearing. "A large dog killed him? A pit bull?"

"I'm not sure."

The other uniform turned to Ross. "Did you see it?"

He hesitated for a minute, then said, "No. I was in the barn—searching his torture chamber."

Ross's gaze caught Thornton's—and held.

"Yeah. He missed the action," the detective said, backing up his story in a strained voice.

Both uniforms went to the body and squatted down, looking at the mangled mess of blood and flesh.

"Jesus," one of them muttered. "His throat's ripped out."

Ross bowed his head, unable to meet anyone's eyes. He'd gone for the carotid artery when he might have simply stopped the man from killing him with the knife. But rage had carried him to the next step.

"Should we put out a bulletin on the animal?" the lead officer asked.

"Sure. Couldn't hurt," Thornton said. Ross was pretty certain the detective didn't think they were going to find anything.

Megan had been sitting with her teeth clamped together. Now she began to speak again, and he could see she was struggling to keep her voice steady.

"He took me to that . . . that torture chamber. I got away, and he came after me with a gun."

"How did you escape?" Thornton asked.

"I pretended to faint. When he came to pick me up, I hit him with the cuffs and ran."

"Good for you," Ross said, his hands clenched at his sides. The need to hold her, press his lips to her pale skin, was an ache inside him. But he could see she didn't want him any closer than he already was.

"I think the room is proof enough of what he's been

doing here," he said. "There was a videocamera. Maybe you'll find tapes."

"Can you show us where it is?" Thornton asked.

"Yeah." His gaze swung to Megan. "But she doesn't have to see it again. Call an ambulance for her. She should be checked out in the hospital."

"I'm okay," she insisted in a thin voice.

"Ross is right," Thornton said, backing him up again.

Ross stood, blood roaring in his ears, his eyes focused on Megan. The pain in his heart was almost more than he could bear, because he knew this was the last time he would ever see the woman he loved. He would remember her like this. And remember the look of joy on her face after they'd made love. And all the other moments of the brief time they had spent together.

She had seen him kill Arnott. Seen the savagery of the wolf and cringed away from the man. And now the only thing left for him was to walk away with what dignity he still possessed.

JACK waited until one of the uniforms put in the call, then helped Dr. Sheridan into the backseat of the cruiser. While one of the officers sat with her, he and the other officer followed Marshall through the woods to a ruined barn.

The PI pointed to the opening in the floor, where bright light flowed up a flight of rough steps. "I guess he wanted to make sure he could see every detail of what he was doing."

"Yeah." Jack let Marshall lead the way down the steps into a room that looked like it had been constructed during the Inquisition—except for the modern lighting and the video equipment.

Gagging at the smell, he looked around at the racks of carefully arranged knives and other implements. At one end of the room was a TV with a VCR, next to videocassettes neatly labeled and stacked on shelves.

Penny Delano. Charlotte Lawrence. Lisa Patterson.

Cindy Hamilton. Mary Beth Nixon. The murder victims.

If the tapes showed what he thought they showed, then there was no doubt that Arnott had killed the women.

And now he was dead. His throat ripped out. Like Crawford. He'd think about that later. First he needed to get official statements from Marshall and Sheridan.

CHAPTER
TWENTY-SEVEN

MEGAN HEARD A car stop in front of the house. Whenever that happened these days, she felt a burst of anticipation—and dread.

Ross. She longed for it to be Ross, and at the same time she didn't know if she could handle seeing him. Not now. Not yet.

Her emotions were still too raw. Her thoughts still in turmoil. Her wounds too fresh.

Crossing to the kitchen window, she looked out and felt a stab of disappointment mixed with relief.

It wasn't Ross, it was the detective—Jack Thornton.

She took a step back, her hands clenching and unclenching as she waited for the doorbell to ring. He'd made her uncomfortable once. Now . . .

Now she was pretty sure the two of them shared a secret that could destroy Ross Marshall.

The bell rang, and she jumped, then tried to will her heart from thumping its way through the wall of her chest as she walked toward the door.

When she opened it, they stood looking at each other for several seconds.

"Can I come in?" he asked.

"Why?"

"I want to make sure you're okay."

"I'm fine," she said without moving.

"Megan, let me come in."

She still had a choice, she thought. But she stepped aside and he followed her into the living room.

"Why are you really here?" she asked.

"To see how you're doing—and to talk about Ross."

She took her bottom lip between her teeth, thinking that they could circle around that latter topic for hours. Instead she decided there was no point in prolonging the uncertainty. "You could have turned him in," she said. "But you didn't. Why not?"

He stared at her, neither of them spelling it out— but both of them knowing exactly what the other meant.

"Can I sit down?" he asked.

She gave a tight nod. He took one of her overstuffed chairs; she sat on the sofa, her fingers closing around the edge of a cushion.

"What purpose would it have served to turn him in?" Thornton asked.

"It depends on whether you think Ross is dangerous."

"Because he killed Arnott?" the detective said.

He was being more direct than she'd expected. If she'd needed proof that he'd lied about the "big dog" that had killed Arnott, he'd just given it to her. Or maybe he was looking for confirmation that *he* hadn't imagined the impossible.

An awkward silence stretched between them.

She was the one who broke it. Ignoring his direct question, she said, "I'm trying to sort through my life, trying to decide what I want to do." She stopped and turned her palm upward. "There are things that are still too hard for me to deal with." She might have been talking about her ordeal at Arnott's. She was pretty sure

Detective Thornton knew she was talking about Ross Marshall, werewolf.

"I understand." He cleared his throat. "I'm sorting through stuff, too."

Her heart leaped into her throat. "You aren't going to . . ."

"I'm not going to talk about him to anyone besides you," he said quickly.

"Good."

He shifted in his chair. "I'd like to come back, if you don't mind. Find out how you're getting along."

"Why are you so interested in my welfare?"

"Because I know you're going through a hard time. Because I know there's nobody else you can talk to about . . . what happened. And there's nobody I can talk to, either," he added.

She hesitated for a moment, torn. Despite his reassurances, she didn't know how far she could trust Police Detective Jack Thornton. But she would find out, because in the weeks ahead she might need a friend.

JACK paused at the entrance to Ross Marshall's property and inspected the No Trespassing signs, then stepped on the accelerator again and nosed the unmarked up the rutted road into the woods.

He negotiated a rickety bridge that crossed a gurgling stream, then emerged into a meadow across which he could see a very nicely proportioned stone and wood house that fit perfectly into the wooded landscape.

The ideal place to live, he thought, for a man like Marshall. Privacy. Woodland. A comfortable home.

It had been a month since Dr. Sheridan had been abducted by Donald Arnott and a gray wolf had leaped out of the darkness to cut the serial killer down.

When Jack turned off the engine and got out of the car, he heard the sound of someone splitting wood—working as if the devil himself were flogging him.

Rounding the side of the building he found Marshall shirtless in the late April sunshine, splitting a log on a chopping block. He stared at the man's tanned skin, seeing his muscles flex. Ordinary skin he told himself. Ordinary muscles.

He waited until the ax had completed its downward swing and the piece of wood had fallen into two chunks before clearing his throat.

The PI turned, looked at him warily as he propped the ax handle against the block. "Did you come to arrest me?" he asked.

"For what?"

Ross shrugged. "You tell me."

"Actually, I came to say that I hope we can keep working together."

Surprise flashed on the other man's face. "Why?"

"You've been a big help to me in the past. It's a good professional relationship. More than that, I think we've gotten to be friends."

Marshall nodded, then asked. "What about that scene at Arnott's?"

Jack had been pretty direct with Megan. This time, he gave a different answer. "I guess you missed it, 'cause you were in the barn."

"Um-hum. And what about Crawford?"

"That's a Stone Who Done It."

Marshall shifted his weight from one foot to the other, still looking uncertain, and Jack understood his reasons. With Marshall, the need for caution must be as ingrained as the habit of looking both ways before crossing the street.

"Why don't you invite me inside? You must be cold now that you've stopped working."

"Okay." The PI picked up a plaid shirt draped across the woodpile and shrugged his arms into the sleeves. As he buttoned the front, he led the way around to the front door. They stepped into a spacious room of gleaming wood and comfortable furniture. Huge windows brought the outdoors inside.

Jack looked around with a touch of envy. "Nice place. I take it you remodeled it yourself."

"How do you know?"

"I did a background check on you when I was investigating the Crawford murder. I know you bought a number of houses and fixed them up. Then put the profits into this place."

"Yeah. It's the American dream—improving your lot in life."

"You seem to have done better than most."

"It depends on the way you look at it."

Jack was wondering how to respond when Marshall spoke again. "I can offer you herbal tea. Water. I don't drink coffee. Or anything stronger." He gave a small laugh. "Caffeine plays hell with my system. And alcohol—forget it."

"Tea is fine."

He followed Marshall into a nicely laid out kitchen with granite countertops that would have made Mrs. Anderson swoon, watched him open a cabinet and gesture toward several boxes of tea.

"I'll have whatever you're having," Jack said.

Marshall filled the kettle and turned on a burner, then pulled down a box of wild blackberry tea.

Propping his hips against a counter, he looked at ease, although the tightness around his eyes betrayed his tension. "So you've decided you don't care how Arnott died or how I get the information I bring you?"

Jack kept his own posture relaxed as he met the other man's gaze. "That's right."

"But you're pretty sure you know."

"Yes."

"And that doesn't . . . make you want to run screaming in the other direction?"

"I believe I'm open-minded enough to handle it."

Neither one of them had said the word *werewolf*, but it hung in the air between them.

"Ross, I liked you from the start. I never understood why you were so closemouthed about your investigative methods. Now I understand better—but it doesn't change my opinion of you. You're a good, solid PI. The information you've given me has always panned out. And I've never had any reason to question your motivation. You're not trying to get even with anybody. Or score points. Or rip anybody off. You're not the Lone Ranger."

Marshall listened, then spoke quietly, almost to himself. "After Crawford, I swore I'd never indulge in vigilante justice again. Never bring myself down to the level of one of the bastards I was tracking."

"But Arnott was pointing a gun at Megan, ready to pull the trigger—you didn't have a choice. Then he went for his knife. Plus you keep forgetting that I would have killed him if I'd been close enough. Now my advice is: stop beating up on yourself."

"Easier said than done."

"Yeah," Jack agreed. After ten years in law enforcement, he had his own burden to lug around.

Marshall got down two mugs, added tea bags and boiling water. "It has to steep awhile."

"Okay."

"Tell me about Walter Galveston. Did you go after him?"

"Megan told him she wouldn't press charges—if he'd agree to psychiatric counseling."

"So you're dead in the water?"

"I'll give you the legal mumbo jumbo on that. The state's attorney could, by law, go ahead with the prosecution, using Megan as a hostile victim. But with the court system so clogged, I'm pretty sure he's decided to nol-pros the case."

"Which means in English?"

"Well, a nol-pros isn't a dismissal. It just means the state's attorney chooses not to prosecute, and the case kind of lies there in legal limbo—unless Walter gets back into criminal activity. Then the state can drag this case out of the archives as an added benefit."

Ross was leaning forward, hanging on the details.

"You haven't talked to Megan about it?" Jack asked, although he was pretty sure he knew the answer to the question. He'd seen her a week ago, and she hadn't mentioned getting in touch with Ross.

"I haven't seen her."

"I'm sorry. I could tell you two care about each other."

He grimaced. "Well, her seeing the wolf take Arnott down had to be a shock even if it was justified. And she'd been treated to a preview of my undesirable qualities."

"It's something genetic? That's why you went to Bio Gen Labs?"

"Yeah. I have a twenty-fourth chromosome. At Arnott's you got a graphic demonstration of the effect it has."

"Your parents had a lot of children who died."

"You *did* dig into my background."

"I interviewed a neighbor, Rosa Lantana."

Ross gave a bark of a laugh. "Is that old bat still alive? I'll bet she gave you an earful."

"Yeah."

Marshall looked down into the mugs, stirred the contents with a spoon. "You want sugar?"

"I'll take it straight."

"Let's go sit where it's comfortable."

They each took a mug and settled themselves into leather chairs in the great room.

When Marshal spoke again, his voice was flat and hard. "To give you the rest of the genetic picture—the girl babies die at birth. The boys hang around until their teens. Then they either turn out like me, or they . . ." He shrugged. "I don't know. Maybe it's a stroke that kills them. It causes a hell of a headache in those who survive, anyway." His hand gripped the mug so tightly that the knuckles whitened.

"I'm glad you trust me enough to talk about it."

"I figure if you tried to tell this to anyone, they'd catch you with a butterfly net and cart you off."

It was Jack's turn to laugh. "Right."

"So you see that any woman who got mixed up with me would be in for a lot of grief." Marshall spoke matter-of-factly, but it was obvious the subject was painful—and one that had been on his mind for a long time.

Jack wanted to tell him that he'd talked to Megan— that she might not make the right decision on her own. He wanted to say that if Ross loved her, he should go after her. Then he reminded himself that things weren't so simple for the man he'd always thought of as the Lone Wolf.

Ross shrugged. "I've been keeping tabs on her, though. I had a chat with Galveston. He's selling her the lab equipment at a very reasonable price. I know she's got financing for her own company and is moving to another location, and that Galveston isn't exercising any claim over research she did while working for him."

Jack already knew those details. He said only, "She deserves that victory—after what she went through."

"Yeah."

When the silence stretched again, Marshall asked, "So what are you working on?"

"Mostly routine stuff. But a few cases you'll appreciate." Over the mugs of berry tea, Jack gave him the details. "Well, call me if you have anything I can use," he finally said, rising from his chair.

Marshall stood, too, facing him.

Jack held out his hand, and they shook, their clasps warm and firm. "Take care of yourself."

"You, too."

He wanted to say more. But he was in danger of embarrassing himself or Marshall with half-baked philosophy about friendship and loyalty. So he turned and left.

* * *

THE next time Megan braved the road to Ross Marshall's house was almost three months after she had first come here. It was late in the day, as the last fading rays of the sun kissed the landscape.

Once more, she cut the engine and stepped nervously out of her car. The trees had leafed out, the canopy of their foliage luxurious against the navy blue of the sky.

She looked at the flower beds near the house, making out the shapes of ferns and hostas interspersed with brightly colored impatiens, the arrangement as natural as if it had simply sprung up. But she knew that an artful gardener had placed the plants to suit his own aesthetic sense.

She took several steps closer, breathing in clean country air—then stopped short when she saw a gray shape moving toward her.

The wolf.

Her heart skipped a beat, then started hammering so hard her chest hurt. But she'd done a lot of thinking since they'd parted, and now she stood her ground as he approached, his head up, his gait majestic.

This was the first time she'd gotten a good look at him when fear wasn't slashing through her.

She looked her fill now, feeling her heart turn over. He was beautiful, a wild creature—totally uncaged, totally at home in the forest. Yet his yellow eyes glowed with the intelligence she'd seen that first time—intelligence far beyond that of a mere animal.

Tangled emotions surged through her as he came forward across the meadow, a challenge in his gaze and his posture. The first night she'd seen the gray wolf, she'd turned and run. Now she went down on her knees in the springy grass, bringing herself to his eye level as he stopped within a few feet of her.

"I missed you," she said, holding out her arms. "Come here."

For several heartbeats, she wasn't sure he was going to accept the invitation. Then he moved toward her with maddening slowness, as if he were giving her a final chance to change her mind.

She stayed where she was. And finally, finally he was close enough so that she could reach out, circling his neck with her arms and laying her cheek against his thick coat.

The contact sent a surge of relief flowing through her. She drank in his woodsy scent. Turning her face, she rubbed her lips against the side of his muzzle.

His tongue flicked out, and delicately licked her cheek, and she felt a shiver go through him.

"Mmm. I'm glad to see you, too." She stroked the silky fur behind his ears, pressed herself more tightly to his side.

"What do you think it means when a woman is turned on by a wolf?" she asked. "Well—not just any wolf. Her mate, actually."

He eased away so that the bright yellow eyes could meet hers.

"I guess you're wondering where I've been. I've had some stuff to straighten out. About the lab and my project. And other things." She swallowed, her fingers playing with the fabric of her cloak. "My research on Myer's disease is going to bring in quite a bit of money. Enough to finance my new project."

The wolf cocked his head questioningly to one side.

"Saving girl babies with the twenty-fourth chromosome. And figuring out what to do for the boys when they get old enough to change."

The turbulent look on his face made her shake her head. "You're not going to frighten me away this time."

The wolf stepped back twenty yards, stood looking at her, and she knew what he was going to do. Despite her bold words, a bolt of fear shot through her. But she stayed where she was, her breath fast and shallow.

She had known she must face this. Known it was the ultimate test—for both of them. Wide-eyed, she watched the shape of his body begin to flow the way it had that first night when fever had almost driven him to change. Then he had stopped himself in time. Tonight, he didn't. Seeing the transformation froze the breath in her lungs, and she felt her face contort.

ROSS stood in front of her, a naked man, watching the horror that twisted her perfect features into something that shattered his heart. The sorrow of it was almost too much for any living being to bear.

He had lain awake at night aching for her, yet he hadn't dared to hope for his heart's desire. Then he had seen her get out of the car—and all the longing had coalesced into one terrible driving need to claim his mate.

He had held back his joy when she put her arms around his neck, telling him she accepted the wolf, because he knew there was one crucial test that the wolf's mate must pass.

And now—

Now he felt as if his body and his soul had been torn to shreds and scattered to the winds.

"No. Please. No." She pushed herself off the ground, and he braced himself for unbearable pain. She had come here and given him hope. Then snatched it away.

But she didn't turn her back. Incredibly, she was coming toward him, her loose cloak flowing around her in the wind.

"Ross. Oh, God, Ross," she cried as she hurtled forward, wrapped her arms around him, holding him as though she never meant to let him go. "It's all right. It's all right," she added, the tears in her voice burning his skin.

"Your face. I saw the look of horror on your face," he managed to get out before his clogged throat made speech impossible.

"No. Not horror," she gasped, tipping her head back so that her eyes could meet his. "I watched you, and I thought how much it must hurt—muscle and bone contorting, internal organs changing shape. And I remembered how you'd done it twice—to save me. From Walter and from Arnott. That's what you saw."

It took several charged moments before the words sank in. Yet he still couldn't quite accept that happiness was within his grasp. "Don't you have the sense to be afraid of me? Of us?"

"I'm not afraid. I love you. That makes all the difference."

He sucked in a breath and let it out before it scalded his lungs. "You saw me kill a man."

"To save my life." She repeated what Jack Thornton had said.

"Arnott never would have come after you, if it wasn't for me. He probably saw us together at the mall."

"Ross, stop! That wasn't your fault. And if I were afraid of you, I wouldn't be here. Don't you know that every man and woman struggles with doubts? Regrets? Fears? You don't have to be a werewolf to doubt yourself."

He stared down into her eyes, trying to absorb the words. "God, what am I going to do with you?"

"Love me, I hope."

His head dropped to her shoulder. For long moments he stood listening to the sound of his own labored breathing as her fingers tangled in his hair, stroked across his broad back, drifted downward to caress his naked hips. Somehow it was that contact—the possessive way her fingers glided over his body—that allowed the miracle of their reunion to sink in.

Lifting his head, he looked down at her in wonder. She gave him a brilliant smile. "We had one unforgettable night together. I want a lot more."

Slinging her arms around his neck, she breached the distance between her mouth and his.

His response came in a flood of physical sensation and emotion, like a dam bursting. His mouth opened, devoured hers with all the hunger that had built inside him over the past lonely days and nights.

She tasted wonderful, and he feasted on her. She felt wonderful, and he gathered her close. Her scent was richer, fuller than he remembered. He might have puzzled over that, but she didn't give him time to think.

She spoke against his lips, nibbling the words, "It's a little too cold to make love out here. At least it is for me. Can we go inside?"

Too overwhelmed to voice an answer, he turned and led her to the house. He'd pictured her there, with him. But he'd thought it was simply a fantasy built from his own aching loneliness.

Now she had come to him, and the reality humbled him.

They made it through the front door, but not much farther. The sight of her eyes bright with need and her lips red and moist from his kiss made his knees go weak.

He laid her down on the rug in front of the fireplace, gathered her to him, rocking with her as they kissed and stroked each other, each touch, each kiss fueling the astonishing sensual pleasure building between them.

"I'm overdressed, I think," she murmured.

"Yes." His hands shook as they worked to pull off her cloak and open the buttons on the simple shift she wore. As they had that first time in her kitchen, two sets of hands tangled.

This time, she laughed, the sound pure joy in his ears.

"We could rip it off," she suggested.

"I'm trying to show you I can be civilized," he answered, his voice rough with barely leashed passion.

Finally, after an eternity, she was as naked as he. On a sigh of gratitude, he bent to press his face against her breasts.

She combed her fingers through his hair, holding him to her. He turned his head to find a hardened nipple with his mouth, teasing her with his tongue and teeth, wringing one glad cry from her and then another as his thumb and finger tightened on her other nipple.

In the dark hours of the night, he'd wondered if he'd made it up, if anything could have been as good as the memory of making love with her.

Incredibly, this was better. The taste of her was exquisite, the feel of her overwhelming.

His free hand slid along the curve of her hip, then traveled inward to the thatch of blond hair at the vee of her legs. His fingers dipped lower, finding her hot and wet and ready for him.

A low hum of pleasure vibrated in her throat as her body arched into the caress. Then he felt her hand close around the hard, distended shaft of his penis, and a jolt of incredible animal sensation surged through him.

"I want this inside me again."

Her words and enticing clasp drove him to the edge of madness. Now. It had to be now! He covered her body with his, his eyes never leaving hers as he plunged inside her, feeling some dark, hidden core deep within him shatter.

"Oh, Ross," she breathed, her arms circling his shoulders, and he sensed that she had felt it, too.

She was his mate.

More than his mate. His love. The other half of his being. And he understood now that his soul would have died if she hadn't come back to him.

He began to move inside her, feeling her match his rhythm. He wanted the incredible pleasure to last an eternity, but nothing so intense could endure for more than moments. He felt her inner muscles contract, heard her call out his name once more. And then he was shaking with the force of his own release, his head thrown back as ecstasy washed over him.

Afterward he held her in his arms, watching the satisfied expression on her face, gently touching the faint scar that ran down her cheek.

She turned her face, closed her eyes as she kissed his fingers.

His hand moved lower, stroking possessively over her flushed skin. When his fingers skimmed over the slight swell of her abdomen, he stopped a tremor going through him.

"Megan?" he asked, his voice hoarse.

She opened her eyes, met his questioning gaze, and gave him a small nod.

"Oh, Christ."

When he tried to wrench away from her, she circled his shoulders, held him beside her. "It's okay."

"You don't know that!"

"Yes, I do. It's a boy. I found out this morning. There's a new technique that gives you the sex early. That's why I waited so long to come back here. I wanted to find out before I saw you."

"And if it had been a girl?"

Her face turned very serious. "I . . . would have tried to save her, although I'm not sure I could do anything at this point. With in vitro fertilization, there's a much better chance. If it's a girl, you can remove the extra chromosome before implanting the fertilized egg."

"And with a boy?"

Her features lightened again. "We've got fifteen years to figure out what happens at puberty. I need to do some tests on you. And on your brother, if he'll let me. I'm betting that the key to survival is hormonal."

He stared down at her in wonder. "You'd do all that for me?"

"For us. I'd do anything for us. The question is: Can you accept the idea of 'us'?"

He bent, pressed his forehead to hers. "God, I want to." His voice turned low and urgent as he went on rapidly. "But . . . you didn't choose me, the way any other woman would choose a man. The extra genes I have forced me to find a mate. You came here and touched me, took care of me. That was how the bond formed between us. Neither one of us could control what was happening."

She let him talk, waited until he was finished. "I

don't think it's so different from the way other women choose a man," she murmured. "They meet. Maybe by chance, the way we met. And some mysterious chemistry draws them together. But they know they've found the one person for them—in all the sea of humanity."

He hadn't thought about it in those terms. Never. The revelation shook him.

She lifted her face, looked into his eyes. "The important thing is, do you love me?"

"You know I do."

"Then stop worrying about the rest of it. Just let yourself take the leap off the cliff. I'll be leaping with you."

She made it sound so easy. And maybe with her beside him it could be. Maybe she was what he needed to rise above the genes that ruled his life. Perhaps he had found the anchor to his humanity in her—this woman who had come back to him against all odds.

"I love you," he whispered. Then said it again louder.

"Did it hurt to say it?" she asked, a smile flickering at the corners of her lips.

"Only a little. It will probably get easier with practice." He pulled the quilt off the sofa, tucked it around them, and nuzzled his face against hers, trailing his lips up her cheek.

Her arms came up to circle his shoulders, pull his body more tightly against hers. "I can't promise everything is going to work out perfectly. We may have some . . . sadness . . . in our life."

"You mean, we may lose some children?"

"I hope that's not going to be true. But there are no guarantees. There never are."

He sucked in a breath, let it out in a rush. "I think I got the closest thing to a guarantee I could get when they sent a doctor out from Bio Gen Labs—and it turned out to be you."

She snuggled in his arms. "You know what Jack

started calling you a long time ago? The Lone Wolf. Ironic, isn't it?"

"You talked to Jack?"

"He came over to find out how I was doing. He kept coming back, and I could open up with him a little more each time. He ended up telling me how much you needed me. That was after he'd been out here and talked to you."

"The sneaky bastard."

"I told him why I was waiting before I came back here."

He thought about that for a moment. "So he found out we're going to have a baby before I did."

Her color deepened. "Do you mind? I had to talk to someone. And he . . . he let me know that he's our friend." She watched his face anxiously.

"I think he is."

He saw the tension ease out of her. Then she gave him a sly smile. "I think if you asked him, he'd be your best man at the wedding."

His face must have told her how unprepared he was for the suggestion.

"That is if you're interested in making an honest woman of me," she added.

"God, yes. I just wasn't thinking that far ahead."

"I'd like to do it soon—before I start showing. I think the ceremony will be a little more decorous that way."

Once the idea took hold, he realized how much he wanted the world to know she was his wife. "As soon as we can," he answered thickly.

She pressed against him, then raised her head. "So now that I know you're not going to send me away, I think you're going to have to feed me. I was too nervous to eat anything before I came here. But now I'm ravenous. I've discovered pregnancy will do that to you."

"You want some chicken soup?" he offered. "I have a bunch of it left."

"Steak, I think. This child I'm carrying is demanding meat."

"Well, then, that's what he'll get." He climbed out of their makeshift bed, hurried down the hall to his bedroom, and pulled on a T-shirt and jeans.

When he returned he saw that she'd dressed in her shift and run her hands through her hair.

He stopped at the entrance to the great room, just staring at the woman who had changed his life, still hardly able to believe she was really in his house—really his. For the rest of his life.

She must have read the expression on his face.

"Believe it," she murmured. Then, *"Go gcumhdaí is dtreoraí na déithe thú."*

He gazed at her in wonder. "You know what that means?"

"Yes. 'May the gods guard and guide you.' I got myself a Gaelic dictionary. I used one of yours when I was here before. I know why you named this place Díthreabh. It's your refuge. Ours, now."

She glided toward him, kissed his lips, his cheeks, his brows as her fingertips stroked lovingly over his back and shoulders.

He gave himself over to her embrace, and in that moment, he finally understood the Lone Wolf would never be alone again.

Turn the page for Jack Thornton's
pulse-pounding story in

EDGE OF THE MOON

Coming in August 2003 from Berkley Sensation

"I'VE GOT SOMETHING more important for you. Come on into my office."

Jack pushed back his chair, then followed his supervisor to the private enclosure in the corner of the squad room.

When they were both seated, Granger said, "I'd like you to interview a woman named Kathryn Reynolds." He consulted a file on his desk. "She turned in a missing person report two days ago on her tenant, Heather DeYoung. One of the uniforms at the Rockville station, Chris Kendall, took the initial report."

"Uh huh."

"We have several other missing person reports in the county. Another woman named Brenda Quinlin. A young man named Stewart Talber. And an eight-year-old boy, Kip Bradley."

Jack felt his chest tighten. A kid. About the age of his own children. He remembered the newspaper accounts of the case. There was some evidence that the boy had been abducted by his noncustodial father, but neither the man nor the boy had turned up in a month of beating the bushes for them. Jack was still hoping it was the father, because the alternative hit too close to home.

"The missing adult male is mentally ill," Granger was saying. "On the surface these cases don't seem related to each other—or to Heather DeYoung. But you're good at digging information out of witnesses and making correlations. DeYoung is the freshest case. I want your impressions—and then I want you to see if you can find any patterns."

Basically, there was nothing strange about Granger's request. Jack knew he was good at connecting the dots on cases that might not seem related. Still, Granger's manner put him on the alert. There was something else in play here. Had a bigwig with an interest in one of the cases leaned on the captain?

Jack knew he might never find out. So he simply said, "Okay," took the offered case files, and went back to his own desk to study them.

An hour later, he pulled up in front of Kathryn Reynolds's nicely preserved Victorian on Davenport Street. Out of habit, his appraising eye took in details. It was early in the season, but the flower beds were dressed with a fresh layer of mulch. Pink and red azaleas and a variety of daffodils were in bloom, along with white dogwoods.

He sat for several more minutes, still grappling with the odd, disquieting feeling that had settled over him in Granger's office. He might have ignored it, but long ago he'd learned to trust his spider senses.

He'd worked with Chris Kendall, the officer who had taken Reynolds's report, back when they were both at the Bethesda station, and he would have liked to talk to him before coming out here. But the patrolman had left the building for a doctor's appointment before Jack had gotten the assignment. Too bad, because the initial police contact was a good source of additional information. Although the uniforms put down what was required in writing, there was usually a whole lot they didn't get onto paper. Jack liked to do a little probing into their casual observations, stuff they didn't think was important enough to go in the report, or stuff they didn't even know they'd noticed, until he asked about it. He also paid attention to their opinions, which gave them a chance to express "gut feelings" that were often useful later.

Of course, Jack suspected Granger was probably planning to do the same thing with him. More than once, the captain had sent him out on an interview that hardly seemed top priority, then quizzed him on his impressions.

After climbing out of the unmarked and locking the door, he glanced toward the second floor of the house and caught a flash of red. Red hair, he realized—as fiery as flames flickering behind the windowpanes.

Was that Reynolds? Or someone else? Whoever it was had pulled back the moment he'd looked up. So was she nervous about getting caught peering out or curious about who had pulled up in front of her house?

He hadn't called ahead. She'd said she worked at home, so he'd taken a chance on catching her in— catching her off balance if there was something going on that she hadn't shared with Officer Kendall.

He tucked the folder unobtrusively under one arm and started toward the front door. According to the initial report, Ms. Reynolds owned the house and lived on the upper story. The missing woman had an apartment on the ground floor.

Jack rang the bell and listened to footsteps coming down an inner stairway. He prepared to confirm the name of the female who opened the door; but the moment the door opened, the breath froze in his lungs so that it was impossible to speak.

He was caught and held by a pair of emerald-green eyes, a sweep of wild red hair, and skin like rich dairy cream.

His muscles went rigid. His arm clamped against the folder tucked against his body.

Time seemed to stop, like a scene from a videotape frozen on a TV screen. Unable to move forward or back away, he stared into her eyes, seeing her pupils dilate and then contract.

Everything around him was out of focus, with the exception of the slender young woman standing in the doorway. She remained sharp and clear. Details came to him: the way her breasts filled out the front of her wildflower-printed tee shirt. The smell of strawberries wafting toward him. The startled look in those green eyes.

Along with the physical awareness came a jolt of pure sexual energy, like nothing he had ever experienced in his life. Lust at first sight. It was almost palpable—arching between them like electricity between two contact points. Dangerous and at the same time so compelling that he would have leaped through a wall of fire to reach this woman if she had been on the other side.

The whole out-of-kilter experience lasted only seconds. Then the world as he knew it clicked back into real time. The moment had passed so quickly that it was easy to tell himself that it had all been in his imagination.

He clung to that theory, because if it wasn't imagination, he was hardly equipped to deal with what had happened.

The woman in the doorway took a quick step back, as if trying to escape from the same emotions bolting through him.

For several heartbeats, neither of them spoke.

Finally, Jack dragged air into his lungs and let it out before asking, "Kathryn Reynolds?" He was surprised that his voice sounded normal.

"Yes. And you are?"

"Jack Thornton, Montgomery County P.D."

Reynolds's hands clenched in front of her. "The police? Have you come to tell me something about Heather? Is it bad news?"

"Are you expecting bad news?" he asked, slipping back into his professional mode, carefully watching her reaction.

"No ... I mean, I don't know. I hope not. I don't know what to expect."

"Can I come in? Then you can tell me what brought you to the station house."

"Can I see some identification?" she countered, as if she'd just realized she should have asked.

"Of course." While he pulled out his ID and shield, he was still mentally shaking his head at his out-of-character reaction in those first few seconds after she'd opened the door.

She studied his ID, then said, "I already filed a report with Officer ..." She stopped and fumbled for the name. "Officer Kendall."

"Yes." Jack put away his credentials, then pulled the folder from under his arm, opened it, and showed her the forms. "I have the report right here. So can we talk?"

This time she nodded and stepped back to let him into a vestibule. He followed her through a second doorway, then up a flight of steps, watching the unconscious sway of her hips in faded jeans.

He was accustomed to making assumptions about people based on their personal spaces. Seconds after stepping into her apartment, he was thinking that Kathryn Reynolds was a study in contradictions.

In one corner of the room was an antique desk with a computer under a set of mahogany wall shelves. Catty-corner to the desk area were more shelves piled with neatly labeled folders and plastic boxes. The office atmosphere was broken by all manner of whimsical objects that adorned the work area. He saw ceramic cats, a papier-mâché rooster, at least ten fancy glass paperweights, a glass unicorn. On her computer screen was an underwater scene with swimming fish and coral. When the computer made a belching, bubbling noise like a toilet flushing, she crossed the room and cranked the sound down.

He cleared his throat. "So when did you first notice that Heather DeYoung was missing?"

She walked toward one of the easy chairs, picked up a paisley pillow, and clutched it to her middle as she sat down. "It kind of crept up on me. Two days ago I realized she hadn't come home since Sunday night."

"She was missing for five days before you reported it?"

Her fingers clamped on the pillow. "You're making it sound like an accusation."

"I didn't mean to. I'm just trying to get the full picture," he said, still watching her reactions, thinking that facts were never the whole story.

"Sometimes she stays away for several days. It suddenly dawned on me that I hadn't seen her in a while."

"Okay." He answered, noting her discomfort, although he still didn't know if it was because of her friend or because of him.

For a split second he thought about what had happened when she'd opened the door. Should he say something? To clear the air? Or to find out if she'd experienced the same thing that he had?

The latter would be his primary motive, he silently admitted. A very unprofessional motive.

Usually he had an excellent sense of what questions to ask a witness or a suspect. Today he fumbled for the right approach.

"Let's see. Ms. DeYoung works for the Montgomery County School System—as a substitute teacher. That pays enough to support her?"

"She says it does."

"But she could have some other source of income?"

"I don't know."

He set finances aside for the moment. He had other ways of poking into the woman's fiscal solvency. Instead, he quickly switched topics. "So Ms. DeYoung is unreliable?"

She tipped her head to one side. "Where did you get that impression?"

"It isn't unusual for her to take off for several days—on a whim." He waited for her to counter the statement.

"Yes, but she pays her rent on time. She doesn't give me any problems."

"What kind of problems are you referring to?"

"She doesn't play loud music. She doesn't have wild parties. She doesn't wake me up at two in the morning if the toilet's stopped up. She gets out a plunger."

He nodded, thinking about what she was saying and what she was leaving out. "Does she have any bad habits? Drugs, alcohol? Something that could get her into trouble?"

"No," she said, but could have sounded more sure.

"But?"

Reynolds swallowed. "I don't like to make judgments. And I don't like to talk about people."

"I understand. But if it will help us find Heather, I'd appreciate your insights."

She swallowed, then answered. "Okay, I don't like her boyfriend."

"Because?"

"He takes advantage. She loves him, but he doesn't love her."

"How do you mean, 'takes advantage'?"

"He's borrowed money from her." She stopped, played with the fringe of the pillow. "I wouldn't tell you this if it weren't important. He told her he'd stop dating her if she didn't have an abortion last year, but she was the one who had to pay for it."

The guy sounded like a real winner, but Jack still didn't know whether or not Reynolds was exaggerating her assessment. "She discussed all that with you?"

"Yes. We've gotten to be good friends."

"What's his name?"

"Gary Swinton."

"Could she be at his house?"

"His apartment," she corrected. "I thought of that. I

called and left a couple of messages on his answering machine."

"Do you have a phone number for him, an address?"

"In my Rolodex." She stood, set the pillow down on the chair, and crossed to the desk, where she flipped through cards—then gave him the requested information.

"What about a work address?"

She thought about that. "I know he's a clerk at Circuit City. The one in Bethesda. I think he's in small electronics—because he got a good deal for her on a floor model table-top stereo. But I don't have the address."

"I know where it is. Can you give me a description? Some way I'll recognize him?"

Her hand skimmed across the desk, settled over a foot-long clear plastic rod with colored liquid and shiny stars and moons inside. When she tipped it on end, the liquid and the glitter began to flow up and down the tube.

She stared at the bobbing glitter, her brow wrinkling. "He's about thirty years old. Blond hair. Light eyes. They're set close together. His hair is usually just one beat too long—maybe to hide his bald spot. He's average height. Not too heavy. He's got a small scar on the left side of his chin. I guess that would be the most identifying mark."

"Okay. That's great," he said, writing it down. "You're good at detail."

"My art background."

"Yeah."

She was still playing with the plastic tube. He watched the swirl of colors. "What's that?"

She gave a small, embarrassed laugh. "A magic wand."

"Where did you get it?"

"Don't tell me you need one."

"Sometimes I'd like to have one. But I was thinking my daughter would like it."

"Oh, you're married."

"I was . . ." He let the sentence trail off. Probably she thought he was divorced, and he didn't want her thinking that he couldn't make a marriage work. Then he reminded himself that it didn't matter what she thought about him. He was interviewing her about a missing person—that was all.

"Oh," she said again, twirling the plastic rod in her hand.

His eyes were drawn to the bits of glitter and the swirling blue liquid. For a moment they both watched the shifting motion inside the beveled plastic.

"What would you do with a magic wand if you had one?" she asked.

"Solve Stone Who Done Its."

"What's a Stone Who Done It?"

"A case where there are no solid suspects and no leads."

"Um."

He watched her lips form the syllable, then roused himself from his study of her—a very unprofessional study. "Would it be possible for me to see Ms. De-Young's apartment?"

She hesitated. "I'd feel like you were invading her privacy."

"Maybe I'd see something that would give me a clue."

"I went down there before I filed the missing person report. I didn't see anything."

"You're not a trained police detective."

She thought that over, then gave a small nod. After putting down the wand, she opened a desk drawer and extracted a key with a pink ribbon threaded through the key chain hole.

She went back down the stairs to the vestibule.

"Did you have the house converted into a duplex?" he asked, already knowing the answer, since he could tell that the work was more than twenty years old.

"No. Grandma O'Shea did it after my grandfather

died. She didn't need such a big place, and she needed the income."

"So how did you end up with the property?"

"My parents got divorced. Dad took off for parts unknown. Mom and I moved into the downstairs apartment. I was just starting college when she got a pulmonary embolism. She died."

"I'm sorry."

"It could have been worse. Grandma O'Shea and I were always close, and I moved in with her."

"She died, too?"

"In her sleep. Five years ago. A heart attack. She was ninety-two and able to take care of herself until the end. I guess that's the way to live—and the way to go."

"Yes," he answered, wondering what his own chances were of dying in bed.

They were still standing in the hallway. "I took the upstairs flat and rented out this one," she said, unlocking the other door. She stepped into an apartment that was similar to her own in layout. But the similarity ended there.

Her abode had been quirky but orderly. DeYoung was—to put it politely—a slob. There were stacks of mail, newspapers, and other paper on every flat surface, including the floor. When he walked farther into the room and looked toward the kitchen, he saw dirty dishes in the sink and on the counter.

"You say she didn't give you any trouble. It looks like you're going to have to blast this place out when she moves."

"Okay, she's not so neat. But she's a good person. She likes children and animals."

"Um hum," he said, thinking it was probably lucky she didn't have custody of either.

He scanned the apartment. To his practiced eye, the owner had stepped out and intended to come back.

He started with the answering machine, pressed the rewind button and listened to the messages. There were several—two from Ms. Reynolds—both asking De-Young to call.

And a message from the boyfriend, Swinton, two days ago. Which proved nothing. If he'd done something to her, he might have left the message to establish his innocence.

The rest of the messages were at least four days old. One was apparently from the office that handled substitute teachers, asking if she was available to take a biology class at Wootton High School on Monday. Another was from her mother with some chatty news about various friends and relatives.

"Did she go to work on Monday?" Jack asked.

"I don't know."

He nodded, then strode down the hall to the bedroom and opened the closet. The hanging rack was full of blouses and jackets, packed so tightly together that they had to come out wrinkled.

"I'd ask if you thought anything was missing, but I imagine it's hard to tell," he said over his shoulder.

"I looked in her storage closet. Her suitcases are there."

"Did you check her dresser drawers?"

She swiped back a lock of fiery hair. "I opened some, yes. But I felt like a sneak thief, so I gave it up."

He opened a dresser drawer and found sweaters in a messy pile. Reaching underneath, he discovered nothing hidden. The next drawer held panty hose—and nothing else. The third drawer was a mass of women's underpants and bras. This time, when he slid his hand underneath, he felt several magazines and a book. When he pulled them out, he saw that they were pornography—S and M oriented. One magazine cover showed an almost naked woman chained to a crossbar. A man was standing over her with a whip. The other magazines were similar. And the book looked like a dominance and submission how-to manual. He made a snorting sound. It seemed that a routine case had just gotten more interesting.

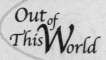

Out of This World